TILL THE END

REMY MARIE

Thank you
for the
review

Remy
Marie

Edited by: Roxana Coumans
https://proofreadebooks.com

Cover by: Sasha Figarella

Chapter Background by: Chinthaka Pradeep.
Instagram: @beefamily8

Interior Design: Damian Jackson

This heart pounding zombie filled love story is dedicated to my wife and kids. Thank you for giving me the time to write this once in a lifetime story. Y'all rock.

ONE

Navy SEALs Malcolm and Zack tossed a football outside in an open grass field inside Little Creek Navy Base. A gentle breeze pushed the blades of grass at their feet as they ran back and forth. The clouds overhead, rolled with the wind, providing the two some protection from the summer sun. The open field where they played was shared with other SEALs and navy sailors. Some trained, others goofed off. Sounds of laughter and orders being yelled could be heard. It was a rare moment of downtime between trainings for both sailors.

Both men were fit for their ages of thirty-five. Lieutenant Malcolm White's dark skin was slick with sweat from his play.

With a short fade, and a stubble beard, he opted to wear his yellow Navy Physical Training shirt. His shirt was neatly tucked into his navy-blue shorts and he wore a pair of white sneakers. Beads of perspiration covered his forehead and dripped down his back from the warm Virginia summer. His silver dog tags bounced on his chest as he leaped high in the air to catch the ball.

"Whoa! Nice catch!" Zack yelled. His voice was filled with a southern Texas twang. Similar to Malcolm, Lieutenant Zack Morris was in his PT, but what he wore was against regulation, as he was shirtless in

1

just his navy-blue shorts and yellow sneakers. The blonde's pale muscles bulged as he flexed to catch the ball thrown back at him. As he ran, his dog tags bounced off his glistening skin.

The two sailors playing catch looked to be taken out of a scene from Top Gun as they were both at their physical peaks. Zack flipped the ball to grip the laces and then zipped it back to Malcolm in a perfect spiral.

Malcolm caught the ball, and then threw it back.

"Thanks, but you forgot that I played ball with the Navy Academy." Malcolm responded. Although Malcolm was from North Carolina, he didn't have the deep southern twang like Zack. His voice was deep and husky, almost like an R&B singer.

"No, I didn't forget." Zack chuckled with his friend and squad mate. With a smirk he tossed the ball back to Malcolm. "I think you remind me every time you can. Just because you played college football, doesn't make you an all-star or something. Last I checked you don't play in the NFL."

"I wanted to serve my country." Malcolm grinned, tossing the ball back to Zack.

"Bullshit," Zack remarked, his Colgate smile was brighter than the sun. He took a few steps back and then yelled, "go long." He grunted and threw the ball as far as he could.

Malcolm ran and got squared underneath the ball and then caught it over his back shoulder. Zack applauded him for the impressive catch.

"Show off!" He yelled.

Malcolm flicked him off, and then threw the ball back to Zack.

He hustled back to Zack and replied, "Don't be an ass because you're trying to avoid the real question."

"Which is?"

"What are you and Kelsey going to do for your honeymoon? You got leave in two weeks, and yet, you still haven't decided on what to do."

"Fuck, please don't remind me."

"You should have booked the hotel and the excursions by now. Instead, you got nada."

"I know. I'm fucked. Any ideas?"

"Hawaii?"

"Are you serious? With what money? Uncle Sam pays us, but we're not millionaires. There's a reason why Kelsey and I had a small wedding. Think cheaper, oh and something on the East Coast."

"Bruh, do I look like a travel advisor?" Malcolm stated, pointing at his friend. "You should have picked out a destination by now."

"You are not helping. Come on, think."

Malcolm grinned and snapped his fingers. "I got an idea. Disney World."

"Seriously? How is Disney World romantic?"

"It doesn't need to be sunsets and long walks on the beach, but y'all need to be doing something besides fucking all night."

"Actually, I was planning on spending all my time in bed."

"Bullshit, you and I both know your shit doesn't last that long."

Zack flicked off Malcolm and they both laughed, almost like they've been brothers all their lives.

"Nah, seriously, I think you should take her to Disney because of Star Wars." Malcolm explained. "Kelsey is a huge geek and loves Star Wars. You can take her to that place where they make lightsabers. You know how much she loves collecting swords and she practices kendo."

"True. She would like it. Plus, they got Marvel and all that stuff."

"Exactly, now you're talking."

"I guess Disney World it is. Thanks, brother, I owe you."

"I'll just add it to the long list of shit you owe me."

Zack flicked Malcolm off again, and then threw the ball hard at him. Malcolm chuckled and caught the pass from Zack. He then returned the ball with the same velocity.

"Speaking of my debt," Zack smirked. "I can think of one way to clear my ledger."

"How?" Malcolm asked, wiping the sweat off his brow.

"Anne..."

Malcolm's heart raced. He tried to keep his emotions at bay, but he had a feeling that Zack could read him like a book based on his smug expression.

"Yeah, I saw the way y'all been looking at each other the last couple of months. Not to mention, you two seemed to be hitting it off as best man and maid of honor."

"That was just for the wedding." Malcolm dismissed. "We both had to take care of your drunk asses."

"Bullshit. If I recall, you and Anne were all over each other on the dance floor, grinding up on each other like it was the senior prom."

"Nah, man, Anne and I..." Malcolm paused and looked at the patch of dirt in front of him. "...Anne and I are just friends. That night at your wedding we were just drunk. Nothing more."

"Sure, well, my wife happens to be best friends with her. If you want a date with her, I'm your man. I'll ask Kelsey to set y'all up."

"Pass. Anne is cool, but I like our friendship. I wouldn't want to ruin it with an awkward date."

Zack laughed and placed the football underneath his arm. "Who said the date would be awkward? Y'all are perfect for each other. Even a blind man could see..."

Before Zack could get his last words out, there was an ear shattering siren and Zack and Malcolm both shared a grave look. They knew that siren was only played for one reason, there's been an attack on US soil.

"Please tell me that we have a drill today." Zack muttered.

"Nope, this shit is real."

"Fuck." Zack growled as he ran to his yellow PT shirt. He quickly tossed it on and then the pair raced towards the command building.

When they arrived, dozens of sailors were already settled in the situation room. The room itself was like an auditorium, with rows of fifty chairs all facing a stage with a podium and a projector screen. Normally, the room was used for briefing SEAL teams before the departure for missions, but today, it was standing room only as every seat was filled with officers and sailors wondering what the hell was going on.

Zack and Malcolm heard every type of rumor as everyone chattered. There were multiple theories on why they were summoned. Malcolm heard whispers that there was an attack from the Russians. Zack heard comments on a bio bomb from a terrorist.

Whichever it was, Malcolm was ready to fight and die for this country. Zack however just prayed that his wife was safe.

"Commander on deck!" An officer yelled and all of the sailors stood at attention, including Zack and Malcolm.

Rear Admiral Reese Wesley was an older navy officer. Although he was over the age of fifty, his body didn't show it as he was fit in his crisp uniform of black and green fatigues. A grey mustache covered his pale skin as he walked towards the podium.

"At ease," Admiral Wesley commanded in a deep voice.

Everyone sat and the captain cleared his throat.

"As of 1200, the commander in chief has ordered us into Code Z."

"Code Z?" Many soldiers muttered, however, judging by the other commanding officers' shallow faces, Malcolm had a feeling that some of them knew what Code Z was.

"What in the hell is Code Z?" Zack whispered.

"It beats me." Malcolm replied.

"For those who don't know," Reese began to say as he gripped the podium tighter, "Code Z is a classified order from the top. It means that there is a zombie outbreak."

More conversation broke between sailors before Admiral Wesley spoke up again.

"Yes, that's right, *zombies*. They are real. What you think you may know of them is true."

The projector started and showed a short film. Judging by the picture quality it looked to be at least fifty years old. A dozen people or so were all wearing medical scrubs and they surrounded a male soldier in an US Army uniform. The G.I appeared to be on the edge of death as there were several bloody bandages all over his body.

"In the sixties, during Vietnam, we did experiments on soldiers, trying to create a cure for lethal injuries. It was called Project Rebirth."

In the video behind Reese, the dying soldier was receiving a shot.

"However, what was discovered was these men still died, but they came back undead. These corpses couldn't be stopped by normal means. Wounding vital organs like lungs and heart had no effect on these creatures. It was like those organs were nonexistent."

As he explained, the dead soldier reanimated, turning into a mindless monster on screen. Several screams and shouts were heard as it took several people to attempt to take down the zombie.

"From this experiment gone wrong, they learned that bites from the zombies can also infect you. The time from initial viral contact to full infection varies. Studies shows it can take seconds to minutes, but what is confirmed is once you're bitten there's only a short time for the disease to overtake your nervous system turning you undead as well."

The video showed several of the soldiers that were bit from holding down the zombie reanimate into zombies themselves. The hospital turned into a violent nightmare, as soldiers shot at the undead moving bodies. Finally, one soldier fired a bullet into the zombie's skull. It fell to the ground and the same soldier communicated to take down the zombies with heads shots.

Admiral Wesley watched the action unfold on the video before looking back at the soldiers. "From what we know the only way to stop a zombie is a trauma to the head."

The video ended with several of the soldiers all getting shot in the head. The Rear Admiral cleared his throat and focused on each Navy SEAL in the room.

"This is the only way to destroy this enemy. There are no other known ways to stop them. After the failure of Project Rebirth, military scientists have been studying the effects of the disease in a secure base for over fifty years. At the time it was secured, until three days ago. When the base was hit by an F-5 tornado. The building housing the zombie was destroyed, along with the scientists in there. When the fire department responded, they didn't know about the zombie threat and one of them got bit. He was transferred to the hospital before the government could contain him and by the time the authorities showed up, it was too late as the infection had already spread."

"Fuck me," Zack muttered as he shifted in his seat.

Admiral Wesley's body language was as stiff as a board as if the news that the world's gone to hell didn't scare him. "Given the nature of how the virus spreads, the Department of Defense came up with a deterrent if ever the virus ever got exposed to the public. They named it Code Z. In this scenario, it's all hands on deck. Every branch and every soldier is called in to contain the threat. Phase one will be various tasks, including bringing local government and military spouses and families on base. Now normally it's not custom to have spouses on base, but during the war game simulations, the DoD determined that there would be less desertion if soldiers knew their loved ones were safe."

"Sir, wouldn't be better to contain the threat now, why waste time trying to protect families and politicians when we can take out the threat before it grows too big?" A commanding officer asked.

The admiral shook his head. "Trust me, I prefer the shock and awe approach too, but these are orders from the top.

DoD has ran simulations on this. For over fifty years they've reviewed scenarios and each time they determined that this will be a long grinding fight, where anarchy and desertion will be high. To curve those things, they've determined that local government and families must be protected first."

"What about girlfriends!" A SEAL yelled out. Malcolm recognized the large man, LTJG Sawyer Knox. He had a full beard of brown hair and wore shades on the back of his head. He was fresh out of working with SEAL Team Four. As he and Zack were both SEAL Team Two, he rarely made contact with Sawyer except for moments when they walked down the hall or when the teams spared against one another.

"No girlfriends. No lovers. No friends. Spouses, sons, and daughters, that's it. Immediate family only. We don't have enough supplies on base to support everyone. Understood?"

"Yes, sir." Everyone responded, however, Malcolm could tell that Sawyer wasn't satisfied with the response as he looked like someone pissed in his cereal.

"Phase two will be law and order. As soon as the president called a Code Z, the nation went under martial law. We will assist the local authorities to contain the threat and establish order. When the code was called, local authorities began setting up containment camps to secure the local population." Admiral Wesley turned towards Sawyer's general direction and said, "this is where your significant others and non-immediate family will go. Once we have established order, you will be able to contact them in these camps."

There was a large sigh of relief from many troops as the commander continued his speech.

"Naturally, anarchy will spread and people will start rioting, looting, and doing various criminal activities. We will be the force to remind them that this is still America. Stealing, raping and killing is still illegal here and we will enforce it. Understood?"

"Yes, sir."

"Good, we have four hours until we go in complete lockdown on base. After that no one will be allowed in or out of the base. Your commanding officers have your assignments. You are dismissed."

The crowd of SEALs dispersed and Malcolm and Zack made their way to their CO, Captain Charles Peterson.

Charles was a broad-chest man with blonde scruff on his face. While he was shorter than most SEALs, Malcolm knew not to underestimate him, as he was the toughest son of a bitch he knew. Malcolm and Zack had both seen the Captain take on an entire platoon of men and walk out without a scratch. There was an ongoing joke that he was invincible, or a descendent of Achilles himself. His deep voice matched his intensity as his blue eyes stared at his troops.

In total, there was a team of seven men and one woman. Junior Lieutenant Sabrina Washington was one of the few women who made it through the brutal training of the SEALs. Like Captain Peterson, she was short, with dark skin, and her curly ebony hair was tied in a tight bun underneath her cap. She was a master with a rifle and could hit anything she put her mind to. Her brown eyes remained on the commander as she waited for the rest of her squad to fall in.

Beside her was Lieutenant Victor Jenkins. Like Malcolm and Zack, Victor was well built, and had seen his share of battle.

Victor was mixed with both African and European features. He had tan skin, cropped brown hair with a fade and a thin brown mustache over his lip. He wore shades as he stared at his CO. His demeanor outside was tough, but Malcolm could see a small twitch in his hands, letting him know he was nervous.

Hell, they were all nervous.

"Skipper, is Admiral Wesley serious?" Victor asked.

"Yes, I always thought Code Z was one of those bullshit scenarios that Washington cooks up, but this shit is real. I've seen the infection in action on tv. It's spreading quickly. We only have a few hours to lock shit down so let's not piss off, got it?"

"Yes, sir," everyone responded.

"SEAL Teams four and ten will be assisting the base with operations to protect the families members. Anyone with spouses or children must reach out to them, and tell them to gather at the community center at the nearby military housing. From there, they will escort them onto base. Anyone who's not there at 1800, will be left behind. Understood?"

"Yes, sir."

"Our team will be spearheading the rescue mission for the governor of Virginia. Lucky for us, he's only a few minutes away in Norfolk. Local PD has him under lockdown, and we will be picking him up along with his family and heading back to base. We will be in the thick of things. From what I understand, this virus moves quickly. Under no circumstances do you let yourself get bit. The undead may be slow, but like the Admiral said, they do not go down easily. Head shots only."

"That shouldn't be too hard," Sabrina grinned.

"Like you could talk, unlike you, not all of us are gifted shooters. Taking away the easy shot of center mass is going to be tough." Victor countered.

"You see? This is why your ass needs to go to the range more often. When you get eaten up by zombies, it would be because your can't-hit-nothing-ass didn't go to the range."

"That's enough." Captain Peterson growled. "This shit is real. Stop fucking around."

"Sorry, sir," Sabrina replied, straightening up.

Captain Peterson stared at Sabrina for a brief moment before looking at the rest of his men. "Be sure to bring your A game. You got ten minutes to get your gear, call your loved ones, and get to the hilo. Let's go to work, SEALs."

The group dispersed as Malcolm and Zack went to the armory to collect their guns, and then to their lockers to place on their tactical gear. As they got dressed, Malcolm whispered to Zack, "Yo, have you gotten in touch with Kelsey?"

"No, I'm worried sick right now that something happened to her. I know she had a Kendo class with Anne earlier today, but that was the last I heard from her. I've called three times and she has yet to pick up."

"I'm sure she's fine. Kelsey has a good head on her shoulders. She'd know what's up and would haul ass to the base."

"I hope so. I don't know what I'd do if I lost her," Zack hesitated and looked down at his gloves. Malcolm placed a hand on his friend's shoulder, and grinned.

"Bruh, it's going to be a'ight. Just keep calling her."

"Thanks, Malcolm. Yeah, I'll keep trying." Zack shook his head, as he zipped up his tactical vest. "This shit is so farfetched. Zombies? It's like something straight out of science fiction."

"I know, but don't lose focus. We got a job to do."

"You're right. Let's go hunting, brother."

TWO

Anne Yamaguchi slurped on her strawberry banana smoothie as she followed her best friend, Kelsey Morris through the lingerie section in the department store. Her arms were sore from the intense training session they just endured with their Kendo Master Sato. Her long jet-black hair was placed in a ponytail and bangs covered her beige skin.

After their class, the two friends decided to get smoothies and go shopping so they didn't bother to change from their clothes after their class.

Anne was wearing a pair of black yoga pants, pink sneakers along with black crop top that showed off her flat stomach. Kelsey had on a pair of hot pink short shorts along with white sneakers and white cami top with a black sports bra underneath. Unlike Anne, Kelsey had her blonde hair untied and it rested on her shoulders as she browsed through the different sensual attires.

"What do you think of this one?" Kelsey asked, holding up a pair of see-through undies.

"I told you, it's a waste of money. Zack only really cares about what's under the clothing. Not this."

Kelsey rolled her eyes. "You're clearly missing the point about lingerie. It's meant to take your man's breath away when he sees you. Of course, I could walk out naked and we'd just start our business. Or I could be walking out in something like this..." Kelsey showed off a silk red camisole. "...something that takes his breath away. Something that makes him forget about the world and only wants me."

"Ha, he's a dude. Dudes only want one thing." Anne made a sexual gesture with her hand and Kelsey rolled her eyes.

"You're not helping. I invited you here to help me."

"Really? I thought it was just for a smoothie."

Kelsey shook her head, laughing as she resumed searching for the perfect outfit.

"Honestly if it was me, with your hips and tits, I would go with lace bra and undies, with a garter belt and some black sheer stockings. You know that classic pin up look."

"Oh, you're right. That would be a good set. You see, you do have taste."

Anne rolled her eyes and then skimmed through some clothes near her.

"You see anything that catches your eye?" Kelsey smirked.

"No, I'm just looking for you."

"Really? Why not shop for yourself?" Kelsey questioned.

"Because you don't wear lingerie to sit alone in your house and watch Netflix."

"Unless there's someone else to watch it with."

Anne scoffed. "Like who?"

"Malcolm." Kelsey grinned.

"Malcolm and I are just friends." Anne quickly dismissed.

"You sure about that?" Kelsey asked. "I mean I saw the way y'all were dancing at my wedding. Y'all were practically having sex on the dance floor."

"Oh God," Anne slapped her forehead and regretted her past actions. "I blame you for that. Why did you have to have an open bar?"

"Don't divert the question. You don't dance like that unless there's something there."

"There's nothing there," Anne repeated.

Kelsey rose her eyes at her tone but didn't push the issue any further.

She continued to browse until she found a pair of black lace lingerie, including a garter.

"Oh, I think I found it. What do you think of this?"

"Oh, that's perfect. I think he'd like that during the honeymoon. Has he told you where you're going?"

"Not yet, he's..." before Kelsey could say more, there was shouting and gunshots.

"Fuck!" Kelsey shrieked as her and Anne both ducked.

"What in the hell?" Anne asked. "Are people shooting up the mall now?"

"It's Norfolk. I wouldn't put it past this city."

The gunfire and the shouts continued.

"We need to get out of here." Kelsey determined.

"Yeah, there goes our fun shopping trip."

Kelsey nodded. "Come on," they both crawled as the screams continued. Crowds of people ran different ways as they tried to escape.

Anne's heart was beating out of control. She'd never been in such a high-pressure situation. She tried to control her breathing like Master Sato taught her, but practice was different from real life.

Kelsey on the other hand was calm. She reminded herself that her husband comes under gunfire all the time, and he tells her the best thing to do is to keep a clear head and focus on surviving.

As they crawled out of the store, towards the exit stairwell, they both gasped as it was pure carnage. Bodies laid on the ground, and people were screaming running for their lives. There was a group of people all moaning and growling. Their faces were covered in blood and gore. Their eyes were soulless and black. It was like they were spawns from hell itself.

Anne couldn't believe her eyes as she stared at the undead, shuffling mindlessly towards anything that had breath.

"What the hell is that?" Anne asked.

"I have no fucking clue, but I don't plan on sticking around. Come on, let's get back to my car." Kelsey whispered.

They both ran to the nearest exit. As they ran, Kelsey pushed open the door to the stairwell and was shocked as there was a man in front of her. His mouth was covered in blood, and his stomach was open, with his guts dripping on the floor.

"What the fuck..." Kelsey exclaimed, and before she could say anything else the man was on top of her, attempting to chomp at her. Kelsey evaded his bites, screaming as she held his face away. Struggling, the man inched closer and closer to her neck until Anne pulled the man off her.

"Get off her!" Anne screamed, shoving the man away.

He growled as he was tossed aside, falling down the stairwell.

"Are you okay?" Anne asked, assisting Kelsey to her feet.

"I'm fine. Thanks for saving my ass. I owe you one. What was up with that man? He was obsessed with trying to take a bite out of me."

"Call me crazy but I think that was a zombie."

"A zombie? Those don't exist, right? I mean that stuff is all fiction."

"Then explain to me why that fucker with no guts was trying to take a bite out of you. Or what about those bodies in the mall. They all had bite marks like they've been eaten. Either they're crazy cannibals attacking the mall or these are zombies. Take your pick."

Kelsey didn't need to reply as her answer was solved for her. There was another loud groan, and the man that attacked her stood off the ground. His leg was clearly broken as he paid little attention to the crooked appendage. He crawled up the stairs attempting to get to the women.

"Well...fuck me. I guess he's a zombie. No normal man would be able to shrug off an injury like that." Kelsey observed.

"So we solved that question. The next question is how. Like you said, zombies don't exist."

"While I would love to have this debate with you, we need to get to my car." Kelsey said, backing up.

Anne followed her climbing up another row of stairs as the zombie crawled after them. They reached the top level and watched as the zombie continued to follow them up the stairwell.

"Well, I got bad news for you. Your car is parked on a level below Mr. Zombie. We got two options. We go back through the mall, dealing with the carnage out there..."

"I'm not going back out there," Kelsey dismissed.

"Or we go through Mr. Zombie."

"I'll take door number two," Kelsey mocked.

"Good, I was thinking the same thing. We can take him."

"But how?"

"Well, if he is a zombie it's safe to assume that a head shot could take him out."

"How are we going to do that? We don't have any weapons."

"What does Master Sato always say? We are the weapon, the swords we use are only tools. We know hand to hand combat. If we can get the zombie closer, we can kick its ass."

"The last thing I want is to have that thing be closer to me." Kelsey replied, disgusted out by the grotesque figure.

"Focus. Breathe. We got this," Anne commanded, as she stood in a fighting pose.

"You're right. We got this. Remember to go for the head."

"Took the words right out of my mouth."

The man approached the duo at the top of the stairs and Anne let out a loud yell, as she struck first. She swept the leg, undercutting the zombie to fall on the ground. In a split second, Kelsey followed with a high leg kick, burying her heel through the skull.

"Ugh, I think I'm going to be sick." Kelsey gagged and held her mouth as her shoe was covered with brain matter.

"Don't say it." Anne coughed and then looked at the downed man. "Well, at least our theory is correct. Zombies are confirmed. Head shots are confirmed too."

"Yeah, let's get out of here."

Anne nodded and the two ran down the stairs towards the parking garage. There were multiple people running and attempting to drive out of the parking deck. Zombies attacked random strangers, as they begged for their own lives. It was violent, brutal, and horrifying.

As Kelsey ran, she spotted a young girl crying for her mother, that laid dead beside her. Kelsey paused and stared at the young girl.

Anne stopped, her eyes opened wide as she looked at her best friend.

"Kelsey, what are you doing? We need to get to the car."

"We can't leave that little girl. Her mother, she's dead."

"We're going to be dead if we don't move. Come on!" Anne

commanded as she grabbed her friend's hand. Before she could pull her away, the young girl shrieked as her mother had awakened. However, her eyes weren't filled with life. Instead they were black and soulless like the rest of the undead.

"Kes! Let's go!" Anne yelled.

"No, we have to save her." Kelsey took a step towards the little girl, but by then it was too late as the mother stood up and ripped into her daughter, biting off large chunks of flesh. The child's wails echoed in Kelsey's ears as she stood frozen in fear. As the mother dug into the kid, she looked up from the child's corpse, blood dripping from her mouth, and stared into Kelsey's blue eyes. She stood up from the child and began her charge towards Anne and Kelsey.

"Come on!" Anne shouted, dragging Kelsey away.

The women both ran as fast as they could towards Kelsey's car. Kelsey took her keys out and unlocked the SUV, and both women got into the car. Kelsey stuck her keys into the car and started the vehicle.

"Go! Go! Go!" Anne yelled.

"What do you think I'm doing?" Kelsey growled as she placed the vehicle into drive and sped off. As she zoomed through the parking lot, she dodged multiple people and crashed cars hoping to get to the exit.

As she drove her car phone when off.

"Shit, it's Zack." Kelsey remarked. She quickly mashed the answer button and she heard Zack take a long sigh of relief.

"Baby? Are you alright?" He asked.

"I am. Anne and I were at the mall and everyone...do you know about the attacks?"

"Yes, the army is in full lock down. We're in route to grab the governor in Norfolk. Where are you?"

"We're at the downtown mall in Norfolk. I'm driving the car out of the parking garage. What should I do?"

"Get to Little Creek base. You have less than an hour. The base is offering shelter to any spouses, but it will lock down at 1800 hours."

"Fuck, well I'm with Anne, can she come?"

There was a long pause before Zack spoke up again.

"No, she can't. I'm sorry Anne, but the military are setting up safe zones. I'm sure you can find one on the way."

"It's okay. I'll find one." Anne replied.

Kelsey looked at her friend and shook her head. "Zack, we can't leave Anne."

"Baby, this situation is a lot worse than it seems. This isn't an argument you're going to win." Zack spat.

Kelsey growled and spat back, "Zack, I'm not leaving... oh shit!" She replied, slamming on the brakes. Her eyes opened wide staring at the mass destruction in front of her. Rows of cars were crashed together as the smells of burning flesh filled the girls' nostrils. Screams of dying victims could be heard as the zombies feasted on the dead remains. From the scene alone, it looked like a horror movie.

"Shit..." Anne and Kelsey both muttered.

"What is it?" Zack asked.

"The exit. It's blocked. There's no way we're getting out of here by car."

"Fuck." Zack cursed. "What?" Zack said, as it was obvious that he was talking to someone else.

"Babe, who are you talking to?"

"Malcolm," he replied. "Man, you know we can't. Our mission is to save the governor. Yes, I know. I know. What? I don't know how far the mall is from the city offices." Zack muttered.

"It's right across the street," Anne interrupted.

"She says it's right across the street," Zack repeated. "Yeah, of course it's risky. On a scale of one to ten, how much shit we'd be in? Ha, of course. Fuck it, let's do it."

"Alright, Kelsey could you and Anne get to the roof?"

"The roof?" Kelsey asked.

"Yeah, we're rescuing the governor next door. If you're on the roof by the time we fly in, we'll get the hilo to drop down and pick you up."

Kelsey stared at Anne and then back at the car phone. "What about Anne? You said she can't get on base."

"We'll figure that step out later, but we need both of you on that roof in the next twenty minutes. Can you do that?"

"Yeah, I think so."

"Good. Be careful, Kelsey. I love you."

"I love you too, babe. You be careful too."

Zack chuckled. "Those zombies don't stand a chance against me. When I show up they'll be running away."

Kelsey cracked a smile on her face as her husband always found a way to make her smile even during her darkest times.

"You're such an ass." She mocked.

"You like this ass, last I checked. I'll see you on the roof, okay?"

"Yeah, see you soon babe."

"Bye, baby."

Zack hung up and Anne looked at Kelsey concerned.

"Not to burst your bubble, but we just escaped hell in that mall, and your husband wants us to go back through it?"

"Yeah, but that's the only way to get out."

"Ugh, why can't it be easy? Why can't we just get on the highway and head to the base."

"You and I both know that we'd rather face a horde of zombies than traffic on 64."

"Ha, true. So what's the plan?"

Kelsey paused and searched their backseat. She spotted their katanas and a smile spread across her face.

"Are you still sore from kendo?"

Anne turned back to see what Kelsey was smiling about, and she smirked. "Not anymore. I'm always ready to practice."

Kelsey laughed, "I think we're far past practice. Let's go."

The women grabbed the swords and exited the vehicle. As soon as they left, a pair of zombies swarmed them, but they were faster as they didn't hesitate stabbing the zombies with the blade. After the zombies fell, Kelsey grinned, "that was easy."

"Don't get cocky. We still have to go through dozens of undead to get to the roof."

"Ugh, you had to bring down the mood."

"Hey, that's why you keep me around." Anne winked.

"Now who's the cocky one? Come on, let's go."

"After you..." Anne replied, getting into fighting position.

Kelsey let out a large roar as she charged ahead, followed by Anne who joined her for the fight of their lives.

THREE

Zack listened to the helicopter rotor as they flew over downtown Norfolk . As they passed over each building, he scanned the roof top, praying that he'd see Kelsey. His foot bounced and he held his M4 rifle tightly as the tension of not knowing if she was alive or not was unbearable. His focus wasn't broke until Malcolm kicked his shoe.

"Yo, where's your head?" He asked through the radio.

"It's in the game."

"You sure? We're about to be dropped into hell. I need my wingman."

"I'm here."

Malcolm studied his friend and shook his head. "You're thinking about her. She's going to be fine. Kelsey is the toughest son of a bitch I know. Anne is a close second. With those two together they probably have the zombies running away from them instead of towards them. Zack shook his head. "I'm just worried, I sent my wife to die. They had an escape route, and instead of leading onto the highway, I led them straight into the monster's mouth."

"Nah, man. We saw the highway when we came up here. It was gridlocked. She would have never made it to base in time. You did the right thing."

"I hope so."

Malcolm nodded and then peered out the window. "We're coming up to the mall now. We should see them."

Zack nodded and scanned the area. As he searched, his frown grew as he didn't spot Kelsey or Anne.

"They're not there." Zack sighed.

"They will be. Perhaps they're held up. The mall is a populated area." Malcolm responded.

"That's what I'm worried about. They could be cornered or worse..."

"Yo!" Malcolm kicked Zack again.

Zack's eyes narrowed at Malcolm, and watched as his best friend shook his head.

"Don't go there, bruh. They're fine." Malcolm comforted.

Zack sighed and flexed his fingers as a nervous tingle surged through his body. He bit his lip and continued to scan the rooftops. His heart raced as a million scenarios ran through his head. Each one was a nightmare to him. Each one finished with his wife not making it out alive. Each one was painfully gut wrenching. Each one scared him to death. He couldn't go on without her.

"Fuck it." He growled. "Skipper!" He yelled towards his CO.

Captain Peterson eyed him, "What is it, Morris?"

"It's my wife, sir. She's trapped in that mall down there. Permission to divert from mission to go in and rescue her?"

"Permission denied. We have orders."

"Fuck those orders. Admiral said it himself, spouses and families will be rescued and granted access to the base. My wife is down there, fighting for her life. At least let me get her."

"Morris, this isn't a debate."

"You're right, it isn't. What would you do if Sheri and Keshia were down there? Would you still follow orders or would you go in there and save their lives?"

Captain Peterson paused and looked out the window. He cursed under his breath and replied, "this hilo leaves in thirty minutes, with or without your ass, got it?"

"Yes, sir." Zack growled, gripping his gun tighter.

"Skipper, permission to tag along with Morris. He needs backup." Malcolm asked.

Peterson nodded. "Go ahead. Thirty minutes!" He yelled back.

The helicopter touched down in an open grassy area, and the team of eight SEALs all exited the black hawk. Their guns were at the ready position as they surveyed the area for any hostiles. After giving the all-clear, Captain Peterson and his sailors diverted towards the city office, while Malcolm and Zack went towards the mall.

Zack held his finger on his trigger as he checked his corners. His heart was racing as he and Malcolm dashed across the empty street. All around them were bodies, wrecked cars, and debris. It was a war zone. Zack had seen this before overseas, but he'd never thought that he'd witness the horrible dismay in his own country.

Zack opened the mall door for Malcolm and his squad mate slowly walked in checking the open spaced mall for any hostiles. Zack was following Malcolm, and halted when he held up a fist. His mate pointed towards a slow-moving zombie as it chewed on a corpse.

Malcolm gave the signal to shoot, and Zack didn't hesitate to take the first shot. It was a clean head shot and the zombie dropped to the ground with a thud.

Malcolm nodded towards Zack and they crept deeper into the mall. Their breathing was shallow, as they held their rifles at the ready. Their heads were on a swivel as they checked each corner and each store. Like outside, complete destruction laid at their feet. Body after body, limb after limb, laid sprawled out in front of them. Their boots became covered in blood as they tip toed inside, making sure not to make a noise.

They've been trained for this, to move without a whisper. To not be detected and sneak up on an enemy. However, this enemy is different. This enemy doesn't want land or money. They aren't killing for religion or prejudice. They are killing based on their basic instincts. They were animals acting only to feed. The hunt was on, and Zack didn't plan on being the prey. He had to save Kelsey.

Normally at this time the mall would be filled with laughs and conversations, instead it was filled with the low growls of the undead roaming about. Natural light poured in from the windows as Malcolm and Zack searched each store.

After going through the hall, they crept into the atrium portion of the mall and as soon as Malcolm saw the large horde, he cursed under his breath. Both sailors ducked behind cover and surveyed the area.

"What did you want to do?" Malcolm whispered.

Zack paused and observed the area, he noticed a mall office sign behind a group of zombies.

"I bet that mall office on your ten goes to the roof." Zack answered in an equal pitch. "I know Kelsey, she would've gone through there."

"Yeah, but there's also like one hundred zombies between us and that door. There has to be another way."

"We're wasting time. That's our path. Let's pave the road."

Malcolm nodded and proceeded to open fire. Zack did the same, picking off zombies one by one. The loud gunfire rang in the empty halls of the mall, causing the zombies to start crawling in Malcolm and Zack's direction.

"Well, we got their attention," Malcolm muttered as he kept firing.

"Yeah, let's move. I don't want to be stranded here as they swam us. On my six."

"Got it."

Zack stood up and began moving towards the main office hall. Malcolm followed, his back was towards Zack as they stayed grouped together. The two SEALs had done this countless of times before as they fire controlled bursts, protecting each other, and making a path to get through.

Sweat beaded Zack's forehead and his hands felt the pressure of the recoil from the rifle. He breathed slowly just like he was taught. His eyes were focused as he took accurate shots at the undead.

In basic, he was taught to aim for critical mass, but all that shit went out the window the moment the undead came to life. On occasion, Zack would hit the heart or lungs out of reflex, and the zombie kept coming. Only when Zack refocused on the head, was he able to finally put the damnation down.

"We're getting closer to the door!" Zack yelled. "Keep up the pressure."

"On it!" Malcolm roared, as he reloaded his weapon.

When Zack neared the door, his gun clicked signaling that he was out of bullets, but he didn't waste time reloading. Instead he switched to his side arm and displaced the last two zombies in his way. He holstered his gun and then grabbed the door handle.

"Come on let's go!" Zack yelled, opening the door.

Malcolm, backed into the maintenance stairwell, still firing his weapon until he was in the room. Once he was inside, Zack quickly closed the door behind him.

"Fuck me, that was close." Zack breathed with his back against the door. Behind him he could feel the zombies banging on the wall.

"Yeah, you said-" before Malcolm could finish his sentence a zombie reached out and grabbed him from behind.

"Oh shit!" Malcolm cursed as he felt the jaws of the zombie near his neck. Acting quickly, he flipped the zombie over his back onto the ground. Pulling his combat knife out, he stabbed its skull.

He breathed heavily as he stood back up. "Fuck!" Malcolm sighed.

"You're telling me. Fucker came out of nowhere. Did you get bit?"

Malcolm checked himself and shook his head. "Nah, I'm good."

Zack nodded, "Good. That was something else."

"Yeah," Malcolm replied, studying the corpse he just killed.

"Every firefight I've ever been in I've had someone shoot back at me. This was the first time my targets just run at me with reckless abandon."

"Yeah, in a way I feel bad though. These were once American people. Hell, we just celebrated the Fourth of July last week. It feels backwards that I'm shooting the people I pledged my life to protect."

"I don't see it that way. These things are trying to kill me. You try and kill me, I shoot first and ask questions later."

"Damn, Bruh. Remind me to never get on your bad side."

Zack winked at Malcolm and then asked, "you good?"

"Yeah, let's keep going."

FOUR
THIRTY MINUTES EARLIER

"Hurry Anne, we're almost there. Keep up!" Kelsey yelled as she sliced through the zombie's skull.

Anne let out a mighty roar as she moved her katana with deadly precision taking a zombie's head off with a clean swipe.

The two women battled their way through the parking lot as zombie after zombie came their way.

To Kelsey, this was nothing like practicing the art of kendo. In kendo there were breaks. There were safety guards and armor to protect her. They used training swords and stopped after someone won a bout. This was different. This was keep moving or die. This was nonstop danger. This was life or death.

Kelsey's arms were tired from the continuous swing of her katana. Sweat covered her pale brow, as she took deep breaths attempting to control her breathing. Her fingers gripped the blade's hilt as she prepared to take on another foe. Without thinking she stabbed the zombie's head with a forward lunge, and white brain matter squirted out. Her blade was covered in bodily fluid as she charged at the next incoming foe.

She fought to see her husband Zack alive again. She fought for her friend beside her. She fought to stay alive.

She now knew what combat felt like. From all the stories that Zack told her. From the examples he gave her of how his mind goes blank, she finally understood that feeling. That rush of adrenaline that pushed her body to the limit. She was a machine, mowing down her enemies as they crossed her path.

Anne was the opposite. Although you couldn't see it on her face, she was scared. All of her life she's been studying martial arts, and while she enjoyed the sport, she's never thought of using it practically. She never thought she'd know the feeling of her sword tearing through flesh. She'd never thought that she'd see the deadly force of what a sharpened blade could do on a human.

She couldn't wrap her head around what was going on. These were zombies. Undead beings crazed and driven by hunger of human flesh. This idea, once thought to be something out of science fiction, was real and her friend and her were fighting for their lives.

Every slice, every thrust, every lunge meant life and death. She understood that, but she couldn't help but think, that she was killing someone's mother, someone's father, someone's lover. She was killing a human being. Someone she saw just an hour ago buying toys, gifts, and clothes. They were old and young, women and children.

These people were innocents, before they were bitten and exposed to this virus. Now they are mindless drones, and in their way of getting to the roof. She felt bad for what she was doing, but Anne knew this was the only way to survive.

The two swordswomen were like a river as they moved with elegance and grace. Their hacks and slashes were accurate, swift and powerful. They covered each other's backs, and when the last zombie in their way fell, both women took long winded breaths.

"Are you okay?" Anne asked.

"I'm good. You?"

"I'm still breathing, and I'm not bit. I'll take that as a victory."

"It's the little things..." Kelsey mocked, placing her katana back in its sheath. She tied it around her waist and then looked at her friend who had done the same with hers.

Both women were covered in blood and God knows what else. Around them laid dozens of bodies of the zombies they slaughtered.

Anne gaped at the mass murder in front of her, wondering what she has done, but before she could get a second thought in, she heard a low growl of the undead.

"Fuck me, here comes more." Kelsey replied, taking her katana out.

"How many are there?" Anne asked, unsheathing her blade.

"This mall is popular. There's no telling."

"We need to move. We'd die if we remain here."

"My thoughts exactly. Let's go."

Anne nodded and charged through the first zombie in her way. Kelsey followed, with a powerful slash that severed the head off cleanly. Both women moved like the wind, breezing through anything that go in their path. They exited the parking deck and entered the mall where they encountered more foes. Dozens of bodies trailed their path as they cut and slashed through the zombies.

"You see that up ahead?"

"The exit stairwell?" Anne grunted.

"Yeah, I bet that leads to the roof." Kelsey yelled.

"Do you think Zack will be there?" Anne asked, fighting off a zombie close to biting her. She kicked him away, and then finished him off, gasping after surviving the close encounter.

"He'd be there. I know my husband. He'd stop at nothing to get us." Kelsey replied, not paying attention as a zombie with no legs knocked her over. She screamed as the legless beast crawled towards her trying to bite into her flesh.

"Kelsey!" Anne yelled as she leaped in front of her friend. She stabbed the head with the tip of her blade, and then assisted her up.

"Are you okay?"

"Yeah, I'm...fuck! Watch out!" Kelsey yelled, pushing her friend out of the way. Quickly she stabbed the zombie through the eye and before she could recover another zombie was on top of her. The two women were being surrounded as they were pushed backwards towards the glass barrier on the second floor.

"There's so many of them!" Anne growled as she killed another.

"Our backs are against the railing if we fall..." Kelsey's heart slumped. For the first time she felt fear grip her chest.

Was this the end for us, Kelsey wondered.

"I know. We can't fight them all."

"Then we run." Kelsey replied.

"Where to?" Anne searched frantically around herself until she saw a red exit sign below that said emergency stairwell. "There! That's the roof access! Come on!"

"I can barely move myself." Kelsey replied, pushing a zombie away.

"We can't stop, or they'll push us over. Come on." Anne yelled as she charged her way through.

Kelsey followed her as she was grabbed several times by the zombies. She screamed as she pushed her legs to move as fast as she could.

When Anne broke through the crowd, Kelsey followed, running as fast as they could. Zombies followed them as they dashed towards the exit.

Anne opened the door to the stairwell, and Kelsey followed. Kelsey tried to close the door after her, but the zombies stuck their legs through the door, making it impossible to close.

"There's no time!" Anne yelled as she ran back down to grab her friend's hand. "We need to get to the roof!"

The duo ran up the steps and seconds later, zombies poured into the stairwell, following them. Their low pitch moans frightened the women.

Anne got to the top of the stairs and jiggled the handle.

"It's locked!" She yelled.

"Move!" Kelsey yelled, pushing her friend aside.

With a loud yell, Kelsey swung her sword, breaking the handle off the door. She pushed aside the broken lock and opened the door.

"Come on!" Kelsey yelled, opening the door.

Anne followed her, closed the door right as a zombie attempted to grab her. Several arms and hands attempted to reach through the ajar door. Holding the door with her back, the weight of the zombies trying to get to the door was too much for Anne.

"Kes!" She yelled. "Cut their arms! Cut their arms!"

"Ahh!" Kelsey screamed as she rose her katana up high. She hacked her way through, cutting through flesh and bone, until no more limbs stuck through. Once the door was cleared, it closed completely, but the horde still pushed the door trying to get through.

Anne was still struggling with the door and Kelsey assisted her, holding the door.

"What are you doing? Stay away. You need to be alive when Zack picks you up. Go over to the corner, where it's safe. I'll hold it."

"No, we need to stay alive. You can't hold this door by yourself."

Anne narrowed her brow at her friend as they both held the door.

"Don't even say it. Your life is as equally important as mine.

Anne smiled. "You're a good friend, Kes."

"Don't talk like that. Zack will be here."

"I know, but in case he doesn't. I want you to know."

"Thanks Anne. I love you too. If we are going to go, at least we got a great skyline to admire."

"Yeah, it's nice." Anne commented, looking at the tall buildings surrounding them. The sun was shining off the towers, giving them a whimsical glow. Behind the buildings they could see the shimmering water of the Elizabeth River that connected downtown Norfolk with the Chesapeake Bay.

The women smiled at each other and held each other's hands. The banging and the low growls were terrifying for them, but their shared company was a bright spot in a dark time.

Anne closed her eyes, praying that the madness would stop. She didn't want to die.

Seconds later, gunfire replaced the growls. Soon the banging on the door was halted and they heard a voice yell, "Kelsey?"

Kelsey stood up and smiled. "Zack!" She yelled back opening the door.

Kelsey was greeted to an image of Zack and Malcolm. Both had large grins on their faces as Zack ran up to Kelsey and picked her up. He swung her around, holding her tightly as he kissed her.

"God, I thought I lost you. Are you okay?" He asked, placing her down.

"I'm good. What about you?"

"I'm fine. Are you sure, any bites or anything?" He asked, reviewing her body.

"No, babe. I'm fine."

His smile grew larger as he dragged her close again. "Damn, I thought the worse. I love you. I fucking love you."

"I know babe. I love you too," Kelsey replied, kissing her husband again.

Malcolm stood smiling at the couple as they embraced each other. He saw Anne doing the same and walked up to her.

"Hey, Anne, are you okay?"

"Yeah, couple of scrapes and bruises, but I'll live."

"Bites?" Malcolm asked concerned.

His hand gently touched Anne's shoulder making her insides quiver. There was something about the way he touched her that made her squirm. No other man did that to her. They gazed into each other's eyes, before Malcolm scanned her arms and legs.

"Ha, no bites," Anne remarked. "You know there are more subtle ways to ogle me."

"Oh, I wasn't ogling. You'd know if I was ogling."

"Yeah, what does that look like?"

"My eyes would bust out of my head, my tongue would drop out and I'll howl like a coyote."

Anne laughed. "You're such an ass. What took you two assholes so long anyways?"

"Oh, we stopped for a mall pretzel, but you know the line was long. It's pretty busy in there." Malcolm chuckled.

"Don't you know it." Anne smirked.

"I'm happy that y'all could handle your own. It's impressive."

"Thank you."

The two smiled at each other, looking into each other's brown eyes. It was as if they both wanted to say something more, but were hesitant to reveal their true feelings.

Their lingering stare lasted longer than Malcolm expected. A stray chill crawled up his spine, causing him to clear his throat and shy away. He focused on to his squad mate who was in a loving trance with his wife as they stared into each other's eyes and held each other.

"Yo, Zack, I hate to break up whatever y'all are sharing, but we are on the clock here. We can't miss our ticket out of here."

"Shit, you're right." He turned to his wife and smiled. "You still got another round in you?"

"You know I do," Kelsey grinned, picking up her katana.

"Good, let's show these zombies what happens when you fuck with us. Let's go hunting."

FIVE

The foursome moved with haste as they went down the stairs. Immediately, they were swarmed by zombies when they exited the stairwell. Zack and Malcolm went first, paving the way for Kelsey and Anne to follow.

Controlled short bursts of gunfire could be heard as Zack and Malcolm mowed down any undead in their path. Behind them, Anne and Kelsey picked off stragglers.

"Well, it looks like those kendo lessons are paying off," Malcolm smirked at Anne.

"Your ass better pay attention. I would hate for you to turn and I'd have to impale you."

"Oh, you can impale me any day. I love how kinky you are," he mocked, firing at a charging zombie in front of him.

Anne rolled her eyes, however, she couldn't help but to smile as she sliced a zombie flanking them.

Kelsey and Zack laughed at the duo, sharing a look that it was obvious the two were flirting. Kelsey shook her head as she covered her husband's six. Like the rest of the group, she couldn't help but to smile as the moment reminded her of the times in their backyard during a cookout, with the four of them together all laughing and having a good time. Kelsey couldn't explain it, but she felt like when they were together they could take on the whole world, and at that moment it appeared like they could have as they moved as one.

The foursome of Zack, Kelsey, Anne and Malcolm were deadly together. Not one zombie got close to the group as they moved down the escalator towards the first level exit.

"Come guys, let's move! We have less than five minutes before that hilo touches down and leaves us high and dry. Let's go!" Zack yelled as they ran.

Zack growled and shoulder tackled a lone zombie in his way before firing at a group of three in front of him. He didn't even bother with the one he tackled as he knew his wife was behind him stabbing the fucker in the face.

He wished he could say that fighting side by side was a joy with his wife, but honestly he was worried about her. At the end of the day, what they were doing was dangerous. Anne and Malcolm might be having fun, but he knew the costs if they slipped up. He knew what would happen if one of them got bit or broke from formation. He prayed that nothing would happen as they shot and sliced their way through the horde.

"Anne, watch out!" Malcolm yelled, shoving a zombie that was flanking her. With the back of his rifle he smashed the zombie's head and then pulled his rifle up to take two clean headshots of the zombies in front of him.

"Thanks," Anne breathed.

Malcolm smirked, "I didn't want you to get bit. I would hate to *impale you* later."

Anne laughed, "you had to make it gross."

Malcolm shrugged, but wasn't paying attention, as a zombie came up behind him.

"Malcolm! Down!"

Malcolm ducked and Anne thrusted her katana over his head into the zombie's skull.

"Wow, thanks. I guess that makes us even."

Anne winked and continued to move with Kelsey and Zack. Malcolm smirked at his friend and followed her.

Malcolm couldn't explain it, but he felt closer to Anne after that. While he liked her as a friend, he couldn't help but to think what if. Normally he wouldn't think this way in a firefight. His mind would be clear, focusing on the task at hand, instead, his eyes kept drifting towards Anne. He watched with amazement as she moved with grace. Kelsey used the same technique, but there was something about the way Anne did it that made his stomach turn. He couldn't put his finger on it, but it was definitely something he wanted to explore.

After killing the zombie in front of her, Anne took a deep breath and checked on her friends. Kelsey and Zack seemed to be doing fine as they mowed down everything in their path. They truly looked like they were made for each other, moving as one, barely communicating as if they knew what each other wanted. Anne's eyes then turned to Malcolm whose eyes were focused ahead. She admired the way he held his rifle and the way he shot it. His form alone made her heart flutter. She didn't know what was coming over her. Perhaps it was the rush of the fight, or the idea that tomorrow might not come, she didn't know, but there was something about Malcolm she didn't see before.

"Anne, let's move, come on! We're almost out." Malcolm yelled as he pushed her ahead of him. Anne followed, Kelsey and Zack out of the mall, and Zack led the group across the street.

Last time, Malcolm and Zack were on the street, there wasn't a soul in sight, however, this wasn't the case now. Dozens of zombies growled and wondered about as they made their way through downtown. The gun fire attracted each one, as they moaned and shuffled their way toward the foursome.

"Keep moving. They should be calling the hilo any minute now. Keep moving! I see the LZ!" Zack yelled, using his side arm to take several shots instead of using his M4.

"Bruh, you said in a minute, but where are they?" Malcolm asked as he covered Kelsey. "Did they leave us?"

Zack double checked his watch and shook his head. "We're on time. Smoke hasn't been popped yet. Plus skipper wouldn't have left early. He would have secured the LZ until the last second promised."

"Fuck! Do you think they're dead?" Malcolm asked.

"No, we're talking about Achilles himself. Skipper had been through a lot worse than this."

"A lot worse than this?" Anne asked, slicing through another zombie.

"Yeah, try firefights with tanks and helicopters. This right here is target practice."

"Show off." Kelsey grinned, stabbing a nearby zombie.

Zack winked and the group continued to push their way to the grassy open area. When they arrived, Zack pointed at a concrete barrier.

"Malcolm, use this area for cover and stay with the ladies. I'm going into the city office to search for everyone."

"The hell you are!" Kelsey roared.

"This isn't a debate, baby. I've already went against orders to get y'all. I can't let my brothers and sisters die on my accord. You're safe with Malcolm, and you've proven that you could handle yourself here. I'll be right back. I promise."

Kelsey sighed and nodded. "Fine. I love you."

Zack smiled, "I love you too." He placed his hand on the small of her back and dragged her close for another kiss.

"I'll be right back." Zack reloaded and prepared to charge towards the city office until the doors of the building opened and he saw Sabrina, Charles, and Victor rushing out.

Sabrina was providing covering fire while Victor was assisting Charles who was limping. His lower left leg was covered in blood.

"Malcolm, lay down cover fire. Kelsey and Anne come with me and help them." Zack commanded.

The group didn't hesitate, as Malcolm remained perched in his position, picking off zombies at a distance. Anne and Kelsey followed Zack, mowing down zombies that got near.

"Here let me help," Zack told Victor as he placed his CO's arm over his shoulder.

"Damn, you're a sight for sore eyes. Sabrina and I had a bet that you two didn't make it." Victor grinned.

"You should've known better to bet against us." Zack mocked.

"Told you," Sabrina responded, taking several shots.

Victor rolled his eyes and fired a few shots with his side arm.

"Skipper, what's going on? Where's everyone else?" Zack asked.

"They're all dead. The rest of the team, the governor and his family and the guard assigned to watch him. When we got in it was already fucked up. The governor and his team lied about being bit and when they turned, they ambushed us. I guess that's what I get for trusting a politician."

"What about you? What happened to your leg?"

"Fucker bit my leg when we were making our way out."

"Skipper..."

"Oh, don't get all emotional over it. When it's your turn to go, it's your turn. Lord knows I've fucked around with death so many times. It was finally time I pay the piper. Just wished it wasn't in the damn ankle. Fucking Achilles. I ought to shoot the fucker that came up with that nickname for me."

Zack and Charles both laughed, before Zack placed him on the concrete barrier. Behind them, Malcolm, Sabrina, Victor, Kelsey and Anne were fighting off the horde that grew near.

"I've already radioed base. They know that the governor isn't coming. You go ahead and get out of here. I'll cover you."

"Skipper, you can't."

"This ain't a debate. You and I both know that I'd turn mid-flight. The last thing I want to do is endanger my team and your wife."

"The only thing I ask is to watch after my family. Make sure Sheri and Keshia make it through this shit."

"I will Skipper. You got my word."

"Good. You're a good sailor, Zack, and by the way your wife is fighting, you picked one hell of a woman."

"Yeah, this is all a reminder to not be on her bad side."

Charles laughed and shook his head. "That's a good one. This is your team now. Take care of them. That's an order."

"Yes, sir."

"Good."

The sound of helicopter blades was heard followed by the loud chain of bullets from the guns as they mowed down the surrounding undead. The helicopter landed in the center of the grass and Malcolm led the group towards it, providing covering fire as they all got on. Zack made sure that his wife and Anne got on before checking back on Charles who didn't move from the spot he was placed on.

The two SEALs didn't need to say much to each other as they both knew what had to happen next.

"I'll see you on the other side, Skipper."

"See you soon. Don't forget your promise. Keep them safe."

"I will." Zack saluted his CO, before turning and getting into the helicopter. As he ran, he heard gunfire and watched as his Captain laid down cover fire, for him. That was his last act of bravery before he was eaten alive by the undead. His screams echoed in Zack's ears as he was taken.

While others shied away, Zack didn't, watching the man he respected most in this life die. No one deserved to go out that way. Dozens of mouths and hands ripping you apart was a gruesome way to go, but at least he went out on his terms. He went out like the hero he always was.

SIX

As the helicopter took off, Malcolm held up his fingers telling Zack to switch to the private line. Once Zack was connected, he held a thumbs sign up, joining the conversation between Malcolm, Anne, Kelsey, Sabrina and Victor. "Where's Skipper?" Malcolm asked.

Zack shook his head. "He got bit. Didn't want to risk turning in the hilo killing us all."

"Son of a bitch!" Malcolm roared as he punched the metal walls of the helicopter. Anne reached out to him and grabbed his knee and rubbed it.

"I'm sorry," she comforted.

"Thanks, Anne. Skipper and I were close. Losing him...losing him hurts. What the hell happened out there?" Malcolm asked, looking at Sabrina and Victor.

Victor shook his head. "It was good until we got the governor. Then shit went to hell. They all lied to us. They had just assumed that we had a solution if someone was bit. We didn't. So when they turned, the fuckers flanked us because our backs were turned trying to defend them."

"We lost good sailors for some bullshit." Sabrina growled.

"The situation was fubar, but we still have a job to do." Zack replied. "Keep our heads in the game. Skipper told me his final wish was for us to protect his wife and daughter. We go before them, got it?"

"Yes, sir," Malcolm, Sabrina and Victor all replied.

"Good." Zack replied, adjusting his tactical vest.

The helicopter ride was silent as they flew over the city. Most of them just stared at the action below in awe. Just like downtown, other parts of the city were hectic. Firefights between people and the undead, lifeless bodies stretched out on the street, houses and cars on fire, hordes of zombies destroying everything in their path. It was a horror that humans weren't meant to see.

Malcolm couldn't believe his eyes. Just this morning, everything seemed normal. He waved good morning to his neighbors. He got his coffee and doughnut from the normal place. He even sat in rush hour traffic like he usually did. Now all of that was gone. The America he once knew was now a wasteland.

Looking away from outside, his vision then focused on Anne. He stared at her, reviewing her body covered in blood that wasn't hers. He was thankful that she made it out of the mall alive. He was even more thankful that she protected Kelsey as Malcolm didn't know how Zack would react if he lost her.

Malcolm's mind replayed their fight to get out of the mall, and the memory of how Anne fought. He was impressed with the way she moved and fought bravely. It was almost like he saw a different side of her. She would've made a good soldier.

The more he thought about Anne, the more he realized the situation that they were going to be in when they landed at the base. His eyes opened wide and he turned towards Zack who was holding Kelsey close.

"Zack?"

"Yeah, what is it?" He asked, turning his attention to his comrade.

"Anne...what are we going to do about her when we get back to base? You heard the Admiral. No friends allowed. Only spouses and kids. We're fucked the moment we land."

"Shit, you're right," Zack replied.

"Can't he make an exception?" Kelsey asked.

Malcolm shook his head. "The Navy doesn't do exceptions. It's one way only. Like us, the Admiral is under orders. He can only do so much. It's probably already hectic on base with all of the civilians around."

"He's right. It's going to be a hard no," Victor added.

"So what would happen to me?" Anne asked, concerned.

Zack, Sabrina, Malcolm and Victor all shared the same grim facial feature. They didn't need to say anything for Anne to know the news won't be good.

Zack sighed, "they would probably force you out to the nearest safe zone."

"Those zones are bullshit. The safest spot is with us. Zack, isn't there something that we could do?" Kelsey complained.

"I'm sorry baby, but my hands are tied. Those safe zones would be secured by the military. So, they would be in the best hands."

"You and I both know that's bullshit. Kelsey's right, the safest area for Anne to be is with us." Malcolm debated.

"I can't see a way to convince the Admiral to let her stay."

Malcolm bit his lip and studied Anne. He could tell that she was worried about going to the camps. Like him, he knew that she didn't want to be separated from Kelsey.

"It's okay, guys. I'm fine with going to the camps. It's only temporary, right?" Anne asked Zack.

"Yeah, it is. Don't worry, the military is going to kick ass once we get settled. Just wait and see." Zack reassured.

Malcolm stared at Anne and she gave him a thumbs up.

Even when she was scared she still put on a brave face, he thought. The longer he kept watching Anne, the more he thought of ways he could help her. Suddenly an idea dawned on him.

"Spouses are only allowed on base, right?" Malcolm asked Zack.

"Yeah, we've been over this million times."

"I know, but hold on I'm thinking of something..."

"This ought to be good," Victor joked.

Malcolm gave Victor the stink eye before refocusing on Zack.

"What if we say Anne is married to me?"

"You can't be serious," Anne interjected.

"Do you have a better idea?" Malcolm replied. "I mean, we won't be actually married, just playing the part. We'd say that we got married over the weekend, you know a spur of the moment type of thing, like we went to Vegas or some shit, and I was supposed to tell everyone but the zombie attack happened and that ruined the announcement."

"They won't believe that," Anne debated.

"They would. Everyone on base knows how close the four of us are. Hell, a lot of them saw us dance at Kelsey and Zack's wedding. We could get away with this."

"I agree with Malcolm, most of the squads know that y'all are tight." Sabrina interjected.

"Yeah, I mean, I wouldn't question it." Victor added. "Also this goes without saying, whatever y'all decide, we got your six."

"Yeah, we'd back up your story if anyone asks." Sabrina confirmed.

"I don't know..." Anne doubted.

"No, it's a good plan." Zack confirmed. "Malcolm is right. Not many people would question a drunk wedding between the two of you."

"Well, that's saying a lot," Kelsey grinned.

"You're not helping," Anne added.

"Anne, come on. This is the only way we can all stay together. I promise, we'd be married just for show, nothing else would go down."

Anne rubbed her elbow and bit her lip. "Are you sure?"

She studied his face as Malcolm narrowed his eyes and held her hand. His eyes showed the true intent that this gesture was only a means to keep her safe. In a comforting way, this warmed her to the idea, easing some of the tension.

"This is the only way." He confirmed.

"Fine." She sighed. "Let's get married. You know I expected a bit more for my first wedding proposal, you know... the man down on one knee, flowers, chocolates. That sorta of thing."

"Well, perhaps if you weren't so high maintenance, you would have gotten married by now." He smirked.

"Please, I'm obviously out of your league. Just be thankful I said yes. As far as everyone else knows, you just captured the great white whale."

"Oh!" Victor and Sabrina joked.

"Funny, I was going to say the same thing," Malcolm flirted.

"Aww, look not even married for a minute and they already have their first fight. Such a lovely couple." Zack joked. "I'm going to radio in HQ letting them know that Mrs. White would be joining us."

"White-Yamaguchi, at least hyphen it." Anne added.

Everyone laughed including Anne, who had a small smile on her face.

"Of course. How could I forget." Zack grinned, before switching off the private line to talk to base.

"Aww, they grow up so fast," Kelsey mocked.

Sabrina pulled up her phone and aimed it at Anne and Malcolm. "Smile, newlyweds!"

Without commenting, both Malcolm and Anne flicked off Sabrina and she laughed, taking the picture.

"Oh, yeah, you two were made for each other," Victor teased, studying the photo.

"On a serious note, there's something missing if this rouse is going to work." Kelsey grinned.

"What's that?" Anne asked.

"A ring," Kelsey replied, pulling off her own golden wedding band.

"Oh, Kelsey I can't. That's yours."

"You're right it is mine, but I want you to wear it. You are my best friend, and I can't picture a world without you in it. If wearing this helps the lie, then I'm okay with it."

"Okay," Anne replied, taking the ring out of her hand. She slipped the ring on and was surprised at how well it fit. She wasn't used to the weight of it though. It wasn't just the metal weighing her down either. The whole idea of having a fake marriage with Malcolm was a lot. She liked him as a friend, but marriage was something else and suddenly she felt a lot of pressure to act like a married couple.

How do you act madly in love when you're not? Anne wondered.

SEVEN

The helicopter landed at Little Creek Navy Base with a hard thud. Once on the ground, Sabrina and Victor left first, followed by Zack, assisting Kelsey. Malcolm and Anne were last out as he carried her out of the vehicle. As Malcolm held her, their eyes met yet again.

To Malcolm, holding her felt different. Before, it was always in a joking or nonchalant matter, but now it felt different. They were married now. Even if it was a fake marriage, they had to act like it was real.

Once Malcolm placed Anne down on her feet, he pushed a stray strand of her hair back. Anne shivered from his touch. She didn't know why. Something about his touch and his deep husky stare made her stomach tremble.

"What was that for?" Anne asked.

"It's all an act, remember? If we are going to sell this, then we sell it." Malcolm explained.

"Yeah, but it felt real."

"The more realistic our love, the more our lie would work. Come on."

He held her hand and Anne stared at his brown skinned hand

wrapped around her beige skin. His hand was larger than hers and warmer. His calloused hands were tougher than her soft skin, and she could feel the years of holding a gun from the rough texture.

As they left the helicopter pad, they were met by three other sailors. Each of them stared at Kelsey and Anne.

"Morris, who is this? I thought your CO said no civilians were traveling back with you." LTJG Sawyer Knox asked.

"This is my wife Kelsey," Zack replied, "and over there is Malcolm's wife, Anne."

"Huh, I've heard you talk about Kelsey before, but Malcolm I didn't know you were married."

"Yeah, I well, we actually got married over the weekend."

"Really?" Sawyer questioned in disbelief. He gawked at Anne and then back at Malcolm.

Right then, Anne's heart started to beat rapidly.

Was their plan going to work, she wondered.

Her hand gripped Malcolm's tighter and he looked back at her. His gentle eyes calmed her. They were comforting and at the same time reassuring, almost as if he was saying it's going to be alright.

"Yes, we all flew out to Vegas over the weekend. Her and I got married in the chapel."

"Hold on…" Sawyer closed his eyes, placed his hand up, and shook his head. "I'm just trying to wrap my head around this. Last I checked you were single and sleeping around, now you're a tied down man in one weekend?" Sawyer pointed out.

"What can I say man, drunken love. Anne and I've been friends for years. When you know, you know." Malcolm replied with a smirk.

Sawyer chuckled. "Yeah, I'm calling bullshit."

"Really?" Malcolm asked.

"Yeah, really, I think this whole marriage thing is fake. You heard the Admiral about no girlfriends and you stuck a ring on her finger so that you could sneak her on base."

Anne's nerves were out of control now. In her head she screamed, *he's on to us!*

Glancing at Malcolm, he appeared cooler than a cucumber as his grin grew.

"Really? Do you really want to question that? Do you want to bother the Admiral to tell him about this special manhunt for my marriage certificate, while the nation is under attack from the undead? Do you think that's a good use of your time?"

Sawyer opened his mouth and then looked away, muttering something under his breath.

"That's what I thought. Excuse us..." Malcolm replied, walking past Sawyer, whose face was redder than a cherry.

Anne double checked on Sawyer and then back at Malcolm and whispered, "I can't believe that worked."

"Me either, but it's best not to gloat. We still have to convince the entire base that we're married."

"Right, good point."

Anne placed her head on Malcolm's shoulder as they walked and it made Malcolm jump. He didn't expect to be this close to her. However, he wasn't going to complain.

Despite the blood and guts in her hair, she still smelled nice. He wondered how that was even possible. He's been touched by a woman before, but he hasn't felt this way. In some small corner of his heart, he actually liked what was happening at the moment.

Most of the families had already arrived on base and were walking around exploring the area that they were permitted to go into. Temporary barracks had been made on the grass field that Malcolm and Zack were playing on earlier that day. Soldiers gave blankets and supplies to the families directing them to various tents. The group of Sabrina, Victor, Zack, Kelsey, Malcolm and Anne all walked together, taking in the sights of the chaotic motion. There were people crying, people yelling and begging for things, soldiers patrolling the area with their hands on the triggers as if everyone was a prisoner. There was a strong tension in the air, and Malcolm could tell that this wasn't the base he was used to. It felt more like a concentration camp than a navy base. As they walked, they heard a voice call out, "Zack!"

Zack searched for the origin of the call, and spotted Sheri and Keshia who both ran towards him. Sheri was a short, bigger black woman, with short hair. Her tan capri shorts were ripped and her shirt was covered in blood. Beside her was a young child, Keshia. She was mixed with light brown skin, light mocha hair and had blue eyes like her father. She trembled as she clung to her mother's leg.

"Zack, thank God. When we got the call to come to base, I expected to see Charles here, but they told me he went on a mission downtown. Where is he? Is he alright?"

Zack bit his lip and hesitated.

"No..." Sheri cried. She covered her face as tears began to flow down her cheeks.

"I'm sorry, Sheri. He got bit and chose to stay behind."

"Oh, Charles!" Sheri wailed, she collapsed in Zack's arms crying. Zack shushed her, attempting to comfort her.

"I'm sorry that I wasn't there. I had to save Kelsey. She was trapped in the mall across the street. Perhaps if I was there..."

"Don't." Sheri snapped, wiping her tears away. "Don't you dare say it. You did what you had to do to save Kelsey. Don't blame yourself for that."

"Yes, ma'am." Zack replied, holding her tightly.

"Did he die with honor?"

"Yes, he covered the retreat for all of us."

"That's my Charles." A small smile appeared on Sheri's face as she wiped her tears away. Zack did the same as he cleared his throat.

"Before I left, he made me promise to take care of you. Anything you need day or night come and see me, okay?"

Sheri nodded.

"And if he's not there, come and see me." Kelsey added. "Us military spouses got to stick together, right?"

"Yes, thank you all."

"No, thank you for your sacrifice." Kelsey replied, giving Sheri a big hug. As they hugged, Petty Officer 1st Class, Richard Green came walking up to Zack and Malcolm. He was a younger man, with a fresh face and only a few years of the Navy under his belt. Unlike the muscular SEALs in front of him, Richard was small, short and skinny. With red hair and black rimmed glasses resting on his freckled nose. His green and black fatigues were crisp and clean unlike the battle worn uniforms that the Navy SEALs had.

"Lieutenant Morris?" He asked, saluting.

"Yes?"

"You and Lieutenant White are wanted In Rear Admiral Wesley's office for a debriefing. I am also supposed to take your wives to your barracks to get settled in. After your meeting with the Admiral, come to zone D, barracks three and four and you will find Mrs. Morris and Mrs. White-Yamaguchi."

Anne's eyes opened up wide hearing her new last name. While it was discussed on the helicopter, it was a different feeling to hear someone else say it. It felt like it was cementing the fact that she was now married to Malcolm. Granted it was a fake marriage, it was still real to the people around her, and that was a fact she had to get used to.

"Yes, we'll be right there." Zack and Malcolm shared a concerning glance knowing that the Admiral wanted to talk to them about what happened downtown.

Zack looked back at Victor and he nodded. "Go ahead, I got Sheri and Keshia. Come on ladies."

Sheri and Keshia began to walk away before stopping.

Sheri turned back and said, "when you guys get settled, come and find me. I'm in Zone D, barracks ten. I'm not too far from you."

"Of course." Kelsey replied, waving back to Sheri as she left with Sabrina and Victor.

"Sir, I'll get Anne and Kelsey settled in the barracks." Richard offered in a stern voice.

"Thank you." Zack replied. Before he left, he hugged his wife and held her close. His hand rested on her cheek and then gave her a passionate kiss. "I'll be right back, okay?"

"See you soon, babe." Kelsey breathed, giving him a loving stare.

Anne and Malcolm both froze as they gawked at each other.

In Malcolm's mind he was wondering if he should kiss Anne as well. He debated since they were married, they might as well act like it, but how far is he allowed to go, he questioned. A hug? A kiss? A simple goodbye. While the discussion of saying that they were married was easy, but everything else was complicated. How far was too far? How much PDA was needed to keep up this ruse?

Anne wondered the same thing. She liked Malcolm, but she didn't like him enough to kiss him goodbye. While the idea of faking a marriage made sense to her, the other small details confused her. What was okay, and wasn't okay? Was he supposed to kiss her or whisper sweet nothings in her ear in front of people, or not?

Anne was partly angry at Kelsey and Zack for being a newlywed power couple.

Why couldn't they be old bitter spouses, that never kissed or said that they loved each other? Anne wondered.

"I love you," Anne replied, dryly. Her words weren't believable to nobody.

"I love you too, Anniecakes," Malcolm grinned, blowing a kiss.

Victor snickered and Sabrina elbowed him in the side, shaking her head.

Zack almost laughed too as he held his breath.

There was an awkward silence between the group as they all looked at each other.

"Umm, yeah I would hate to break up you two lovebirds, but Malcolm and I need to debrief." Zack replied, dragging Malcolm away from the horrible situation.

Walking away Zack chuckled. "Anniecakes?"

"Don't start. You put me in that situation."

"What did I do?"

"Oh, you know what you did. Being all romantic and shit. Making Anne and us look bad."

"Umm you did that yourself. You should've just kissed her."

"Kissed her? This is Anne we're talking about. We're just friends... well, I guess husband and wife, but you get what I'm talking about."

"Actually, I don't know. I saw the way y'all were admiring each other. There's something there."

"There's nothing there."

"Okay," Zack rosed his eyebrows, and then winked at his friend.

Malcolm rolled his eyes as he walked through the door to the officer's offices.

"On a scale to one to ten, how much shit do you think we're in for disobeying orders?"

"About as much trouble you're in for using Anniecakes."

"Fuck," Malcolm grumbled.

ANNIECAKES? Anne wondered as she followed Richard around the barracks. *What in the hell did he mean by that? Next time I see him, we have to talk about pet names. I hate them. God that was awkward,* she thought.

"Hey, are you okay?" Kelsey asked.

"Yeah, I was just thinking to myself that I have to talk to my husband about random pet names."

"Anniecakes?"

"Please don't repeat that." Anne laughed.

"Yeah, that was the highest of levels of cringe." Kelsey confirmed.

The two friends followed the sailor through the rows and rows of outdoor tan tents. Each tent was about ten feet high and ten feet wide. Outside it seemed like there was a small village of spouses and their children. Some were talking, others were organizing their assigned spaces. Multiple kids were running around playing tag. While the threat of zombies was present, it seemed like none of the families were overwhelmed.

"It looks like everyone is settled. I'm impressed that everyone got so comfortable so easily." Anne observed.

"Don't underestimate military spouses. These people understand what it is to be uprooted in a day. I'm more impressed on how the Navy set up this little village of tents." Kelsey added.

"The Navy always had these temporary barracks. Normally these tents would be used overseas, but given the situation we put them up in the yard to take in the overflow of families." Richard replied.

"Ahh that makes sense," Kelsey confirmed.

"As far as the barracks go, please refrain from going out of your zone. Each zone has male bathrooms and female bathrooms, with showers in each. The mess area for each zone is at the end of the column, near the bathrooms. Breakfast, Lunch and Dinner is served for only an hour, at 0700, 1200 and 1700. You miss a meal, there's no substitutes. Your tents have already been furnished to suit you and your husbands. There are double beds along with lights, and cubbies for your personal items."

Anne's eyebrows rose at the mention of beds. She didn't even think about the sleeping situation until then.

"Since you weren't able to grab any of your belongings, we have provided you towels and some PT clothes to wear. Feel free to look through lost and found if you want other clothing options. Any questions?"

"No, sir," Kelsey replied. "I think you explained it all."

Richard nodded and then guided them to their barracks with an open hand. "If you need anything please come and find me. I am in charge of zone D. The Admiral is planning on having a community meeting at 0900 tomorrow. Attendance is mandatory. Other than that, you ladies have a wonderful evening."

"Thank you," Kelsey replied.

Richard nodded and walked away.

"So what did you want to do first?" Kelsey asked.

"Is that even a question? A shower would be lovely. I really want to get the smell of the dead off me."

"You see...there's a reason why I like you. Come on, let's go get our towels." Kelsey grinned.

ZACK TOOK a deep breath and glanced at Malcolm before they entered the Admiral's office.

"You wanted to see me, sir?" Zack asked.

"Yes, close the door." Admiral Wesley commanded. The older commander scratched his chin as he stared at the two Navy SEALS in his office.

"You know I ought to bust your butts right now. Not following orders and splitting off on your own mission. You're lucky that the mission went to shit and the governor was bit beforehand. Any other way, I would have your ass." The Admiral growled.

"Sir, if I may, our wives were in danger. They were across the street. We had to save them." Malcolm interjected.

"Don't even get me started with you Lieutenant White. Married? Since when?"

"I got married in Vegas over the weekend, sir. I'm in love with Anne." Malcolm replied.

Admiral laughed and shook his head. "Is that so?" He stared at Malcolm studying his mannerisms before sighing and shaking his head. "Honestly, if this was any other situation and the world didn't go to hell, I would bust your ass right now. However, I do understand the situation. Phase one of Code Z was all about protecting families. This is exactly why Washington ordered the families on base first because they knew soldiers would not follow orders to get their loved ones. You two did exactly what they thought, and went off mission. We lose command, we lose this war. Now that your wives are here and protected by the military, I expect no more deviations. Orders are orders, understood?"

"Yes, sir."

"Good. Zack, with the absence of Captain Peterson, I'm promoting you to team leader and captain."

"Thank you sir."

Admiral Wesley nodded. "While Phase One was successful, it came at a cost. This virus knocked the nation hard, in attempting to protect our own, we lost a lot of military service members and are limited with air and naval support. I'm keeping the remaining air support here on base. Your team will also be smaller. Sabrina and Victor will remain and as of right now I won't add anyone else."

"Sir?" Zack questioned.

"We're stretched thin as it is. I'm breaking up the units into smaller man units. Keeping some on patrol here, while sending out a few to help with other safe zones. Command is focused on keeping the living alive, the last thing they want is to add to the army of undead. Therefore , at 0200, you and your team will leave via Humvee to patrol safe zone B." He explained pointing to an area on the map on his desk. He stared at both SEALs and said, "You will patrol the area keeping any undead from entering and perform search and rescue for any survivors. Near Safe zone B is a hospital, so keep your head on a swivel as many people would be coming and going to that area. The hospital already knows not to allow people with bites in, but you know people won't follow the rules, so you may be called in to defend the hospitals from hostiles."

"You think people will be violent if they are denied entry?" Malcolm questioned.

"I wouldn't be surprised. Hell, nothing surprises me anymore given that we have the undead walking around. Any more questions?"

"No, sir." They both replied.

"Good, get some rest and chow, as in the next hours you'd be going back out there. Good luck men."

"Thank you sir," Zack and Malcolm both saluted and left the office, heading back to zone D to get a well needed rest.

———

WHEN MALCOLM ENTERED the tent it was empty, but Malcolm could tell that Anne had been in there given how things were shuffled around. He spotted her dirty, bloodied clothes on the ground and noted that a towel was missing and figured that she left the tent to take a shower.

Thinking of a shower made Malcolm want one too as he was covered in dirt, grime, and blood from their earlier skirmish with the zombies. He wasn't even thinking as he began to undress. Right when he removed his boxers, Anne walked in with a towel draped around her body. Her eyes grew wide as she spotted Malcolm naked.

"Shit! I'm sorry, I should've knocked."

"It's cool, it's cool." Malcolm repeated, quickly covering himself up with a towel. "Remember we're married. We should have already seen each other naked by now."

"True. I guess me getting changed somewhere else is out of the question?"

Malcolm laughed. "Yeah. Don't worry, I'm going to give you the room. I have to take a shower myself. How was it?"

"Cold and there was barely any water pressure. It was like taking a shower underneath a water hose."

"Ha, only the best from the US Navy. A'ight, well, I'll be right back."

"Yeah, see you soon." Anne smiled as Malcolm exited.

Once he was gone, Anne quickly changed into a pair of PT shorts and shirt. The navy-blue shirt was too big for her, and the shorts kept sliding down her small hips, so she ended up rolling the shorts to keep them upright.

Climbing into the bed, Anne felt exhausted, but there was something on her mind. Well, something big. Really Big. Malcolm. She'd never seen him naked before and when she walked in and saw him naked her whole body seemed to shake. His muscles alone twisted her stomach into knots. Just thinking about his body made her insides quiver. She couldn't stop herself as her head became filled with sensual thoughts. A vivid image of him inside her projected in her brain, she tried to think of something else, but her mind was on auto control as the erotic image left her in shambles.

What in the hell is in the water here? Anne asked herself as the naughty thoughts continued. Anne laid in bed, trying to compose herself, but the swoon worthy sexual imagery kept replaying in her mind. It was pure torture for her. Her mind was adrift until Malcolm returned from the shower.

"Ah, that was amazing."

"Ha, if you like cold showers. The shower back at my place was one of a kind. Massaging jets, removable shower head. Most importantly, it has *warm water*." Anne smirked.

"Oh, don't tease me." Malcolm grinned. "I'm about to change now...so..."

"Yeah, sorry," Anne looked away and Malcolm began to get dressed, but Anne didn't shy away for long as she had to confirm what her eyes saw earlier. Judging by what she saw, her assumptions were correct.

Once Malcolm was dressed he grabbed a blanket and laid it on the ground beside Anne.

"What are you doing?" Anne asked.

"We don't have to keep up the charade all the time." Malcolm explained.

"True, but we also don't need Richard or anyone else poking their head in and seeing you sleep on the floor. Newlyweds don't have their spouses sleep on their floor."

"True, good point. Newlyweds are usually fucking their brains out."

"Umm..."

"Yeah, don't worry we're not going to do any of that. Unless you want to..."

"No, no, no. I'm fine. No need to push the rouse that much."

"Okay, good. Glad we can draw that line." Malcolm grinned.

The two shared a curious glance once more. Both wondering what the other was thinking about at that moment.

Malcolm cleared his throat and then pointed to the bed. "I guess I'm getting in. Scoot over."

Anne made room for Malcolm and the two laid together silently staring at the green tent ceiling.

"Well, this is a bit awkward." Malcolm admitted.

Anne laughed. "It really is. It could be the way you are laying down. You're like a log. It's okay to cuddle me up a bit."

"You sure?"

"Yeah, this bed is definitely made for one person, both of our asses are hanging off the edge. It's cool to get a little closer to me."

"Okay," Malcolm replied, wrapping his arms around Anne. As they laid there cuddling, Anne smelled Malcolm's manly scent and it made her heart flutter.

"Thank you for saving my life today."

"You're welcome, Anne. You're special to me. I'd do anything for you," Malcolm said before falling asleep.

Anne listened to Malcolm softly breathe wondering what in the hell was going on. These new found feelings for Malcolm kept appearing. She didn't know what to do with them, but she did know that he was a good friend, and being wrapped in his arms was all she wanted at the time.

EIGHT

It was early in the morning when Anne woke up. She stretched her body and turned to place her arm on Malcolm, but he wasn't there. Part of her missed his warmth as the time they spent together sleeping was comfortable, like a warm blanket on a cold winter day.

Laying there she thought of the past hours and how she became Mrs. White-Yamaguchi. It all happened so fast. One minute they were being evacuated from downtown, the next she was in a fake marriage with a ring on her finger.

Malcolm was a good man, he was honest and kind, however, he wasn't what she thought she wanted for a romantic partner. Malcolm was a good friend, nothing more.

The more she thought about the marriage the more she wondered how long they would have to play this charade. It was obvious that they had to stay married during their time in the barracks but what about after? What will happen to their relationship once they manage to contain the zombie threat? Would they get a divorce or would they be forced to play house for the rest of their lives?

Question after question rolled through her mind as she realized that she was trapped. While she's grateful for the situation and being safe inside the navy base. She was concerned that the choice she made to marry Malcolm had locked her into a relationship she didn't choose. What if she met someone that she liked. What would happen to Malcolm. Would he be punished for deceiving everyone?

The more she thought about it, the more her head hurt as she rubbed her temples.

Sitting up in the bed, Anne heard Kelsey's voice outside.

"Anne? Can I come in?" She asked.

"Yeah, come on in."

Kelsey walked in with a large smile on her face. Like Anne, she was wearing a yellow and navy-blue physical training shirt and shorts. Unlike Anne, Kelsey's outfit actually fit her petite frame. "So how was your first night as a married woman? Did anything go down?"

Anne rolled her eyes. "No, we just passed out. We did cuddle though."

"Ohh!" Kelsey squealed.

"Please, don't. Malcolm and I aren't like that."

"Like what?"

"This marriage or whatever you want to call it is just for me to stay here with you on base. Malcolm and I will never get close."

"Never?"

Anne shook her head. "I'm sorry, I know you and Zack have this fantasy of the two of us being married, but I can't see it. I like Malcolm, but not as much as you guys think."

"Oh..." Kelsey looked away and rubbed her elbow. "Sorry, I didn't mean to push you..."

"It's okay," Anne grinned. "I don't mind the teasing. I just wanted to let you know where I stood."

"I gotcha." Kelsey replied.

"Speaking of Malcolm, do you know where he went?"

"Patrol, he and Zack are defending a safe zone. They left late last night."

"Oh, I didn't even hear him leave. He didn't even say goodbye."

"Perhaps, he didn't want to wake you."

"I guess so..." Anne's voice trailed.

"I'm sure they're safe. Take it from one military wife to the other, it's best not to think of that."

Anne rose her eyebrows at her friend's remarks.

Kelsey read her mind and replied, "oh you know what I mean. Romantic partners or just friends, you still care for him. All I'm trying to tell you is not to worry."

"I guess you're right. So what's the plan for today?"

"Well, we have an hour before breakfast. I figured we go outside and practice our forms."

"Sounds good to me, let me grab my katana." Anne replied.

Anne strapped her sheath around her waist and followed Kelsey into her tent so that she could grab her blade. The two then walked to an open area in zone D and began practicing doing various slices and thrusts.

It was picturesque of the two women practicing as the sun was beginning to come up. As the two trained, it looked like it was taken out of a movie, with the sun raising in the background, their shadows were being casted, sweat beaded their foreheads as they repeated the same technique over and over again.

Anne made sure to breathe as she channeled her ki. She narrowed her eyes, stilling herself as she became one with her blade. She shuffled her feet shoulder length apart, and with a grunt, she swiped her sword, going through her motions of hacks and slashes. Each time she roared, she channeled her ki into powerful strikes.

Kelsey did the same, moving like Anne's twin. Both women moved with deadly grace as they practiced their forms.

When they were done, they sheathed their blades breathing heavily.

Applause erupted from the distance making Anne and Kelsey jump, and when they turned to discover the origin of the sound, they saw Admiral Wesley watching them with admiration. He was wearing his brown service dress uniform, with two silver stars attached to his collar.

"That was impressive." He complimented.

"Thank you Admiral." Kelsey replied.

"Were you practicing Kendo? When I was stationed in Japan, I've seen similar forms." He asked.

"Yes, we were." Anne replied. "Have you studied?"

"I've taken a few lessons when I was stationed there. Never kept it up." With a smile on his face he asked, "is it true that you both survived on your own against the undead using only your swords?"

Anne laughed, "I wouldn't say survived. I don't think we would've made it if Malcolm and Zack didn't show up when they did."

"Yes, sir. They saved our lives yesterday. We were stranded on the roof before they came."

"Yes, I know I've seen the debrief. I was just impressed that two civilians handled themselves like you did. From the way Malcolm described you Anne, you were like a samurai slicing up zombies left and right."

Anne laughed and rubbed the back of her head. "Malcolm likes to bend the truth sometimes. I was just doing what I could to survive."

"Huh..." the Admiral paused and then crossed his arms. "I won't hold you up much longer, but I was curious, how would you two feel about teaching a kendo class to the families on base? Bullets can only go so far, and if we need a call to arms we will need a way to defend ourselves in case of breach."

"Sir, with respect, kendo takes years to master. Kelsey and I've been training most of our lives to get to the level we're at."

"I'm aware. I'm not asking for an army. Just teach some techniques to properly swing a sword. We have some lying around in the armory, and in case of emergency, I would like everyone to know how to defend themselves."

Kelsey and Anne shared a look before, Anne nodded, and shrugged giving the silent agreement to Kelsey.

Kelsey smiled and faced the Admiral. "We'd be happy to assist, sir."

"Perfect. Well, I won't hold you two up. Remember breakfast is at 0700. After that I will be speaking to all of the families about the duties on base. Have a good morning."

The Admiral walked away leaving Kelsey and Anne to stare at each other.

"What was that about?" Anne asked.

"I'm not sure, but it's not everyday an Admiral gives us praise, so I'll take it."

"You would. Are you going to brag about this to Zack?"

"You know I will. Master Morris has a nice ring, doesn't it?"

"Don't push it." Anne joked.

The friends finished their training and went to breakfast together. With their katanas on their sides, they drew a few eyes, but neither of the women cared as they were waiting in line for food. As they approached the serving table, they spotted Richard who was spooning out portions of oatmeal in people's bowls. Like yesterday, the sailor was wearing his green and black fatigues and his black boots were shined.

When the petty officer noticed them, he gave Kelsey and Anne a large smile. "Mrs. Morris and Mrs. White-Yamaguchi. Good morning."

"Morning," they greeted.

"Is everything okay with your barracks?"

"It is, thank you," Kelsey smiled.

"Oh, Richard, you mentioned that you had clothes in the lost and found. Where can we find that?" Anne asked.

"If you come and find me after breakfast and the briefing from Rear Admiral Wesley, I'd help get you sorted."

"Perfect. Thank you, Richard." Anne replied.

"Mmm, smells good. What are we having for breakfast today?" Kelsey inquired.

"Just oatmeal, and a side of apple sauce. There's also coffee , juice, and water if you want it on the drink table." Richard pointed down the buffet line at each item available.

"Sounds delicious. We're both starving as we barely ate anything after escaping from the mall." Anne admitted.

"Oh, well, don't tell anyone, but here..." Richard gave both women another serving of oatmeal. "To fill up those stomachs."

"Ahh, thanks Richard." Kelsey smiled.

"Yeah, you rock Richard."

"Anything for zone D. We have to stick together, am I right?"

"Of course," Kelsey grinned. "We'd see you later, Richard."

"Yep, bye!" He smiled before serving another woman in line.

"He's nice," Anne observed, as they collected an apple sauce pouch and headed to the drink table.

"Yeah, I'm glad he's in charge of our zone. It seems like we lucked out. Did you want me to grab you coffee?"

"Yes, please." Anne replied.

Kelsey grabbed two coffees from the server and then handed one to Anne. She then looked down the rows of tables. "Where did you want to sit?" Kelsey asked, observing the four long rows of tables. By her guess, there had to be at least twenty-five people on each row.

Anne scanned the tables before spotting Sheri and her child, Keshia. They were sitting alone at the end of the table.

"Did you want to sit with Sheri and Keshia?"

"Yes, I've wanted to check up on them anyways."

Anne and Kelsey walked towards the family and when they got near, Kelsey smiled and asked, "Good morning Sheri, can we sit next to you?"

"Sure," she replied.

"How are you feeling?" Kelsey asked.

"I'm still a bit raw. I woke up this morning and I realized that Charles was no longer in my life. I cried a bit when I woke up and I cried a bit more again. It's been a tough grieving process. I've been through it before with other spouses who've lost loved ones overseas, but I never thought I would have to go through it myself. I guess that's the duty that all military spouses have. Anne, you'll learn soon enough. You think you'd get used to it, but it's hard. Every mission they go on, you hold your breath, until they come home and are in your arms again."

Anne looked away and thought of Malcolm. Although she wasn't in love with him, she was concerned over his safety. Watching the emotional toll that Sheri went through, Anne wondered if she could take the same heartache of losing Malcolm. As a friend she cared for him and didn't want to see anything bad happen to him.

"True, Zack's been on my mind since he left camp."

Sheri nodded.

"Zack's promise extends to us too," Kelsey explained. "Anything you need you got it. If you want, we can hang out more. I don't know many of the people here, but you and I go way back as Zack served under Charles for many years."

"Sure, I'd like that. I think I'd go crazy with how locked down this place is."

"Me too," Anne replied. "I feel safe within these walls, but do they really need patrols watching our every movements?"

"They are here for our protection." Kelsey added.

"I'm aware of that, but it's a lot to get used to."

"You'd get used to it. I know you and Malcolm are newlyweds so the whole idea of being on base throws you off, but every time I've been on base, it's about the same tension. It's just how this place feels. You tend to forget about it after a while." Sheri added.

Anne nodded as she ate a spoonful of oatmeal.

The group was quiet until Keshia pulled her mother's shirt. "Mommy, can I go play with those kids over there?"

"Yes, you may, but remember to stay where I can see you."

"Okay. Love you, mommy." Keshia yelled before giggling with glee to join the other kids nearby.

Kelsey smiled watching the kids play and then asked Sheri, "how is Keshia taking the news?"

"Surprisingly well. Charles and I have had talks with her explaining daddy's profession and how dangerous it is. We had a long cry last night, but since then she's been brave. She told me she wanted to be a hero like daddy. Once again that broke my heart." Sheri sniffed, wiping her eyes.

"She has Charles' eyes," Kelsey noted.

"She does. She has his heart and spirit too. It's almost like he left me a part of him down here. It's nice. Are you and Zack thinking of kids?"

"We were," Kelsey admitted. "However, with all that's going on, I'm having second thoughts. Do I really want a child to be born in a world with zombies?"

"Kids get born into war torn countries all the time. Only difference is they don't have the US military protecting it. We're in a very secure base. I don't think you should hesitate. Creating life with someone you love is one of the most fulfilling things you could go through. My advice is if you want kids don't wait. Just do."

Kelsey smiled. "That's a good point. Perhaps I'll try to convince Zack to start creating life tonight."

"Ahh, could you not talk about that? I'm eating." Anne exclaimed.

Kelsey and Sheri both laughed loudly and Sheri clutched her sides from her uncontrollable laughter.

"Oh, I needed that laugh." Sheri admitted. "So Anne, are you and Malcolm wanting kids?"

Once the question was asked, Anne felt a lump in her throat. The oatmeal suddenly felt dry and she was feeling light headed.

"I...umm..." Anne stuttered. "It's not that I don't want kids..." Anne began to say trying to figure out her words. "It's just Malcolm and I haven't really discussed having children. We're sort of just having fun and living in the spur of the moment."

"Oh, I remember those days," Sheri grinned. "Fucking until you can't see straight and couldn't walk. I met Charles when he was stationed in San Diego. I was a server at a local bar near base. He only had eyes for me when he first saw me. Then again a lot of guys did. I had curves for days." Sheri laughed, glancing away as if she was reliving the memory.

"Hey now, Sheri, you still look good." Kelsey responded.

"Ah, girl, not like then. I had those Navy boys drooling. All of them wanted a piece of this ass, if you catch my drift. However, I would always shoot them down. Charles on the other hand. He had no quit. That man never took no for answer." Sheri chuckled.

"I remember when he once tried to hire a singer just to serenade me."

"Did that work?" Anne asked.

"Nah, like I said, I don't fold easy. No, what I fell for wasn't his terrible pick-up lines or his elaborate ways to ask me out, what I fell for was his determination, his grit and never give up attitude. The man never took no for an answer. After a couple months of hitting on me, I finally said yes." Sheri gave Anne a naughty smirk. "After that we were like rabbits. I tell you, those Navy men have stamina for days. Of course, Anne, you would know, with you being a newlywed with Malcolm." Sheri rose her eyebrows at her.

Anne's face grew red as the sex talk was focusing on her. Kelsey snorted and then started laughing as she knew Anne's secret.

"I betcha Malcolm is good too, you got yourself a good-looking man. Better hold on to him." Sheri joked.

At that time, all Anne wanted to do was duck her head underneath the table. However the more she thought about Malcolm the more she remembered his sculpted godlike figure. Her body trembled at the thought of having sex with him. She squirmed in her seat as her thoughts got more vivid. Like an unstoppable train, naughty thoughts continued to become more rampant in her mind. She saw herself on the bed, he was on top of her, her legs were spread as he buried every inch of himself into her. Her heartbeat started to rapidly increase and she breathed heavily, trying to keep the lustful thoughts at bay.

"Oh, dear, I'm sorry to make you embarrassed. Your cheeks are more red than a cherry pie." Sheri snickered with her hand over her mouth.

"It's okay," Anne admitted, however, she would love to have a distraction to get her away from the awkward conversation about children. Her prayers were answered when Admiral Wesley walked to the center of the rows.

"Could I have everyone's attention?" He asked loudly.

Everyone stopped their conversations and stared at the Admiral. Even the kids stopped playing and stood at attention.

"Thank you. This won't be long, but I wanted to brief you on the situation. As of right now, the American government is still stable. As I speak multiple branches of the military are conducting strikes to defeat the undead threat. There's no timeline on when this could be met, so the government has decided to make these barracks temporary housing until we can be sure that the area outside those fences is safe. Since there's no timeline, and getting food in and out of base will be difficult, we will also be growing food inside the base. We have selected land plots that each zone will farm and grow their own vegetables and fruits. In addition, we will be having self-defense classes, just in case there's a breach. From what we've seen the zombies aren't strong enough to push down our fences, but if one does get through, we want everyone to be ready. Petty Officer Richard Green will teach gun safety, and Kelsey Morris and Anne White-Yamaguchi, will teach kendo for anyone who's wanting to know the basics of sword technique."

Sheri grinned at Anne and Kelsey. "Well, sign me up for your class," She whispered. "I want to be a badass like y'all."

Kelsey smiled and whispered back, "you're a badass in your own regard."

Sheri scoffed and waved off Kelsey as she resumed listening to the Admiral, like Kelsey did.

Anne however wasn't paying attention. She was too concerned over what the Admiral said about conducting strikes against the zombies. She didn't feel it before, but after talking to Sheri and Kelsey and listening to the Admiral speak about the aggressive offensive that they were going to do, she began to worry about Malcolm, and prayed that he was okay.

NINE

"Contact left! Contact left!" Victor yelled, firing quick bursts of gunfire.

"I see them. I see them," Sabrina repeated, assisting Victor with the additional zombie crawling towards them.

Zack and Malcolm were covering their flank, picking off zombies one by one as they approached them.

Victor moved swiftly down the street of the apartment complex. In the neighborhood, there were eight three-story apartment buildings in all, and they were ordered there to save a group of survivors who were holed up in building in the far end of the complex. It would've been an easy task if it wasn't for the dozens of zombies in their path.

The SEAL team fought off each zombie they encountered. They moved as one, taking out anything that got near.

"How far are we from the building 2241?" Malcolm asked, after shooting a zombie.

"I can't imagine that we have to go much further." Victor replied.

"Over there! I see it!" Sabrina yelled.

"Yeah, I see it too. Let's move people. Double time it. Those people don't have much time."

"Yes, sir," the group yelled as they pressed on.

Zack was still getting used to being in command. Two days ago he was just another member on the team, but now his squad looked to him to make decisions and not only did he have his life to consider, but his own team's making each of one of his decisions have weight.

They neared the building and saw the makeshift sandbags in front of it. The barrier kept most of the zombies out, but there was a small breach allowing a small number to flow in.

The Navy SEALs took out the group of zombies in front of the complex and then went up the stairs.

"Intel says they are on the third floor. Apartment 303." Zack relayed.

"Got it." Victor replied as he quickly took out a zombie on his way with the butt of his rifle. With a grunt, he smashed it skull with his foot giving it the killing blow. At the top of the stairs, Victor held a fist and everyone stopped. He then pointed toward the door to apartment 303 which was ajar with a dead corpse in the middle of the doorway.

"Fuck me. That's not good." Sabrina commented.

"Malcolm, tell them we're friendlies." Zack ordered as he covered the bottom of the stairwell.

"We are US Navy SEALs. Please acknowledge." Malcolm yelled out.

He received no response, but repeated his message. "This is the US Military. We got your distress message. Please acknowledge!"

Malcolm looked back at Zack and shook his head.

"Victor, take point. Don't shoot unless you are sure they are undead." Zack commanded.

"Yes, sir." Victor took a deep breath and then entered the apartment. The SEALs didn't see anything but the undead. The zombies admitted a low growl as they turned at attention.

"Drop them..." Zack growled.

With quick precision, the SEALs disposed of the six zombies with little effort, and when they were down, Zack surveyed the apartment. Malcolm bent down and reviewed the zombies they killed while Sabrina and Victor provided cover.

"What do you think?" Zack asked.

"I think we were too late. Judging by the woman and the man, I'm willing to guess this was the family that called us." Malcolm observed.

"You see a kid?"

"No..." Malcolm and Zack both shared a look. Malcolm immediately grabbed his rifle and crept towards the bedroom. "If you were a scared kid, where would you hide?"

"Mom and Dad's room."

"Yep." Malcolm entered the bedroom and noticed the closed closet door. Behind it he could hear shuffling and smiled as he nodded towards the door.

Zack nodded and provided cover as he stood back.

"Hey, kid. It's the Navy. We're here to save you. It's okay to come out. The monsters are gone." Malcolm said in a soft voice.

There was movement again, but the door didn't open.

Malcolm double checked with Zack and he shrugged, "perhaps the kid is deaf?"

Malcolm inched forward. He opened the door and sighed once he saw the horrible sight. The young boy, not older than three, was lying on the ground, his chest was wide open, as a zombie chewed on his insides.

"Fuck..." Malcolm groaned as it was a depressing sight to see such a small child mauled like that. Taking his pistol he shot the zombie chewing in the head. Malcolm sighed and shook his head.

"That's fucked up." Zack replied.

"This whole situation is fubar. He's just a toddler. What the fuck?"

As the two SEALs stared at each other, they heard a low-pitched growl. Malcolm turned around and saw the young boy reanimate as a zombie. His body wiggled as he came to life. He struggled to move, as he barely had any function in his body, due to most of it being chewed off. Howling, the tiny zombie attempted to crawl towards Malcolm.

Malcolm glanced at Zack and shook his head. He then turned back to the child and aimed his gun.

"Damn. I'm sorry kid."

Malcolm felt a horrible feeling in the pit of his stomach. He knew what he had to do was right. That kid was no longer a boy, he was a zombie. He was a threat to himself and his teammates, yet killing it didn't sit right with him. In little boys' eyes he was a hero. Heroes save kids, not let them die.

"You okay, brother?" Zack asked.

"Yeah, just a bit shaken up."

"You did what you had to do."

"Yeah, I know, but a kid?"

"There's going to be a lot more. It's just what this virus does." Zack walked closed to Malcolm and placed his hand on his shoulders. He stared deep into his eyes. "You can't let that shit throw you off. You good?"

"Yeah, I'm good."

"You sure?"

"Yeah, let's keep searching."

"Okay," Zack double checked his partner before yelling out, "hey, the apartment is cleared. Let's move out." Zack left the room, leaving Malcolm by himself.

Malcolm stared at the corpse one last time before departmentalizing the image. Like the other horrible things he's experienced in war, he learned a long time ago not to dwell too much on the past. However, this one stung a bit more than the others.

He was just a kid, Malcolm repeated in his head.

Closing his eyes he prayed that he could save a life, because he knew eventually all of this death and destruction was going to get to him.

Walking out of the room, Sabrina, Victor, and Zack were all waiting for him.

"You ready?" Zack asked.

Malcolm nodded. "Yeah, let's go hunting."

The team left the building, taking out any zombies that got in their way. After clearing the complex, they marched back to the safe zone nearby.

"Is it weird that we haven't seen any zombies?" Sabrina asked scanning the area.

"Don't jinx us. I'm getting low on ammo." Zack replied.

"Nah, she's right. I haven't seen a soul. It's eerie almost, as this street would normally be jammed back with traffic at this time. Now it's just us." Malcolm observed.

"Isn't it obvious? We're kicking ass. The zombies know what's up and they know if they fuck with us, they get a bullet to the skull." Victor laughed.

"In your case it's two bullets in the chest, then maybe one in the shoulder and then finally one in the head." Sabrina mocked.

"Hey! Headshots are hard!"

Everyone laughed and Victor's smile grew a bit wider as he looked towards Malcolm. "Let's change the subject. Since we've left base we haven't had a chance to talk to Malcolm about his romantic first night as a married man."

"Ohh!" Sabrina made a kissing noise. Victor and her laughed.

"Nothing happened." Malcolm replied.

"That's what they all say." Victor quipped. "I heard a cot creaking last night. You know how good my ears are."

"Oh, that's my bad," Zack grinned. "Kelsey and I had some we-nearly-died-sex."

"Oh, you see, these ears don't lie. Malcolm, since you are quiet I'm assuming you guys had we-nearly-died-sex as well." Victor questioned.

"We didn't have any type of sex at all. We're just friends."

"Bullshit. Two attractive people like yourselves didn't screw last night. Hell, y'all are married too."

"Technically married," Malcolm corrected.

"Whatever you want to call it, if I was in your situation I would be buried in it. Worst marriage ever. This is why I chose the single life. It's too much to be tied down. You have to beg for scraps. Hell, the only reason why Zack got some was because his wife and him were about to die."

"Yeah, that's not true at all," Zack added, but Victor ignored him as he continued his rant.

"Being single is much better. I love the ladies and the ladies love me." Victor exclaimed.

Malcolm laughed. "Last time I checked, you were in the same boat as me, the No Sex zone. When was the last time you got some? Your right hand doesn't count."

"Ohhh!" Sabrina and Zack both laughed, and then high fived each other.

Victor shook his head. "That's beside the point."

"Good recovery." Sabrina mocked.

"Hey, now. We haven't even heard about your exploits."

"Don't ask. Don't tell." Sabrina smirked.

"Well, I am asking now."

"Don't ask. Don't tell..." Sabrina crossed her arms, "that's all I'm going to say."

Victor and Sabrina stared at each other before Victor asked, "is it someone on base?"

"I'm not telling you."

"Oh, it's someone on base. Do we know them?"

"No..."

"Oh, is it Chris from Gate Three?"

"I'm not telling," Sabrina laughed from Victor's attempts to get an answer out of her. Zack laughed as they approached the check point to the safe zone. A large barrier made up of an orange traffic dividers laid in a zig zag pattern was in front of them. Ten yards from that, was a guard who stood at the ready with his rifle. He was in the army reserves and Malcolm could tell, as he was green in the face with no combat experience.

"Captain Morris, were you successful at the rescue?"

"No, another dead end."

"I'm sorry to hear." The soldier moved out of the way letting the group inside the safe zone. The safe zone itself was made up of a block of three-story apartments, that was surrounded by fences. The community was already gated making it an easy transition for the military to come in and set up operations. The first two buildings in the complex were housing for military while the other buildings behind it were for any civilians.

"You guys hungry?" Zack asked.

"Starved." Malcolm grinned.

"Yeah, let's see what the mess hall cooked up." Sabrina replied.

The team began walking towards the eatery when they heard someone call out, "Captain Morris!"

Zack stopped, and turned to find Captain Fred Wallace of the US Army Reserves trying to get his attention. Fred was an older white man, with peppered black and white hair, wearing a green, black and tan army uniform.

"Yes, Captain?" Zack asked.

"We just got new orders. You and your team will go to a hospital and evacuate a Virologist that the military thinks will be an asset to fighting this virus, Dr. Emily López. She's been holed up there since the fall, but the military had decided that she would be safer on base than working in the field."

"What's so important about her?" Zack asked.

"She's the best in her field. She's created more vaccines than anyone could count. The army believes that she can create a cure for the zombie plague."

"Well, that's good news." Malcolm added.

Zack nodded and then turned his attention towards the Army Captain, "How soon do we need to go?"

"ASAP." He replied.

"Do we have access to any vehicles or air support?"

"You and I both know we're stretched thin, sailor. You're going to have to hump it on foot."

"Yes, sir." Zack nodded then faced his team. "It looks like we're having lunch to go. Sabrina and Victor, secure some food for the trip. Malcolm, you're with me to the armory. You got five minutes, let's move."

Malcolm followed Zack to the armory nearby and they began to collect mags for their handguns and rifles. Zack and Malcolm were silent as they took the items needed.

They've done this countless times before. They were used to barely eating anything, grabbing more ammo and heading back out to a fight. They were used to fighting hours on end, with little rest and food. This is what they trained for. This is what they were built for. They were the tip of the spear, the elites, and the best of the best. They were focused and ready for the task at hand.

Loaded with a collection of ammunition and night vision goggles, they met up at the gate where Sabrina and Victor were located.

"I got y'all more mags," Malcolm said, passing them out.

"Thanks," Sabrina replied. "Here's water." Malcolm took it from her and downed half of the bottle.

"I got protein bars." Victor replied. He handed them out to Zack and Malcolm, who both ripped into them eating them quickly.

"Victor and Sabrina, here's night vision. By the time we get back it's going to be dark." Zack replied, handing out the kits.

"Thanks," they both replied, placing the gear on their hip.

"Y'all ready?" Zack asked.

"Yes, sir." Everyone replied.

"Good, let's go hunting."

The group left the safe zone and headed west towards the Virginia Beach Hospital. The hike was five miles away from the safe zone, and the group marched in a light jog. As they ran, sweat poured down their backs and covered their brows.

They were all exhausted but didn't admit it as they knew the task at hand. They knew that not only did they have to be strong to complete the mission, they also had to be strong for one another. That bond of family and fighting for the person beside you kept them going.

Along the way, they encountered zombies, but Zack chose to not engage. He wanted to save ammo, as he had a feeling they were going to need it when they arrived at the hospital. After an hour long run, the group made it to the hospital, just as the summer sun was setting.

The hospital itself was a four-story brick building, with piles of dead bodies out front. In front of the emergency entrance was a large horde of zombies. They all moaned and groaned as they attempted to cram inside the blockaded doorway. In the distance, they could hear gun fire and they knew that time was running out for the soldiers defending the place.

Zack stopped at a car and the group halted, and got in cover.

"What's the plan?" Malcolm breathed.

"Find another way in. We don't want to disturb those zombies all trying to get in that one way. The way that we find will also be our exit so we don't want to draw attention to it either." Zack replied.

"So knifes only?" Malcolm asked.

"Yes, until we get inside. Once there, we can move to guns. Is everyone okay with that?"

Sabrina and Victor nodded.

"Alright, let's go." Zack replied, removing his combat knife. The others did the same and followed their leader as he crouched down and slowly made his way around the building.

The team encountered a few stragglers, but they were able to take them down easily, with a simple slice to the head. The team worked together in silence, clearing out any zombies in their path.

They found an exit stairwell, and Zack and Sabrina placed their backs on the wall, while Victor and Malcolm, tried to pry it open.

"Damn, this fucker is tough." Victor growled, pulling.

"Keep at it." Malcolm heaved. On a final tug the door opened, but three zombies came pouring out too..

"Fuck me!" Victor growled as he toppled over with one on top of him. Sabrina was quick to the draw, and pulled the zombie off Victor. She stabbed the foe in the head and it dropped harmlessly to the ground.

Malcolm took out the second with ease. He shouldered into it, knocking it off balance before landing the killing blow. Zack crept behind the third and before it would register what was happening, Zack's blade was stuck in its skull.

When the last body fell, Zack checked his crew. "Y'all ready?"

They all nodded.

"Alright, let's find the doctor. I can hear gunshots on level four."

The SEALs entered the building and didn't bother checking the other floors following the sounds of danger. When most people heard gunfire, they ran, but not this foursome who charged into the fray unafraid of the danger that laid near.

There was no light in the building, so the team placed on their night vision goggles and made their way through. When they made it to the fourth level, they found a group of survivors holed up in the lobby fighting off zombies who came up the main stairwell in the hospital. The lobby had minimum light, so the SEALs turned off their goggles and placed them on their heads.

"Friendlies! Friendlies! This is the US Military!" Zack yelled as they approached. "Victor and Sabrina, assist with cover fire."

"Yes, sir," Victor and Sabrina moved up to join the three soldiers at the edge of the stairs. They fired their guns in controlled bursts, while Zack and Malcolm stayed behind with the group.

"My name is Captain Zack Morris, this is Lieutenant Malcolm White. We are US Navy SEALs, sent here to rescue the crew here. Is this all of you?" Zack asked, staring at the five people left in the lobby.

"Yes, Sergeant Ryan Jones of the US Reserves, sir." The soldier saluted Zack and he returned the gesture. The Sergeant appeared to be in his late twenties. He had brown crew cut and wore the U.S. army uniform of green, brown, and tan.

"What's your situation, Sergeant Jones?" Lieutenant Morris asked.

"The zombies broke through our defenses, we've been falling back to here. Thank God you guys are here. We weren't sure if we were going to make it." Ryan replied. He then looked behind Zack then asked, "Is this all the reinforcements they sent? We won't be able to take back the hospital with just you four."

Zack shook his head. "We're abandoning the hospital."

"We're what?" A female asked. She was in her late thirties, and was wearing purple scrubs, with a white doctor's jacket. She was a curvy woman, with a pear-shaped frame, tanned skin, and dark brown hair that was shoulder length. Her glasses on her eyes were dirty as she stared at Zack.

"Leaving," Zack repeated. "This hospital is unsafe, we're to take you all to the safe zone and Dr. Emily López is supposed to accompany us back to Little Creek Navy Base."

"And what if I don't want to come?" the same woman asked.

"You must be Dr. López..." Zack guessed.

She nodded. "I have patients that need me. They are still recovering from their vaccines." She pointed to two women on hospital gurneys.

"Are they contagious?" Malcolm asked, studying them.

"No, but they've been my patients since the start of all of this. I can't abandon them."

"Can they walk?" Zack asked, studying the women lying in the beds.

"No, they can't."

Malcolm and Zack looked at each other, and Zack shook his head.

"We had a tough time, getting here as it was. Two people in stretchers ain't going to work." Zack said.

"So, what are you thinking?" Malcolm asked.

"We leave them here."

"Absolutely not. I will go with you on the base, only if you can guarantee that you take them to the safe zone. I know doctors there that could look after them." Dr. López pleaded.

"Well, that complicates things..." Zack replied.

"We could take an ambulance. I saw one downstairs."

"That could work." Zack replied.

"That ambulance could only take one of them. We need to transport both." Dr. López interjected.

Zack sighed and then turned to Malcolm. "Any more ideas?"

"One, and you're not going to like it."

"Let me guess, we carry the other back to the safe zone?"

Malcolm nodded.

"That's five miles. Five miles between us and God knows what." Zack explained.

"I know, but it's the only way to transport everyone. Victor and I can carry her. You and Sabrina take point, and guard us."

"I can come too. You'll need a doctor on site in case something happens to her during transport." Dr. López offered.

Zack bit his lip and shook his head. "Fine, but if I say we run. We run. Your safety is what matters most."

"Why me? Why does my life matter more than anyone else's in this room?"

"The US government believes that you are the key to stopping this virus."

"This zombie plague is a virus?"

"Yes, it's an experiment gone wrong in the 60s. For years, the government has kept the virus locked up until a tornado destroyed the building and the virus got out. The government needs you to help us cure it."

Dr. López paused and looked down at her shoes. She nodded and then looked back up, "Fine. What do I need to do to insure the safety of my patients?"

"Malcolm and I will go downstairs and secure the ambulance. When we come back up, we will carry down both patients, and allow the soldiers here to escort one of them back in the ambulance. Sergeant Jones will lead that unit."

Ryan nodded, in agreement to his orders.

"We'd take the second out on foot. When we do, I'm in charge, Dr.

López. When I tell you to stop, you stop. When I tell you to run, you run. Do you understand?"

"Yes." She replied.

"Do you know how to use a gun?" Zack asked.

"No, I trained myself to save lives, not take one."

Malcolm rose his eyebrows at Zack as both of them knew that comment was meant for them.

Zack muttered something under his breath before handing Emily his handgun. "Just point and shoot."

Her eyes opened wide as she held the gun in her hands.

"And for the love of God, don't shoot us." Malcolm added.

Zack laughed and then nodded his head towards the stairwell. "Come on Malcolm, let's get the ambulance."

Malcolm nodded and the two navy SEALs left the lobby to head back downstairs. They only encountered one zombie and disposed of it easily to make it to the ambulance in the parking lot.

"Do you know how to hot-wire it?" Zack asked.

"Why you asking? Is it because I'm black?" Malcolm joked.

Zack laughed. "You had to make it racial."

Malcolm winked at Zack and then broke the window to unlock the door. Grabbing underneath the steering wheel, Malcolm hot-wired the vehicle and it started with a roar.

Malcolm and Zack both gave each other worried expressions that they disrupted the horde of zombies nearby, but Zack gave the signal that they were in the clear.

The two hopped into the ambulance and then drove it to the back of the hospital where the back stairwell was located. When they got back to the fourth floor, Victor, Sabrina, Ryan and Emily had already assisted with organizing the survivors for the trip, as each sick patient was in their own stretcher.

"The ambulance is outside. Once you get the patient in, you just have to drive it. No need to start it up as it's hot wired." Malcolm told to Sergeant Jones.

"Thank you, Sir. Alright, men, let's move." He ordered, before his two other guys picked up the stretcher.

"Do you know where you're heading to?" Zack asked Ryan.

"Yes, it's the safe zone on the Oceanview, right?"

"Yeah, good luck. Take it slow out there, the road back had a lot of obstacles."

"I will. Good luck to you, sir." Ryan gave Zack a crisp salute and then left.

Zack returned the gesture and watched as the soldiers carried the stretcher away.

"Okay, that means Dr. López, you are with us. Are you ready to go?"

"About as ready as I need to be..." she replied.

"Good enough. Alright, Victor and Malcolm, grab the stretcher. Sabrina, you are with me, guarding everyone. Not a thing gets within five feet of us, understood?"

"Yes, sir." Sabrina replied.

"Good, let's move out."

The group moved as one, with Zack and Sabrina on the outside of Victor, Malcolm and Emily. By the time they made it down the stairs, the ambulance had already left, and it was just them. They managed to sneak past the horde in the hospital and were met with little resistance as they traveled.

A mile into the trip, Zack noticed the turned over ambulance. "Shit, I hope they're okay."

"The doors are open, you think they are humping it like us?" Malcolm asked, scanning the area.

Zack was about to say yes, before he saw the body of the dead soldier nearby. "Fuck me. No, I don't think they made it out."

"What? No!" Emily shrieked. "What about my patients? I have to check on them!"

"Shit, Dr. López, please stay with us!" Zack yelled, but it was too late as the doctor had already broken rank and ran towards the down truck.

"Victor, go and get her back her. The rest of us would guard the patient." Zack commanded.

Victor nodded and chased after the doctor. "Dr. López," Victor yelled as he chased after her.

Dr. López approached the vehicle and covered her face when she saw the carnage. Blood was everywhere as it looked like a wild animal had been through there. Before she had a chance to react, she felt a hand on her shoulder and screamed as an undead Sergeant Ryan Jones tried to eat her.

"Sergeant Jones!" Emily cried upon seeing the man who protected her was dead. It was a mixture of shock and fear as she fell backwards with the zombie. She screamed, as his mouth got close to her neck. His teeth chomped at her as it attempted to bite into her flesh. She struggled, trying to push him away, but the soldier was too strong and too heavy for her.

"I got you!" Victor yelled as he ripped the zombie away from Dr. López. Once she was clear, he took his pistol and shot it in the head.

"Are you okay?" Victor asked.

"You saved me. Thank you."

"All in a day's work, ma'am." He grinned. "Now we need to get back with the group. Come on!"

"Okay," she replied, she looked back at the corpse of Sergeant Ryan Jones once more, and silently thanked him for everything he did to keep her safe. She thought it was such a waste of a good life. Not only that, but she was also upset that he didn't get a proper funeral, instead, his body was left out in the open.

As they ran back, more zombies began to make their way towards the group, and Zack, Sabrina, and Malcolm had to lay down cover fire to keep them away from the stretcher. Once regrouped, the Navy SEALs team and Dr. López all ran for their lives. Zack, Sabrina, and Emily all fired blindly as they made their way to the safe zone.

Everyone was scared, as endless waves of zombies continued to attack them. Zack tried to put on a brave face, but even he was concerned about their survival.

Emily had never fired a gun before and every time she hit her mark, killing a zombie, she swore apart of her died too. She'd made an oath to protect life and to be taking it felt wrong to her. However, she knew that she had to protect her patient. The zombies that attacked her were gone, but her patient wasn't, and if taking life was the answer, she was ready to make that call.

Malcolm's legs burned and his arms grew tired from carrying the stretcher, but he pushed himself to make it to the safe zone. For some strange reason, he thought of Anne, and how he had to get back to her. He had to survive for her. That thought alone gave him strength to get through it.

When they finally made it to the gates of the safe zone, flood lights turned on, and they heard a soldier yell, "Announce yourselves or you will be fired upon."

Zack yelled, "US Navy SEALs! US Navy SEALs! We have civilians! Zombies are hot on our ass."

"Roger, come on in." The gates opened and as soon as they made it past the gate, the zombies that followed them were mowed down by machine gun cover fire.

Entering the gated community, all five of them gasped for air as the run was breathtaking. A group of doctors came running out to check on the patient that they saved.

Watching her get carted away, Dr. López smiled. "Thank you for saving her. While I know we lost one of them, we managed to save one. Thank you. You could have easily just picked me up and carried me on your back but you didn't. You chose the hard way, and I respect you for that." She told Zack.

Zack nodded, "Trust me, I would have put you on my back if it was my decision. You should be thanking Malcolm. It was his idea."

Dr. López turned to Malcolm and gave him a slight head nod. "Thank you."

"You're welcome," Malcolm replied. "I'm sorry about the other patient. I thought the ambulance would have been the safer mode of transportation."

"It's okay. When do we leave for Little Creek?" Dr. López asked.

"In the morning. It's five hours till dawn. I suggest we all get some shut eye until then." Zack commanded.

"Sounds good to me, Dr. López, perhaps I can find a cot for you," Victor grinned.

"Oh thank you, you're so nice."

Once Victor and Dr. López were out of listening distance, Sabrina leaned closer to Zack and Malcolm, "Is Victor hitting on the doctor?"

"Yep," Malcolm grinned.

Sabrina shook her head. "He would." She muttered.

"Ten says he scores." Zack replies.

"Easy money. Ten says that she shuts him down." Sabrina said, as they all walked together into the barracks. When they entered, Victor was already cozying up to the doctor making the threesome laugh. Zack held up the money sign to Sabrina as he rubbed his fingers together. Sabrina flicked him off, before lying down on a nearby cot. Zack and Malcolm took the cots next to each other, and both sailors groaned as they'd been on their feet for over twenty-four hours.

"Damn, this feels good." Zack said.

"I know, right? Goodnight, bruh." Malcolm replied.

"Yep, night brother." Zack replied.

Malcolm turned on his side, trying to get comfortable, and then moved once more to see Zack staring at a picture of Kelsey. Zack was smiling as he was rubbing her face with his thumb.

As Malcolm watched him, he wondered if he would ever love someone like Zack loved Kelsey. His mind immediately thought about Anne, and how she could be someone like that. He dismissed the thought like he always did, reminding himself that he was just friends with her, but strangely there was a part of him that wondered, what if they weren't just friends.

As Malcolm's eyes got heavy, he thought of Anne and her smile. His mind went adrift thinking about what her lips would taste like in a kiss. The more he thought of her, the more relaxed he became, until he drifted off to sleep.

It was less than twenty minutes after Malcolm had fallen asleep that he was awakened by gunfire. He stood up and looked at Zack, who had also sat up wide eyed.

A soldier came running into the barracks, "All hands on deck! All hands! A horde just showed up and we need every man fighting on the line."

Zack sighed and grabbed this rifle nearby. "I guess that's all the rest we're going to get."

"Yeah, I guess so, let's go hunting," Malcolm replied, reloading his gun to head outside to join the fight.

TEN

"Retreat! Retreat!" A shadowy figure yelled.

"Help Me! Oh god! Help me!" A bloodied corpse yelled.

"No, no, no! Don't let them eat me! Don't let them eat me!" A young woman begged as dozens of zombies ripped into her body.

"I don't want to die. I don't want to die." Screamed a young boy as he bled out.

"Please save me!" A pregnant woman pleaded being dragged away from the horde.

"They're breaking through!" A voice gasped as the walls of the safe house collapsed.

Malcolm woke up gasping for air as his nightmare ended. A cold sweat dripped down his shirtless body as he relived the horrible memories of the safe zone firefight from three days ago. He rubbed his head, attempting to keep his breathing under control.

Looking to his left, he saw Anne who slept peacefully in her sleep. Her eyes were closed, and she was wrapped in a blanket.

He tried to departmentalize it like all the rest of his terrible memories, but this one was tough. This one didn't seem to go away.

He shivered as the dark images swirled in his head.

That night at the safe zone when they were called to fight it was like an army of dead descended upon them. The fighting was intense. A lot of people lost their lives. To make things worse, those who died came back and joined the horde of undead.

The gruesome memories of the people dying, begging for their help repeated in Malcolm's head. His hands shook and he held a distant stare towards the end of the tent.

He was focused on the screams in his head until he felt a hand on his arm. He jumped and turned to see that Anne had awakened.

She had a worried expression on her face as she studied him. "Malcolm, are you okay?"

"Yeah, I'm fine."

"Are you sure?" She questioned.

"Yes," he lied. "Just go back to bed. I'm going on a quick run to clear my head."

Anne didn't reply as she looked at Malcolm once more. She gave his arm a gentle squeeze before falling back to bed.

Malcolm stared at the spot she touched. It still felt warm. She felt warm. His hand touched the spot she touched and then glanced back at Anne.

Her eyes were closed yet again as she drifted off to sleep. He smiled at the way her black hair covered her face. When the safe zone was going to hell, she was on his mind. He fought to survive not only to keep his brothers and sisters in arms alive, but to see Anne again. Something about her calmed him down. Her presence made him happy and feel at peace.

Reaching over, he pushed a strand of her hair away from her face, placing it behind her ear and then tucked her in. He looked back at her once more before getting out of bed to change into his jogging attire. He didn't bother to wear a shirt, instead he just wore navy blue shorts and sneakers.

Walking out of the tent, not a soul was insight, and the pale moon still shined above his head. Checking his watch, he realized that the time was four a.m.

Stretching, he heard a noise behind him and jumped to see Petty Officer Richard Green walking down the rows of tents.

"Lieutenant White?" He asked. "What are you doing up?"

"Couldn't sleep, you?"

"I always walk the grounds before everyone gets up. I check the tents for any visible damages and then I start prep for breakfast."

"Oh, that's kind of you. Anne...I mean my wife tells me that you're doing a good job with keeping up zone D. She says you're the heart of the area."

A large smile spread across Richard's face. "She said that?"

"Yeah, she did. She says you make this place like home for her and Kelsey."

"I try to, it's good to hear that they're enjoying their stay. I know that you and other soldiers will contain this threat. I just feel bad that I'm not contributing in any major way in the fight."

"Don't be brash. You're the glue that holds everything together. You do more than you know."

"Thank you, sir. I just wish I had a chance to actually prove my worth fighting wise."

"Let's hope that day never comes, because if it does, the enemy is at the gates. You're the last line of defense, the person who will keep Anne save when I'm gone. I think that's more valuable than you know."

Richard chuckled and nodded. "Thank you, sir. Those words were what I needed this morning. Do you need anything before your run?"

"No, thank you, I'm good. Carry on."

"Yes, sir," Richard saluted and then walked away from Malcolm, continuing to review the tents' structures. Malcolm smiled at Richard before taking off on a brisk jog.

As he ran, he came upon a shadowy figure, and he thought it was strange that someone else would be running outside like him. As he approached the figure, he realized that it was a smaller woman, with a curvy frame. Five yards out, he figured out it was Dr. López who was also jogging. Her white shirt was drenched in sweat, and she wore red yoga pants that covered her thick thighs, ankle high socks and sneakers.

"Morning, Dr. López."

"Good Morning, Malcolm."

"You're up early today."

"I could say the same about you," she chuckled. "I'm up early because I plan on getting a head start on my research."

"Ah, I saw that Admiral Wesley gave you a nice lab to work in."

"Yes, it has all the bells and whistles. As we speak I'm running an analysis on the zombie blood."

"Any initial thoughts?"

Dr. López shrugged, "I've never seen a virus work so fast before. There's no way that we'd be able to administer it after the fact as there's not much time after the turn once someone gets bit, so I'm thinking of a preventive vaccine, like a rabies shot."

"Ah, well that makes sense."

"Yes, easier said than done though."

"Besides the science, how are you feeling? Are you settling in on the base?"

"I am, but I still keep thinking of how we lost the safe zone. It was horrible that night."

"It was. I'm sorry about your patient."

"Thank you. Mary was a good woman. It was a shame we lost her like that. If anything that attack motivated me to find a cure. Think about how many lives would be saved if we were all vaccinated."

"That's a good attitude, doctor."

"Thanks," she breathed. "I just hope to find it before it's too late. Well, break's over. I'm heading back to the lab. I'll see you later, Malcolm. Don't be a stranger."

"Yeah, I won't. Bye," Malcolm waved, watching her jog away.

He took a deep breath and continued his work out.

He ran around the base, checking the fences' dexterity. Unlike the gated community in the safe zone , the fences around Little Creek Base were designed to keep people from attacking, and were strong enough to withstand several zombies pushing and pulling on it.

Little Creek Base had three entrances, but two of them were blocked off and destroyed leaving one way in and out. Half of the compound was surrounded by fences while the other was water, as a beach covered the rear of the base. The rest of the perimeter was marked with proximity alarms, and if anything got within five feet the alarm would go off. There were also three roaming patrols around the fences that took care of any zombies that got near it, along with an entire platoon of men at the front guarding the entrance.

As far as Malcolm was concerned, Little Creek base was a fortress, but even fortresses have cracks and he was determined to plug all the holes.

His time at the safe zone taught him that no matter how something is secure, it could still be overrun. As he ran he could still hear the screams and the pleas for help. With every cry he pushed himself to run faster.

Overall he blamed himself. He thought that if he was faster, stronger or quicker to the draw he could have saved more lives. Hundreds of lives were lost at the safe house. They only returned with a handful including Dr. López.

To make matters worse, the base lost all of its air support trying to defend their retreat. Now the base is left with only a few vehicles and tanks. Malcolm thought the whole zombie apocalypse was fubar. Who would have thought that the grand army of the United States of America would be taken down so quickly.

He was angry. He was angry that he couldn't save them all. He was angry that the government was failing. He growled pushing his body to the limit as dirt flew from under his shoes. His lungs burned with exhaustion, but he kept pushing himself. He wanted to punish himself for losing all of those innocents. It was his fault they were dead. He was supposed to protect them. They looked to him to save them and he didn't.

"Argh!" He roared when his body finally gave out.

He gasped for air and doubled over, breathing quickly. He stood up, wiped his brow, and watched as the sun was coming up over the base. His eyes watched the amber light stretched out, pushing away the darkness that was once there. The clouds were a bright red orange, and he could hear birds sing almost like they were presenting the morning to him. The sun glistened off the morning dew on the grass making the grass even greener than it usually is.

As his eyes admired the sunset, another beautiful thing caught his eye. Anne walked out onto the grass and began stretching her body. She was wearing a sports bra along with a pair of short shorts. Her flat toned stomach was revealed as he bent her body left and right.

Although they were just friends, Malcolm thought Anne and an amazing body. Fit, athletic, petite, each trait described his perfect woman.

After stretching, Anne got into a yoga pose and held her position. Walking up to her, Malcolm waved, "good morning, Anne."

"Morning, Malcolm. I was wondering when you were going to come and say hi, instead of creepily watching me from the bushes."

"Oh I wasn't..."

"You don't have to lie, I know I look good," she winked.

Malcolm laughed and rubbed the back of his head. "Busted."

"It's cool, you're easy on the eyes too. Not every day you see an eight pack. God, how is that even possible?" Anne asked as her eyes lingered on Malcolm's chest watching a sweat droplet roll down the multiple ridges on his dark skin.

"Diet and exercise."

"And a thousand sit ups daily."

"It's actually a lot more core exercises than just sit ups."

"Ha, do you have to correct me every time you get a chance?" She asked.

"Force of nature," Malcolm replied with a grin. "Why are you up so early?"

"One could ask the same of you. Are you okay after that nightmare you had?"

"Yeah, I'm good."

"Are you though? It's not good that you push that stuff down. If you need to talk, I'm here."

"Thanks, but I wouldn't want to bore you with my troubles."

Anne grabbed Malcolm's hand and peered into his eyes. "I am never too busy to listen to a friend. If you have something that you want to get off your chest, I'm all ears."

Malcolm hesitated and questioned if he should say anything. As he stared at Anne, he remembered how much he respected her opinion. Even before the zombies, she was always the person who listened and gave useful information.

"I'm upset about losing the safe zone," Malcolm admitted.

Anne shook her head. "That wasn't your fault. It got overrun."

"Was it though? We just finished saving Dr. López and there was a group of zombies that were chasing us. We were saved by the guards at the gate. A part of me can't help but think that we brought that horde to the area. We attracted every zombie around us with our gunfire. That was us."

"You can't blame yourself for that," Anne comforted Malcolm and placed a hand on his shoulder.

"That horde could've came from anywhere. You don't know that."

"I do know those people were counting on me. They all died."

"Not all of them. You saved Dr. López and a few others."

"Yes, but at what cost. This war, isn't like what I've been trained to fight. These people are Americans. They were once fathers and mothers, sons and daughters. Now I'm slaughtering them. I can't..."

"Shhh..." Anne hugged Malcolm and rubbed his back. He buried his head in her shoulder and held her tight.

"I'm not sure why I'm getting caught up about this..."

"It's because you're human and we're in a fucked-up situation. At the end of the day, think about the people you're protecting. You're protecting Victor and Sabrina. Zack and Kelsey. You're protecting me..."

Malcolm leaned back and stared in to Anne's eyes. There was a silent tension between the two as their eyes were locked on each other. He held her chin as if he wanted to say or do something more, but he hesitated.

"Malcolm?" Anne asked, her breath heavy with need.

"Yes..."

"I just wanted to say...thank you for earlier. I know that our fake marriage wasn't an easy decision to make but..."

"Stop it," he shook his head. "You're one of my best friends. I would have done anything for you. I would lie, cheat, and kill for you. You mean that much to me. You understand?"

Anne smiled, and nodded. Malcolm hugged her once more holding her tightly.

Wrapped in his arms, he said, "thanks for being a good friend, Anne."

"Don't mention it," she breathed, allowing herself to get engulfed in his aroma.

The two broke apart and smiled at each other. While their words said one thing, their grins told a different story as if there was more to be said.

Malcolm cleared his throat and asked, "Now, what exactly are you doing up at this time?"

"I'm meditating using yoga. Would you like to join? It could actually help you."

"Yeah, sure I'd like that."

ELEVEN

Malcolm stood, watching Anne and Kelsey train. He couldn't help but to smile as his eyes remained on Anne. Once more her beauty seemed to capture him, as she wore a pair of navy shorts and yellow T-shirt. There was something about her toned legs that made him crazy. Her jet-black hair was tied in a ponytail, and her bangs rested on her forehead. Her enchanting brown eyes were focused as she instructed the several attendees on how to swipe their swords up and down.

He couldn't help but to smile at her form. As she held her katana above her head, her fingers, gripped the sword as she hacked and slashed. The other students followed, copying her movements.

He straightened his green military uniform, and looked down at his black boots as he was swelled with an emotion he only felt when he saw Anne. A military cap covered his head, as a gentle breeze swept through the base on the warm August morning.

When the lesson broke up, Kelsey and Sheri both waved at Malcolm.

"Hi Malcolm," they both replied.

"Ladies..." he grinned. "How was the lesson?"

"Strenuous!" Sheri replied. "This girl got me out here sweating, but

I swear I feel like I'm ready to take on a whole army with these moves!" She mocked, swinging her sword.

Malcolm laughed. "I guess you have a good teacher," he replied, looking towards Kelsey.

Kelsey chuckled. "Anne's the true teacher. I'm just her pretty side kick."

"Is that so?" Malcolm asked.

"Yeah, what's up? I thought you were training with Zack today?" Kelsey asked.

"Oh, I am, but I have some free time for lunch. I wanted to see if Anne wanted to grab a quick bite to eat."

"Is that so?" Kelsey rose her eyebrows and Malcolm laughed it off and looked uneasy at Sheri.

"Ah, don't get all timid around me. I know about you and Anne. Kelsey filled me in on your secret. Answer the question."

"It's not like that, we're just friends."

"Funny I keep hearing that from you too. It's like a catch phrase."

"It's because it's true." Malcolm admitted.

Kelsey leaned closer and whispered, "Is it though?" She rose her eyebrows. "There's only one person in the world that looks at me like you do with Anne, that's my husband. That's saying a lot."

"Kelsey, we're just *friends*."

"Leaning on that word hard today, aren't we?" Kelsey winked and then left with Sheri. They were both giggling like two school girls as they walked away.

Malcolm shook his head and walked over to Anne who was gathering the rest of the materials from the class.

"Do you need a hand with that?" He asked.

Anne had a nervous smile spread on her face as she pushed a strand of her hair behind her ear. "Yes, I would love one."

Malcolm grinned and helped pick up the other materials.

"I thought I saw you stalking me in the corner."

"I wasn't stalking. I was trying to learn a few moves," Malcolm replied, pretending to swing a sword.

"Oh, that's even worse. Stealing classroom time? I rather have you gawk at me."

"What's my punishment?"

"Push ups, fifty." Anne gave him a toothy grin.

"With pleasure..." Malcolm got down to his hands and squared up his body.

"Oh, Malcolm, I was kidding. You don't have to do anything."

"Oh, but I want to. You said fifty, so you get fifty," he grunted as he began pushing his body up and down. His eyes didn't leave Anne's as he bent up and down. Anne couldn't look away as she stared at his form. His ass was ridged as he pushed himself up. Ogling him, a stray tingle crawled up her spine. She tried to fight it, but it was no use as the foreign feeling she felt for him was taking over.

As she gazed upon him she wondered what was wrong with her.

"Done," he smiled.

"I'd be lying if I said I wasn't impressed." Anne replied, biting her lip. "I have half a mind to ask for another fifty."

"More? Just say the word. I can do this *all day*."

"Is that supposed to be a sexual innuendo?" Anne asked.

"You want it to be?" He flirted.

Anne rolled her eyes, "you are too much. Please tell me you have a reason to be hovering."

"I did. I wanted to see if you wanted to get lunch."

"Lunch? Don't you have some place to be?"

"I don't go on patrol until tomorrow. Until then, I'm all yours."

"Really? What does that entail?" Anne took a step forward, allowing only a few inches of space between the two.

"Whatever you want it to be."

"Well, I am hungry, so I guess you're buying."

"I figured. You're always extra."

Anne gasped and clutched her chest as if she was easily offended. They both laughed and walked away from the open grassy toward the beach that was on the base.

"You know I hate surprises. Just tell me." Anne smirked.

"No, I can't. It's supposed to be a surprise."

"Oh, I have ways of making you talk."

"I'm a Navy SEAL. I've been trained in advance interrogation techniques. You can try but I won't break."

"Advanced interrogation techniques my ass. You've obviously haven't been tickled by the tickle master. Let me get my hands on you and you'll squeal like a pig."

"Pretty cocky."

"When you have skill you don't need to be cocky. Come here!"

Malcolm laughed and ran away from Anne as she chased him. Both were giggling with glee as they ran through the compound to the beach on base. When they arrived, Anne's jaw hit the ground looking at the beautiful picnic set up by Malcolm.

On a red blanket in the sand was a picnic basket along with a bottle of wine. The setting was picturesque with the blue waves of the ocean crashing into the white sands of the beach. A gentle breeze blew Anne's hair as she looked at her surroundings.

"Malcolm, you shouldn't have. A picnic? Is that my surprise?" She asked.

"Umm, this is not mine. I have no idea where this came from. My surprise was me taking my shirt off for you."

Anne laughed and slapped his arm. "You're such an ass."

"Yeah, I know. I hope this picnic isn't too much."

"No, it's fine. I mean, we're supposed to be married, so romantic gestures like this are supposed to happen, right?"

"Exactly my thoughts. I mean, it's hard to keep up with perfect couple, Zack and Kelsey Morris." Malcolm mocked.

"Yes! I feel like they are purposely making out in front of us, to pressure us to do the same thing."

"Yeah, we're just friends. Stop pushing us!" Malcolm chuckled.

"Exactly! I repeat this fact to Kelsey daily and she expects my answer to change everyday. It won't. I mean this marriage is all a show, just for us to stay together on base."

"Exactly! There's zero romantic feelings between us, right?" Malcolm asked.

Anne hesitated and glanced at Malcolm as if she was expecting him to say something else. She coughed and then nodded, "yeah, of course. None."

The two fell silent, and Malcolm looked out to the ocean. Anne rubbed her elbow and then nodded towards the wine bottle.

"Where did you get wine from?"

"That? I had to give an arm and a leg for that. Let's just say I owe a couple of favors on the base."

"Wow, way to make a girl feel special." Anne laughed.

The couple sat down on the blanket. Anne sat her knees, while Malcolm sat cross legged. Malcolm pulled out the cork to the wine bottle and then poured it into two red plastic cups.

"Cheers," he grinned, handing her a cup.

"Cheers," she replied, touching her glass to his before drinking its contents. Upon the first sip she coughed and covered her mouth. "Oh, shit, this is terrible."

"You get what you get."

Anne laughed. "Some romantic you are. *You get what you get?* Damn, I feel bad for your future wife."

"Hey, I haven't had any complaints about my romance skills."

"You know you actually can't count booty calls, right?"

"Hey now, those count as relationships."

Anne laughed, shaking her head. "They do not!" She playfully slapped Malcolm's shoulder, and then pointed to the wicker basket. "Please tell me you have two delicious sandwiches in the basket."

"Even better. Two MREs. Standard issue for all US military."

"You have to be kidding me... Worst. Picnic. Ever."

"Don't blame me. Blame the zombies."

"Always passing blame to others." Anne teased. "What flavors do we have?"

"Chicken Chunks or Ground Beef."

"Which one is better?"

"None," Malcolm laughed.

"Damn, you really have no shot with the ladies."

"Lucky for them, I'm already married."

Anne rolled her eyes, "oh no, your ass is going back on the market because of this shit. MREs? That's it, I'm getting a divorce."

"Now, who's the ass."

Both of them laughed and Anne pointed towards the ground beef. "I'll try that one."

Malcolm tossed the bag to Anne and then assisted her with the heater to warm the beef. He did the same with his chicken. While they waited they tried the other contents in the MRE including, the rice and beans, corn and they swapped the fruit bar and trail mix. When the meat was cooked they both spooned the contents on the tortillas and added the given cheese sauce.

"Oh, God, what am I eating?" Anne asked.

"Welcome to the Navy. Bottoms up." Malcolm said, taking a bite.

Anne did the same and then coughed, "Oh God. It's horrible."

"Really? I think mine tastes like a five-star restaurant."

"You're so full of shit." Anne laughed.

"You wanna swap?"

"Yes, please."

They traded burritos and Anne took a bit of Malcolm's taco and Malcolm did the same with Anne's.

"Oh, this is worse. You're such an ass!"

Malcolm was laughing uncontrollably and in retort, Anne tossed the taco at Malcolm. He dodged it and then tossed his own at her.

"You!" She laughed. "It's official this is the worse date I've been on."

He laughed and took another sip of his wine. "Ah, that was good."

"You're such an ass. When this shit is over, you owe me a proper dinner."

Malcolm grinned and stared into Anne's eyes. His deep brown eyes made Anne squirm. Looking at him, she was wondering how it was possible for a man to make her feel this way.

"Where did you want to go?" He asked.

"Together?"

Malcolm nodded.

"Hmm...Italian." She grinned, scooting closer to Malcolm. He leaned closer to her, and placed his arm behind her, allowing Anne's head to rest on his shoulder. Anne smiled as she watched the seagulls hover the blue ocean water.

"You talking about that place off of 5th street?"

"Yes, Mario's Italian Grill. Oh, my mouth is watering thinking about that place. I'm talking good bread. Good wine, not this shit..." Anne admitted, holding up her wine cup. "...And then the eggplant parmesan." She moaned, closing her eyes. "Oh, my mouth is watering. What would you get there?"

"Steak cooked medium rare, side of spaghetti, to dip the steak in the sauce and all the garlic bread in the basket."

Anne smiled. "Sounds like we're going to clear the restaurant of bread."

"They don't stand a chance. What do you miss most since the fall?"

"Candy. I want a peanut butter chocolate cup so bad."

"Really?"

"Yes, I would flash you for that candy."

"Really? Are we talking about a quick glance or a long lingering look?"

"What?" Anne took her head off of Malcolm's shoulder and playfully shoved him, while smirking, "Creeper."

Malcolm placed both hands up and shrugged. "Hey now, I'm just trying to figure out how far I need to go to catch a look at the girls."

Anne rolled her eyes. "I swear you only think with the thing between your legs."

"Hey, you've seen mine, it's only right I see yours."

"Yeah, nice try that's not how it works."

They both laughed, before the two fell silent. Malcolm grabbed a nearby shell and tossed it towards the ocean.

"So, how's class? You and Kelsey seem to be popular on base?" Malcolm asked.

"It's going good. A lot of people are learning a lot of things. I'm impressed with Sheri, she's really determined to learn."

"Do you think it has something to do with the loss of Captain Peterson?"

Anne shook her head. "No, I think she wants to be able to defend herself when the time comes."

"That's good to hear. From what I've seen, she's going to need those skills if this place ever falls apart."

"You think that?"

"It's only a question of when? I hear reports all the time of safe zones and bases falling to zombie hordes. It could be a month, it could be years, but these fences won't last forever. What happens when a horde breaks through. She will have to know how to defend herself."

"You sound like Admiral Wesley."

"He's a smart man. He's been in the military long enough to know to always expect the worst. Take the fruits and vegetables you're planting. Admiral Wesley knows the food we have isn't going to last forever, and since there's no end in sight with this zombie threat he has everyone planting and jarring food for later."

"I agree it is smart. I'm glad I'm on base, I can't imagine life in the safe zones."

"It's not the best. It's like the Wild West out there and every day we spend in this zombie apocalypse, the worse the world gets. It's horrible."

Anne's smile disappeared as she looked down at her shoes.

"What is it?" Malcolm asked.

"It's my parents. They were in a safe zone in Norfolk, but I haven't heard from them in the last three days. I'm worried. We usually reach out to each other daily, but this long period, I'm concerned."

"Really? That is strange." Malcolm paused and then asked, "did you want to go and see them?"

"Is that possible? Admiral Wesley says that civilians aren't allowed off base."

"Don't worry about the Admiral. Zack and I will convince him."

"Oh, thank you," Anne replied giving Malcolm a big hug.

TWELVE

"You wanted to see me?" Admiral Wesley replied as he reviewed a few papers in his office. Despite the world going to hell, Admiral still never broke dress code wearing his tan officer uniform. His two silver stars shined in the limited light of the office.

"Yes, sir," Malcolm replied, standing straight. "It's my wife, sir..."

"Anne? She's been a breath of fresh air. That kendo class she's teaching with Kelsey has really taken off."

"Yes, sir. She enjoys it. Well, I was talking to her earlier today and she's concerned about her parents' safe zone."

"Really? Why?"

"She's lost contact with them. It's been three days since she's last talked to them."

"Perhaps they've lost connection? The world isn't what it used to be."

"I understand, but she has talked to them every day since the fall. This is out of order for them to randomly lose connection. As an officer, you have contact with all of the safe zones, could you reach out to them? Perhaps see where her parents are?"

"Malcolm...While I respect you as a sailor and what your wife is doing for the community, I can't break protocol."

"Sir, please. What if this was your family?"

The Admiral paused as the question hit hard. He loved his wife and daughter and thought what he would do in the situation if they were still alive. He sighed and shook his head.

"What safe zone are they in?"

"Safe Zone A2, in Norfolk."

Admiral Wesley walked towards his bookcase and pulled out a manual. After searching through the log, he found what he was looking for.

"Captain Bates runs that zone. I'll call them now." He muttered, dialing the number. The room was silent as the Admiral waited for someone to pick up.

"That's strange, someone should have answered it."

"Perhaps the connection is bad too?"

The Admiral shook his head. "No, this phone line is battery and satellite operated and manned 24/7. Someone should've answered it by now."

Admiral Wesley hung up the phone and sighed. "That's not good."

"Sir, permission to check out the base, sir."

"Granted. Tell Zack to gather his team and do recon on the base."

"Sir, if I may, can we invite Anne and Kelsey along?"

"Lieutenant, we're not sure if that zone is safe or not. You'd be walking two civilians in a hornet's nest."

"With all due respect sir, Anne and Kelsey can handle themselves. They are more than capable to defend themselves. Their history has shown it."

"I'm aware, but I will not put civilians into harm's way."

"Sir, it's Anne's parents. Both her and Kelsey have volunteered to go. Please, sir. All Anne has is her parents. Give her the comfort just to check on them."

Admiral Wesley sighed and stared at Malcolm as he bit his lip. "Fine, but I'm adding an extra man to your team."

"Sir? We do better as a four-man team."

"I wasn't asking. These are orders. LTJG Sawyer Knox will report to your unit, you leave at 0600 hours. Understood?"

"Yes, sir!"

"Since all my birds are gone. I'm assigning you two Humvees to take to the zone. I expect you bring my vehicles back in one piece. Because my sailors keep getting bit, I'm losing my valuable resources in the field. Don't get bit and bring my stuff back."

"Yes sir, there won't be a scratch on them."

Rear Admiral Wesley nodded. "You're dismissed."

Malcolm saluted and then left the Admiral's office. He made his way out of the command office towards the common area for zone d barracks where he found Zack, Kelsey, Anne, Sabrina, and Victor all waiting. No one else was in the area, as the fivesome sat talking. When they saw Malcolm, they stopped their conversation. Judging his face, Anne began to worry.

"So?" Anne asked.

Malcolm shook his head. "It's not good. Admiral Wesley called the commander's line, but no one picked up."

"Oh, God." Anne rubbed her temples as her worst fears were beginning to take hold.

"Did he say if we can check it out?" Zack asked.

"He did, he also gave us permission to take Anne and Kelsey with us."

"Well, that's good news, right?" Kelsey asked.

"I guess, he also ordered that Sawyer tag along and join our team."

"Fuck! Sawyer? He's the worst," Victor moaned as he slapped his head.

"Wait who's Sawyer?" Kelsey asked.

"He's another SEAL, but he's a total jackass." Zack replied, crossing his arms. "How long is he supposed to be on our team?"

"Admiral didn't answer that, but judging by his tone, indefinitely."

"Fuck, well there goes the neighborhood." Sabrina growled.

"Exactly. From here on out, no jokes about our fake marriage." Malcolm reminded. "Sawyer wasn't too happy that he couldn't get his girlfriend on base. The last thing we need is him finding out about Anne."

"Yeah. Good point." Anne replied.

"When do we leave?" Zack asked.

"0600, I suggest we get some shut eye for the next few hours and then get ready to head out."

"Sounds good. We will meet at the armory. I'll find Sawyer and tell him to meet us there too. Get some good rest everyone, I have a feeling we won't be sleeping for a while." Zack said.

Everyone nodded and then dispersed towards their own individual barracks, while Zack left to find Sawyer.

Anne and Malcolm walked back towards their tent. When they got to their barrack, they both lied down on the bed, and Anne placed her head on Malcolm's chest. What started out as an awkward placement for the two, actually became second nature as the two became used to cuddling with each other. Malcolm held Anne's shoulder as she began to cry.

"What's wrong?" He asked, rubbing her.

"It's my parents. What if they're dead?"

"They're not dead. They raised the toughest SOB I've met. Those zombies don't stand a chance." Malcolm touched her cheek wiping away a tear. Anne sniffed and stared into Malcolm's eyes.

"Thank you, Malcolm for everything. I have no idea what I'd do without you. You're a good friend."

"So are you," he replied. "Come on, let's get some sleep we have a long day ahead of us."

Anne nodded and placed her head back in his chest. He gave her a big hug, and continued to comfort her until they both fell asleep.

ANNE PULLED at the uniform she wore. The fabric felt different than what she was used to. Like Kelsey, they both wore Navy combat uniforms, matching Victor, Sabrina, Zack and Malcolm. Around tied on her hip was her katana, and holstered to the opposite hip was a pistol. She wasn't the best shot, but Malcolm insisted that she'd take it to protect herself. Personally all she needed was her blade.

It was Zack's idea to wear the uniform, as he didn't want to raise any suspicions on why two civilians were traveling with them. To Anne it didn't make a difference, she figured with her sword sheathed on her back, she stood out like a sore thumb.

The group walked out of the armory to find Sawyer leaning on a post.

"About time you pussies showed up," Sawyer spat chew onto the ground and grinned at the six walking out of the armory.

Sawyer was wearing a camo baseball cap backwards along with amber lens shades on his face, even though it was still pitched dark outside. Sawyer was easily the biggest man in the SEALs, at six foot six, and three hundred pounds, he was more football player than sailor. Outside of the standard US camo gear, Sawyer didn't follow dress protocol, as his beard wasn't regulation size nor were his habits, but he didn't give a fuck about rules. He knew the Navy cared more about his skills with a rifle than his dress appearance.

He was leaning on the post as he picked his teeth.

"There are ladies present." Sabrina growled.

"Shit Sabrina, you and I both know that you ain't no lady. I'm convinced that you have balls down there. Come on, pull your pants and give us a show." He mocked.

Sabrina flicked Sawyer off and then gave Zack a glare.

Zack didn't need words to know what Sabrina was thinking.

"Cool it, Sawyer." Victor growled.

"Hey *Bruh*, no harm no foul." He told Victor with a mock tone. "We're on the same team, well at least half of you is. The other side of you is on Sabrina and Malcolm's team, right?"

Victor shook his head mumbling as he joined Sabrina near the Humvee.

Sawyer chuckled and then spat his chew once more as he eyeballed, Kelsey and Anne. It wasn't a curious stare either, it was one of those gawking lingering stares, that made Anne feel like he was undressing them with his eyes.

Anne and Sawyer made eye contact and he winked and then blew a kiss at them, before looking at Zack and Malcolm. "Why are we bringing civies on this mission. This ain't no sightseeing tour."

"We can handle ourselves." Anne snapped, as she adjusted her katana at her hip.

"Ohh, I forgot, you're like some samurai warrior princess or something like that?" He teased as he punched and kicked the air.

Anne sighed and rolled her eyes.

"You can sigh all you want baby, but there's a reason why those samurai went extinct. There's nothing like a good ole American rifle. Guns beat swords all the time."

Anne flicked off Sawyer and joined Kelsey who was shaking her head at Sawyer's remarks.

Sawyer laughed watching the two women whisper to each other. "I like this one. Beauty and she's got a *mouth*. No wonder you locked this one up, Malcolm. If you didn't, I sure would have."

"Don't you have a girlfriend?" Malcolm growled.

"Ex-girlfriend I'm sure she's dead just like the rest of the population," he winked at Anne and Kelsey. "That's right ladies, I'm back on the market."

"We're married duchebag." Kelsey stated.

"That's never stopped nobody. Hell, Anne apparently you just got married last week. A shotgun wedding if I remember. You barely stuck your foot in it. If you get tired of Malcolm's shit, I'm only a couple tents down. I can show you what a real man feels like."

"That's enough..." Malcolm growled as he stepped forward placing Anne behind him.

"Oh, did I strike a nerve?" Sawyer grinned.

"Say something else. Give me a reason..." Malcolm barked as his eyes narrowed.

"A true man doesn't have to give a reason. If he wants it. He takes it."

"Excuse me?"

"You deaf, *boy*?" Sawyer chuckled.

Malcolm shoved Sawyer hard before Zack got in between the two. "Hey! Hey! Hey! Same fucking side! What the hell is wrong with you?" Zack glared at Malcolm.

"Zack he's..." Malcolm began to say before Zack placed his hand on his chest and frowned at him.

"I don't fucking care. Go over there. Cool off."

"Zack..." Malcolm began to say, but Zack cut him off.

"Over there!" He barked, pointing at the Humvee.

Malcolm shook his head and walked away.

"Yeah, that's right. Listen to your Captain like a good ole boy..." Sawyer mocked.

"And you..." Zack yanked Sawyer by the collar, and shoved him hard against the wall. Zack's voice was filled with fire, and his eyes were wide, glaring at him.

"Step out of line one more time in my unit, and I'll kick your ass myself. Got it?"

"Touch me and you'd lose your command."

"It's well worth it for an asshole like you. Get in line or get left behind. Your choice."

Sawyer smugly winked at Malcolm before walking away. Malcolm continued to scowl at Sawyer as he walked away.

"You good?" Zack asked.

"You can't be seriously considering letting him stay with us? He's toxic. In a matter of seconds he put all of us on edge." Malcolm growled.

"I am. He's a good shot. You and I both know that. For right now, let him tag along. After this, I'll speak with the Admiral to see what he can do to transfer Sawyer to a different squad. Okay?"

"Yeah, that's fine."

"Good, let's go hunting."

Malcolm nodded and they bumped fists, getting into the vehicle.

Sabrina, Victor and Sawyer were the lead truck, while the others trailed behind. Malcolm drove while Zack sat in the passenger front seat and the women sat in the back. As they zig zag through zombies and car debris, Malcolm cleared his throat.

"Zack, you radio clear?"

"Yeah, hold on," Zack switched his radio to only listen to the broadcast that was shared with Sabrina, Victor and Sawyer. "You're good. What's up Malcolm?"

"Can we talk about the monkey in the room, known as Sawyer Knox? He's only been on the team for five minutes and he's managed to piss everyone off. I have no idea how Victor and Sabrina could keep their cool with him right now."

"Yeah, I know, but there's not much I can do."

"Really, babe?" Kelsey asked.

Zack nodded as he looked out the window to stare at the lead vehicle. "Sawyer is an ass..."

"That's an understatement." Anne muttered as she watched a few zombies stumble along the road.

"But he's a SEAL. A brother. He's only with us for this one mission, after that we're parting ways."

"God, I hope so." Malcolm sighed.

After thirty minutes of careful driving, they arrived at the safe zone in Norfolk. The morning sun was just starting to come up, giving the group light. Unlike the last safe zone full of apartments, this was in a neighborhood, with several million-dollar homes. The neighborhood was Anne's childhood. She remembered spending summers at the club's pool and having community parties. She'd made a lot of memories in her home and prayed that it was still there when she neared.

Her community was fenced in, making it an excellent candidate for a safe zone. The HOA agreed for the military to move in there and set up a base of operations. They accepted anyone into their community and set up temporary tents along the street. During the first week of the fall, everyone was surprised that a once thought snobby rich neighborhood would open up their doors for everyone showing how down to earth they were.

As the vehicles turned down the street, they could see plumes of black smoke rising in the air.

"Please tell me they are planning a barbecue." Anne groaned.

Zack rolled down his window and sniffed the air. He frowned at Anne. "Smells like burnt rubber. That's not good."

"Oh God, Malcolm, please hurry!" Anne begged.

"On it," Malcolm replied speeding up. He passed the lead Humvee and drove as quick as he could to the safe zone.

Anne prayed that her parents were okay, but as they approached the complex it seemed like her prayers weren't going to be answered. The closer they got, the more bodies they found. Each one looked to be either eaten or undead at one time. It was almost like a war was fought in front of the safe zone. Military vehicles were burning with charred corpses inside. Bullet casings lined the streets, with their copper casings shining in the sun.

Anne felt like she was having a heart attack as the vehicles stopped at the entrance of the complex, and Malcolm and Zack both shared a concerned look.

"That's not good." Malcolm muttered, studying their surroundings.

"Why?" Anne asked.

"The amount of bodies and bullet casings everywhere. It doesn't look like a random zombie horde passing through. It looks like an actual battle was fought here between humans." Zack replied, searching the area.

"Oh, no!" Anne started running toward the gate, and Malcolm cursed under his breath.

"Anne! Wait! It's not safe. Wait for us!" He yelled, but Anne wasn't listening. All she cared about was her parents. She feared the worst as her heart began to beat rapidly.

Anne hopped over the gate and ran into the complex. As soon as she did, she was frozen with fear as there were dozens of zombies all grouped together at the entrance. The moment they saw Anne, they all made a low pitch growl and began to crawl towards her.

"Mom...Dad..." Anne cried as her body trembled with regret and fear. Soon those emotions morphed into rage as the thought of being without the people she loved blinded her with hate. Without thinking she unsheathed her katana and screamed as she charged into the horde. She wasn't thinking of her own safety, just her parents. As she hacked and slashed through the dozens of bodies, she focused on seeing their smiling faces once more.

Behind her she could hear Malcolm shout for her. She could hear the bursts of gunfire and the dropping of bodies. She heard Kelsey scream come back, but she was too far gone. She wanted blood.

She then felt someone's hand around her waist. She kicked and screamed, begging them to let her go.

"I would love to, sexy samurai, but you're going to get us all killed," Sawyer growled, firing from his hip. He tossed her backwards towards the group, "cover her!" he yelled.

"I got her!" Malcolm responded as he pulled her back behind Zack,

Sabrina, Victor, and Kelsey. The threesome of SEALs joined Sawyer firing in controlled shots, while Kelsey took care of stragglers that came near. For a brief moment she looked back at her friend with a worried look on her face.

"Hey, are you okay?" Malcolm asked as he touched her cheek.

"Mom and Dad...they're dead." Anne cried.

"We don't know that yet. We just got here. They could be holed up in a house, waiting for the horde to disperse. The worse thing we can do is charge at this mass head on. It makes no sense to kill yourself for unanswered questions, understand?"

Anne nodded.

"We need you. I need you." Malcolm replied, wiping a stray tear off her cheek.

Anne trembled from Malcolm's touch. Looking up from the ground, she placed her hand on Malcolm's. The two shared a passionate gaze as they stared deep into each other's eyes. Malcolm was lost in her eyes before he cleared his throat and attempted to refocus himself.

Looking away, Malcolm called out to Zack, "Yo, we should split up and search for survivors."

"I was thinking the same thing. You, me, Kelsey, and Anne look for her parents while the rest of the team secures the area and searches for other survivors?"

"Yeah." Malcolm nodded.

"Okay, Sabrina, Victor and Sawyer, secure the area and then do a search and rescue for survivors. Try and figure out what the hell happened here."

"Yes, sir," they responded .

"Okay, y'all are with me, let's go." Zack led Kelsey, Malcolm and Anne away from the main herd. They ran down the street, in a tight group of four, killing anything that got close to them. "Stay close!" Zack ordered. "Anne, where's your house?"

"Keep going down this street and then at the intersection, take a left."

Zack nodded as they fought their way through. Dozens of zombies attempted to break their ranks, but the group stayed strong taking on any that got in their way.

"What in the hell happened to this place?" Kelsey asked as she sliced through an undead soldier.

"I'm not sure, but it's strange to hear a safe zone falling like this without calling us first. There was no warning. Whatever happened must have just occurred." Malcolm guessed.

Anne's heart slumped at hearing that they were possibly too late to save everyone. As they neared her childhood home, she pointed to the two-story brick colonial with green shutters.

"There it is! That's my home." Anne shouted.

"Okay, Anne and Malcolm go in and look for her parents. Kelsey and I will stay out here and cover you."

Anne nodded and broke off, running as fast as she could towards her home.

"Anne wait!" Malcolm yelled, chasing after her.

"Mom! Dad!" Anne yelled. There was no reply. She ran up the porch and tried opening the door, but it was locked. Anne cried as she tried to kick the door down, but it was no use.

"Here, move. I'll help you." Malcolm replied.

Anne sidestepped out of the way and Malcolm took his foot and executed a door breach. The door splintered and Anne was the first to run in. Zack and Kelsey remained outside providing cover.

"Mom! Dad!" Anne yelled, searching for her parents. Looking around her home, her house appeared normal. Nothing was out of place. All of the pictures of her family picnics and vacations were still up. Nothing was broken or misplaced. The house was just as she remembered, but at the same time had an eerie aura inside.

Anne frantically searched the first floor, calling out the names of her parents. While she did, Malcolm studied the house for clues and his heart dropped the moment he saw the blood on the stairs.

"Anne!" He yelled.

"What? Do you see something?" She responded, running towards him.

He pointed towards the steps, and Anne gasped. "No, no, no..." she rushed up the stairs and Malcolm followed her.

"Anne, wait!" He yelled.

However, there was no stopping her. She had to know. She knew the answer, but she was afraid to see it with her own eyes. She followed the blood trail down the hall and every step she took she could hear the low growl of a zombie.

She prayed as hard as she could. She prayed that this was all a horrible nightmare. She would wake up and none of this would be real. She would be back at her parents' home, they would hold her tight and tell her that everything was going to be okay.

Tears rolled down her eyes as she got closer to her parents' bedroom. Her hands trembled as she reached for the closed-door knob. Upon opening it, her worst fears were realized when she saw the undead corpses of her father and mother. They stood aimlessly moaning, and turned once their daughter entered the room. Her father still had his glasses on, and like his shirt, his glasses were covered in blood. His stomach was torn open and his guts rolled on the floor as he crawled towards Anne. His mouth was chewed off with barely a few pieces of skin keeping it together. His arms went out stretched as he shuffled towards his daughter.

Anne's mother had blood dripping from her mouth. Her brown eyes which were once filled with wonder and love were now filled with the soulless black eyes that all zombies had. Blood covered her neck and shirt, as she stumbled, following her undead husband towards fresh meat.

Just by looking at the two, it was obvious what happened. Her mother turned and her father was eaten by her, thus turning him as well. By that fact, Anne broke down crying.

In the distance she could hear Malcolm running towards her. His voice was faint as her whole world seemed to be tumbling down. She knew that she'd find them like this, but she wasn't prepared for the horrible feeling in her gut. She'd never felt this way before and it made her sick.

As her parents approached her, Anne tightened her grip on her katana and screamed as loudly as she could muster. With two clean swipes, she severed the heads of her parents. When the bodies and heads hit the ground, she collapsed, sobbing. Her whole body trembled as her emotions took its toll on her.

"Anne!" She heard Malcolm yelled. She then felt his arms wrap her up and her face was on his chest as he rubbed her back.

"Oh God, I'm so sorry Anne," Malcolm whispered.

"I was too late. I was too late." Anne repeated.

"It's okay, Anne. I'm here."

"I didn't even get to say goodbye. They were fine last time we spoke. They were fine."

"Words can't heal a broken heart, Anne. Just know that I'm here for you. No matter what. I'm here."

Zack and Kelsey came up the stairs to see what made the noise they heard previously. When they arrived in the master bedroom room they found Anne and Malcolm together. He was rocking her back and forth, holding her as she let out every single emotion in her body.

Kelsey took a step forward and reviewed the room. She stared at Anne's parents before turning towards Zack and breaking down. Zack rubbed her back and looked at Malcolm.

"I'm sorry Anne. I really am, but we can't stay here. We have to get back and report our findings in this zone."

"Bruh...just give us a minute. Please."

Zack opened his mouth to say something else, but Kelsey squeezed him and gave him a look. With saying a word, Zack knew what his wife was signaling towards him and he sighed.

"Anne, take five more minutes. We'll be outside." Zack and Kelsey began to walk away before Anne called out to them.

"No, wait, I'm ready." She wiped away her tears and stood up.

"Are you sure?" Malcolm asked with concern in his voice.

"Yes, Zack is right. This isn't the place to be grieving. Not here. I will not have the people I care about in this fucked up world die because I couldn't keep it together for a few damn minutes. Now is not the time to grieve. Let's go."

Everyone nodded and began to leave, as they did, Anne stopped at the doorway and stared at her motionless parents. She sniffed and whispered in Japanese, *mata aeru hi made.*

Malcolm stood near her watching as she turned and followed him out.

"What did you say?" He asked.

"I said, *until the day we meet again.*"

"That's sweet." Malcolm replied.

"Thank you, I just wish I could say a different goodbye."

On their way out, Anne grabbed a picture frame of her and her parents. She was a young girl on the picture, as she sat on her father's shoulders posing for the picture with her mother beside her. The picture was taken in a park during a warm sunny day. She rubbed the frame with her thumb before slamming it on the ground, breaking the frame. She took the picture out from the shards and then folded into her pocket. She took a deep breath and looked back at Malcolm.

"Let's go."

Malcolm nodded and together they left the house, as they did, Anne didn't look back. She couldn't as it hurt too much to look at the past.

THIRTEEN

Zack, Kelsey, Malcolm and Anne caught up to the group who'd secured a command tent nearby. Victor was playing with the radio trying to contact Little Creek Base, Sabrina checked for supplies nearby and Sawyer stood by keeping watch.

Sabrina noticed the foursome first, and she frowned when she saw Anne's face. She didn't have to ask, as she knew that her parents were gone.

"Anne?" She began to say.

Anne shook her head and Sabrina opened her arms to give Anne a hug.

"I'm sorry," Sabrina replied, rubbing Anne's back.

"Sorry Anne..." Victor added.

"Ugh, yeah, sorry." Sawyer replied, but he didn't look away from the street he was patrolling.

"It's okay guys. I'm okay," Anne lied. In truth, she was going through a mix of emotions but she didn't want to let everyone know what she was thinking. Not here. Not now.

"Victor, what's the situation?" Zack asked.

"No survivors, sir. We checked most of the houses, but we're only met with biters."

131

"Damn. Any idea what happened here? It looks like a war zone was here with the amount of shell casings laying around."

Sabrina and Victor both shared a look.

"Yeah, that's what we thought too. So we started to inspect the zombies. During our search, we began to notice some things. Follow me." Sabrina said as she led the group outside the tent to a pile of bodies nearby. Some wore US military outfits while others were in standard street clothes.

"Upon further review of the bodies, we realized that many of the military members weren't bit. They were shot."

"Shot? That can't be right. Why would anyone shoot someone?" Kelsey asked.

"Exactly. Who were they shooting and who were they firing at?" Sabrina added.

"My theory is that it's a group of bandits." Victor added.

"Why would you say that?" Zack asked.

Victor nodded his head to a body with street clothes on. He turned the body over to reveal a corpse with the initials SS carved into his forehead.

"What the hell? Who would mutilate a body like this?" Malcolm asked studying the body.

"That's the thing this wasn't recent. Look at the scarring, it looks like it was beginning to heal. This wound is at least a few days old, way before we lost contact with this safe zone," Victor added.

"What the fuck..." Zack whispered. "Why would someone do that to themselves?"

"Clearly, they aren't in the right mind." Sabrina added.

"Yeah, we think that they are the ones responsible for this. Think about it, the zone gets attacked, there's a firefight between us and them. Bodies drop from bullet wounds, but rise again as the undead if they get bit too. It's a bad combination. That's how this place fell so quickly."

Anne gripped her katana tighter as she stared at the body. Rage flowed through her as she realized that her parents' lives were taken by these goons.

"Any idea of where they came from?" Zack asked.

"No, but whoever they are they're not in their right mind."

"The apocalypse would do that to someone. Before all of this we had order. We had psych wards and police. Now these people are free to do whatever the hell they want. It's their world now, and we're just living in it." Malcolm replied.

"Fuck…" Zack wiped his face observing the carnage in front of him.

"Let's head back to base, and tell the Admiral. He's going to need to increase the security around Little Creek. Not only for zombies, but for these freaks as well. Let's get out of here." Malcolm said.

Everyone agreed and got into the Humvees to head back to base. Kelsey sat in the back with Anne, holding her for support, Malcolm sat up front while Zack drove. The ride was quiet besides the sounds of Anne's occasional sniffs and the condolences from Kelsey as he rubbed her back.

Along the way, Anne shushed everyone, "do you hear that?"

"Hear what? I could barely hear anything over the engine." Zack replied.

"No, I hear it too," Kelsey confirmed. "It sounds like screams."

"It's coming from the woods. Perhaps it's a survivor. Stop the car!" Anne yelled.

"No, Anne wait!" Malcolm snapped but before he could say another thing, Anne jumped out of the moving vehicle, and ran into the woods.

"Ahh shit! Anne!" Malcolm yelled, chasing after her.

Zack stopped the car, and hopped out along with Kelsey following the two. The lead car stopped as well, and they could hear Victor's voice yell, "what the hell!"

Anne didn't stop despite the calls from everyone. She knew someone needed help, and they were close by the safe zone, so that person could've been from that zone. They could have known her parents, and that pushed her to help that mysterious voice. In her mind, she has lost her parents and she didn't want to lose anyone else.

As she got closer and further in the woods, the voices started to be more clear as she heard a male and female voice. The female seemed to be struggling as she begged for the man to stop. Anne could hear his sinister laugh as the woman cried out.

When Anne cleared the bushes, she came to a clearing and saw a man on top of a woman. The man was twice the skinny woman's size, as he pinned her against the forest floor. His pants were around his ankles as he attempted to have his way with her. The woman's clothes were ripped, and her pants were undone. Her red hair was tussled, with dirt and leaves mixed in. Tears rolled down her cheeks as she begged for the man to stop.

"Hey asshole!" Anne yelled.

The man looked up, and Anne froze the moment she saw the SS carving on his head.

"You're one of them!" she screamed.

"Anne!" Malcolm yelled as he caught up with her. His eyes opened wide when he saw the man next to the woman. "Don't you fucking move!" Malcolm yelled as he took aim with his rifle.

Zack and Kelsey showed up afterwards and Zack joined by aiming his gun at the stranger.

"Stay right there or we will shoot!" Malcolm commanded.

The pariah smiled as he placed his hands above his head. "You wouldn't shoot a man with his pants around his ankles would you, friend?"

"I'm not friends with rapist assholes like yourself," Malcolm growled. "Keep your hands where we can see them, and step away from the woman."

The outsider grinned and took a couple steps towards his left, allowing Anne and Kelsey to aid the woman.

"She okay?" Zack asked not taking his eyes off the man.

"Yeah, just a little shaken," Kelsey replied.

"Good. What the fuck is wrong with you? We don't have enough on our hands with the fucking zombies and you have to be a rapist prick too?" Zack growled.

"The end of humanity is here. The devil has brought Hell on Earth, and his children now roam these lands. I am his disciple, a Son of Satan. You can kill me now, or you can kill me later. It makes no difference, as I will be reborn again."

"What the fuck is wrong with you?" Malcolm asked. "This is not the work of the devil. It's a virus."

"A virus that the devil created. The undead are his sheep, and we the Sons of Satan are his Shepherds."

"Last I checked Shepherds don't rape innocents."

The man laughed. His cold laugh made Anne shiver as she peered into his crazed eyes. "We take what we want in the flesh. In his eyes, all sins are pathways to hell. The more I rape and kill the closer I am to him." He smirked looking back at Anne.

"Yeah, bullshit. Are you assholes responsible for what happened at the safe zone back there?" Zack asked.

"Yes, we are. There was a flock that needed to be herded. We did that."

Zack and Malcolm glanced at each other before Zack said, "You're coming back with us, for questioning."

"Sure, but can I pull my pants up? I'm sure that you don't want me walking around with my pants down."

"Fine, pull them up slowly." Zack replied, keeping his gun on him.

"Of course," the man replied as he grabbed his pants. As he lifted them up, he reached in his back pocket, and brandished a gun.

"Gun!" Malcolm yelled, and before the man could aim, Malcolm and Zack opened fire, killing the man on sight.

When he laid dead, Zack shook his head and mumbled, "Good riddance." Before shooting the man in the head for a final kill shot.

He then looked towards Anne, Kelsey, and the mystery woman.

"Hey, are you okay?"

"Thank you," she replied

"You're welcome." Malcolm replied.

Seconds later, Victor, Sabrina and Sawyer, appeared from the bushes.

"Hey, are you guys alright? We heard gunfire." Victor asked.

"Yeah, just taking out the trash." Zack replied, pointing to the dead Sons of Satan member.

"What the fuck?" Victor uttered, looking at the man.

"What happened?" Sawyer asked.

"We followed Anne who heard the screams and when we came through this clearing we saw the woman over there being raped by that fucker over there." Zack explained.

"Damn..." Sawyer stared at the man and saw the gun in his hands. "And then he drew on you?"

"Yeah, he was messed up in the head, talking about Sons of Satan and how they're going to take over the world."

"What a nut job."

"You're telling me."

Sawyer ogled the redhead and a small smile cracked on his face. "Who's the gal?"

"I'm not sure yet. Kelsey, care to make an introduction?" Zack asked.

"Yeah, this is Sophia. She's from the Norfolk safe zone we were just at. She's a bit shaken up so I don't know how much help she'd be." Kelsey replied.

Zack looked back at the lady as she was being consoled by Anne.

"What are you thinking?" Malcolm asked Zack.

"She could probably give us a detail attack of what happened. If she was there, she knew why the Sons of Satan would have attacked the safe zone."

"True, you want me to talk to her?" Malcolm asked.

"Yeah, you've always had that smooth tongue compared to me." Zack replied.

Malcolm nodded and slowly approached Sophia. As he did, he saw that the woman had been through hell. Her clothes were ripped, her red hair was in shambles. Her pale skin was covered in cuts and bruises.

No woman deserves to be treated like this, Malcolm thought. In his mind he was pissed. He knew that this shit would have never happened if the world hadn't gone to hell.

"Hi, my name is Malcolm."

Sophia trembled as she stared into Malcolm's eyes. She shivered and leaned away from him.

"I'm not going to hurt you." He replied softly, holding up his hands.

Sophia didn't say anything.

"He's a good guy," Anne admitted. "Trust me, I know Malcolm. He's the sweetest man around. He's not going to hurt you."

Sophia looked at Anne and then back at Malcolm.

"My name is Sophia." She stuttered.

"Nice to meet you, Sophia. I was wondering if you could tell us what happened at the safe zone. We're US Navy SEALs sent out to check out this safe zone and when we arrived it was destroyed."

"Yes, they came out of nowhere."

"Who came? The Sons of Satan?" Malcolm asked.

Sophia nodded. "They claimed that they were sent there from Satan to purify our camp. The soldiers that protected us fought bravely but there was more of them than us. These people aren't humans they're evil monsters. They killed for sport and raped women in the middle of the street. It was horrible."

Malcolm breathed deeply and turned to Anne who was still comforting Sophia. He knew whoever these Sons of Satan were they were dangerous and unhinged, the longer their alive the more danger Anne and everyone else would be in and he couldn't have that. He could lose her to those savages.

"How did you get here?" Malcolm asked Sophia.

"After they raided the safe zone, they took the women whom they thought were favorable, and killed and burned the rest of the area. They took me and a few other women. We were in a group going through the woods, and that asshole over there..."

Her head nodded towards the dead Son of Satan.

"Decided that he couldn't wait to get back to their base or whatever and decided to rape me here. That's when you guys came in."

Malcolm nodded. "Did you overhear where their base was?"

Sophia shook her head. "No, I just know that they were heading that way." She pointed towards the west.

"Yeah, I'll see if I can track it. I'm sure these fuckers don't cover their asses. I'll see if they made a trail." Victor replied as he left the group.

"I'll help him." Sawyer added, following Victor. As he left, his eyes lingered on Sophia before following Victor.

"What are you going to do when you find them?" Sophia asked.

"We're going to rescue those women and show those men that the law still exists in America." Malcolm told her.

"Are you going to kill them?" She asked.

"Depends, on how much they want to meet their maker." Zack replied.

"They all deserve to die. Those men are lower than scum." Sophia growled.

"Well, take care of it." Malcolm replied.

For the first time, Malcolm saw Sophia smile at him and it warmed his heart to see that expression of joy on her face.

Victor and Sawyer rejoined the group.

"What did y'all find?" Zack asked.

"We found a large amount of tracks heading West. We're sure it's them." Victor answered.

"Good. We got ourselves a trail. Sabrina, take a Humvee and take the women back to base. Let the Admiral know what we found." Zack ordered.

"Yes, sir." Sabrina replied. "Let's go ladies," Sabrina replied as she helped Sophia up.

"Wait, Zack, I want to go with you." Anne replied. "I want to make those fuckers pay for what they did to my parents."

"While I respect the gusto, those guys have guns. Fighting men with guns is a bit different than zombies. You can't charge at them with a katana. Sit this one out, help protect Sophia when y'all are heading back to base. Trust me, I'll make those fuckers pay for everything."

"Thank you Zack."

Zack nodded and then looked towards Kelsey who approached him. She wrapped her arms around his neck and placed his forehead on hers.

"Be careful, and come back to me."

"I will. I will come back to you every fucking time. I love you."

"I love you too," Kelsey replied. She leaned forward and grabbed the back of Zack's head as she gave him a passionate kiss. As the two shared their embrace Malcolm and Anne stared at each other.

Anne placed her arm behind her back, playing with her hands, while Malcolm rubbed his chin.

"Well..."

"I just..."

They spoke at the same time before Anne cleared her throat. "Go ahead."

"Be safe." Malcolm told her.

"I was going to tell you the same. I'll see you back at base, okay?"

"Yep, see you soon." Malcolm smiled at her while they shared a tame hug. Anne smiled once more at him before her and Kelsey followed Sabrina and Sophia.

A small smile curled on Sawyer's face as he watched the couples interact.

"Sabrina?" Zack called.

"Sir?" She replied.

"Thank you."

"You're welcome, sir. Alright, let's go ladies. Kelsey and Anne take point."

"Okay," Anne and Kelsey replied, unsheathing their blades and leading the way back to the vehicle.

Once they were gone, Zack grinned at the remaining three, "Boys, let's go hunting." Zack commanded.

"Yes, sir." Malcolm, Victor, and Sawyer replied.

FOURTEEN

Victor led them down the path, with Malcolm, Zack and Sawyer following behind.

"That was some goodbye, Malcolm. Is everything okay with you and the misses?" Sawyer smirked.

"What do you mean?" Malcolm asked as he searched the area around him.

"Well, you know we got treated to the heavy pda session between Kelsey and Zack..."

"Sawyer...choose your next words carefully." Zack interrupted.

Sawyer laughed and then shrugged. "No offense, Captain. I was just wondering, Malcolm, is the honeymoon phase over? You just got married two weeks ago as you were both madly in love with each other. Not even a kiss or an I love you. Just a straight up goodbye hug. Trouble in paradise already?"

"Not the least. Anne and I just have a different love language."

"Really? Sounds boring. All I'm trying to say is if I was still with my ex, and we randomly decided to get married, we'd be all over each other."

"Key word in that statement is, *if*. Last I checked you were single.

What Anne and I have is special. We may not be like Zack and Kelsey, but there's something there."

"A.K.A y'all are freaks in the bedroom. Tell me, what does she sound like when you're hitting that tight ass from behind?"

Zack and Malcolm shared a look and shook their heads.

"Yeah, I'm not having this conversation with you." Malcolm replied.

"Seriously it's just us guys shooting the shit. Everyone does it."

"No, Malcolm is right. We're walking into a hornet's nest. Keep your head in the game. No outside talk. That's an order." Zack growled.

"Yes, sir." Sawyer shook his head and walked ahead to join Victor as he tracked the path.

Malcolm and Zack shared a final glance and Malcolm didn't need to say a word to know what Zack was thinking. Sawyer was digging and if he dug any further he would have pieced together that his and Anne's marriage was a scam.

Malcolm was thankful for the silence as it gave them time to forget about Anne and his awkward goodbye, a few minutes later, they came to a clearing where a warehouse stood. Outside of the warehouse was a guard taking watch. The warehouse was surrounded by a rusty fence and dozens of zombies roamed around the outside like sheep. Hanging on the fence were severed bloodied limps where zombies chewed at them like dogs.

"Fuck me, that asshole wasn't kidding about being shepherds." Malcolm expressed, witnessing the bodies of undead roaming around chewing on the hanging flesh.

"No shit," Zack replied.

"So what's the plan to get in?" Victor asked.

"Well, the zombies are acting like a guard between us and the entrance. We won't be able to get in with force." Zack reasoned.

"What about a distraction?" Malcolm asked. "We can take some grenades and cause a loud enough distraction in the woods. When the zombies roam over there, we should have enough space to slip in."

"It could work, but we'd also be out in the open, if any guards come out, they would pick us off as there's no cover between the tree line and warehouse."

"I can handle that. I'll cover you." Sawyer replied.

"You'll be alone." Zack told him.

"I'm fine with that. I work better alone anyways. I'll climb a tree that way none of the zombies would sneak up on me from behind."

"Good idea. Sounds like the plan is laid. Everyone give Malcolm your grenades. He's going to toss them and once the zombies disburse we'll go in."

Everyone nodded and split up to do their separate tasks. With a grunt, Sawyer jumped and began climbing a tree until he was at a small nook at the top of the tree. He attached his scope to his gun and began to take aim at the guard in the distance. Malcolm snuck away from Victor and Zack, holding multiple grenades, waiting for Zack's call.

Zack and Victor squatted at the end of the tree line and Zack got on the radio.

"Do it." He commanded.

Malcolm removed the pins and tossed the grenades. Several explosions occurred drawing the zombies away. Simultaneously, Swayer took his shot killing the guard with an accurate head shot.

"You're clear." Sawyer radioed in. "I'll stay up here and cover y'all."

"Thanks Sawyer, okay, let's move out." Zack commanded. Malcolm rejoined them, and the threesome took out any remaining zombies in their path. Using a pair of cutters they sniped the metal in the fence and made a small hole for them to enter.

Clearing the fence, they snuck into the warehouse and covered each other as they cleared each corner. The deeper they got into the warehouse the more noises they heard. When they arrived at an opening, Zack held up his fist telling his group to halt.

The group of SEALs were on the second floor looking down at a wide-open floor of the warehouse. In front of them was a large gathering of men. They were drinking and dancing to heavy metal music. Spread throughout the warehouse space were pallets full of boxes of food. In the corner of the room, behind the multiple boxes, were makeshift beds, where the Sons of Satan were raping a group of women.

Zack was sickened at the brutal image and clutched his gun tighter. The prisoners who were taken, laid there pleading for their capturers to stop. In the opposite corner was a raised stage with a cage ring on top of it. It was surrounded by men, drinking and cheering as a naked woman tried fighting off a zombie from eating her. Tears streamed down her eyes as she attempted to keep the biter at bay.

"What the fuck is wrong with these people?" Malcolm whispered.

"The world has truly gone to hell. Our main objective is to save these women. Got it?"

"Yes, sir."

"Malcolm, do you have any flash grenades?"

"Yeah..."

"Good. This is the plan. We toss them into the crowd. We help the woman fighting the zombie first, then we move across the room, getting the women who are with those men. After that, we bug out. Sawyer provides cover fire, and we take the second Humvee back to base."

"That Humvee ain't going to fit all of us." Malcolm whispered.

"I know. The women can sit on each other's laps, while one of us drives back the vehicle. I'll stay and run back." Zack volunteered.

"Those Sons of Satan are going to be on us like white on rice. I'll back you up." Malcolm added.

"Me too," Swayer replied over the radio. "I've been inching for a good fight. Perhaps these fuckers could provide it."

"Good, then it's settled. Victor, take the women back to base. Don't wait for us. That's an order."

"Yes, sir." Victor replied.

"Okay, Malcolm, get ready with that grenade."

Malcolm held it up waiting for Zack's command.

Zack held up three fingers and counted down to one. At one, Malcolm tossed the flash grenade into the center of the room and a loud bang went off. Everyone covered their ears, and the SEAL team moved quickly towards their first target. They didn't even announce themselves before firing. They took clean center mass shots, and the several men watching the cage fell with ease. Zack opened the cage and Malcolm followed, killing the zombie that was on top of the woman, attempting to bite her.

"Are you bit?" Zack asked, inspecting her for any bites.

She shook her head. "Are you military?" She asked.

Zack nodded. "Yes, we're here to save you and the rest of the women."

"Oh, thank god." She replied.

"Zack!" Victor yelled as he tossed some clothes he found nearby.

"Here put these on, hurry the effects of the flash grenade are going to be wearing thin soon." As soon as Zack said those words, the Sons of Satan shook off the concussions, grabbed their guns and began firing at the three Navy SEALs.

"We got to move! We got to move!" Victor yelled, firing back.

"Get in cover!" Zack commanded, as he helped the woman behind a box. "Malcolm, we need to get to the other women! I'll hold off the main group. Go!"

"A'ight! Victor! Cover me! I'm advancing towards the other women!" Malcolm roared as he left his cover, moving up towards the four men, who had gotten off their prisoners and began firing at SEALs as well.

Malcolm killed two of the men with ease, before shifting back into cover. Checking his corner, he spotted the two other men, firing blindly and laughing as if it was a game.

"Sick fucks." Malcolm muttered, before taking a deep breath.

He peeked his head from cover once more taking aim of where the men were, before ducking once more behind cover. He closed his eyes, and then turned to fight them. First shot hit the man in the shoulder, second shot hit him in the center chest.

The second man, shocked that he was the last man standing, screamed a high-pitched battle cry, firing multiple shots away from cover. Malcolm remained behind cover waiting for the man to run out of ammo.

When he did, Malcolm left his cover and was surprised to see that the women had joined the fight by jumping on this guy's back and tackling him to the ground. One woman managed to grab another Sons of Satan's gun and shoot the man.

To his surprise the woman, then aimed the gun at him and Malcolm placed his hands up. Tears rolled down her cheeks as she held the gun at him. Her hands trembled with the weapon in her hands as she took aim.

"Whoa! I'm US Military. My name is Lieutenant Malcolm White. We saw what happened to your safe zone and we're here to rescue you."

"What if I don't believe you?" she asked.

"You have to trust me, okay? I know that's saying a lot given what you've gone through, but I'm a good guy. My team and I are going to get you out of here and take you to Little Creek Navy Base, it's safe there. There's food and medical supplies there. You'll be safe."

"That's what I thought when I went to the safe zone. I'm sorry, but I was told that those zones were safe, but I ended up right back here. I don't want to go through what I've gone through again. What those men did..."

"I won't make you come. If you want to go, leave. Take a gun with you though. If anyone wants to come with me, come over here."

Two women walked closer towards Malcolm, while the others grabbed the Sons of Satan's guns and ran the opposite way.

"Okay, follow me. Stay close." Malcolm told them. The two women nodded and held Malcolm's back as he left cover.

Zack and Victor had already advanced as they continued their firefight with the Sons of Satan.

"I got two, Zack." Malcolm yelled.

"Others?"

Malcolm shook his head. "Didn't feel safe with us. Went on their own."

"Understood. Okay, we're getting out of here. Ladies stay with us, and cover your ears." They all nodded and placed their hands over their ears.

"Malcolm, another flash!"

"On it!" Malcolm yelled as they tossed the grenade in the center of the room. Another loud screech occurred and the Sons of Satan covered their ears, groaning in pain. Victor, Malcolm and Zack, fired quick controlled bursts at any man in their way as they led the women out of the warehouse. As they ran, Zack got on the radio and yelled, "Sawyer! We're coming your way."

"Okay, you better hurry, those zombies are making their way back the fence."

"Shit, let's move!" Zack yelled as they ran outside. Victor, Malcolm and Zack made a circle around the woman as they cleared a path through the group of zombies in their way. Hot on their trail were the Sons of Satan. They roared and growled as they fired off multiple shots.

As they retreated, Malcolm got clipped by a bullet in the shoulder and growled. "Son of a bitch!" He roared, falling down.

"Malcolm!" Zack yelled.

"I'm good, keep going. Don't worry about me!" Malcolm attempted to get back up, but came under fire once more. He quickly crawled to the nearest cover he could find and resumed firing back.

"Malcolm, keep moving!" Zack yelled.

"It's fine! Go! Get the women to safety. I'll draw their fire."

"Malcolm!" Zack responded in an exhausted plea. He didn't want to leave his best friend. He couldn't live with himself if he lost Malcolm.

It was the first time Malcolm was scared in a fire fight. He wasn't afraid to die, he was afraid of what he would lose. Once more Anne came to his mind. It was strange how she was always on his mind when times seemed at its darkest. Her smile was the light and strength he needed to fight the evil that was in front of him. As he fired, he prayed that Anne would be safe. He prayed that she'd find someone to be with. Someone who would care for her like he did.

Malcolm's eyes opened wide as the men drew closer and closer. He knew his time was running thin. Just in the last second, when all hope seemed lost, there was shot from the distance hitting the man closest to Malcolm.

Over the radio Malcolm could hear Sawyer laughing, "I got your back buddy. Keep moving back to the tree line."

"Zack and Victor..." Malcolm began to say, but Zack cut him off.

"We're clear back in the tree line. Sawyer will guide you out. Move your ass. I would rather face a whole horde than to deal with Anne if you don't come back."

"Yeah, you got it." Malcolm fired another shot and retreated. As he did body after body around him fell as Sawyer covered him. As he shot each man, you could hear Sawyer laugh hysterically almost like he lost it and enjoyed taking the life of every man he shot.

"Move your ass, Malcolm. I thought black people were supposed to be fast." Sawyer joked.

"I'm going to pretend like I didn't hear that."

"I'm just fucking with you. You want to see something funny. Son of Satan's meet karma." Sawyer fired a shot, to a fence nearby, and opened the gates. Zombies came flooding into the space and attacked the Sons as they fired their guns attempting to protect themselves.

"Looks like you're cleared. All of the other Sons of Satan are busy dealing with their sheep."

"Thanks Sawyer. I owe you one." Malcolm replied as he ran from the warehouse into the tree line.

Sawyer hopped down from the tree and grinned, "I'm going to hold you to it."

"Enough with the chit chat. Let's go!" Zack yelled as the group retreated back towards the Humvee. Since the two women left, there was enough space in the Humvee for the women to double up and sit on each other's laps. The space was cramp in the four-seat vehicle, but they all managed to fit. Driving back to base, Zack checked out Malcolm's wound.

"How bad is it?" Malcolm asked.

"Looks like a through and through. You'll live." Zack replied.

"Ahh, another scar to add to my fine collection." Malcolm joked.

"If you think this is bad, wait till Anne sees you. You'd take the bullet every time, compared to a worried wife."

"You talking from experience?" Malcolm asked.

"And then some."

When they arrived back at base, the rescued survivors and Malcolm got taken to the hospital. Zack, Victor and Sawyer left with Admiral Wesley to debrief him on the situation.

An hour later, Malcolm sat on the hospital bed, getting stitched up. From the corner of his eye, he saw Anne walk in with tears in her eyes.

"How are you feeling?" Malcolm's doctor asked.

"I'm good. Been through worse."

The doctor chuckled. "Okay, you're going to feel some soreness for the next couple of days, but you should be combat ready by then."

"Thanks doc."

The doctor smiled at Malcolm, gathered their medical materials, and then left the room.

Once the doctor was gone, Anne took a step forward. She sniffled and held Malcolm's hand. Malcolm gave her a small smile, admiring her doe eyes. Reaching up he wiped a tear away, and allowed his hand to rest on her cheek. Anne placed her hand on his and took a deep breath. He peered into her eyes and grinned, "Are you okay?"

She grinned " Shouldn't I be asking you that question? Zack told me you'd been shot. I thought the worst ..." Anne breathed once more and shuddered, looking away.

"Hey..." Malcolm touched her chin and turned her eyes towards him. "It's just a couple of stitches, I'll be fine." Malcolm chuckled and replied in a deep husky voice, "Besides, chicks dig scars."

Anne rolled her eyes at his attempts to be suave. She couldn't help but to laugh. "Is that so?"

"Yeah, is it working?"

Anne shook her head. "No, it's not. Not in the littlest bit."

"Really, then why are you looking at me that way?"

"I am not. I'm just concerned." She smirked, crossing her arms.

"I appreciate it, but seriously I'm fine."

"Good to hear." Anne hesitated and then gazed into Malcolm's eyes. "Do you mind if I stay here with you a bit? Everything that happened in the last twenty-four hours is a lot."

"No, I understand. Here, lie next to me." Malcolm offered as he scooted over in the bed.

Anne laid next to him. He groaned as he stretched his arms out and placed his arms around her.

"Are you okay?" Anne asked.

"Yeah, I'm good. Just a bit sore. You feel good on top of me."

"Yeah?"

Malcolm nodded. "Like a warm blanket."

She laughed. "Good." She cuddled closer to him and placed her hand on his chest. Malcolm's hand rested on her thigh as they relaxed together. They held each other, silently basking in their embrace together. It stayed that way until Anne broke the silence.

"I miss them," She admitted.

"I know, it's going to be okay. Did you want to know what I was told after my mother died?"

"Oh, Malcolm I know you don't like talking about her."

"It's okay." Malcolm sighed and closed his eyes as the tough memories of the funeral replayed in his brain. He was only twelve when his mother got gunned down in his neighborhood. Her death was unexpected and when he saw her in the hospital bed, it felt like he lost a part of himself. After he lost her, he was all alone as his father left when he was younger. She was the last one who cared for him. Just thinking of her pained him. "At the funeral, the pastor told me that life finds a way to bring people into your life to love again. I think life is doing that with you."

"That's sweet Malcolm. I think life is telling me that too."

"I've never had a friend like you, Anne. I'm so happy that you're in my life."

"Me too," Anne smiled. The two shared a look, but didn't say much after that as they held each other silently enjoying each other's company.

FIFTEEN

Malcolm knocked on the open door of Admiral Wesley's office.

"You wanted to see me, sir?"

"Yes, Lieutenant. Please take a seat."

"Sir." Malcolm replied, walking in and sitting down in the seat in front of the Admiral's desk. Both sailors were wearing their black and green navy uniforms.

"How's the arm?" Wesley asked, pointing to the area that Malcolm got shot in.

"It's healing. I'll be ready whenever you say go."

"That's good to hear. We'd need warriors. This fight with the zombies has taken more lives I'm willing to admit. We need men and women who are trained, not new citizens who've just learn to fire a gun last month."

Malcolm nodded, but wondered if he was referring to Anne.

"I've already spoken to Captain Morris about your findings on the Sons of Satan, but I wanted to get your take."

Malcolm nodded. "They're horrible people, showing the worst side of human nature. They believe that they are disciples of the devil and the zombies are his sheep that they must herd. Even worse they think that killing and raping of innocents will bring them one step closer to the devil, whom they worship."

"Yes, that's what Zack told me. Sick individuals."

"I agree."

"What's your threat assessment on them?"

"High. We don't know many lived after Sawyer unleashed the zombies on them. Not to mention, they have guns. They could easily attack us and we'd be vulnerable to attack. It was wise to train the families how to defend themselves."

"Yes, I was hoping that they wouldn't have to use their skills that they've learn, but as time goes on and more safe zones fall, I'm afraid that we will be seeing more and more people lose their minds. It's crazy how much society has fallen in a month."

"Yes, it's sad because if you think about it, this society was already at its breaking point before the undead. Now, with the zombies, it was the push it needed to turn everyone insane."

"Hopefully not everyone. It may not be tomorrow, but this country will be made whole again, and those people like the Sons of Satan will pay for their sins that they've committed."

"I hope so too, sir."

"Thank you, Malcolm. You, Victor, Zack and Sawyer did a brave thing and those survivors that you brought back are grateful to be here. You are dismissed."

"Thank you, sir." Malcolm stood and gave a crisp salute before leaving. Walking out of the admiral's office, Malcolm headed back to his tent to find Anne who was staring at the picture she took from her family home. She was wearing a red spaghetti strapped cami top with a pair of black leggings and sneakers.

"Hey Anne, how are you feeling?" Malcolm asked.

"I'm still a bit numb. I mean, just when I think I'm going to be fine, a memory of my parents pops up and I'm right back to feeling terrible."

"Oh, I'm sorry." Malcolm replied. He sat next to Anne and rubbed her shoulders. "While I've never met your parents, I knew that they were good people."

"How?" Anne asked, wiping her face. She looked up from the picture to stare into his eyes.

"Because they raised one hell of a daughter."

"Aww, Malcolm that's sweet." Anne placed her head on Malcolm's shoulder as she rubbed his hand. The two were silent as they embraced each other.

Anne sniffed and wiped her face once more. "I don't want to keep you. I know that you're a busy man."

"I'm actually not as busy as you think I am. I'm grounded for a day or two to heal."

"Oh, I didn't know that. How is your wound by the way?"

"It's sore, but I've been shot before. It's nothing new."

"You've been shot before? How have I not heard of this?"

Malcolm chuckled. "Yeah, getting shot is like a rite of passage for Navy SEALs. I've taken one in the arm, and a graze on the leg."

"And you laugh at this? You could've been killed!"

"Comes with the territory."

Anne laughed and shook her head. "You know you're not Superman."

"No, I'm even better, I'm Captain America."

"You would want to be Captain America."

"What's that supposed to mean?"

"It means that you're in the military and guys like you gravitate to characters like him."

"True, either him or Punisher."

"Aww, yes. The famed marine."

"Who would you want to be?"

"Is that even a question, Black Widow. She's such a bad ass. She'd take on any man or alien, without breaking a sweat, and she could hang out with the boys."

"Yeah, she was pretty awesome. Plus she's hot."

"Oh! You would! You're such a guy!"

"Yo, do I detect a hint of jealousy?"

"You wish." Anne laughed as she playfully pushed him.

Malcolm chuckled and tickled Anne, who squealed as she flailed about in the cot.

"Oh you! Stop it!" she begged.

"Make me." Malcolm replied, falling back on top of her as he tickled her arms and neck. Anne laughed and wrapped her legs around him attempting to tickle him back. She couldn't contain her smile as the two played.

Anne looked into Malcolm's eyes and then she hesitated. Malcolm noticed Anne's pause and stared at her, breathing heavily, waiting to see if Anne was going to make another move. The room was quiet until Malcolm cleared his throat and inched away from her.

"Sorry, got carried away." Malcolm replied, rubbing the back of his head.

"Hey, it's cool." Anne shuffled in the cot and sat up. She pushed a fallen strap of her cami top back on her shoulder and then took a deep breath. "Talking about the Avengers makes me miss their movies though."

"Really? Which Avengers movie is your favorite?"

"It's hard to pick. All of them are so good, but I liked the first movie best."

"Me too."

A smile spread across Anne's face as she pushed a strand of her hair behind her ear. "Did you want to hear something crazy. I used to watch that first movie whenever I was feeling sad or alone. I don't know, but something about that movie brings me back to 2012, when I was still in college and the world didn't seem as confusing back then."

"I hear you. Was your theater packed when you saw it?"

"Yeah, every seat was taken. You?"

"Same." Malcolm grinned. He rubbed his chin and soon his smile got wider. "Hey, what are you doing later tonight?"

"Nothing, why?"

"I think I have an idea to make your day. Do you know where the rec center on base is?"

"Yeah, I've walked past it several times."

"Good, meet me there around eight p.m." Malcolm stood up and placed his hat back on. "I gotta go."

"Alright, I'll see you soon," Anne replied, watching him leave.

ANNE DIDN'T KNOW what to wear. Normally, she'd have a whole outfit picked out if she had her massive wardrobe at her apartment, but her options were limited as her and Kelsey could only pick up clothes that were on base. She decided on a pair of skinny jeans and a flannel shirt. She decided to let her hair down as it covered her shoulders, and the only make up she could wear was some cherry lip gloss. With a final check in the mirror, she left the tent and headed down to the rec center. As she did, she ran into Kelsey and Zack.

"Oh, hey guys. Are you going to the rec center too?" Anne asked.

"Yes, Malcolm asked us to be there. Said he had something fun planned for us to get our minds off of zombies for a night." Zack replied.

"He's so sweet. Thinking of all of us like this. I heard he invited, Victor, Sabrina, Sheri, Keshia, and Dr. López too. It should be a fun night."

"That was generous of him." Anne replied, wondering who else was going to be there. She also felt like a fool thinking that she was going to be the only one there.

Of course, he'd invite others. We're just friends, Anne reminded herself.

"I agree, we all have been through it." Zack replied.

As the threesome walked towards the rec center, they were surprised to see Sophia and Sawyer.

"Hi, guys! Are you going to the rec center too?" she asked.

"Yeah, did Malcolm invite the other women too?"

Sophia nodded, "Yes, but they didn't feel comfortable in a large crowd."

"Oh, I understand." Anne replied. "How are you holding up?"

"It's been tough, but Sawyer's been an absolute gentlemen. He's allowed me to break down so many times. Who would have thought that this big lug would be mister sensitive."

"Hey now, don't be spilling all of my secrets." Sawyer joked.

Everyone laughed and as they neared the doors to the building, Sawyer opened the door for everyone.

"Here y'all go."

"Thank you, Sawyer." Sophia grinned.

Sawyer winked at her, and then held the door open until the last person came in.

"Did Malcolm tell you where to go?" Anne asked.

"Yeah, he told me. Room A3. It's this way follow me." Zack led the way down the hall towards the multi-purpose room. As they got closer, Anne could detect the smell of buttered popcorn and questioned if her nose was playing tricks on her.

They opened the door to the room, and to Anne's surprise she saw Avengers on the projector screen. In front of the screen were dozens of chairs, and Anne recognized Victor and Sabrina who were sitting next to each other, while Sheri and Keshia sat in the front row eating popcorn together. Richard was there too as he popped the popcorn on a hot plate.

On the table with the hot plate, was an assortment of drinks and snacks. Right then, she realized what his surprise was going to be, a private screening of Avengers.

"You guy's made it!" Malcolm grinned, dabbing up Zack and hugging Kelsey and Anne.

"Yeah this was amazing. How did you pull this off?" Zack asked.

"With the help of Richard over there. I told him my idea, and he just rolled with it."

"Oh, damn, nice one Richard!" Zack grinned.

"Thank you, thank you!" Richard waved, before cursing as he started to burn the popcorn in the pan.

"Yeah, so help yourselves, there's drinks and popcorn over by Richard, and then take your seat. As of right now we are waiting for Dr. López to show up."

Kelsey rose her eyebrows at Anne.

Anne shrugged as if she didn't know what Kelsey was implying, but it was obvious what she was thinking. Anne was in shocked that Malcolm did all of this for her. Kelsey and Zack grabbed a few things from the concession table and sat down in the third row, cuddling together.

Sawyer squeezed Malcolm's shoulder and said, "I think I underestimated you, Malcolm. This is nice."

"It really is, Malcolm. Anne, you're one lucky girl to be married to him." Sophia told Anne.

"Thanks." Anne replied. It was weird to hear that she was lucky to be married to Malcolm. She always thought of Malcolm as a friend, not a prize to be shown off to women.

Sawyer and Sophia grabbed a few things as well, and took their seats in the back row, leaving Malcolm and Anne together.

"Malcolm, words can't express how shocked I am. I can't believe you did this for me." Anne complimented.

"Anne, you're my friend. I do anything for my friends. You said Avengers is your favorite movie, and the movie that makes you feel better. So I got Richard's help to track down a copy of it in the rec area."

"Wow, Richard is the best."

"He really is."

Once more the two locked eyes and smiled at each other, both waiting to say something, but unsure how the other would take it.

"Malcolm?" Anne asked.

"Yes?"

"I have a question for you…"

"What is it?"

"Can…" before Anne could get her final thoughts out, Dr. López came into the room.

"Sorry, I'm late. I lost track of time." She apologized.

"It's okay. There's some snacks and stuff on the table, if you want it."

"Oh, good I'm starved. I haven't eaten anything today, but been stuck in that lab."

"You should come out more. Hang out with Kelsey or Anne." Malcolm suggested.

"Yeah, we would love to pick your brain." Anne added.

"I would love too, but the science can't wait. Honestly, I'm only here for an hour as a break. I'd been working on this virus for a while and didn't want to get cross eyed."

"Well, happy to provide the rest and apparently the food."

Dr. López laughed, "That's a good one. Thanks again." She added before walking away. She filled her plate to the brim with snacks and then sat next to Victor.

Victor attempted to grab some food off her plate, but she smacked his hand away causing them to both laugh.

Malcolm shook his head watching them interact, and refocused on Anne.

"Anne, sorry about that. You were going to ask me a question?"

"Yeah..." Anne hesitated as the thing she was originally going to tell him, suddenly felt like it was in bad taste. Quickly she made up something to ask him. " I was going to ask you to teach me how to shoot."

"Shoot? I thought that you were already taking class with Richard."

"I am, but feel like I'm missing something. Perhaps you could assist with that."

Malcolm laughed, "sure. I would love that. Come on, everyone is waiting for us, let's get our snacks and watch the movie."

"Sounds good," Anne smiled, following her to the snack table. They grabbed two bowls of popcorn and two sodas.

"Well, it looks like everyone is served. I'm gonna go back on patrol of zone D." Richard told everyone.

"Richard, where are you going?" Malcolm grinned.

"It's a private group. I don't want to impose."

Malcolm laughed. "Yeah, and you're a part of it."

"Really?" He smiled.

"Yeah, Richard. You're the glue in this place. Take a few hours off." Anne added.

Richard looked down at his shoes as his face couldn't contain his smile. "Thanks, guys." Richard grabbed himself a bowl of popcorn and sat in the back next to Sawyer and Sophia. Malcolm and Anne chose to sit in the third row near Victor, Sabrina and Dr. López.

"It's about time, y'all lovebirds showed up. We were afraid that the movie wasn't going to play." Victor replied.

Malcolm threw a popcorn kernel at Victor's head, and Victor laughed.

"Alright, I'm starting the movie now." Malcolm replied, grabbing the remote and pressing play. As the movie began, Malcolm and Anne got closer and closer together. Soon Anne found herself putting her head on Malcolm's shoulder and rubbing his arms, as they shared a close embrace.

"Thank you for doing this. I needed this." Anne whispered.

"You're welcome." Malcolm replied in an equal tone. "I'd do anything for you Anne. You mean that much to me."

"Aww, you're so sweet Malcolm." Anne replied, caressing his chin before turning her attention back to the movie.

SIXTEEN

As the credits of the movie rolled by, everyone clapped and
cheered.

"See what I was saying. Best movie ever." Anne told the
group.

Zack rolled his eyes. "Nah, the best movie ever is Top Gun."

"Yes!" Victor yelled.

"I feel the need!" Zack yelled.

"The need for speed!" Victor completed his sentence and the two
slapped hands like two fraternity brothers.

"We should totally watch it." Victor suggested.

"Yes, double feature! Do you know where they keep the DVDs,
Richard?"

"Yeah, down the hall. I'll go get it for you."

"Oh, you're a lifesaver. I could kiss you now," Victor puckered as he
made kissing sounds.

"Please don't." Richard replied, walking away.

Everyone laughed and Zack looked at the rest of the group, "so
who's up for the encore?"

"I've been here longer than I should have. I have to get back to the
lab. Victor, don't be a stranger." Emily grinned.

Victor winked at the doctor, watching her curves sway as she left the room.

"Sheri and Keshia?" Zack asked.

"We like Top Gun , but it's getting close to Keshia's bed time. We best be going too. Say goodnight to everyone," Sheri told her daughter.

"Goodnight," she yawned, before placing her head in her mother's hip.

"Aww," Anne and Kelsey both chorused.

"Sabrina?" Zack asked.

"You know me, I always got your six and you never leave your wingman," she grinned.

"Ah, I saw what you did there. Sawyer and Sophia, y'all in?" Zack asked.

Sophia shook her head. "I'm calling it a night. Sawyer, care to accompany me back to my tent?"

"I would love to," he grinned, walking away with her. He placed a hand behind her waist and turned to the others winking at them.

Zack shook his head at Sawyer and then turned his attention to his wife and Anne. "Now come on. Don't abandon us now in our biggest hour of need."

"Yeah, I'm ejecting from this," Kelsey replied. "You know I hate the scene Goose dies."

"Ahh come on babe. What about you, Anne?"

Anne looked at Kelsey and then towards Malcolm trying to decide. As she stared at Malcolm, he gave her a shrug which she interpreted as her choice. While she wanted to watch the movie with Malcolm especially if she got to cuddle him, she didn't want her friend to walk back alone.

"I'm heading out too."

"What! And miss out on a chance to cuddle your handsome husband? Is your marriage okay? Did you lose that loving feeling?"

Suddenly Victor and Sabrina broke out in song singing the classic ballot. Anne and Kelsey laughed as the Navy SEALs made a fool of themselves.

"And on that note we're leaving. Come on Kes." Anne held out her arm and Kelsey took it as they walked out of the red center.

"Bye guys. Enjoy your heavy macho man flick." Kelsey waved.

"We will!" Zack yelled back causing Kelsey and Anne both to laugh.

Walking out of the building, Kelsey asked Anne, "so what was with you and Malcolm cuddling. You like him now or something?"

"No, we're just friends." Kelsey rolled her eyes. "Damn girl. You and I have different definitions of friends."

"And what is that?"

"If I have to spell it out to you, then you really are clueless."

Anne gave Kelsey a light playful shrug. "You're such a bitch."

The friends looked at each other and laughed once more. As they walked down the path towards their barracks they spotted Sawyer and Sophia on the wall. He was leaning close to her, his lips barely touching hers, as he fondled her red hair with his finger.

"Well, it looks like not all of us are missing out." Kelsey smiled.

"Yeah, I guess so. Sawyer works fast." Anne added, watching the couple's romantic embrace. However the more Anne observed the more she realized that something was wrong. Sophia was struggling to escape as Sawyer pinned her against the wall.

"Something is wrong," Anne stated as she ran towards Sophia. Kelsey followed after her.

"Sawyer no! Stop it. Please. I don't want this." Sophia cried as she attempted to push the big man away.

"Shh, you told me you did, remember? You were putting it out there. Just let it happen." Sawyer muttered as he forced his tongue into Sophia's mouth.

"Hey! Asshole, she said no." Anne growled.

"Stay out of this, you don't know the conversation that we had before. She told me she wanted this."

"Well, it looks like she doesn't want it. Get off her. Now."

"Fuck off," Sawyer growled.

"Hey, what's going on here?" Richard asked, walking up to the group.

"Nothing. People are interrupting me and Sophia."

Richard narrowed his eyebrows and looked towards Sophia. "Are you okay?"

She shook her head.

"Okay, Sawyer, this has gone far enough."

"Excuse me?"

"Leave her alone." Richard commanded.

Sawyer turned and glared at Richard. "And if I don't? You're half my size, runt."

"Leave her alone, or else...." Richard repeated.

"Or else what? What are you going to do? I'd snap you in two before you'd lay a finger on me. " Sawyer left Sophia in the corner and turned to hover over Richard. He easily had ten inches of height on Richard as he hovered above him. He shoved Richard hard and chuckled from Richard's worried expression.

Richard stumbled back. "Sawyer, stop it! We're on the same team."

"Are we? Last I checked we're not on the same team. My teammates would've turned their heads, looked the other way, but you seem to be in my way."

"Sawyer, stop it!" Anne yelled as she grabbed his hand.

Sawyer narrowed his brow and pushed her on the ground. Upon seeing this, Richard punched Sawyer in the face, drawing blood.

"You son of a bitch!" Sawyer growled as his hands collapsed around Richard's throat. They fell to the ground and Sawyer started to punch Richard multiple times. Every time his fist made contact with Richard's face, his fist became bloodier. Richard's face was covered in blood as he attempted to fight back, but it was no use as Sawyer was too strong. Kelsey and Anne tried to pull Sawyer off, but they were too weak due to his massive size.

"Sawyer! Stop this. Stop!" Kelsey yelled.

"Get off him!" Anne screamed.

Sophia stood in the wall crying as she watched the mayhem.

Richard coughed blood and soon became motionless as Sawyer continued to pummel him.

"Sawyer!" Anne yelled. She felt helpless as she tried to push the giant, but it was no use.

Soon she heard Malcolm and Zack yelling. Looking up, she saw Sabrina, Victor, Malcolm and Zack running out of the rec center.

"Sawyer! What the hell!" Zack yelled.

Zack and Victor tackled Sawyer, pulling him off Richard. Sabrina bent down and checked on Richard, who was unrecognizable as his face was cut and bruised.

"He's still breathing." Sabrina told everyone.

"Get off me!" Sawyer yelled, struggling against Zack and Victor. Both of the sailors struggled to keep Sawyer at bay as he looked wild and unhinged.

"What in the hell happened?" Malcolm asked Anne.

"When we walked out, Sawyer was taking advantage of Sophia." Anne gasped.

"That's bullshit. She wanted it. That's fucking bullshit!" Sawyer screamed as he kicked attempting to break out of the hold of Zack and Victor.

"Is that true, Sophia?" Malcolm asked, checking with Sophia.

Sophia didn't say a word as she stared at the motionless body of Richard.

Zack shook his head. "Regardless of what the hell happened, you should never put your hands on another sailor. We're on the same side, Goddamnit, Sawyer! What in the hell were you thinking? Come on, let's move." Zack replied, dragging Sawyer away.

"Get the fuck off me." Sawyer roared.

"I wasn't asking sailor. Do you want to disobey orders again?" Zack growled. "Give me a reason to kick your ass. Move or I'll move you." Zack glared at Sawyer.

Sawyer shook his head while walking away, with Victor and Zack following him.

Anne glared at Sawyer as he walked away and then looked back at Malcolm, "I do not feel safe with him here. What he did...that wasn't right. He just snapped. He nearly killed Richard, if it wasn't for you guys coming out."

"I understand. Come with me, we will go and tell the Admiral. Sabrina could you take Richard to medical to get checked out."

"Yeah, I got him." Sabrina picked up Richard and placed him in a fireman's carry.

"I'll come with you." Kelsey added.

"I'll come too..." Sophia squeaked, following them.

"A'ight, come on Anne." Malcolm said, grabbing her hand. "On the way, tell me everything that happened."

As they walked, Anne repeated all the details that she saw including how Sophia was begging for help and how she tried to get Sawyer to stop, but he didn't. Malcolm nodded in understanding as they walked into the commander's office.

To their surprise, Sawyer, Victor and Zack were already in Admiral Wesley's office. Sawyer was sitting in the far chair and when Anne entered he glared at her. Zack was in the middle of telling the Admiral what he saw. The entire time, Admiral never took his grey eyes off Sawyer as he glared at him.

"Any news on Richard?" Admiral Wesley asked.

"No, but he didn't look good. He's going to need at least a day or two in medical though."

"What in the hell is wrong with you, Sawyer?" Admiral Wesley growled. His glare then shifted towards Anne and Malcolm who entered his office.

"Malcolm? What is Anne doing here?"

"Sir, she saw the whole thing. I thought that she could give some insight on what we missed."

"Okay, Anne what was going on?"

"After the movie, Kelsey and I were walking out when we saw Sawyer assaulting Sophia."

"That's bullshit. She wanted it. She told me so." Sawyer replied.

"That's not the point. She told you to stop. You should have stopped." Anne snapped back.

Sawyer rolled his eyes. "You women are all the same. You don't know what the hell y'all want. You may be saying no, but really all you want is something in between your legs."

"You disgusting little pervert."

"You wouldn't be saying that, after a night with me..." Sawyer grinned.

"That's enough out of you! Another word out of you and you're done. Got it?" Admiral Wesley yelled. His voice shook the walls of his office. His grey eyes were wide as he stared at his subordinate. He rubbed his temples and shook his head.

168

"Go ahead and finish Anne. What else happened?"

"She tried to escape, but Sawyer wouldn't let her. We tried to intervene, but Sawyer wouldn't stop. I attempted to pull him away, but he pushed me down."

Upon saying those words, Malcolm's hand clenched into a fist. He hated hearing how Sawyer touched Anne. The fact that he placed his hands on her made his blood boil.

"That's when Richard showed up. He tried to defend us, but Sawyer was too strong. He overpowered him and even when Richard was already beaten, Sawyer kept punching him. Kes and me tried to get him to stop, but he wouldn't budge. That's when Zack and Victor stopped him."

Reese nodded and rubbed his chin. He crossed his arms and was deep in thought. He cleared his throat and then turned to Anne.

"Anne, you're saying one thing while Sawyer is saying another. It's hard to pinpoint what happened since you weren't out there the entire time."

"You can't be seriously taking his fucking side," Anne interjected.

"I'm not." Reese sternly replied. "What Sawyer did is inexcusable. He attacked another sailor. That's not okay. He'll be punished accordingly for that, but I will not cast him out. We need warriors. We need men who know how to fight. Every day we lose people to zombies or the crazies like the Sons of Satan. We need as many bodies that we can get."

"Seriously? You can't just push this under the rug." Anne expressed.

"Another outburst from you and we'll be having another conversation." Admiral Wesley growled.

Anne pressed her lips together, crossed her arms, and looked away.

"Now, I understand this event may put a wedge on your team, Zack. I will transfer Sawyer to another team."

"Thank you, sir." Zack replied.

Admiral Wesley nodded. "You are all dismissed, except Sawyer. You stay here so we can discuss what in the hell I'm going to do with you."

The three sailors all saluted the Admiral before leaving with Anne. Closing the door, they could hear the Admiral yell at Sawyer.

"What do you think will happen to him?" Anne asked.

"He's probably going to be spending some time in the brig." Malcolm replied. "After that, he'd be back in another unit."

"The Admiral was wrong, he should be thrown out."

"I agree, but it's not up to us." Malcolm replied.

The group was silent walking out of the commander's office. Each one had a blank stare as the previous drama was emotionally draining.

Victor cleared his throat breaking the silent tension in the air. "Hey, y'all I'm going to check on Dr. López. I'll see you later." Victor waved at everyone and split off to go to the medical area.

"Victor, wait up, I'm going to check on Richard and see if Kelsey is still there with him." Zack added, walking away with him. "Goodnight guys."

"Night," Anne waved as they left.

Malcolm and Anne walked down the path towards the tent. With each step, they inched closer and closer together. Anne sighed and placed her head on Malcolm's shoulder and he wrapped his arm around her. It was a familiar embrace by the two friends as they walked down the path. Anne reached up and held Malcolm's hand that dangled over her shoulder. Her fingers rubbed his palm, as she silently listened to his heartbeat.

Drained from the drama, Anne sighed, "I feel so bad about Richard. I wish I could have done more. If I had my sword, I would've been able to take down Sawyer with ease."

Malcolm chuckled as a smile spread on his face, "he wouldn't have stood a chance."

"Thanks for tonight by the way. It was sweet, but I guess it ended on a sour note."

"Yeah, sorry about that. Besides the drama, tonight was fun though, wasn't it?"

"It was. I can't wait for you to take me shooting tomorrow."

"Is that what you want to do?"

"Yeah, you promised you'd train me."

"Then it's a date. Come on let's head to bed. We have a long day of training tomorrow." Malcolm grinned as they walked back to their tent.

SEVENTEEN

Anne woke up next to Malcolm who was sleeping shirtless next to her. She couldn't explain why but ogling his godlike figure gave her butterflies in her stomach. She didn't even know a man could have so many muscles. Like a moth to the flame she was drawn to his dark complexion. Her eyes lingered on his brawny arms, buff chest, and rippled core. She thought that Malcolm's fit body rivaled even Thor's.

She squirmed at the thought of his body over hers. Her erotic thoughts got the better of her as her mind drifted. She saw a vivid image of herself on her back, her beige fingers sinking into his dark skin. His muscly forearms pinning her down, as he buried every thick inch inside her.

She fought the urge to touch herself. It had been so long, and the fact that she had to sleep next to Malcolm nightly and be subjected to his husky exterior was torture enough. For a brief moment, she wondered what if.

She wondered what would happen if they would throw out all reason. What if they lost the idea of just being friends and became intimate. What would it feel like to kiss him. What would it feel like when he fucks her. What would it feel like when he made her come. The dirty thoughts alone made her body shiver.

She had to close her eyes trying to keep her natural urges at bay. After counting back from ten she breathed and reopened them. She wished the urge would disappear but it didn't. It still lingered like a bad hangover.

Sighing she tried to focus on something else. Her eyes then drifted to his shoulder where it was still patched by a bandage. Unlike the other nights, there was no blood on the white cloth letting her know that the wound had healed.

Even though Malcolm says he's been shot several times, she was still concerned about his well-being, especially since the fall. Over the past couple of weeks she'd been slowly falling for Malcolm, and the thought of losing him was unsettling.

It was strange sleeping next to Malcolm every night. At first it felt weird sleeping next to her best friend, especially since he slept shirtless and she slept pantless, but now it was a nightly task she was used to. Strangely it was the one moment in the day she looked forward to. There was something about the way Malcolm wrapped her in his large arms that made her feel safe. His body heat felt like the warmest blanket on the coldest winter day. She didn't want to admit but she loved cuddling him.

Sitting up in the cot, she smiled knowing that today was the day she will train with Malcolm. She was excited to pick his brain on how to shoot and defend herself.

She got off the cot and grabbed her skinny jeans that were on the chair nearby. She shimmied them on, and didn't bother to put a shirt on as she opted to wear her tank top. After placing her hair in a ponytail she checked on Malcolm and saw that he was still asleep. He looked peaceful as his eyes were gently closed. Watching him rest, Anne realized that she'd rather have him wake up in his own and get the sleep he needed than to wake him up bright and early.

Anne thought on what she could do to pass the time, and an idea dawned on her as she remembered that Malcolm told her that Richard woke up from his coma, so she decided to go out to the hospital to check up on him.

Walking out of the tent, Anne walked down the path towards the medical center. Along the way, Anne observed zone D and appreciated the work that Richard did as everything was spotless and in order. As she walked, she replayed the night and the brutality that Sawyer showed.

What man would do such a thing, she wondered. *He was unhinged. It was like nothing was going to stop him from destroying Richard. A man like that is dangerous.*

The medical center was a three-story brick building, much like the command and the rec center, the building's outside was built in the 50s, but the interior was updated. Anne took the stairs to the third floor and found Richard's room down the hall.

Walking in she found a bandaged and bruised Richard. His face was covered in cuts as he slept in the bed. Anne was surprised to see another guest already in the room, Sophia. She was sleeping on his lap. Anne smiled as she realized that Sophia must have stayed by his side the entire time.

Anne cleared her throat and Sophia woke up. Her red hair was matted on one side and she was still wearing her jeans and blouse from last night.

"Anne?" She asked.

"Hi," Anne whispered back. "I wanted to check up on Richard."

"He's doing better than yesterday. Doctors say that it will take weeks for his face to heal."

"Oh my..." Anne clutched her chest. "Have you been by his side the entire time?"

"Yes, after what happened I felt so bad. I don't know why I do it. I'm attracted to macho assholes like Sawyer when I should be with nice guys like Richard. Granted he's a skinny twig, he has heart. Did you see the way he defended me?"

"I did. He has a good heart. Have you seen the smiles around zone D? Everyone in our group loves him. He's a good man."

"I know, and because of me I got him hurt. I should have never led Sawyer on. I thought I wanted it, but then I got cold feet and he just kept pushing."

Anne narrowed her eyes and crept closer to Sophia.

"Listen to me, it's not your fault. Sawyer is an asshole who will get his due."

"Yes, I'm happy he's spending time in the brig, but why didn't the Admiral kick him out for what he did to Richard?"

"He claimed that it's because they needed to keep good fighting soldiers around. It's total bullshit. As far as I'm concerned, Admiral Wesley is just as guilty for being compliant in it."

"I agree," Sophia replied. "But I feel still like this is my fault. I kissed Sawyer first. He wanted more. Perhaps if I just gave it up, we wouldn't have..."

"Don't. As a woman, you have the right to say yes or no. It's your choice."

"I know but..."

"Sophia..." Richard muttered as his eyes fluttered open.

"Richard!" Sophia reacted as she held his hand.

"It's not your fault," he groaned.

"Richard..." Sophia cried as she caressed his face.

"It's not your fault," he repeated. "I would gladly take this punishment a thousand times over to defend a woman as kind as you. No means no. Sawyer should have respected that."

"Thank you, Richard. That's so sweet of you." Sophia grinned.

"Richard? How are you feeling?" Anne asked.

"Like I've been hit by a truck. What happened to Sawyer?"

"He's in the brig."

Richard nodded. "That's good to hear. Thanks for checking up on me, Anne."

"You're welcome. If you need anything just let me know."

Richard laughed and then groaned as he touched his ribs. "Ouch. It hurts my ribs to laugh."

"Sorry..."

"It's cool. I was just going to say, usually that's my line."

Anne laughed. "Well, now it's my turn to take care of you."

"Thanks, Anne."

"You're welcome. I'll check up on you later. Sophia, did you want to walk out with me?"

Sophia and Richard shared a look before Sophia faced Anne.

"Actually, I'm going to stick around here for a bit more."

Anne smiled and nodded. "Yeah, I understand. I'll see you guys later."

Anne left the medical center and went back to her tent. When she arrived she found that Malcolm was up and dressed in his military uniform.

"Anne, is everything okay?"

"Yeah, I went to go see Richard."

"How is he?"

"He's doing well, Sophia was there too. I think she might be falling for him."

"Why do you say that?" Malcolm asked.

Anne laughed, "woman's intuition."

"Ahh, one of the many superpowers y'all have."

"Of course we do. If you play your cards right, I might show you more," she winked.

Malcolm laughed," I'd like to see that. Are you ready for your first lesson?"

"Yes, I've been waiting for it. Of course someone had to sleep in."

"Ah, I see the jokes are starting early today."

"Yep, so what's my first lesson?"

"Well, I wanted to see how good your aim is first."

"No need, I have top marks in our gun class. I know how to clean and assemble a gun, aim and fire. Perfect head shots every time."

"Really, and why do you need my help again?"

"I want to be put in the field. There's no point of shooting at something that isn't coming at you."

"So you want live fire practice?"

"Bingo."

"I guess I could do that. We would have to sneak off base though, as I doubt the Admiral would let us leave just to shoot some random zombies."

"Okay, so what's the plan?"

"Come on, let's head to the armory."

"Okay, let's go." Anne picked up her katana and placed it on her hip.

"Leave that here. We're learning how to shoot, remember?"

"I take this katana every time I leave those gates. We may be learning to use a gun but if we get bogged down, I'm using my blade."

"Fair enough. Come on," Malcolm replied.

They left the tent and walked down the path towards the armory.

"So how do you propose we sneak out?" Anne asked.

"I know some paths I've used before the fall."

"Really, what were you sneaking in or out?"

"That's classified." Malcolm grinned.

"Was it a woman?"

"I can't confirm or deny." Malcolm smirked.

"What? Captain America himself is breaking some rules! There's a little bad boy in you. I'm shocked. I'm not going to lie, that's sorta hot."

"Really? So all it takes to get in your panties is breaking a couple of rules?"

"What can I say, I'm a sucker for bad boys."

"Yeah? You're hopeless. You really need to adjust your standards."

Malcolm and Anne looked at each other before bursting out in laughter. They arrived at the armory and the guard was sitting taking watch. When he saw Lieutenant White walk in he sat up straighter.

"Sir? There should be no civilians in here."

"It's okay. She's with me. I need my M4 and side arm, I also need an extra M4 for her and a side arm. Along with two rounds of ammo for each gun."

"Sir," the man saluted and walked back into the gun cage.

"You have some power around here." Anne observed.

"I'm a rock star. That's why."

"You are full of it." Anne crossed her arms and rolled her eyes.

"Admit it, you like it."

Anne couldn't help but to smirk.

The sailor came back with the multiple guns and ammo and placed them on the table in front of him.

"Anything else?"

"Fries and a Milkshake," Malcolm joked.

"Like I haven't heard that before. Happy hunting, sir." The man saluted.

"Thank you. Come on Anne, I want to get you to the storage room to find you some proper gear."

"What's wrong with what I have on right now?"

"You'd need something to keep all of the ammo and the holster for the gun. Come on."

In the same building beside the armory was the supply room, where all the uniforms and flak jackets were located. Malcolm walked in and was muttering to himself as he searched through the articles of clothing.

"Ah, here's the woman's section."

"First things first, you need a tactical vest."

"I don't get a uniform?"

"You don't really need one. The vest is only needed. This keeps all you ammo on a belt so that it's easier to grab. Here put this on." He tossed her a green flak jacket over her body.

"It's heavy."

"Yep, you'll get used to the weight."

Anne placed the vest over her tank top. Upon wearing it, she felt like a bad ass, as the vest made her feel like a commando.

"Go ahead and place these ammo packs in your front pocket. It should make it easier for you to grab, when you need to reload."

"Okay," she replied, stuffing her pockets.

While she did that, Malcolm also got his gear on. Once he was done, he grabbed a pistol holster. He approached her with the Velcro band on the holster.

"Is that for my pistol?" Anne asked.

"Yeah, the holster goes around your leg of your primary shooting hand which is..."

"My right."

"I use my right too," Malcolm grinned. Holding the leg holster, he got on one knee and then asked, "may I?"

"Yeah sure," Anne stuck her leg out and Malcolm knelt to slip the band over her foot and up to her thigh. As he did, his fingers graced her upper thigh.

There was something about the way Malcolm touched Anne that stirred her core. As he sat there, he looked up and the two stared at each other like they've done countless times before. Gazing into each other's eyes, both shared the same hesitation. Both wanted the other to make a move. Both wanted something more. The opportunity was there, but neither wanted to be the first.

Malcolm shied away and cleared his throat.

"There you have it. You're a regular G.I Jane." He smirked, admiring her attire.

"Well, you're missing one thing." Anne took her scabbard and tied it around her hip, to have her katana hilt on her left side. She tested out the placement by removing her blade and sheathing it several times.

"Well, that's certainly not military issue. You look like a bad ass ninja, like the G.I Joe Snake Eyes or something."

"That's because *I am a bad ass*. Are you ready to go?"

Malcolm chuckled and shook his head. "Yeah, let's get out of here. Follow me."

Malcolm led Anne out of the armory and across the base towards a less populated area. Nearby was a portion of the fence that was a gate that was locked. Malcolm took out a lock pick set and began to pick the lock.

As he did, Anne asked, "You look like you've done this more than a few times. Exactly how many times have you snuck out women from this base?"

"Anne White-Yamaguchi, are you jealous?"

"No, but as your fake wife I need to know about all your strays."

"Oh, that's cold." Malcolm replied as he unlocked the padlock. "Alright, come on," He opened the gate and allowed Anne to get through before closing it after himself and locking it. Anne followed Malcolm as he led her though a semi cleared trail in the woods.

"You weren't kidding about this being a secret path. How many women have you sneaked in and out again, this path looks worn down?"

"That's the second time you've asked. You getting jealous?"

"No, I'm just curious if I'm next to a walking STD. I don't want to catch anything from proximity."

"I'm clean. It wasn't just me who snuck women on and off base."

"Sure," Anne winked. "So where are you taking me?"

"There's a small strip mall near the base. We can make an impromptu choke point and we'd have our target practice."

"Sounds good to me. Question for you, do you ever feel bad about killing zombies?"

Malcolm paused as he looked down at the ground as he walked. "When the world first fell I did. It felt weird shooting these beings who used to be human, but now I don't. These things aren't humans. I've seen horrible things from the undead. I've seen these things rip into children without hesitation. They've killed people who are begging for their lives. As far as I'm concerned they're not human anymore. Now, I see them as monsters."

"I hesitated at first too. I remember that day in the mall. I've never been more scared in my life. Watching the zombies attack those innocents. Right there, I realized that we were dealing with something else. I agree with you. They are monsters."

Malcolm turned and briefly smiled at Anne before turning back around to continue to hike through the forest. Anne smiled back as once again they shared another thing in common.

They soon came to the clearing and then the strip mall. As they approached the building, they encountered their first zombie. Malcolm held up his hand and pointed to the shuffling groaning monster. Silently he gave the order to kill it and Anne nodded and aimed her rifle. She missed her first shot and second one clipped the zombie in the shoulder, sending it staggering back.

"Fuck," Anne growled.

"Just breathe. Don't think. Just do. Let it come to you. Only take your shot when you're confident." Malcolm instructed.

Anne took a deep breath and aimed once more. Her rifle followed the biter as it drew closer to them. She took a second deep breath and then fired. Her third shot was a clean head shot, dropping the zombie down. "Good kill." Malcolm grinned.

"I had a good teacher." Anne smiled back.

"Come on, that shot should have attracted more to the area. Let's get our kill zone set up.

Anne nodded and followed Malcolm towards a nearby alley way.

"This looks like a good spot. We'll move these cars over here and form a narrow entry way. The zombies will filter through here and we'll shoot them. It would be like fish in a barrel.

"And if shit goes south?"

"We run."

"Okay, let's do this." Anne replied.

Malcolm nodded and walked towards a broken-down car. He broke the window and hot-wired it. He then drove the car into the alley way to make a choke point. He hot-wired another car and did the same thing. Anne kept an eye out for any incoming biters. As she searched she heard the familiar low growl in the distance. She looked towards Malcolm and yelled, "I hear them. They're coming."

"Good, fire a few shots and lead them here."

"Okay," Anne shot at the sky three times, and then the growls got closer. Soon Anne could see dozens of zombies heading their way.

"I see them!" Anne yelled.

"Okay, come over here and get into position." Malcolm yelled.

Anne nodded and ran through the zigzagged cars, through the open kill zone towards Malcolm who was squatting behind a car.

"Are you ready?" He asked.

Anne nodded.

"Remember, don't think and breathe. If you miss, don't worry. Regroup and keep trying."

"Okay."

Malcolm and Anne aimed and when the first zombie noticed them, he shuffled his way through the two cars into the open area.

"You got him?" Malcolm asked.

"Yeah, I got him." Anne breathed and then took her shot. It was a clean headshot and the zombie fell to the ground. The shot attracted more zombies as they began filtering through into the kill zone. It was a steady stream of undead walking through the cars but soon the stream turned into a flood as multiple zombies rushed at them.

Anne's eyes opened wide as she looked at Malcolm.

"Don't panic. We're fine. Take your time. Breathe."

Anne nodded and kept firing. Bodies of the zombies began to pile up and multiple shell casings covered the ground around Malcolm and Anne.

"Better than hitting targets?" Malcolm laughed in between shots.

"Yes, much better. I might say, I might be a Navy SEAL myself."

"Don't push it." Malcolm quipped.

Anne gave Malcolm a wide grin before resuming shooting. Dozens of zombies came and the duo mowed them down. As the last began to filter through, Anne reached down to her tactical vest and brought out her last ammo cartridge.

"I'm running out of ammo."

"Switch to your pistol. Don't give up. We're almost through this." Malcolm yelled over the constant fire.

Anne continued to fire and when her gun clicked, she knew her ammo for her M4 was through. In a clean movement, she dropped her rifle and switched to her pistol taking out several zombies until the gun was empty.

Even though there were still ten zombies left, Anne didn't hesitate.

"I got them!" Anne yelled as she leaped over the car's hood with her sword in hand.

Malcolm followed her with his jagged ten-inch knife in his hand. Together they slayed the remaining zombies and when they were through, multiple bodies laid stretched out between them. Both of them stared at each other, gasping for air as their faces were covered in blood. Anne smiled at Malcolm and Malcolm smirked at Anne.

"Some target practice. You're a great teacher Malcolm."

"And you were a good student. I was impressed with that move you did when you were losing ammo. The switch between M4, pistol, and then sword was impressive. Looked right out of an action movie."

"Thanks," Anne replied. She observed the corpses around her and then asked, "now what?"

"Let's head back to the base. I could use a shower."

"Same here. I got blood and guts in my hair."

"Are you kidding me, I think it looks amazing," Malcolm joked as he plucked a piece of brain matter from her hair. "I'd still do you."

"Ha, you're such a guy. I'm pretty sure you'd hump a piece of dirt if it let you."

"Oh, you know about Charlene, the mud pile."

Anne laughed. "Case and point. Come on Romeo, you can tell me all about this mud pile." Anne winked and then walked ahead of him back into the woods.

Watching her ass sway, Malcolm chuckled, "Yes, ma'am."

EIGHTEEN

"So you're going on a date?" Zack asked, watching Malcolm count his ammo cartridges.

"It's not a date," Malcolm replied, placing the ammo in his tactical vest.

"Really? It sounds like it? I mean y'all are going off the base to go shopping. That sounds like a date."

Malcolm laughed, "we're getting clothes for her because she's tired of wearing clothes that aren't hers. Besides we're looking for clothes for Kelsey too."

"No, don't shift the conversation. Just admit it's a date."

Malcolm laughed. "If I say it's a date, would you get off my case?"

"Yes," Zack grinned.

Malcolm hesitated and then sighed. "It's a date...as friends."

"Oh, you..." Zack and Malcolm both shared a look and laughed. "You're lucky I like you."

Malcolm winked at him. "So are you going to cover for me or not?"

"Yeah, I got your back, you got two hours. That should be enough time for you, minute man."

"Minute man?"

Zack made an obscene gesture humping the air and then groaned quickly. Malcolm laughed and pushed him.

"Two things. One, none of that will be happening. We're friends."

"Ah there's your classic catch phrase."

"And two, I'm not a minute man. I'm far from it. I have my references."

"Sure," Zack winked.

Malcolm shook his head and grabbed two rifles along with a couple of pistols from the armory. Zack followed him as they left the building heading towards their barracks. The morning sun was just beginning to come up, and most of the base was still sleeping. After the armory the two Navy SEAL, hiked back towards Zone D to Malcolm and Anne's tent. Inside their tent, they found Kelsey and Anne talking. Anne already had her tactical vest on, along with her katana tied on her hip. With a pair of jeans and boots, she looked ready to take on an entire army.

"Hey Anne, you look stunning," Malcolm complimented. "Honestly, I wish I was wearing jeans too. This uniform is a drag."

"Nah, I think you look handsome. I always like a man in uniform," Anne smirked.

"Yes, our everyday uniforms are perfect for every occasion. Between firefights and shopping trips this uniform does it all."

"Don't forget about using it for dates," Zack added.

"It's not a date!" Anne and Malcolm both snapped.

Zack placed his hands up in defense, and looked at Kelsey who was giggling.

"Point taken. It's not a date." He laughed. "Y'all be safe on your non-date."

Anne shook her head and then asked Kelsey, "Did you want me to pick you up anything from the store?"

"Yeah, a new pair of jeans would be nice, you know my size."

"Yep, I got you. Malcolm, did you bring me something special?"

"Yeah, one M4, a pistol, and two mags each." Malcolm replied, handing her the items.

"Perfect. You sure know a way to a gal's heart. Thank you." Anne replied, taking the guns and ammo from him. She placed the magazine cartridges in her vest, checked the ammo on both guns, and strapped the rifle to her shoulder and holstered the pistol. "Let's go."

Zack and Kelsey smirked at the duo like proud parents sending their kids off to prom. Zack stood behind Kelsey and teased, "Have fun you two, don't do anything I won't!" Zack teased.

"Nothing will happen. We're just friends!" Malcolm and Anne chorused together.

"Yeah, yeah, have her back here by ten! No funny business!" Kelsey chimed in.

Anne rolled her eyes and sighed, and Malcolm playfully flicked them off as they exited the tent.

"When are they going to learn?" Anne whispered.

"I have no idea..." Malcolm replied as they sneaked out of zone D. The pair crept towards the back unguarded gate. Like last time, Malcolm opened the lock and the two left the base, heading through the woods. They were met with little resistance as they traveled through the forest to the open area, where a truck that they hot-wired previously was waiting. Malcolm started the vehicle again and they drove to the nearest department store a mile away.

As Malcolm drove, Anne smiled at him, "Can I ask you a question?"

"Yeah, sure," Malcolm replied as he dodged multiple broken-down cars in his way.

"Do you get annoyed when Zack and Kelsey tease us about hooking up? I mean it's gotten a bit old, right?"

Malcolm shrugged as he kept one hand on the steering wheel. "I think it's their way of telling us that they want us to be together."

"I know, but they should know by now that we don't see each other like that."

"Exactly! I think it's just wishful thinking on their part. I wouldn't let it bother you."

"Ha, easier said than done." Anne sighed and looked out the window watching random zombies stumble about in the background.

"Hey..." Malcolm replied, touching her shoulder. Anne turned her attention to Malcolm. "I'm serious on this part, we're just friends. We know that and that is all that matters. Let Kelsey and Zack have their fun, but at the end of the day, if we know where we stand, that is what counts."

"You're right, Malcolm. Thanks."

Malcolm winked at her and when they arrived at the department store, his smile disappeared. "We're here. There's a couple of zombies in front, let's clear them out. You get the ones on the right. I got the ones on the left."

"Yeah, got it?"

Malcolm nodded and stopped the truck in front of the store. As soon as he did, the duo hopped out of the vehicle, and took aim at the zombies in front of them. After the last zombie fell, Malcolm checked his surroundings and then looked back at Anne.

"Clear."

Anne double checked and nodded. "Yeah, clear."

Malcolm nodded and then pointed towards the store. "Let's go shopping."

"Oh, yes, I've been dying for a new pair of jeans."

Malcolm laughed and then led Anne to the store. The department store that the duo went to was a big box store, that had multiple departments including, clothes, grocery, outdoor, and electronics. The windows were shot out, and the only light source in the store was from the sun, as it was pitch dark the deeper the two traveled inside. Judging by the disarray in the store, the store had been looted several times, but as Anne and Malcolm walked in they noticed the woman's clothing department still had multiple options.

"Oh, these are cute, what do you think?" Anne questioned, showing him a pair of skinny blue jeans.

"I like the black ones." Malcolm replied as his eyes continued to scan the area.

"Oh, good eye, I think I'm going to try this one on."

"Yep, I'll be right here."

Anne walked towards the changing room that was nearby. The room had a hallway , with several doors on each side. Anne hummed to herself as she casually chose the closest door to her left and opened it.

To her surprise, the room was occupied, as a zombie came tumbling out. She screamed as a zombie attacked her. It growled and it tried biting her. Anne quickly shoved it away, unsheathed her blade and sliced it's head off.

"Anne!" Malcolm yelled, running up to her. "Are you okay?"

"Yeah, I didn't see that coming." She laughed, placing her katana back in its sheath.

"Maybe, I should stay outside your door?"

"Not the worst idea. I'll be out in a second."

Malcolm nodded and turned back away from the dressing room door. Inside the room, Anne removed her pants and placed on the first pair of blue jeans. Looking in the mirror, she checked out how the jeans were fitting her. Biting her lip, she felt as if the jeans were missing something, and she decided to walk out to get a second opinion.

"Hey Malcolm?"

"Yeah?" he called out.

"Could you come in here for a second?"

"Umm...sure." Malcolm replied, opening the door to get inside the dressing room.

"What's your opinion on these?" She asked, turning around in the jeans.

Malcolm paused staring at her slim figure. He shrugged and shook his head. "Honestly, I'm a dude, so my opinion isn't the best."

Anne laughed. "Spoken like a true man. Just tell me what you think. No bullshit."

"Your ass looks great in them."

Anne laughed once more. "Really? I've never pegged you for an ass man. Besides my ass, what else?"

"Umm..." Malcolm hesitated and studied Anne. He hated to admit it, but she looked stunning in the jeans. Along with the tactical vest, she made his heart pound like nothing he's ever felt before. "The blue really matches your tact vest."

Anne placed her hand on mouth and laughed. "Wow, that was cringy."

Malcolm chuckled. "Sorry, maybe you should have brought Kelsey with you."

"Nah, Kelsey would've had my ass here for hours. Plus, last time I went shopping with Kelsey we barely survived the mall, until you and Zack saved us."

"Ha, true."

"Come on give me a good opinion. Not about my ass, and please don't say anything about tactical vest. Entertain me." She grinned.

Malcolm rubbed the back of his head and it was hard to erase the smile that grew on his face as he stared at Anne. His fingers rubbed his chin as his eyes looked her up and down.

"The blue jeans match your eyes."

Anne was taken back by the comment and tilted her head. "In what way?"

"You have these gorgeous brown eyes that you could just get lost in. The blue jeans compliment them."

"That's sweet." Anne replied. She looked back in the mirror judging the jeans, before unbuttoning them. "Let's try your choice."

"Oh, you're getting undressed now. Did you want me to leave?" Malcolm asked.

Anne shrugged. "You've seen me in my underwear all the time in the tent. This is no different. Besides who will protect me when my pants are down and a zombie comes in. I do not want to die with my pants around my ankles."

Malcolm laughed. "Yeah, good point. Here lies Anne Yamaguchi, she died with her pants around her ankles."

"Ouch. Sounds terrible. Also correction, Anne White-Yamaguchi, we're married, remember?"

"How could I forget," Malcolm grinned.

Anne winked at him and proceeded to remove her pants, and Malcolm couldn't help but to ogle her toned curves.

"Yo, my eyes are up here." Anne joked.

"Sorry."

"It's cool, just busting your balls." Anne grabbed the pair of black skinny jeans and tried them on. She looked in the mirror with them and bit her lip. "Hmm, what do you think?"

"I like the blue jeans better."

"Really? Well, I like these better. Damn."

"Why don't you just get both? I mean, it's not like we're paying for these."

Anne laughed and slapped her forehead. "Shit, you're right. Why am I in here trying on multiple clothes like I only have a budget for one when I can just take whatever I want?"

Malcolm laughed. "I have no idea."

"Shit, well, I'll take both of these."

"Good choice."

Anne laughed and grabbed the second pair of blue jeans behind her.

"Hey, are you going to take your old jeans with you?"

"Nah, perhaps the person who originally lost them will find them here."

"Oh, how considerate you are." Malcolm joked.

Anne flicked him off and then walked back to the jeans area where she proceeded to look for a couple of pairs of jeans for Kelsey. As she browsed, Malcolm walked towards the men's section and looked at a pair of board shorts.

"You plan on going swimming?"

"Actually, I was. The beach is on base, figure it would be a nice break to get away from it all. Perhaps we can invite everyone with us to hang out. Especially since all the drama with Sawyer. It would be nice to just relax."

"Yeah, that's a good idea. Let me see if I can find a bikini to wear."

Malcolm nodded and grabbed a pair of shorts for himself, and then followed Anne who was browsing through the women's swimsuit section.

"Find anything?" Malcolm asked.

"I did, but I can't decide between the red or green set." She held up both to show to Malcolm.

"Why not both. I mean that's what you did with the jeans."

"I don't plan on swimming every day. One set is good."

"Did you want to try them on?"

Anne rose an eyebrow. "So you can see me try on different suits for you?"

"Of course not. I don't want one being loose on you. You know. I would hate for a boob to pop out or something. I can be the judge of a bounce test or something."

"Oh, I'm so glad you are concerned about the safety of my breasts."

"I mean who else is going to be?"

Anne rolled her eyes and shook her head. "I'll go and try them on."

"Perfect. You need someone to guard you in the room?"

Anne laughed, "nice try. Let's try and leave some mystery in our relationship, shall we?"

"Yeah, sure."

"Okay, I'll be right back." Anne grinned as she disappeared in the dressing room. Malcolm could hear her remove her flak jacket and other clothes and as she did, Malcolm looked away from the dressing room, towards the checkout lanes near the women's section. As he did, he noticed the familiar orange wrapper of the peanut butter cups and chuckled. He took one of the candies, as he remembered what Anne said she would do if she got her hands on the candy again.

"Alright, Malcolm, what do you think of this outfit?" she asked walking out.

Malcolm's hands were behind his back as he looked out her swimsuit. He whistled and couldn't help but to gaze Anne's petite form. "It's nice," Malcolm grinned.

"Yeah? Is that all you're going to say? You seemed really adamant to get me into this two piece, and now your only words are, *it's nice*?" She mocked inching closer to him.

Malcolm shrugged. "What can I say? I guess I'm not a man for words."

"Really? I find that hard to believe. Perhaps, I look so smoking hot in this that you just can't come up with any other words."

"You got me."

"Bullshit, what's behind your back? And why are you giggling like a teenager?" Anne asked.

"Well, I remember a certain someone saying that if they had a particular type of candy..." Malcolm removed the candy from his back and showed her. "...You'll get to flash me."

Anne laughed and covered her face. "Really? God, I didn't peg you for a perv."

"What? You said it, not me."

Anne rolled her eyes laughing. " I swear men would do anything to get shown a little skin. So the deal is I'll show you my tits for the candy, right?"

"Yeah," Malcolm grinned, holding the candy up.

"Alright come closer."

"Why?"

"Because I want you to get the full view."

Malcolm laughed and got closer.

"Yep, that's it. Closer." Anne grinned as she grabbed the string on her top. "You ready?"

Malcolm nodded, as his eyes focused on her chest.

"Okay, here we go!" However, instead of pulling the string to her bikini, Anne punched Malcolm in the nose and stole the candy from his hand.

"Hey! That's cheating!" Malcolm groaned. "Come here!" he yelled.

Anne screamed as Malcolm chased her through the store. He finally caught up with her and picked her up. He swirled her around and the two laughed. Placing her feet on the ground, he looked down at her, breathing heavily. Anne did the same looking into his eyes. The sexual tension that was between the two returned as they took labored breaths. Both hesitated as if they wanted to do more, but didn't want to over reach.

"So about the bet..." Anne asked.

"Nah, it's off. Don't worry about it. I just wanted to see how far I could go. The chocolate is yours."

"What if I wanted to show you?"

Malcolm hesitated. "I mean, you can if you want to but..."

"But what?" Anne asked.

"Don't you think that's a step too far?"

"You didn't sound like you thought it was too far a minute ago."

"Yeah, but standing here with you right now, made me realize how good a friend you are. I mean, friends don't go around flashing each other. Do they?"

Anne looked down and bit her lip. "No, I guess they don't."

Malcolm let her go and rubbed the back of his head. He looked outside and frowned. "It's getting late, we should head back soon. Go ahead and get dressed. We should head back to base."

Anne frowned as well, sensing that something changed between them. She didn't know what Malcolm was thinking, but it seemed like all the fun was sucked out of the room from their close encounter. As Anne walked back out to the dressing room, Malcolm took watch in front of it, guarding the area.

Wanting to brighten his mood Anne grinned and untied her top. "Hey Malcolm!"

"What?" He turned and saw her topless. He laughed and shook his head as Anne danced in front of him.

She placed her top back on and winked at him. "We're not that type of friends, okay? We're the type of friends that flash each other!"

"I guess we are." Malcolm laughed.

"It's nice to see you smile again." Anne grinned before heading back into the dressing room to get changed. A few minutes later, Anne walked back out dressed in her jeans, tank top, and tact vest on. In her hands were a bag of clothes that she took.

"You ready?" she asked.

"Yeah, let's go."

Anne began to walk out of the store back to the truck when Malcolm walked beside her, and nudged her with his shoulder. Leaning close to her ear, he whispered, "I just wanted to let you know that you have a nice pair of tits."

"Ha, I know you talk big game, but I'm questioning it now. Were those the first pair of knockers you've seen? You were drooling and everything."

"Hey! I've seen some."

"Your mother's don't count."

"You're such an ass," Malcolm grinned, giving her a playful shove.

"Umm, last I checked, you're married to this ass."

"Ugh, don't remind me. Worst decision of my life." Malcolm grinned.

"You kidding me? Guys are lined up around the block for a piece of this. Apparently, I still got it judging by your deer in headlights look."

"I'm never going to live this down, am I?"

"Nope," Anne grinned. She opened the candy package and handed him a peanut butter cup. "Chocolate?"

"Sure." He grinned taking a bite.

"Hmm, totally worth it. Best shopping trip ever!" Anne groaned, taking a bite of the second peanut butter cup.

Malcolm laughed, shaking his head, as the two got back into the truck to head back to base.

NINETEEN

"Did you guys grab the sunscreen?" Zack asked.

"Yeah, mission accomplished." Kelsey replied, lifting the bag of goods in her hand.

"We also found some great shades to wear." Anne pointed to the glass on the top of her head. "We got some for you guys too."

Malcolm laughed. "We have shades covered." He pulled out his aviator sunglass and placed them on. "Beefcake airlines is now open." He joked.

"Anne, you seem to be a frequent flier on that airline. Tell me how's the ride?" Zack grinned.

"I wouldn't know, but it sounds like you also may want to ride." Anne smirked. Malcolm and Anne shared a look and they both laughed.

"What about you? Did you get the snacks?" Kelsey asked.

"Yeah, we got them." Malcolm replied.

"Then I guess we're set. We were supposed to meet everyone at two. Come on." Anne replied.

The foursome left the tent and headed outside. Walking towards the beach, they could feel the sun on their skin as it was a hot August day. Anne and Kelsey were both wearing bikini tops, short jean shorts, and flip flops. Their shades were resting on the top of their heads as she followed the men carrying a cooler of food. Like Zack, Malcolm was shirtless wearing his board shorts and sandals. It felt great to not be restricted to the standard army uniform or on patrol fighting for their lives outside the gate. It was a rare day of rest for the group and they planned on enjoying every second of it.

When they got to the beach, everyone was already waiting for them. They had already set up their area with beach umbrellas, beach chairs and towels. Everyone was in their swimsuits enjoying the sun and water. Emily was taking to Sheri as they lounged on the beach chairs. Across from them, Sabrina, Keshia and Victor were playing with a frisbee. Richard and Sophia were floating in the water by the time Zack placed the cooler down next to the group.

"The snacks and drinks are here!" He grinned.

"It's about time. I think I was going to die from dehydration." Sheri joked.

"Yes, the sun is terrible!" Emily added.

"That's one way to say you're welcome." Zack grinned, taking out two waters and handing it to the women. "How long have y'all been out here?"

"About thirty minutes. What took you four so long?" Sheri asked.

"Hey, finding ice was tough enough. We had to bribe the kitchen staff for this stuff." Malcolm added.

"We would've been on time, but Kelsey had to choose the perfect suntan lotion." Anne replied.

"You make fun, but the options on base were terrible. I had to do proper research, y'all will thank me when none of y'all burn."

Everyone laughed and Kelsey tossed a bottle of the lotion towards Sheri, who reviewed the bottle. She nodded reading the label. "Good choice," Sheri replied. She squeezed some lotion onto her hand and applied it to her dark skin.

Emily took the bottle and reviewed it. "Yeah, Sheri's right. Good choice," she replied, placing the lotion on her tan skin.

"You see? Priorities."

Malcolm laughed, shaking his head. "So how are you doing, Sheri?"

"Good, it feels good to get out of that tent." Sheri looked towards her daughter who was giggling as Victor chased her. "Thanks for inviting us."

"Are you kidding? You guys are family. You are always invited."

Sheri smiled and gave Malcolm a big hug. "What about you, Emily?"

"I'm like Sheri. I'm happy to be out of that lab. I've been working like a dog trying to find a cure for this virus."

"Any luck?"

Emily shook her head. "None, and I hate it. I've never met a virus I couldn't cure, but this is different. Everything I think of ends up being a failure."

"Don't worry, you'll figure it out. We have faith in you."

"Thanks, it's tough though. All of the pressure to save the human race. It's a lot to shoulder."

"Try not to carry it all. That's why we're here. You need to vent, let us know." Anne added.

"Thanks, everyone." Emily smiled.

Sophia and Richard ran out of the water towards the group standing around the cooler.

"Zack and Malcolm, you're finally here with the drinks!" Sophia grinned, grabbing a soda.

"Hi, guys," Richard waved, joining everyone.

"Sorry we're late." Malcolm apologized. "Richard, it's good to see you. It looks like your injuries are healing well."

A smile cracked on Richard's face. "Yeah, Sophia's been awesome helping me heal. She's been my rock." He grabbed Sophia's hand and she smirked at him, rubbing his palm.

Malcolm rose his eyebrows and looked at Anne who also had a large smile on her face. There was no secret that there was something growing between Richard and Sophia.

Victor, Sabrina and Keshia joined the group.

"It's about time you showed up." Victor mocked.

"Save it, I think I heard it from about everyone. We get it. We're late." Zack groaned.

"Yeah, just making sure. We also wanted to let you know that we took the liberty of picking teams for football. Zack, Keshia and Sabrina are on a team, versus Malcolm, Richard and me. Sorry that you got on the all-girls team."

"Are you kidding me. This is perfect. You lose, I'm forever letting you know that you lost to a bunch of girls." Zack challenged taking the ball from Victor and ran away with it. Victor chased after him and tackled Zack to the sand. The two wrestled on the beach, while their two teams laughed at them.

"Well, then ladies, I guess that leaves us as the cheerleaders." Kelsey replied.

"Or perhaps, the gawkers as we watch the men play." Anne added. Her eyes lingered on Malcolm and she felt a shiver up her spine. There was something about his shirtless body that made her quiver. She'd seen him shirtless before, but there was something sexier about him that day. It could have been how the sweat was rolling down his dark skin or the way his skin glistened in the sun. It could have been how each one of his muscles had a ridged shape. She particularly loved his abs.

She loved the V that formed at his lower abdomen, that led to the bulge in his shorts.

Watching him run, she saw the outline of his length jiggle causing her heart to flutter. She didn't know why lust was taking over her, they were just friends, but it was hard to deny the sexy spartan like physique that Malcolm had. It was breathtaking.

Anne tried to settle herself focusing on something else, but her eyes kept drifting back to Malcolm. She didn't know what spell she was under, but it was hard to resist it.

"Very true." Kelsey corrected herself.

All of the women laughed, as they got settled in on the beach chairs. Eventually Zack and Victor ended their squabble and a game of football began.

Kelsey was half paying attention as she looked towards Sophia who had all eyes on Richard.

"Sophia?"

"Yeah?" she replied, not taking her eyes off Richard.

"How are you and Richard doing? I've noticed that you two have gotten a lot closer in the last coming days."

Sophia's smile doubled on her face. "Richard is a dream. To be honest, if it wasn't for this zombie apocalypse, I would have never paid him any mind. Before all of this my types were muscle head assholes, not skinny sweet guys like Richard, but since that night with Sawyer, Richard showed me who he was. He's a down to earth guy, and every time he speaks he melts my heart. Did you know he writes his own poetry?"

"No, I had no idea."

"Yes, he's written me several poems each one, makes my heartbeat triple its pace."

"So have y'all hooked up?" Kelsey asked.

Sophia looked down at her feet as she buried them in the sand. "Yeah, we have. A couple of days ago."

"And?"

Sophia shook her head and covered her face. "He was good. Really good."

"Ahh!" Kelsey and Sheri both yelled out loud. They both sounded like two school girls as they snickered.

"Yeah, I'm going to need more details." Sheri interjected.

"Well, he was walking me back to my tent, and I kissed him. He kissed me back. He wanted the night to end there, you know after the way things ended with Sawyer, but like I said, I never met a man like Richard, so I took him back into my tent. I didn't think he'd be so good at sex. What that man could do with his tongue. Fuck me."

"Huh, I didn't think he had it in him." Kelsey observed as Richard missed a wide-open catch that was thrown by Malcolm.

"He may be skinny, but the man knows what he's doing." Sophia breathed as if she was reliving the memory in her mind.

"Who would've thought? You see? Friends always make better lovers." Kelsey replied, but as she said the words, her eyes remained on Anne's.

Anne knew that she was talking about her and Malcolm's situation, and shook her head in response. Kelsey winked at her and then turned her attention to Emily.

"What about you Dr. López? I've noticed Victor has been spending time in your lab."

Emily's plump cheeks got flushed as she looked away towards the ocean.

"Oh, Victor..." her hands reached to her brunette hair and she twisted it, as if she was trying to find the right words to say. "Victor and I are just friends. He likes to come by my lab and just talk."

"Really? No hot sex going on in the lab?"

"That's unsanitary."

"I figured, but just once, wouldn't it be hot to just have Victor, lift you on a desk, hike up your skirt, and have his way with you?"

Emily breathed deeply again and touched her neck. Her eyes lingered on the shirtless Victor as he ran back and forth in the sand. She was in a daze as if she was in deep thought about the sensual image described by Kelsey. She then shook her head, as if she awakened from it and cleared her throat.

"Like I said, just friends. You seem to be focusing on everyone's sex lives. You sure you're not missing out on something?"

"She's not." Sheri and Anne both said at the same time. They then looked at each other and laughed.

"Please don't get Kelsey started on what her and Zack do on their spare time. They'd make a paster blush." Sheri told Emily.

"She gets graphic." Anne added.

On cue, Kelsey winked at Emily. "If you want details let me know."

"I'll pass," Emily replied.

"You know I'm down. I love your stories." Sheri grinned. Kelsey smirked and proceeded to tell her a dirty story of her and Zack from a few days ago. Anne, Sophia, and Emily ignored the details of Kelsey's juicy affair with Zack and turned their attention to the group men playing football.

The game looked intense as both Malcolm and Zack were the quarterbacks. Anne was surprised that little seven-year-old Keshia was able to hold her own against the grownups. However, it was obvious that they were going light against her as they missed obvious tackles with her. Eventually, Kelsey and Sheri stopped sharing dirty secrets and all of the ladies each cheered for a team.

Anne didn't know what the score was, but she heard Zack yell,

"Match point." He lined up with the football, yelled, "hike," and ran backwards with the football. Sabrina drew Richard and Victor's guard, while Malcolm guarded Keshia. Zack pump faked the ball and then aired it out to Keshia. She shuffled her feet and Malcolm pretended to get juked by the move as she ran past him and caught the ball, running as fast as she could the opposite way. Twenty yards later, she stopped and spiked the football cheering.

"We won!" Zack cheered.

"Malcolm let you win." Victor complained.

"Nah, that move was good." Malcolm admitted, dusting himself off.

"Coming from a college football player. No wonder Navy lost to Army when you played."

"Bruh, I played on the offensive not defense."

"Football is football."

Malcolm laughed and then looked towards the ladies watching them. "Yo, does anyone want to take a dip? That game left me hotter than the sun."

"Yeah, I'm game." Anne replied, sitting up.

"Me too." Kelsey grinned.

"Yeah, I'm coming." Sophia followed the two women as they walked towards the group.

Sheri and Emily stayed behind as they continued to chat. Sabrina and Victor picked up Keshia and ran her out to waves before tossing her in the water. Keshia giggled as she hopped out the water and splashed them. The three proceed to have a splash war as they threw water all over themselves.

Kelsey and Zack cuddled each other in a shallow area. Zack held Kelsey by her back, while Kelsey placed her arms around his back. The two stared at each other before making out. Sophia and Richard shared the same romantic energy before kissing each other.

"Whoa, when did that happen?" Malcolm asked Anne, looking at Richard and Sophia.

"That's been going on for the last couple of days," Anne responded as she treaded water. "They've hooked up already too."

"What? How did I miss that?"

"I thought the same thing. I guess we sorta lost ourselves in our adventures in target practicing."

"Yeah, I guess so. Good for them. They make a cute couple."

"That's what I was thinking too. Kelsey gave me a look after we found out that they're hooking up."

"Really? Sorry, I know it's getting old of those two pushing us together."

"I agree. I mean, if it hasn't happened now, it's never going to happen. Right?"

Malcolm paused and looked away. He was going to reply to Anne until he saw Sawyer standing on top of a dune looking down at him and Anne.

"What are you staring..." Anne turned to follow his line of sight and saw Sawyer. "Malcolm..."

"Yeah, I'll handle it." Malcolm replied. "Yo, Zack."

Zack stopped dancing with Kelsey and looked at Malcolm, then towards Sawyer. Zack growled and shook his head.

"What the fuck is he doing here?" Zack asked.

Malcolm looked towards Sophia who had a worried looked on her face as she clutched Richard tighter. No words needed to be shared to show how scared Sophia was of Sawyer.

"I have no idea, but I'm going to tell him to get lost." Malcolm replied, swimming back to shore.

"Yeah, I got your six." Zack reaffirmed.

"I'm coming too." Richard added.

"You don't have to..." Zack replied.

"No, Sawyer needs to be put in his place."

Zack nodded. "Come on then."

Malcolm jogged off the beach and onto the dune where Sawyer was standing.

"What the hell are you doing, Sawyer?" Malcolm asked. Zack and Richard followed Malcolm and stood behind him.

"I'm just looking at the ocean. I'm not going anywhere near y'all."

"This beach stretches on for a mile, and this is the place you decide to go see the water?" Malcolm snapped.

"I like the view better here." Sawyer nodded towards Sophia who was getting out of the water with Kelsey and Anne.

Richard noticed that Sawyer was staring at Sophia and got into Sawyer's face.

"You touch a hair on her." Richard growled, as Zack held him back.

"Or what? What are you going to do, Richard? I've already kicked your ass once. Let's not make a mess out of things again. Shall we?"

"You're a fucking asshole, Sawyer." Richard added.

"I am, but women like Sophia like assholes like me. All I have to do is bide my time, and she'd get tired of your skinny ass, and come to look for a real man."

"Real men don't beat woman like you did."

"Really? That's a lot of talk coming from a toothpick," Sawyer quipped.

"That's enough!" Zack roared. "Sawyer, what the hell? Just leave. Stop this. You're already in enough trouble as it is. Why can't you just leave us alone?"

Sawyer smiled at Zack and then looked towards Malcolm. "I'll leave, if Malcolm could answer one of my questions."

"What?" Malcolm asked annoyed.

"Why don't you kiss Anne more often? When I was up here, I saw Sophia and Richard and Kelsey and Zack in this romantic trance, but looking at you and Anne in the water, you two looked like friends. You were barely touching each other. Why is that?"

Malcolm hesitated and looked back at Zack who shared the same worried expression. Malcolm thought of something to say quick and replied, "we don't like expressing PDA."

"Is that so?" Sawyer asked, raising his eyebrows. "Well, I guess that answers my question. Thanks."

He began to walk away, and after a few steps he turned back around and smirked, "I just think that it's weird that a newlywed married couple doesn't kiss often. If she was my woman, I would kiss her nonstop." He winked at them and then waved goodbye. "Enjoy your beach day everyone."

Once he was gone, the remainder of the beach day fell flat as everyone had this uneasy feeling that Sawyer was watching them.

Malcolm on the other hand couldn't shake off what Sawyer said. He didn't like how Sawyer kept poking holes in their lie. The more Malcolm thought about it, the more concerned he became. Finally, a stray chill went up his spine as he worried about his fake marriage to Anne coming to light to the others.

TWENTY

Malcolm tugged on the fence testing its dexterity before walking away and joining Zack who was standing watch.

"How's the fence?" Zack asked.

"It's good. I'm amazed with the amount of zombies we catch the perimeter it's still standing."

"That's because the Navy is always prepared."

"You're starting to sound like a recruiter."

"Haha, join the Navy and see the world."

"Or join the Navy and fight zombies on land, screw the sea."

Zack laughed. "Yeah, some Navy service members we are. We've been demoted down to an army service member."

"Ugh, don't say that." Malcolm chuckled.

The duo continued their patrol as they checked the fence every five yards. As they circled the base, the sun was coming up on the early morning, and the dew was beginning to roll off of the grass. As they walked they saw Ann and Kelsey leading a group of people through kendo lessons. It was the normal group, but Malcolm was surprised to see two additional members to the class.

"Huh, when did Sophia and Emily join the class?" Malcolm asked.

"I'm not sure, but Anne or Kelsey must had convinced them to join." Zack replied. "It's good that they're learning. They're going to need those skills if this place ever falls."

"You think we'd get overrun?"

Zack shrugged. "I'd like to think this place is a fortress, but it's not. It's too big, even with multiple patrols, we can't guard every inch. Because of that, it leaves us vulnerable. I mean hell, you and Anne sneak off every once in a while to get some nookie."

"I told you that's not what we're doing. We're training."

"Sure..." Zack winked at Malcolm.

Malcolm shook his head and then looked at Anne who was helping Sophia with her stance. Malcolm thought Anne looked great this morning. He noted how she seemed to glow in the early morning sun. Not to mention, she was wearing a sports bra and yoga pants, making it hard not to look away. Friends or not, Malcolm couldn't deny that Anne had an impressive body.

Anne noticed Malcolm and waved at him. Malcolm smiled and returned the gesture.

"Hey, Malcolm are you going to ogle her all day?"

"I'm not ogling her." Malcolm replied, turning back around to face Zack.

"Brother, you were gawking at her like a hawk looking at prey. Seriously, y'all just need to hook up."

"We're just friends."

Zack sighed and shook his head after hearing the same thing over and over again. "Would you quit with that same line? Even friends slip up and hook up every once and a while."

"That's not us." Malcolm replied as he walked away. Zack joined him as they continued to walk around the perimeter.

"Really? Bullshit. What have you two been doing every time you sneak out?"

"We're training."

"Nope. I know you two are getting it in. I mean that's what I would do with Kelsey."

"That's because you and Kelsey are sexual freaks."

"Hey now. I take offense. We just happen to enjoy expressing our love."

"Well, next time you two are expressing your love, remember that the tent walls are thin and Anne and I can hear everything."

"Oh we only do that to put you two in the mood."

"Oh God..."

Zack laughed as his eyes continued to scan the wooded area behind the fence. "From what I've heard, you two had a perfect opportunity when she flashed you. You should have acted on it."

"I'm beginning to regret telling you about that."

"Please Kelsey would have told me anyways. You two should have hooked up then."

"Her flashing me had nothing to do with sex. It was just a joke."

"Are you that naïve? Come on. It was clearly a sign that she wanted more from you."

Malcolm shook his head. "I'm telling you. We've discussed this. We like what we are as friends. Nothing you say is going to change our opinion on that."

Zack sighed and scratched his chin. "I just don't get it man, I would be losing my mind going without sex. How long has it been for you?"

Malcolm looked down at his boots and shook his head. "Six months."

"Six months! I'm surprised that thing hasn't shriveled up into a raisin."

"Hey!" Malcolm playfully shoved Zack.

Zack laughed and shrugged. "I just can't see why you two can't just hook up a la friends with benefits."

"You and I both know that friends with benefits never works out."

"What's that supposed to mean?"

"Remember Debora? That chick you were *friends with benefits* with in San Diego? How well did that turn out for you? If I recall, she drove cross country to stalk you here."

"Debora was a complete psycho and I feel bad for any man who gets caught in that witch's web. Anne is different than Debora. She's not crazy."

"She isn't, but sex just ruins what we have."

"You and Anne have this flirty *wouldn't they won't they* chemistry. Everyone sees how you are around her. You're completely smitten.

211

The stares. The flirting. The jokes. It's suffocating. Just do her already."

"The flirting is all for the ruse of us being married."

"Bullshit, y'all flirt when no one is even around. Watching you two gives me blue balls."

Malcolm snickered as Zack continued his rant.

"Seriously though, if this was a romance book, you two would've been hooked up. What's taking so long?"

"We can not just gloss over the fact that you mentioned you read romance books."

"Don't change the subject!"

"I've known you for over ten years. In that span, I've never seen you pick up a romance novel."

Zack laughed and rubbed the back of his head. "It's the zombie apocalypse. What do you want from me? Kelsey keeps bringing them in our tent and I end up reading them. They're not as bad as they sound. Besides I got into reading that stuff because watching you and Anne interact burns my soul. You're the worst slow burn ever."

"There's nothing burning, because we're just friends."

"No, there's some smoke I see it. I just got to find me some lighter fluid to get you two going."

"Please don't burn us alive."

"I will if I have to," Zack smirked.

Malcolm chuckled and through his laughter he heard movement behind the fence. His smile disappeared as did Zack's as they became serious.

"You heard that?" Malcolm asked.

Zack nodded, "the nearest gate is two hundred yards away."

"Then I suggest we hustle."

Zack agreed and the two SEALs ran towards the gate. After getting it open, they followed each other into the woods searching for the origin of the sound.

"This is patrol 233, we heard a noise at gate 25. We're going to investigate." Malcolm radioed in.

"Roger, that patrol 233. Radio if you need back up."

"Copy." Malcolm replied.

Malcolm followed Zack as he took point in the woods. They crept quietly with their guns at the ready. They saw a group of twenty zombies all shuffling towards them and Zack held up a fist and Malcolm stopped. Zack gave the kill order and Malcolm acknowledged.

Zack counted down and on one they opened fire in controlled clean bursts. As they fired, Zack pressed, along with Malcolm behind him, until the last zombie fell. When the last one was slain, Zack studied the bodies.

"That's strange that they would be so close to base. Have you ever seen them this close before?"

"No, when Anne and I go out we normally see one or two at the end of the tree-line but after that they're only in populated areas. They don't roam in the woods."

"Yeah, them getting so close to us concerns me."

They heard a low growl and Malcolm cursed. Fuck! Zack, behind you!"

Before Zack had time to react, the zombie was on top of him. Malcolm didn't have a clean shot as the zombie and Zack fought.

"Stay still so I can get a clean shot."

"Don't. I got it." Zack barked. The zombie was a bigger man, probably around three hundred pounds, his clothes were torn and he has a large bite mark on his neck. He looked freshly turned unlike the others that they've encountered that day.

Malcolm removed his knife and approached Zack. "Hold him steady. Let me get him in the head with the blade."

"Easier said than done. The fucker is huge. Let me deal with it. I got it."

Zack tossed the zombie to the ground and before the zombie could stand back up, Zack removed his pistol from his holster and fired a quick shot at his head, and then holstered his gun like a cowboy.

"And that's why you don't fuck with Texas. Fastest hands from Waco."

"Show off." Malcolm smirked.

Zack flicked him off and then double checked his surroundings. "I don't see any more."

"Me either. I think the coast is clear." Malcolm replied, looking

"I wonder where they came from."

"I think I have an idea. Check out the guy you killed. That symbol on his forehead look familiar?"

Zack inspected the body and saw the bloodied SS carved on his skin.

"Sons of Satan." He muttered. "I thought those fuckers were gone after we raided that warehouse."

"Me too. Apparently some survived and have been recruiting." Malcolm observed.

"Fuck. What are you thinking?"

"Perhaps the guy was taking his pet zombies on a walk and one of them turned and bit their master."

"Sounds plausible, but why here? You think he was scoping out the base?"

"We haven't seen any tracks before on patrol, but it's best not to discuss this here. Admiral Wesley would want a full report. Let's hustle back to him." Malcolm suggested.

"Yeah, that's a good idea. Come on."

The two left the bodies and ran back to base. When they arrived back at the Admiral's office, they knocked on the door and the Admiral looked up from his notes on his desk.

"Just the men I've wanted to talk to..." he paused and looked at their exhausted faces.

"What is it?" His eyes narrowed, looking back at the sailors as he sensed something was off.

"We were patrolling and heard a noise around gate twenty-five, upon further inspection we found about twenty zombies and a man who identified as a member of the Sons of Satan." Zack explained.

"I thought you guys buried those sons of bitches."

"We did too, sir, but somehow they survived. At least their ideology did."

"I'm not surprised. This zombie apocalypse is a perfect breeding ground for those nut jobs. Any idea why he was so close to base?"

"We're not sure if he just stumbled upon us or was scouting the area, regardless you and I both know that is not good they're too close. This base isn't designed to keep large hordes out." Malcolm added.

"I'm aware. Until we can know more, I'm going to increase the patrols around the perimeter, plus I want your team to scout the woods. See if you find any more traces of any other Sons of Satan poking their heads where they shouldn't be."

"Yes, sir. I'll get the team ready." Zack and Malcolm saluted and began to leave the office before the Admiral called out to Malcolm.

"Lieutenant White. Stay where you are. Captain Morris, you are free to go."

Malcolm and Zack shared a look before Zack exited.

"Sir?" Malcolm questioned.

Admiral didn't say a word as he sat up from his desk, walked to his door and closed it. As soon as the officer closed the door, Malcolm began to worry. Whatever the conversation was about it wasn't going to be pleasant.

Admiral Wesley sat back at his desk and stared at Malcolm before clearing his throat.

"I'm going to go ahead and come out and say that I know about you and Anne."

"Sir?"

"Don't speak, just listen. I know about you and Anne. I knew from the moment you landed with her in the helicopter that she wasn't your wife. You might be able to lie and confuse everyone on base about her, but I wasn't fooled. I'm not sure how many people are in your little ruse, but I don't care. What I do care about is that you broke the rules. You knew the rules. No friends and girlfriends. Only spouses, but you went against them. I could have easily thrown Anne out of the base, but I didn't. She became an asset and no one was aware of your lie. So I let things slide. However that has changed. People are starting to put two and two together realizing that you two aren't as close as you say to be."

"Who is saying those things?"

"It doesn't matter who, what matters is if people figure out your lie. Once that happens the flood gates will open. The base will be in disarray as everyone who couldn't get a loved one or friend on the base would be upset and unhappy."

"Are you going to kick Anne out?"

"No, she's safe. However, the more people talk, the bigger target you paint over yourselves. I don't care how you convince people on base that you're together, but figure it out. I don't care if you have to make out with her or hold her hand every second you're together. I really don't need details, but I don't want another person to question the legitimacy of your lie. Understood?"

"Yes, sir, but if people don't believe us..."

"Then Anne goes."

Malcolm's heart sunk as he didn't want her to leave. Beyond these gates it was dangerous and he couldn't let Anne face those dangers alone.

"And if I refuse to let her go?" Malcolm asked.

"By that you are refusing a direct order from your superior?" Admiral Wesley glared at Malcolm as he stood up. "Refusing an order is punishable. Under normal circumstances, I would have thrown you in the brig, but since you've defied my orders from the start, there's no point of punishing you that way. Instead you will be executed by firing squad."

"You can't be serious..."

"I am. The world isn't like the one three months ago. Before the fall, soldiers listened to orders and didn't disobey as they were afraid of the consequences. However, we now live in a world without consequences. Soldiers now think they are Gods among men, and the rules don't apply to them. I have dozens of soldiers, including you and Sawyer, breaking rules and not following command. Ever since Washington fell..."

"Sir, there's no commander in chief?"

Admiral Wesley stared at Malcolm and shook his head. "A month ago, central command lost contact with the president. They sent a team in and confirmed the kill. The Vice President died three days into the fall. The speaker of the house and Secretary of State are gone too. The heads of our government have been dropping like flies."

Malcolm was in shock as he stared at Admiral Wesley. "Why doesn't anyone know about this?"

"Do you realize the panic that would spread? There's already disorder, imagine what it would be like if everyone knew."

"Why are you telling me this?"

Admiral Wesley shrugged as he walked towards his cabinet and pulled out a cigar. He smelled the tobacco before snipping its end and lighting it.

"Besides lying to me about Anne, you're a good soldier and one of the few senior officers still alive on base, however, I do know that if this leaks, you'd be the first I'll come find. This stays between us. If not, I'd deny it and you'd be on my shit list. Got it?"

"Yes, sir."

Admiral Wesley nodded and smoked his cigar letting out a puff of smoke. He sighed and continued. "It was under agreement in Code Z that the commanders of each base would govern their own men if the government failed. That's why I'm instituting capital punishment. I can't have disorder here. If we can't keep order here we're just as bad as the places outside these walls. We are holding on by a string in this place. Every day, I get news of something drastic happening. I can barely keep it together."

"Sorry, sir."

The Admiral shook his head and took another puff of his cigar. He had a distant stare as he looked at the small American flag in his desk. He sighed and then looked back at Malcolm. "If you ask me, this country went to shit as soon as they called Code Z. Gathering up the families was a waste of time and resources. Most of my problems in this base stem from the families we brought in. The fat cats in government had it wrong. They should have had us sweep the zombies off the face of the earth before we saved everyone. We should have called in air strikes wiping cities off the face of the Earth, dropped soldiers on the ground, and fired at anything that growled at us. Instead we wasted half our strike time and man power trying to collect people's wives, kids, and bureaucrats too afraid to hold a gun. If we could have contained the threat, it would have never gotten worse. Instead we were worried about saving lives. Bunch of bullshit if you ask me." Admiral scratched his chin and left his cigar in his mouth. He looked back down at the papers in his desk and with his mouth filled with the tobacco, he mumbled, "Anne and you... Find a way to keep people from talking about you, otherwise you'll see a different side of me. Understood?"

"Yes, sir."

"Good. You are dismissed."

TWENTY-ONE

"What did y'all talk about?" Zack asked as he waited for Malcolm in the hall.

"Not here. Follow me back to my tent. We need to have a meeting with Kelsey and Anne."

Zack nodded and followed Malcolm as they searched for the women. They found Kelsey and Anne eating lunch in the mess area for zone D. The two were talking and the moment Anne saw Malcolm's face, she put her bowl of pasta down and frowned.

"Is there something wrong?" She asked.

"Yeah, not here. Come back to the tent." Kelsey and Anne nodded following Malcolm and Zack to their tent. The foursome were quiet. Once everyone was in the tent, the foursome all stood in a circle looking at Malcolm.

Anne had a concerned look on her face as she asked, "what's wrong?"

Malcolm chuckled, "honestly I don't even know where to begin."

"Just start from the beginning." Zack offered.

"Admiral Wesley knows that we're not married."

"How did he find out?" Anne asked.

"He says he always knew. However, now even more people are

catching on. He's willing to go along with our lie, if we can convince others that we're actually married."

"What do you mean?"

Malcolm sighed and then pointed towards Zack and Kelsey. "Basically we have to act like these two love birds whenever we're in public. That includes kissing, hugging, getting close to each other. The full ten yards."

"Does that include fucking each other loudly too?" Anne mocked.

"Hey! That was once." Kelsey complained.

"No, that was multiple times. I'm pretty sure everyone in zone D knows you're fucking."

Kelsey and Zack looked at each other and laughed.

"Our bad," Zack smirked.

Malcolm rolled his eyes and looked back at Anne. "No, we don't have to do that. I'm pretty sure we can get away with not actually going the distance, but the kissing part. I know we're just friends..." Malcolm hesitated as he knew kissing would change their terms of friendship. He stared into her eyes and offered, "if you don't want to do it, I understand, but you have to know if people discover your secret, you'd get thrown out."

"And what would happen to you?" Anne asked.

"Admiral Wesley was very clear, he said either I comply with his orders or I will face capital punishment via firing squad."

"You can't be fucking serious? What is this the 19th century?" Zack growled. "The US military has clear rules about that shit."

"Apparently there's no military anymore. Hell there's no government in the US."

"What?" Zack's jaw dropped. Anne and Kelsey had the same expression.

Malcolm nodded and then added, "what I'm about to tell you doesn't leave this tent. However, the Admiral let it slip that the president and all other chains of commands are either missing or dead. There's no leadership in Washington."

"So, wait who's in charge?" Zack asked.

"No one knows, but Admiral Wesley told me that the military leaders on each base are governing themselves, which explains why he's bringing back capital punishment. There's no one above him to say no."

"Wow, so what now? We just follow orders like everything is fine?" Zack asked.

Malcolm shrugged, "that's why I'm meeting with you. What did y'all want to do? It's obvious that the military is no more. Did you want to stay here and take our chances or leave and see what else is there."

"I want to leave. I don't feel safe with him." Kelsey replied.

Zack shook his head. "Although I think capital punishment is extreme I trust Admiral Wesley. I've served under him for a while and he's a good man, despite his rules. Malcolm?"

"I say the same, but Anne it's up to you. If you feel like getting close to me is too much, then I'll draw the line. We'd run away together, and take our chances."

Anne smiled, "you've give up everything you have for me?"

Malcolm nodded, "for you it's worth it. I can't let someone I care about go and fend for themselves."

Anne's grin grew as she reached out and grabbed Malcolm's hand. She rubbed it and replied, "thank you. You're a good man, Malcolm." Anne sighed and looked back at Zack and Kelsey. "I have to agree with Malcolm and Zack. Outside these walls it's dangerous. Kelsey you've seen this first hand. On top of zombies, we have to worry about the Sons of Satan and anyone else who wants to kill us. It's not worth it. Here we know it's safe, and if I have to kiss and hug Malcolm in front of people to prove that we're married so be it. I'm down. As long as we're all safe. That's all that counts."

"Then it's decided. We stay here." Malcolm confirmed.

Everyone agreed.

Zack and Kelsey shared a look and Zack nodded as if he was agreeing to their silent conversation. A small smile curved on his lips as he looked at Anne and Malcolm.

"And on that note, I think we should all get some rest. Big day tomorrow you know."

"Really? We're just patrolling tomorrow." Malcolm replied.

"I know. Judging by this conversation, you and Anne will need some alone time to catch up. It could take hours, minute man." Zack winked.

Malcolm shook his head.

"What does that mean?" Anne asked.

"Aw, girl, you know what we mean." Kelsey gave her a hug and rubbed her back. "We'll see y'all tomorrow. Don't stay up too late."

"What?" Anne asked, oblivious to their hints.

Kelsey and Zack laughed at Anne and said their final goodbyes before leaving the tent.

"What was that about?" Anne asked.

"You know them, always trying to get us to hook up."

"Oh...right, I get it now."

Anne and Malcolm shared an awkward stare. Both of them looked like they wanted to say something else, yet their mouths were glued together. As they lingered, Anne finally coughed and looked away. She pushed a strand of her hair behind her ear, and began to pick up things around the tent, putting clothes and various items in their correct spots.

Malcolm couldn't take the uncomfortable tension anymore and cleared his throat. Anne looked up, and stared at him.

Malcolm shuffled his feet and played with his hands, as suddenly he felt like the entire weight of the world was on his shoulders. "Are you sure you're okay with all of this?" He asked.

"I am..." Anne hesitated and continued to clean.

"Are you sure? While we haven't been faked married for years, I know your tendencies. I know when something is bugging you."

Anne sighed, "you can read me like a book, can't you?"

"Yeah, I guess living with someone does that. Here sit down next to me. Tell me what's wrong." Malcolm replied, as he took a seat on the cot.

Anne followed and sat next to him. "It's just this fake marriage. When I agreed to it I didn't think much of it at first, but now I'm realizing what it is. To me it's almost like we really are married."

"But we're not."

"Are we though? I mean like, the moment we stepped foot on this base I declared myself married. Right there I went from a single lady to a married lady. I mean what happens if I met someone I want to date?"

"Then we just get a divorce."

"Really? You think it's going to be that easy with the newly crowned

King Wesley? He's not going to let us get a divorce. He's pissed that we outsmarted him and in retaliation he's going to force us to stay married. God I would hate to see what he'd do to us if we decided to get a divorce."

"He wouldn't do that. He'd be reasonable."

"Ha, like firing squad reasonable?"

Malcolm didn't say anything as he looked away.

Anne sighed and shook her head. She rubbed his hand and got his attention. "Hey..."

Malcolm looked back up at Anne, peering into his eyes almost like a desperate plea.

"I know the ruse was to keep me here and safe but now it's become more than that. Now I'm expected to show people how much we love each other when there's no love there."

"I mean we care for each other as friends..."

"We do, but how far will that take us? Kissing someone and convincing them that we're in love is more than just a peck on the lips. There's emotion and passion behind it."

"What if there was."

"What do you mean?"

"Let's face it, we've been heckled nonstop from Kelsey and Zack for not doing more. What if what's holding us back is the idea of friendship. Let's just say for one moment. Right here in this tent, we forget what we always tell people and ourselves and just act upon what they see. We don't think, we just do."

"What are you suggesting, Malcolm?"

"Kiss me."

Anne hesitated and bit her lip. Her heart beat seemed to triple as she looked into Malcolm's eyes. Her fingers felt like they were made out of electricity and her breathing was labored.

"Malcolm ..." she muttered.

"Don't think, just do." He replied, leaning in close. He paused, hovering over her lips before Anne closed her eyes and completed the space in between the two.

Anne was surprised how good a kisser Malcolm was. As soon as his lips touched hers there was sparks. While her eyes were closed, she could sense him with every fiber in her body. His lips were smoother than she imagined, but the feeling was out of this world. She loved the smell of his woodsy scent as it gave her butterflies. She could hear him gasping for air as his lips never left hers. She could taste his tongue on hers as they deepened their kiss.

They both took shallow breaths as if they couldn't stand being away from each other for a moment. Opening her eyes, she gazed upon his brown eyes, and Anne could see the lust that drove him. He looked like a man on a mission as he was guided by one thing. Her.

Combined with the way that he held her and the way his tongue felt on hers she was in heaven. His kiss was hot-blooded, pulse-pounding and passionate. All she wanted was more. She didn't know what came over her as her emotions took over all control. Her hands reached up and grabbed Malcolm's back dragging him closer to her.

The two fell onto the cot, and Malcolm was on top of Anne.

For a brief moment, he hovered above her and admired every inch of her. He loved how soft her skin felt as his hand slowly slid across her curves. Her perfume drove him mad, driving him to kiss her with more intensity. The feeling of her tongue dragging across his was erotic and breathtaking. He could feel himself grow in size the longer their session grew. He didn't know what the next hour would bring, all he knew was he wanted her. He wanted to continue listening to her moans. He wanted to continue tasting her soft lips and skin. He wanted to keep looking into her exquisite eyes. He wanted her.

Malcolm's hands combed through Anne's jet-black hair and Anne's rubbed his muscly forearms. The two explored each other's bodies as they slowly ground themselves on top of one another.

His fingers graced her breasts. Her fingers graced his abs. She felt his stiffness. He felt her crotch. The two wove their bodies together, arms crossed with arms, legs crossed with legs, their sexes a mere inch apart. Only cloth separated the two from meeting.

Their bodies filled with excitement as they unleashed the tension that they felt for months. By the second their kiss became more passionate and what started as a curiosity ended in a definitive answer. There was no denying what each other felt.

Anne crossed her legs around Malcolm torso, and her fingers moved with haste as she began to unbutton his jacket. He assisted her, and tossed the clothing away. He leaned forward and sucked on her neck. Anne moaned as she felt his tongue grace her skin. Her toes curled as she felt his teeth nibble her body. She closed her eyes and held him tighter.

Malcolm leaned back and ripped away his shirt revealing his ridged hunky shape. Anne's eyes grew wide as her fingers caressed his muscles. Her hands rested on his defined abs and she felt her body tremble. Her fingers slipped lower to his pants and her hands hovered at his zipper.

She hesitated, and bit her lip. She wanted to continue. She wanted to feel him inside her, but there was something that was bothering her. The idea was small at first but soon it spread through her brain like a virus.

She was worried if she continued, what would happen to their relationship? Would they still be friends or something else, she wondered. The more she thought about it, the more she realized that she didn't want to carry the burden of caring for someone that deeply. She'd already lost her parents and she was afraid that if she opened up her heart again she would feel that same pain. Thinking of that made her pull her hand away from his pants line.

Malcolm looked at Anne and held her hand.

"Are you okay?"

"Yes, why?"

"You're shaking."

"Sorry. It's just..."

"What is it?"

Anne sighed. "Don't get me wrong I find you incredibly sexy, but this whole make out session was to prove that we could kiss each other with passion, which we clearly proved that we could."

"Yeah...and then some." Malcolm grinned, rubbing the back of his head.

"Exactly, so what I'm trying to say is going any further with you, could compromise what we have."

"Our friendship?"

"Yes, we're good together. Obviously we can be that sexy couple in public, but in this tent, let's just remain friends. You're okay with that, right?"

Now it was Malcolm's turn to hesitate. While he did like Anne as a friend, kissing her awakened something in him. He felt something for her, something that he didn't know was there. He had a desire to be with her. It was an unquenchable thirst for her to be his. He wanted more, not just to be friends and have a fake marriage. He wanted the real thing. He wanted to hold her like he did before. He wanted to kiss her all night, and make love to her all day. He wanted to claim her and tell the world that she was his. However, he could sense that Anne wanted the opposite.

Not wanting to upset her, Malcolm was prepared to lie to tell her that he wanted to be friends, but there was a loud blaring alarm that went off, that took his breath away. His eyes opened wide as he immediately recognized the sound.

Anne covered her ears and looked at Malcolm. "What is that sound?"

"It's not good. It's an all hands call. We're being attacked."

Anne's jaw dropped as she suddenly felt a surge of adrenaline. She watched Malcolm crawl out of the bed, picking up his shirt off the ground. His loving expression was gone as his eyes narrowed at the incoming danger.

He looked at her and growled, "Get your gear on, it looks like we're about to jump two feet into hell."

TWENTY-TWO

Anne was in the middle of putting on her tactical vest, when she looked up to stare at Malcolm, who was doing the same. As the "all hands" alarm blared not once did they talk about their kiss. She wondered what Malcolm was going to say to her. She felt like something was at the tip of his tongue before the siren went off. Since then, he's flipped the switch going from gentle romantic to aggressive warrior. His eyes were focused and it was as if he completely ignored everything that happened to them in the last five minutes.

Malcolm tried not to think of the last five minutes. Part of him did. Part of him wanted to tell Anne how he really felt, but he knew all of that had to wait. He knew that going into a battle with a clouded mind was the easiest way to get killed. Like the other things before it, he departmentalized his thoughts and only focused on the task at hand.

He doubled checked the ammo in this side arm and holstered it, along with strapping his M4 around his back.

Malcolm looked across the tent at Anne who like him wore her tactical vest. However, instead of standard issue military fatigues, Anne wore a grey tank top and jeans underneath her jacket. Anne placed her hair in a ponytail and then tied her katana to her hip.

"You ready?" Malcolm asked.

Anne nodded.

"Good, come on, if it's an all hands call we're needed to fight something. We'll head to the armory to get your guns and additional ammo first and then find out where we're assigned. Come on."

Anne took a deep breath and followed Malcolm out the tent. Her heart was racing as they quickly jogged down the path towards the armory.

She had been in combat before, but this was different. Before she was always aware of the danger. This was sudden and out of nowhere. It reminded her of her time in the mall as the unknown fear gripped her chest. She looked ahead at Malcolm who seemed composed and collected.

Anne had drilled for the "all hands" call before. She'd been trained to know where to go and who to listen to, but through all the drills and practice, the real thing made her stomach turn upside down.

Hundreds of people all scrambled to different places along the base. What was usually structured and efficient was now chaotic and unorganized. Anne could hear people screaming for their kids while different soldiers barked out orders on where to go.

She repeatedly heard them bark, "Move! Move! Move! This is not a drill. This is not a fucking drill! Go to your station! Go to your station!"

Upon hearing those words, Anne's hands began to tremble. There was an eerie feeling of what to come that made her nervous. She didn't know what was coming next, but she was glad she was with Malcolm.

When they arrived at the armory there was already a line of people collecting their guns to defend the base. Men and women all over the age of eighteen each collected a rifle and headed towards their zone's officer. The line moved quickly as there were several soldiers handing out arms and ammunition.

"What do you think is happening?" Anne asked as they moved into the line. She almost had to yell as her voice was drowned out by the siren.

"I'm not sure," Malcolm replied. "I do know that shit hasn't gone down yet."

"Why is that?"

"No gunfire. Whatever made the Admiral call for the alarm isn't attacking us yet."

"Sons of Satan?" Anne asked.

"Possibly. That's what I'm thinking. Zack and I found freshly turned zombie with SS carved on his forehead earlier today. We thought it was a stray zombie trying to find a way into our base, however if it is the Sons, then this wasn't just a coincidence, that was a scout. They came to our base, just like they've come to the others."

Anne fear gripped her chest after hearing Malcolm's guess. Her mind shifted towards the day she went to her parents' safe zone. She relived the nightmarish scenes of the corpses that she saw littered across the neighborhood. Looking around the base she imagined their same fate here, making her fear grow. Reaching out she grabbed Malcolm's hand and Malcolm turned and looked at Anne with a concerned look.

"What's wrong?"

"Do you think what happened at my parents' safe zone would happen here?"

"No, I don't. Those fuckers got lucky there. Here they're walking into a hornet's nest filled with armed civilians and Navy SEALs. If anyone should be scared it's them."

Anne smiled and nodded. "Okay."

"Come on, we're next."

Anne followed Malcolm as they were handed additional ammo and guns. Anne holstered her side pistol and strapped her M4 around her back. She then followed Malcolm towards zone D's gathering spot. Everyone was already gathered around Richard who stood in the center of the semi-circle counting up the group of people standing around him. In the crowd, Anne recognized, Kelsey, Zack, Sabrina, Victor, Sheri, and Sophia. Each one held their guns in their hands, waiting for Richard to speak. Malcolm and Anne stood by Kelsey who smiled at Anne, "look at that we match!"

Anne rolled her eyes at Kelsey. "It's more like you copied my style, Combat Barbie." Anne mocked, looking at Kelsey's jeans, grey tank top combo, and green tactical vest. Kelsey opted to tie her blonde hair in a bun, but like Anne, Kelsey has her katana strapped to her hip.

"It's such a good look though. What says sexy and deadly, but a katana and tank top."

Anne laughed, shaking her head.

"What took you y'all so long?" We figured you two would be the first ones out here." Kelsey asked.

Anne and Malcolm shared a look and before they could answer, Zack growled.

"Kill the chit chat. Richard is about to speak."

Anne took a sigh of relief as speaking about Malcolm was the last thing she wanted to do.

"Now that it looks like everyone is here, I will go over our assignments. As we've drilled before, parents of any children will be responsible for them during the all hands on deck. You have taken enough combat classes to defend yourself and your kids. You are to shelter in place at the Rec center. You are not to move from that building unless the all clear signal is given or if the building is overrun. As for anyone else who doesn't have kids, and the soldiers of the spouses themselves, we are to meet the Admiral at the main gate."

"Do you know why the all hands call was made?" Someone asked.

"No, these were the only orders that were given. Any more questions?"

The group stood silent before Richard yelled, "Fall out. Move to you position. Be ready to defend this place with your lives, zone D. Let's move!" Richard led the group towards the main gate and as everyone shuffled to their assignments, Sheri stopped and waved at Anne and Kelsey.

"Good luck you two." Sheri encouraged with a half-smile.

"Thanks," Kelsey replied. "Are you sure you'll be okay with Keshia?"

"Yeah, those zombies won't know what hit them. Between your training and the weapons training, I'll be fine. Besides I'm a tough Navy wife. Nothing phases me, Really. Go!" She commanded, pointing towards the group leaving.

Anne and Kelsey both nodded and caught up with the group. Zone D was made up of thirty men and women. Most were the surviving spouses of the military members who'd past away, while there was a small number of military personal sprinkled in the group, including

Malcolm, Zack, Sabrina and Victor. When the group arrived at the main gate, a row of vehicles blocked the entrance, including five Humvees with machine guns mounted on top and a tank. Admiral Wesley stood in the center Humvee with a bullhorn in his hands. His grey eyes were narrowed as he looked past the main gate towards a man that was standing on the top of a trailer. Each trailer rocked back and forth and Anne could hear the low feral growls of zombies.

Looking at the man closely, Anne spotted the craved markings of SS on his forehead and she knew he was a member of the Sons of Satan. Looking past the man, Anne also spotted a dozen others all with the same symbol cut in their skin. Each man looked unworldly with blood splattered and tattered clothes. To Anne it was hard to distinguish between them and a zombie. Both looked to be spawns of hell.

"Attention! You are in front of a US Military base. You come any closer you will be fired upon." Admiral Wesley warned.

The man on top of the trailer laughed unfazed by the threat. He lifted his arms and grinned, "Hear me and rejoice! We have come to cleanse you and your flock. Your time of suffering is over! We, the Sons of Satan, are here to deliver you to our savior."

"I'm sorry, but no one here needs deliverance. You enter this base and you will only be met with death."

The man laughed hysterically. Hearing his ear shrieking crackle scared Anne to the core. It was obvious that his man was no longer sane.

"Death will be a welcomed friend. I am not afraid, are you? Either in this life or the next you will meet our maker."

"I don't count on it. You have thirty seconds to turn your trucks around and leave. Never come back here, or you will be killed."

"We have come to save you all, why do you turn us away?"

"Because you are deranged hell-bent freaks. Final warning. Leave."

The man's sinister smile grew. "No. This is our final warning. Lay down your arms and take us in. Accept our terms that the strongest men will become our disciples, the weakest ones will join our army and the women will be our slaves. That is our offer."

"Fuck your offer. We have an entire army with their guns on you. You only have twelve men. We will kill you before you even have a chance to even get off that truck."

"On the contrary our army is much larger than yours." He laughed hysterically and stomped the top of the trailer. "Sons of Satan! Unleash hell!"

The men standing outside the walls, walked towards the gates of the truck trailers and opened the doors. The roars got louder as the zombies came piling out of the trailers.

"My God..." Admiral Wesley muttered as he saw hundreds of zombies roam about the main gate.

"Sons! Pass me the key!" One of the Sons of Satan handed him a rocket launcher and Admiral Wesley's eyes got wider.

"Fuck. Sniper, take him down!" Admiral Wesley screamed, but before the sniper could take the shot, the rocket was already fired at the main gate, blowing it up, making a giant hole in the center of the main entry way.

The impact of the blast knocked Anne off her feet onto the ground. Anne hit her head hard and her world went black.

TWENTY-THREE

Anne awakened to the sound of gunfire and screams. As light returned to her, she saw Malcolm holding her and yelling at her. His voice was inaudible at first as her ears rang. As his mouth moved, her hearing slowly was restored and she could hear him yell, "Anne! Anne! Are you okay?"

Anne nodded and held the back of her head, where she felt something wet. She brought her fingers back to her eyesight and saw the crimson-colored blood.

Malcolm saw the blood and his eyes opened wide as he checked the back of her head.

"Am I hurt?" Anne asked.

"It's a scratch. Nothing serious. Here..." he reached into his pocket and brought out a small first aid kit. He applied a bandage and held it to the back of her head.

"This should stop the bleeding, okay?"

Anne nodded and looked behind Malcolm to see Zack and Kelsey providing covering fire. Her back was against something hard. Upon further inspection, she realized that it was sandbags.

"Where are we?" She asked.

"After the blast, the zombies got through the gate. They're everywhere. Admiral Wesley ordered us to fall back. I carried you to this nest, where Zack and Kelsey have been providing cover fire for us."

Malcolm touched the back of her head and saw that the bleeding had stopped.

"The blood clotted," He yelled. "You ready to get back in this fight?"

Anne nodded and grabbed her rifle. Malcolm helped her on her feet, and she turned to see what she'd missed.

At the main gate, where the hole was blown up, a fire burned the structure, black smoke rose from the top of it, and walking and crawling out of the fiery blackness was a massive horde of zombies.

Anne's eyes opened up at the horror as it truly did look like the spawns of hell were at their gate. There were hundreds of them coming through, she'd never seen so many in a group as they all shuffled their way into the base. Some were on fire, others had their limbs missing, some of their bellies were opened with their entrails dragging. Their putrid smell filled the air, and made her stomach turn.

A cold sweat engulfed her hands as the creatures charged at her. The monsters that attacked them showed no fear as they walked into a wave of bullets. Their fiendish growls shook the ground they walked on.

Spread out were groups of soldiers and civilians, each in small firing squads as they took on the horde that attacked them. They fired quick bursts as they retreated backwards. Anne could hear the panic in their voices as they attempted to keep the beasts at bay.

The zombies had managed to break through some lines of defense, attacking soldiers and civilians. Their terrified screams echoed in Anne's ear as she watched with horror as the monsters attacked. The fiends moved with no regard, biting at any victim in their way. Their teeth ripped through flesh like paper, and blood rolled down their dismembered bodies. Seconds later, their dead meals reanimated, joining their army of undead to attack another. It was pure evil. It was a living nightmare.

In front of her, Anne spotted Sawyer who looked unhinged. He was alone and surrounded by undead. He was laughing like a madman as he killed endless foes. Admiral Wesley was still in the bed of the Humvee truck, he was shouting out orders and firing his rifle occasionally.

"Sawyer! Get back in formation!" The Admiral ordered, but Sawyer was too far gone as the sailor was in his own world, joyfully killing any zombie that got near him.

Near the Admiral was the remaining machine gun Humvees. Before the explosion there were five of them, now only two remained. The others were struggling not to be overrun and the other three were swamped by zombies.

A tank was attempting to bottleneck the massive crater made by the rocket, firing several rounds into the crowd of zombies, but they still managed to filter through.

Looking to her left, Anne saw Sophia, Sabrina, Victor, and Richard. They were nearby in another nest of sandbags like hers. They were working together to cover a machine gun Humvee that was getting dangerously close to being overran by zombies.

Anne didn't hesitate as she took aim at her first zombie. Firing in a controlled burst, she began taking out zombies one by one. The foursome were deadly, killing zombies left and right. They were efficient and lethal with every shot.

Anne lost focus when she heard nearby screams coming from the area that Sabrina, Sophia , Victor, and Richard were located. She prayed that none of them were hurt as she took a quick glance at their location. They were fine, but the operator of the machine gun wasn't. He was pulled off the gun by zombies, and then eaten alive.

Despite seeing several people being eaten alive, the savagery of seeing someone's flesh being ripped into while blood spurts from their body still upset Anne.

"Someone needs to get on that 50 cal!" Admiral Wesley barked as he fired multiple shots. "Get on that 50 cal!"

"I got it!" Sabrina yelled. "Victor cover!"

"I got you! Go! Go! Go!" Victor assisted her firing at any zombie that got in her way. Sabrina charged bravely into the horde. She was fearless, almost like a fictional Amazonian. Her battle cry shook Anne to her core watching the woman charge with reckless abandon. She fired several shots with her rifle until she ran out of bullets. She then gracefully switched to her pistol, pulling it out of her hostler, firing several rounds, until she got to the massive gun. She cleared the Humvee, and then looked back at Richard."

"Driver's dead, I need a pilot so I don't get jammed up like the last guys."

"On it!" Richard didn't hesitate as he advanced forward.

"You're going to need a copilot. I'll sit in the front seat and cover you." Sophia replied.

"No, stay here. It's too dangerous.!" Richard replied.

"Baby, I'm with you until the end. Let me help." Sophia begged.

Richard stared at her and then kissed her. "Goddamn, do I love you. Okay, we go on three. One. Two. Three!" They both hopped over the cover of the sandbag and towards the Humvee. Victor provided cover fire as Richard, pulled out the dead driver. Sophia sat in the front seat and fired out the window, killing anything that got near the Humvee.

Richard put the vehicle into reverse and then backed it towards Victor.

"Get in!" Richard told Victor. "Sabrina is going to need help with that fifty cal!"

"On it." Victor hopped into the back seat and then slammed his hand on the door. "Drive! Drive! Drive!" The wheels spun out and the foursome were on the move, firing at the horde and holding them back.

"Yeah that's it. Give those fuckers hell!" Admiral growled watching the group push back the zombies on their flank. He continued to fire, but noticed that there were more zombies collapsing on to his Humvee. The Admiral slammed the top hood of the vehicle, "Alright, move back! Move the Humvee, it's starting to get heavy here."

Admiral Wesley expected the Humvee to move back, but it didn't. He narrowed his eyes and peeked his head through the rear-view glass. "Goddamnit, Williams! I told you..." before Admiral Wesley could say anything he gasped as he saw a zombified Williams attempting to bite him.

"My God..." Admiral Wesley muttered watching his undead sailor. He looked back at the landscape and saw the sea of undead that covered the landscape grow twice the size from before. They were everywhere as his soldiers and civilians under his care got swept up by the horde.

The Humvee rocked back and forth as zombies attempted to get inside the truck.

"Fuckers!" The Admiral yelled as he fired multiple shots into the crowd. He killed several but it was no use as the horde collapsed onto him. Another zombie climbed into the bed of the truck behind him, but before its teeth could sink into the Admiral's neck, a shot rang out and split the zombies head in two. The Admiral looked for the origin of the shot and saw Anne holding a rifle. Several more shots were fired and all around him zombies fell. He saw Zack and Malcolm make their way towards the Humvee, laying bodies in their path. Malcolm ran to the front seat and stabbed the driver zombie in the head with his blade. He dragged him out and sat in the front seat. Zack hopped in the bed of the pickup truck and provided cover fire.

"It looked like you needed some help, commander."

"Damn am I glad to see you."

"Thank you, sir."

Zack slapped the side of the truck and yelled, "we're clear. Back up, Malcolm!"

Malcolm moved the vehicle backwards towards the sandbag nest where Kelsey and Anne were located. Malcolm hopped out of the truck, firing at the crowd as he retreated back into the nest, while Zack and Admiral Wesley hopped out of the truck into the nest.

"Thank you for saving my ass back there," Admiral Wesley told Zack.

Zack nodded, "You're welcome sir. What are your orders?"

The Admiral looked at the chaotic scene in front of him and bit his lip. He then looked back at Zack and replied, "we hold them here. We're gaining ground and if we kept at it we can turn the tide."

"Sir?" Zack questioned. "The battle for this base is over. There's no one left but a handful of us. We should gather as much supplies as we can and leave."

"Abandon the base? For what? A few zombies. We can take them."

"Sir, it's more that. We lost all of our man power. Even if we won, running normal ops in a large base like this would be impossible. We need to leave. Perhaps we can find a smaller safe zone we could protect."

"I will not leave."

"It's not the right play."

"You don't get to decide that!" The Admiral growled.

Zack hesitated and looked away. In the background he could hear the struggle of Malcolm, Kelsey and Anne as they continued to fight off the horde.

"I'm running out of ammo!" Kelsey yelled.

"Same here! Fuck it, I'm going to my blade!" Anne roared as she placed her rifle behind her back and pulled out her katana. In one clean sweep, she severed the head of a zombie and moved on another one beside it. Kelsey did the same as she charged into a group of zombies slashing and hacking though the group. Malcolm continued to fire his gun until it clicked signaling no ammo.

"Shit," Malcolm cursed as he took out his own combat knife and began to kill zombies as they attacked him.

Zack shook his head. "Can't you see? We're running out of ammo. This battle is lost. We need to retreat."

"We're not retreating. This base has never fallen into enemy hands. I will not allow it to happen on my watch."

"Sir, with respect it already has. We're leaving, you can either come with us or stay here. Your choice. Malcolm!"

"Yo!"

"Get in the truck, we're getting out of here."

"Gotcha."

"You'll need cover. Come on!" Anne charged over the barrier and killed the first zombie in her way. Malcolm followed her and stabbed the nearest zombie to Anne. The duo worked through the crowd until they got to the front seat. Anne got into the truck first, and slid to the passenger side, while Malcolm got into the driver's side.

"Zack and Kelsey! Let's go!"

Zack helped Kelsey into the truck and then looked at the Admiral.

"You coming?"

Admiral Wesley glared at Zack and then spat beside him.

"I guess that answers my question." Zack turned his back preparing to climb into the truck, until he heard the hammer of a pistol being pulled back.

"You know I'm getting tired of the men below me not following orders. I told Malcolm the next man who disobeys my orders will be shot. I guess you're the first."

"Zack?!" Kelsey yelled as she took out her own side pistol and aimed it at the Admiral. Zack held up his hands and shook his head at Kelsey. "It's okay," he whispered.

Kelsey furrowed her brow trying to understand what Zack meant by that.

"You wouldn't shoot an unarmed man, would you?"

"I would if it restored order on base."

"We're no longer sailors answering to the commander in chief, sir, but we both know that we will be judged by our actions by a higher power. Did you really want to explain to him why you shot an unarmed man in the back?"

The commander hesitated before cursing under his breath. "You can go."

"I didn't need your permission." Zack growled before hopping into the truck. "Malcolm, let's get out of here."

Malcolm nodded and drove away. As they left the nest, Zack watched as the Admiral took his foolish last stand against the horde. As he fired a zombie flanked him and bit his forearm. Admiral Wesley cursed under his breath as he dragged the zombie who bit him to the ground and took a head shot. Dozens of zombies swarmed him. There were too many of them to handle and he was mauled as several zombies ripped him to shreds. Zack sighed and shook his head as he knew his time at Little Creek Navy base was coming to an end.

TWENTY-FOUR

"Fall back! Fall back!" Zack ordered to the remaining soldiers on the battlefield as he fired off a couple of shots. He held on to the truck's tailgate as Malcolm was fishtailing back and forth to avoid the zombies. Most people who were still alive managed to follow his orders, but the battle was becoming worse by the second as most retreating were attacked and eaten alive by the massive undead army.

Malcolm eventually drove up to Richard and his Humvee.

"We're falling back deeper into the base. The main gate is lost." Zack shouted.

"Are these Admiral Wesley's orders?" Richard asked over the gunfire from Sabrina.

Zack shook his head. "Admiral Wesley is dead. This base has fallen. It's time for us to regroup and leave. Follow us to the armory."

"Yes, sir!" Richard replied.

Malcolm peeled off and drove down the path towards the armory. Richard followed and when they arrived at the armory, zombies had already managed to creep past the main gate infiltrating to other parts of the base.

Zack hopped out of the truck along with, Kelsey, Anne, and

Malcolm. They waited for Richard to pull up beside them. Sabrina and Victor stayed in the Humvee providing cover fire while Richard and Sophia got out of the vehicle.

"Are we seriously abandoning Little Creek?" Richard asked.

Zack nodded. "The base is lost. Our defenses are destroyed. There's nothing for us here."

"What about everyone else?"

Zack shrugged. "I only care about the people here, plus Sheri, Keshia and Emily. Everyone else is on their own. To be honest there's not many people left here. I don't even know if Sheri, Keshia and Emily are still alive, but we will go and get them before we leave. Understood?"

Everyone nodded.

"What's the plan?" Malcolm asked.

"We split up taking the Humvees with us. We will meet back here, and then go together, escaping through gate twenty-five. There's enough space at the gate for the Humvees to drive through. Let's load up everything we can fit in the Humvees first, food, supplies and ammo. After that, Kelsey, Anne, Sophia, and Richard and me will take the truck Humvee to get Sheri and Keshia. Victor, Sabrina, and Malcolm, take the fifty cal to pick up Emily."

Everyone nodded and split up. Anne, Sophia, Kelsey and Richard left to get food and supplies from the nearby depot. While the SEALs collected additional ammo. They picked up several crates of ammo, plus additional guns. When they loaded the last crate into the truck, The foursome of Kelsey, Anne, Richard and Sophia returned pulling a wagon filled with food and supplies.

"We got enough MREs to feed and entire platoon, plus tents, and med packs." Richard replied.

"Perfect. Okay, get in the truck." Zack replied.

Richard nodded and everyone piled into the vehicle. Zack got into the driver's side and looked at Malcolm.

"You have thirty minutes. If you're not back by then, I'm leaving without you."

"Got you, bruh."

"Alright, brother. You do the same for me."

Malcolm hesitated as he looked towards Anne, who gave him a small smile. In his heart, he didn't want to leave Anne, but he knew Zack was right. If they're not back in thirty minutes something had gone wrong, it was possible that they were dead and they could be too if they didn't high tail it out. He didn't like the idea, but Zack seemed to have the clearest head in all of this.

"Okay, Thirty minutes," he confirmed. "Be safe."

"Always am." Zack winked.

"Anne..." Malcolm began to say.

"Yes?" She looked back at him. She pushed back a strand of her hair.

Malcolm wanted to tell her how he felt. He wanted to tell her what that kiss meant to him but he realized that now wasn't the time for romance. They were both fighting for their lives and if he took her head out of the game, he could get her killed. Instead of baring his true feelings to her, he gave her a straight face.

"Come back to me."

"I will." She replied as she got back into the Humvee.

Watching the truck pull away, Malcolm wondered why he told her to come back. That wasn't what he wanted to say. He wanted to tell her how he felt.

He was deep in thought before Sabrina banged the top of the hood.

"Yo! You good?"

"Yeah. I'm good. Let's go." Malcolm didn't think of the thought again as he drove away, towards the medical center.

The medical center was a half mile away from the armory. As they drove they kept encountering more and more zombies, slowing down their advance.

"This is not looking good," Malcolm replied. "Odds that Emily is alive..."

"Don't say it. She's alive. I know she is." Victor growled.

Malcolm nodded and kept weaving through the crowd of undead. When they arrived at the medical center, several guards were already dead, and had either joined the horde or were actively being chewed on.

Sabrina cleared a path for them with the machine gun, killing any that were near. Once it was clear, the threesome left the Humvee and went inside.

The medical center was a three-story brick building. It served as the infirmary and science research laboratory. As they went through the building they saw more bodies stretched out. Each one shared a similar fate as the guards outside.

"Please let her be okay," Victor prayed as they pushed their way through.

The threesome fought their way to the hall towards Dr. López's lab. They encountered several zombies but they put down each one with ease. The closer they got to the lab they began to hear screams and Victor shared a concerned look with Malcolm.

"That sounded like Emily!" Victor yelled and rushed towards the door. Victor busted into her lab and saw Emily struggling against a Sons of Satan. Standing around them, were additional nine men. He was squeezing her neck while Emily attempted to escape.

"Do you think you are God? You will never be able to cure this! This is an act of his will! You will die for it!" The insane Son of Satan screamed.

"Hey asshole!" Victor called out before shooting the guy. The man holding Emily dropped to the ground dead. Emily squealed as she was freed and scrambled for cover. Soon afterwards, the other Sons grabbed their guns and began firing at Victor, Sabrina and Malcolm. The Navy SEALs took defensive positions and fired back. The two groups traded blows. The sailors had managed to kill half the group before Victor heard Emily cry out for him.

"Victor! Help!" She wailed from behind her cover.

Victor looked past his cover and saw another Sons of Satan in Emily's face. Tears rolled down Emily cheeks as she stared into the barrel of the pistol. Her lip quivered with fear as she didn't want to die. She looked towards Victor, crying as she begged for her life.

"Victor...please..." she stuttered.

The deranged man gave Emily a toothy grin, aiming his gun at her head. Victor's eyes went wide, and in that split second, he only saw Emily.

"No," he screamed. He didn't think, and only acted as he left his cover sprinting towards Emily.

"Victor! What are you... shit! Sabrina cover fire!" Malcolm yelled attempting to distract the other Sons in the room from shooting Victor as he was exposed. Beyond cover, Victor was shot twice. Once in the leg once in the upper shoulder. Victor growled from the pain of the bullets, but he didn't let them stop him. He had to get to her. He had to protect her. To him she was the most important person in the world.

He didn't hesitate once as he aimed his own gun and killed Emily's gunman with a clean shot to the head.

Malcolm and Sabrina had managed to kill all of the Sons in the room before Victor fell to the ground.

"Clear!" Malcolm yelled.

"Clear!" Sabrina confirmed. Sabrina and Malcolm's eyes fell on Victor who was laying down in the center of the lab. Blood was oozing out of his wounds onto the white tile floor. Victor's body trembled from the pain of his wounds.

"Fuck me..." Malcolm mumbled towards himself before looking at Sabrina. "Sabrina, go and find a stretcher for Victor. We have to keep moving."

"On it!" She replied, running back into the hall.

"Victor! No, no, no!" Emily cried as she ran to his side. She picked his head and place it in her lap. Victor held her hand and smiled at her.

"Doc? It's good to see you. I know I've never said this before, but I'm loving this whole nerdy vibe you got going. The ponytail, the glasses, the white lab coat and those thick curves in those jeans are doing it for me. It's very sexy."

Emily laughed and rolled her eyes. "Thank you for saving me."

"Pleasure is all mine."

"You're shot though."

"I'll pull through."

Emily reviewed his wounds and smiled, "good news is no major organs were hit."

"Bad news?"

"Looks like the bullets are still in you. I'm going to have to take them out and stitch you up."

"You're going inside me? I like the sound of that."

Emily laughed again and caressed Victor's cheek. "Why do you have to be so nasty?"

"Second nature I guess."

"Well, I like that about you."

"I like you too..." Victor admitted as his bloodied hand rested on hers. Emily's eyes opened at his admission. The two gazed at each other, while Victor grasped the nape of her neck. Slowly the two leaned forward for a passionate kiss.

When they were through, Victor breathed deeply and grinned.

"Damn, girl. Those lips must have healing powers, because I don't feel a damn thing."

Emily's cheeks went red as she looked down at the ground, pushing a strand of her brunette hair behind her ear.

"Hey..." Victor touched her thigh and Emily looked back at him.

"Don't you go anywhere. Stay right here in the moment."

"I won't. I promise." She whispered leaning forward to kiss him again.

A smile crept across Malcolm's face watching the romance blossom between the two. He gave them a second to bask in their newfound love before clearing his throat.

"Sorry to interrupt, but Emily, the base has fallen we need to get you out of here."

She sighed and rubbed Victor's cheek before looking back up at Malcolm. "I figured, especially with the Sons here. I was already packing up my research before those men came in here."

"Good, how much more time do you need to collect the research?"

"Maybe five?"

"Okay, but we need to leave ASAP."

"We can't leave here until we get those bullets out of him."

"We don't have time." Malcolm snapped.

"He's not going to make it if we leave them in. Trust me, if you want him to live, like I do, give me ten minutes to pull the bullets out and stitch him back up."

Malcolm looked at his watch and knew they were already cutting it short.

"Fuck. Ten minutes. No longer."

"Yep." Emily replied as she grabbed a nearby suture kit. She ripped open the packaging and grabbed the tongs. She looked down at Victor. "I'm going to have to remove your jacket and pants."

"Usually women like to take me out to dinner first."

"Some other time?" She smirked as she took off his clothes. Once she could see both bullet wounds she looked at Victor.

"This is going to hurt."

"Just do it..." he growled.

She nodded and began to remove his bullet from his shoulder. Victor screamed from the intrusion and shook. Malcolm assisted Emily and held Victor down. Sabrina walked in with the stretcher and her eyes opened wide.

"We don't have time for this!" She yelled.

"I'm aware, but we've started it. Hold him down over there!" Malcolm barked.

Sabrina cursed under her breath, placed down the stretcher, and helped hold down Victor.

Victor roared in pain as Emily tried to find the bullet.

"I'm sorry. I'm sorry, Victor. I'm almost there. I feel it." Seconds later she pulled the metal out and tossed it to the side. "One down. Now the leg."

"Fuck me..." Victor muttered.

Emily got up and ran down to the leg that got shot. She pulled out the bullet from the leg and grabbed the suture kit. She quickly stitched his leg and shoulder up and looked back at Victor.

"Not my best work, given the time, but you will heal with a scar or two."

"That's fine. Scars are sexy." He winked.

Emily laughed and Sabrina rolled her eyes.

"I hate to break it to you, but we have to go!" Malcolm yelled.

"Right," Victor rolled on to the stretcher and nodded to the group. "Let's go!"

Sabrina and Malcolm picked up the stretcher and ran out to the Humvee, followed by Emily who provided cover fire. After securing Victor inside, Sabrina got back on the 50 cal, while Malcolm got in the driver side. Emily sat next to Victor in the back.

"What's our time!" Sabrina yelled as she fired at zombies that got near.

"It's going to be close! Hold on!" Malcolm yelled as he drove back to armory. Malcolm prayed that they weren't too late. They arrived within a minute of thirty minutes and was surprised that Zack wasn't there.

"What's our time now?" Sabrina asked.

"We're on time, but I don't see Zack."

"Do you think he left us?"

"No, I would have seen him leaving. We were only a minute out. Zack would have waited until the last second before leaving."

"Do you think that something happened to them?"

Malcolm thought of Anne and gripped the steering wheel tighter.

"We're going to get them."

"Malcolm, Zack told us not to check on them. He said that if they're not back by thirty minutes we're supposed to leave."

"Fuck, Zack's orders. We're going to go check on them." Malcolm replied, driving towards zone D.

TWENTY-FIVE
THIRTY MINUTES EARLIER

Z ack looked in the rearview mirror of the Humvee watching Malcolm drive away. He didn't want to give his best friend an ultimatum, but he knew it had to be done. He knew they had to survive. He had to survive for Kelsey. Looking back at his wife, Zack gripped the steering wheel tighter as he saw the blood dripping down her face. She had a long distant stare as she looked out at the horizon.

He'd seen that look before. It was a look shared from soldiers in war. He knew with every fight she was losing a piece of her. He didn't want that for her. He didn't want her to become a hallow shell of herself. He had to fight to keep her safe. He didn't want to lose her, like he lost so many brothers and sisters to their own minds.

"Kelsey, are you okay?" Zack yelled towards the back.

"Yeah, I'm good." Her blank stare morphed into a smile as she gave him a thumbs up.

Zack knew it was just a show, but he didn't question it.

He turned his attention to Anne who had a similar look to Kelsey. He knew that she was thinking of Malcolm. It didn't take a genius to know she was worried about him.

"Anne, Malcolm is going to be on time. He's going to save Dr. López and meet us back at the armory." Zack comforted.

"How do you know?" Anne asked.

"Trust me. He's the toughest son of a bitch I know. He's never failed a mission. He'll be there."

"And if he's not?" Anne asked.

Zack paused. He didn't want to think that way. He didn't want to think about leaving his best friend, but if the choice came between Malcolm or insuring Kelsey's safety, he would choose Kelsey every time.

"He's going to make it." Zack repeated as he drove down the road towards the zone D barracks.

When the group arrived it was hectic as everyone ran away from attacking zombies and Sons of Satan members.

"Zack! Stop the truck! I have to help them!" Richard demanded.

"No! We're finding Sheri and Keshia and then getting the fuck out of here. The base is overrun. It's every man for themselves!"

"Zack, please! Where is your humanity? We can save them. They can come with us!"

Zack shook his head. "We don't have enough supplies for all those mouths. You can hop out of the truck and help them or you can come with us. It's up to you."

Richard and Zack stared at each other. Richard looked away and mumbled something under his breath. He was beginning to hop out of the truck before Sophia grabbed him.

"Don't go!"

"Sophia, those people need me. They can't defend themselves. I can lead them out."

"Please don't go. Stay. Stay with me. I need you."

Richard hesitated and then caressed her cheek. "Sophia...I can't."

"Please..." she begged. She leaned closer and kissed him. "You're the only thing right about this whole fucking apocalypse. Before I met you I didn't know how I'd survive. I don't know our future, but I know I love you. Please don't leave me."

Richard smiled and kissed her again. "I love you too. Fine, I'll stay."

Anne stared at their romantic interactions and thought of Malcolm. She wondered what was he going to say before the alarm went off. Watching Sophia and Richard she pondered if her and Malcolm would be at that level. While she liked him, the idea of being in a relationship scared her. What if he had deeper feelings than she did? She questioned. However, the question didn't linger long as she reminded herself that they were just friends.

Zack looked back at Richard and then stared at Kelsey. She gave him a small smile as she knew that the choice he made wasn't easy. She knew that he was making the tough choice to keep them all alive.

As Zack got closer to the rec center, they encountered more zombies.

"Fuck," Zack muttered as he zigzagged through them all. When he arrived at the rec center, he saw Sheri, posted in a defensive position with Keshia behind her. He could tell that her situation was deterring as she fought off the waves of zombies.

"Sheri! Just hold on!" Zack yelled, as he hopped out of the truck to kill two zombies in front of him.

"You guys stay here. Guard the truck. Richard and Sophia, lay down cover fire for me while I get Sheri and Keshia. Anne and Kelsey, cover Richard and Sophia, got it?"

"Yeah, we gotcha!" Anne responded hopping out of the bed of the pick-up truck. She kicked a nearby zombie in the face and then brought down her blade into its skull. Another zombie approached her from behind, but Anne was quicker as she spun around and sliced its head off. Two more approached her, but Kelsey covered her stabbing both of them in the head. With a mighty war cry, Kelsey and Anne stood back-to-back, taking on any zombie that neared.

Sophia and Richard laid on top of the truck, picking off zombies with their guns. One by one they took them down, making a path for Zack to run towards Sheri.

"Hang on Sheri!" Zack shouted as he ran. He pushed his legs as fast as he could. Any zombie that got in his way met his wrath as he moved at a frantic pace to reach her. He didn't want anything to happen to Sheri. He made Charlie a promise to not let anything happen to his wife and kid and he planned on keeping that promise.

Sheri ran out of bullets on her rifle, and screamed as a zombie neared Keshia. She covered her daughter, but before the zombie had a chance to bite her, Zack arrived and pulled the zombie away. In a swift move, Zack took his pistol out and fired a single shoot in the zombie's skull.

"Are you two okay?"

"Yes, thank you for saving me Zack." Sheri cried as she wrapped her arms around him.

"You can thank me later. We need to get out of here. Keshia, come here." Keshia ran up to Zack and he placed her on his back.

"Hold on tight. Don't let go, okay?"

"Okay." Keshia replied.

Zack stared into Sheri's eyes and yelled. "Whatever you do, don't stop moving. Richard and Sophia will cover us as we make it to the truck, okay?"

"Okay, I'm with you." Sheri replied.

Zack nodded, and then reloaded Sheri's rifle.

"You're good to go now. On three we run. One, two, three!"

Zack ran, and Sheri was behind him, as they fired blindly at anything that got close to them. As they ran, the zombies around them fell as they were picked off by Richard and Sophia.

"Whatever you do, don't stop running!" Zack yelled.

Sheri tripped and Zack gasped as he watched the zombies close around her. His heart pounded as he took aim quickly picking off multiple zombies that attempted to grab her.

Sheri cried evading the monsters' grasp. She rolled on the ground towards Zack. She didn't stop moving. She didn't want to die. Sitting up, she felt a hand on her back and she screamed.

"Sheri! It's me. Come on!"

She looked up and saw Zack standing in front of her. Keshia was still holding on to his back, with tears in her eyes.

"Mommy?" She whimpered.

"I'm okay, baby. I'm fine."

"Let's go! Come on Sheri!" Zack growled, as he pushed her behind him. "Stay by me. Let's move!" The captain killed two zombies before turning and retreating towards the Humvee.

They fought their way through the thick crowd of zombies back to the truck, where Anne and Kelsey had made a small clearing for them. Once they neared Zack looked at his group and yelled, "we're back! Everyone back in the truck!" Zack helped Keshia into the truck and then placed Sheri into the bed. "You guys stay here. Sheri, provide cover fire while I get Kelsey and Anne back into the truck."

"You got it!" Sheri replied, as she began to fire out.

"Kelsey and Anne! Let's go!"

"We're working on it!" Kelsey replied as she slayed another body.

Zack shook his head, and continued to fire. "We don't have time for this, we are going to get bogged down. We have to move."

"Easier said than done!" Anne grunted, stabbing another foe.

Zack growled annoyed at the two until he heard a scream. His heart fell as he turned back the truck hoping that it wasn't overrun, instead he saw a person he least expected, Sawyer. He had Sophia by her red hair as he dragged her off the Humvee.

"Let go of me!" she yelled.

Sawyer shushed her. "I'm doing this for your own good!" He snapped. Sawyer had this crazed look in his eyes as blood covered his face. Zack could tell that the sailor he once knew before the fall was gone. Instead, something else was replaced.

"Let go of her!" Richard growled.

"Or you'll do what? I've kicked your ass once, and I'll happily do it again. If you know what's best for you, you'd leave me and Sophia alone."

"Sawyer! This isn't right. Just let us go our separate ways."

"You're right it isn't right and we should go our separate ways, except Sophia is coming with me. I am the only one who can protect her."

"Don't you dare touch me you fucker!" Sophia growled as she slammed her foot on his toe, and elbowed him in the gut.

"You bitch!" Sawyer snarled as he slapped her hard to the ground.

"Sophia!" Richard growled as he ran to defend her. He tackled Sawyer to the ground, separating Sophia from him. Richard sat on top of Sawyer, punching him left and right. As Sawyer's face became bloodied, Sawyer laughed hysterically as if he'd gone mad.

"Is that all you got! You think that because you are fucking her that makes you more of a man? Think again!" Sawyer headbutted Richard, and then pulled his blade from his pants. Before Richard could register what was happening, Sawyer stabbed Richard in the gut several times, before pushing Richard off.

"Richard, no!" Sophia screamed as she picked him up.

Richard coughed up blood and a bloodied hand reached up to touch Sophia's face.

"I love you..." he said weakly.

"I love you too." Sophia cried, as she leaned forward to kiss him. Sophia didn't get a moment to morn before she was dragged backwards.

"Let's go!" Sawyer growled.

Sophia kicked and screamed as she was taken away.

"SAWYER!" Zack yelled as he rushed to Sophia's aid. Zack tackled Sawyer, and the two rolled around on the ground. Sawyer pushed Zack off of him, and recovered his blade in his hand. Zack removed his knife as the two circled around each other.

"Just stay out of this, brother." Sawyer snapped.

"You are not my brother. My brothers would have never stooped this low. Let Sophia go." Zack growled.

"Or what? You thinking of putting a bullet in me?"

"Thinking about it." Zack replied.

"Figured. Bitch move. You can't take me down like a man, so you'd have to resort to guns."

"I can take you down any way you want."

"Bring it then, knifes only."

"Fine with me."

Sawyer roared as he charged with his blade, but Zack was quicker as he parried the attack. He flipped his blade to the opposite hand and cut Sawyer's backside. Sawyer gritted his teeth in pain, but it didn't stop him from attacking. He took wild slices at Zack, attempting to stab him, but Zack evaded each attack and countered with his own. His blade went into Sawyer's gut as Sawyer gasped for air. Zack removed the blade and watched as Sawyer fell to the ground.

"Finish me you fucking pussy!" Sawyer yelled.

Zack shook his head. "You don't deserve that mercy. You deserve death by a thousand bites. I'll let the zombies take care of you."

Zack turned around and walked away from Sawyer.

"You come back here, pussy! Finish the job! Kill me! Kill..." Before

Sawyer could finish his last words, he screamed as the horde circled around him. Zack didn't turn back, as he heard Sawyer yelling and the bodies of zombies dropping. He didn't care if Sawyer killed a few of them. He was eventually going to tire and when that happened, they would rip him in pieces.

Zack squatted next to Sophia and placed a hand on her shoulder. She was still holding Richard as she sobbed quietly.

"We have to go."

"We can't leave him like this."

"He doesn't deserve this death, but we are running out of time. It's getting close to thirty minutes. We need to go. We need to survive. Richard wouldn't want us to stay here. He would want you to go. Come on."

Sophia closed her eyes and nodded. "Okay, I'm coming." She leaned forward and kissed Richard's forehead. "Good bye my love." She got up and followed Zack back to the truck. As she ran she could hear the zombies feasting on his corpse making the pain of losing him even worse.

By the time Zack arrived back at the truck, Anne and Kelsey had gotten back in. When they saw Sophia, they quickly comforted her as she cried on their shoulders. Zack didn't say a word as he stared up the Humvee and drove back towards the armory.

As he did, Zack cursed underneath his breath as he stared at his watch. They were two minutes over, and he knew the chances of Malcolm leaving were high. He was upset with himself that he allowed the group to get separated. He felt even worse for Anne as he was the main cause for their split.

However, Zack didn't get to wallow in his self-pity for long as another Humvee drove down the road. Zack recognized it was Sabrina on the machine gun and grinned knowing that they didn't leave him.

The two met on the road halfway, to see Malcolm's smiling face. "I figured y'all were held up."

"Yeah..." Zack's voice trailed and looked down.

Malcolm's smile disappeared as he quickly looked towards Anne and saw a crying Sophia on her shoulder. Malcolm looked back at Zack, "what happened to Richard?"

"He didn't make it. I'll fill you in when we make camp. We've overstayed our welcome long enough here."

"I understand. Let's go." Malcolm replied.

Zack nodded, and did a U-turn back towards gate twenty-five. They didn't bother unlocking the gate as they busted through the fence. As they drove through the woods, Malcolm looked back at Little Creek Navy base, watching it burn. He felt bad abandoning it. He also felt fear as they were no longer protected by fences. They were in the outside world now, and he prayed that they would be able to survive it.

TWENTY-SIX

T he group made it to the outskirts of Suffolk about thirty miles outside of Little Creek Navy Base before Zack signaled to Malcolm to stop at a nearby gas station on the side of the highway. The gas station wasn't large with only a couple of pumps and it had a store with its windows broken into. Behind the gas station was a grassy clearing stretching out for about twenty-five feet before the grass met the tree line which went on for what looked like miles.

Malcolm was tired from the long drive. What would normally take an hour to drive took five hours as the group had to navigate through hordes of zombies and other hazards to avoid being seen. The sun was beginning to set as they parked their vehicles.

Compared to the city, there weren't many zombies roaming around, making it easy to clear the area. Zack and Malcolm scouted the area, killing any zombies they found with their blades to keep from attracting any other attention. While they searched, the group stayed in the Humvees guarding each other. The group has been through hell and you could read it on each of their faces.

After walking around the gas station, Malcolm found Zack poking around inside the store. Most of the food and supplies had been raided with various items scattered on the ground.

A sign on the counter said, *take what you need. God bless.*

"The area is clear. Did you want to stop here for the night?"

"Yeah, we'll get the Humvees in a defensive V around the back of the gas station. That way if anyone drives past, they won't see the trucks."

"Good idea."

"Yeah, I figured it would be the best spot. We'll rest here until we can decide on where to go next."

"Sounds good to me. What are you looking for?"

"For starters I was looking for a fuel pump gauge to see if those tanks had any fuel. Also I was thinking of getting a map of Virginia. I don't know about you, but I'm going to avoid all major highways. If this ride here taught me anything it's avoid highways at all costs as they are magnets for zombies."

"Yeah, I agree. I'll go and let everyone know."

Zack nodded and continued to look around the station. Malcolm walked out of the building and found everyone talking.

"What's the plan?" Sabrina asked, noticing Malcolm getting closer.

"We'll stop here for the night. We will park the Humvees behind the back of the store in a V formation and we'd used the back of the store and Humvees for protection. Sabrina, help me move the Humvees to the back."

"On it." Sabrina replied, hopping off the turret to get into the Humvee. Malcolm and her moved the vehicles to the back of the stores and then assisted everyone out.

"I can make a fire." Sheri suggested.

"Yes, that would help. Thank you Sheri. Don't go too far into the woods. Stay within yelling distance."

"I will. Come on Keshia. Let's go and find some dry branches in the woods nearby." Sheri took her daughter's hand and held her rifle in the other as they ventured into the forest nearby.

Malcolm looked back at the group that managed to survive from Little Creek. Victor was being helped out of the Humvee by Dr. López and Kelsey, while Sophia and Anne walked out. Sophia's shoulders were slumped, while Anne comforted her. Malcolm could tell that Sophia was still upset about Richard.

"Sophia..." Malcolm began to say. "I'm sorry for your loss."

Sophia wiped a tear away and looked at Malcolm. "Thank you. It gives me some comfort to know that Sawyer was killed. I miss Richard though. He was my light in all of this darkness."

"Losing someone you love is hard. I can't say that I've been through your pain, but I can say that I will be here for you. Anything you need I'm there for."

"Thank you, Malcolm. It just hurts so much. Why is love like that?"

Malcolm paused and then looked at Anne who was also staring at him. The two were both silent as their lingering stares remained on each other.

"Love is hard to explain. It can be a welcomed friend, but it can also be your worst enemy. Right now you feel like love has betrayed you, but it hasn't. Love will keep you alive. You will fight for Richard's memory. He wouldn't want you to quit. He would want you to keep going. Push ahead. He would want you to survive." Malcolm replied.

Anne felt something in her heart from Malcolm's strong words. The two stared at each other once more before Malcolm looked back at Sophia.

"Thank you Malcolm. That was sweet." Sophia wiped away a tear and nodded. "You're right, Richard wouldn't want me to dwell on him. He would want me to fight on." She took a deep breath and looked Malcolm in his eyes. "Whatever you need from me, I'm there."

"Good to hear. Zack is in the store right now, and there's tons of supplies and food that was picked over. Do you mind helping him to see if there's anything salvable in there?"

"Sure." Sophia wiped her eyes once more and took a deep breath before standing and leaving Anne and Malcolm together. The two looked at each other before Anne cleared her throat.

"That was nice what you said to Sophia."

"Thanks, she's had it rough between the safe zone and Little Creek falling. I can't imagine what she's going through. She's a strong woman though, she'd get through it."

"Yes, she is." Anne replied. There was an awkward tension between the two as it was the first time they've been alone together since the fall of the base.

"How are you doing?" Malcolm asked.

"Just shaken up. I'll be fine though. What about you?"

"As long as you're okay, I'm fine too."

Anne felt that stray chill up her spine once more. She couldn't place the feeling that she felt while looking at Malcolm, but she didn't know if she should act upon it or let it be. She wanted to ask him about what he was going to say to her in their tent before their world got turned upside down, but she hesitated as she figured he probably didn't even remember what he was going to say.

Anne cleared her throat once more and then pointed towards the shop. "Sophia probably needs help sorting through all that's left in there. I'm going to head inside and help her."

"Yeah, sure. I'm going to check up on Victor. Talk later?"

Anne hesitated once more as she realized that he wanted to talk about their kiss. She couldn't explain why she wanted to avoid that talk. She liked him, but she was worried that Malcolm wanted more and she just wasn't at that level yet.

"Yeah, sure." She replied before walking away.

Malcolm sighed, watching Anne leave him. A part of him wanted to grab her by her arms and tell her how he really felt, but he had this feeling that his thoughts didn't match hers. Once Anne was gone, Malcolm turned his attention to Victor who was propped up on the wall. Emily was sitting next to him holding his hand, while helping him drink some water.

"How is he?" Malcolm asked.

"The stitches are holding up. I hate that I had to rush like that."

"You did good. He's alive. That's what counts."

"True, but those stitches will leave some scars."

"Scars are just trophies in my line of work," Victor winked.

Emily rolled her eyes and looked back at Malcolm who was laughing.

"Classic Victor. Well, it sounds like he'd make a full recovery."

"It appears that way." Emily chuckled. "I'm just glad I took the antibiotics and the painkillers. He's going to be out of commission for the next couple of days to heal."

"Of course. You keep an eye out for him?"

"Certainly."

"Who are you kidding, Malcolm? I'm going to be looking out for her." Victor grinned as he squeezed her leg.

"Oh you!" Emily playfully slapped Victor and the two laughed as they both seemed to be lost in each other's worlds. Malcolm smiled at the two as it seemed that a deeper relationship was growing between the two. Watching them interact he wondered if he could have the same relationship with Anne. Judging by her reaction when he requested that they talk later, it wasn't a good chance that she'd wanted to be more than just friends. They were out of the base, therefore their husband-and-wife act was over, and he hated that idea. Playing house with Anne was the best thing that came from this shitty zombie apocalypse.

Malcolm sighed and walked towards Sabrina and Kelsey who were chatting with each other in front of the Humvees.

"Hey y'all." Malcolm greeted.

"Hey, we're just talking about you. Any idea on where we're going next?" Sabrina asked.

"None, Zack is in the store right now, studying maps to figure out our next move."

Sabrina nodded.

"Where's Anne?" Kelsey asked.

"She's in the store with Sophia looking for supplies to take with us."

"Oh, okay, I think I'm going to help her."

Malcolm nodded and then took a step next to Sabrina.

"Hey, did you want to go on patrol with me?"

"Sure," she grinned. The two walked side by side around the Humvees and around the store. As they did, they kept their eyes peeled looking for any hazards coming their way.

"How'd you feel?" Malcolm asked Sabrina as they walked.

"Like shit. Losing Richard hurts. Not to mention, we almost lost Victor." Sabrina shook her head. "I've lost people before, but these stung."

"Yeah, we lost a lot of good people today. It's crazy to think that Little Creek is gone."

"Yeah, I used to think people would be crazy to attack that base, but now that's gone, it's a somber feeling."

"True, at least we're alive. That's what counts."

"That's right. I think we'd be okay as long as we stick together."

"Me too," Malcolm grinned.

The duo walked in front of the store and saw Zack huddled over the counter mumbling to himself as he reviewed the map. In front of him were Sophia, Anne and Kelsey who were picking up various objects and placing them in a cart nearby. Anne and Malcolm shared a look before Malcolm looked back down the street.

Sabrina chuckled. "What's going on with you two? You seem more uptight than usual?"

Malcolm shrugged. "Honestly, I'm not sure. We've been avoiding each other since the fall of the base. Every time the conversation gets about us, one of us always seems to turn and leave. Did you know that we kissed each other before the base fell?"

"Seriously?"

"Yeah, I mean the kiss started off as an experiment to see if we could display emotion during a kiss. You know to keep our lie alive..."

"Yeah..."

"But it then morphed into something else. I mean, it got hot and heavy, we nearly went all the way before we stopped to discuss our true feelings."

"And how does Anne feel about you?"

"She clearly wants us to remain friends."

"How do you feel about her?"

"The jury is still out on that decision, but I don't want to go back to the way things were before."

"Does she know that?"

Malcolm shook his head.

"Then you need to tell her that. Don't wait either. As soon as she's done in there, pull her aside and tell her how you really feel."

Malcolm nodded, "Yeah, good idea." He looked back at Anne who stared at him before walking away.

Anne continued to watch Malcolm as he walked around the building. In the dimly light shop, Sophia, Kelsey and her sorted through various items in the store. So far they had a nice collection of water, chips and some other non-perishables that they could take with them.

Kelsey looked at Anne and rubbed her back. "Hey, are you okay?"

"Yeah, I'm fine."

"Really? You've been holding the same water bottle for the last-minute gawking at Malcolm. Is there something you wanted to get off your chest?"

Anne paused and then looked at Sophia who was still collecting and looking at various items scattered on the floor.

"Hey, Sophia?"

"Yeah?" She responded looking up.

"Kelsey and I are going to carry some of these items back to the Humvees."

"Yeah, sure go ahead. I'll get another pile for you ready by the time you come back."

"Sounds good." Anne responded, picking up a crate. Kelsey did the same and followed Anne out of the store.

"Spill it," Kelsey demanded once they were outside.

Anne sighed. "Malcolm and I made out."

"You did what! When did this happen?"

"Right before the base fell."

"Oh! No wonder y'all keep looking at each other. So, why the long face? Was Malcolm a terrible kisser?"

"No, he's actually really good. I mean things got really hot and heavy."

"Really? I'm not following then."

"I'm worried about us. I like us just as friends, but I'm afraid that he sees us as something more."

"What's wrong with being more?"

"You've seen Sophia. I don't want to live going through that pain again. After seeing my parents die, I don't want Malcolm to go through the same."

"I don't understand. Why do you block yourself off like that? Opening yourself to someone is always a risk. Hell, before the zombie apocalypse, Zack and Malcolm were constantly in danger overseas. This isn't anything new. Not wanting to like someone because you're afraid to lose them isn't a good reason. Malcolm is a good guy and he won't wait for you forever. You guys are a good couple. Just go for it."

Anne looked at Malcolm who was laughing with Sabrina and bit her lip. She looked back at Kelsey and shook her head.

"I'm sorry, I can't. That pain, it was too hard to bear."

Anne placed the crate back on the truck and then grabbed the ring off her finger.

"Here, take your ring back. The ruse of us and Malcolm being together is over. There's no point of me wearing this anymore."

Kelsey stared at the ring, before taking it back and slipping it onto her ring finger. She looked back at Anne. "Anne, are you sure this is what you want?"

"Yes, Malcolm and I are done playing house. It's time for us to reset the clock and go back to being friends. The kiss was nice, but..." Anne closed her eyes and breathed deeply. "Being with him isn't want I want."

"Then you need to tell him. Set the record straight. Go talk to him now."

"I'm helping you with the supplies."

"Sophia and I got it. Go talk to him."

Anne nodded and left to go talk to Malcolm.

"Malcolm? Can I speak to you for a second?"

Malcolm looked at Sabrina and then back at Anne. "Yeah sure. Do you mind?"

"No, go ahead. I'll keep watch." Sabrina replied.

Malcolm nodded and walked away with Anne towards the open field.

"What's up?" Malcolm asked.

"I wanted to speak to you about our kiss."

Malcolm smiled. "I actually wanted to talk to you too."

"I..." Anne and Malcolm both spoke at the same time. Anne rubbed the back of her head and then pointed at Malcolm.

"You go first."

"Anne, what I wanted to say before the attack was that I feel like we should be together. I mean I know we had a fake relationship but through that time, I've grown closer to you, and I feel like you have too. I want to see where this goes. We can take it slow at first, but I just want to be with you."

Anne sighed and rubbed her elbow. "I was afraid you'd say that."

Malcolm's smile turned into a frown as he looked back at Anne, "what do you mean?" He asked.

"I like you Malcolm, but I just want to be friends." Anne lied as there was a part of her that didn't believe what she was saying.

Malcolm narrowed his eyebrows. "I don't understand. The kiss..."

"That kiss was just to prove that we could fake a marriage in front of others, but that part of our lives is over. We're out of the base. No need to lie to the people here because they already know our lie."

"So what? We just destroy everything we built?"

"What was there to build? We were friends faking a marriage. I know you caught feelings, but I didn't. We're just *friends*." The way Anne said friends made her sick to her stomach. The longer she stared into his eyes the worse she felt.

"I'm sorry," Anne replied as she turned and walked away. She felt tears fall down her cheeks and she wiped them away. She felt like the worst human on Earth. She couldn't understand why she felt so shitty. What she was doing was the right thing. She knew she couldn't get close to him because she couldn't deal with going through that pain of loss again, yet the feeling of walking away from him felt exactly like she lost him. Anne didn't dare to turn back and look at him. The damage had been done.

By the time Anne rejoined the group, Sheri had already lit the fire and everyone was standing around it. When she joined them, Kelsey stared at her, and then her eyes shifted towards Malcolm who stood on the opposite side of Zack. Malcolm looked defeated as he had a long distant stare peered into the fire. Kelsey could sense the tension between them but didn't push further. No one else was paying attention to Malcolm and Anne, instead their focus was on Zack who after an hour of researching was finally ready to discuss his plans.

"What's our next move, Zack?" Sabrina asked.

"We have two options, and since we are no longer a military unit, I will put it up to a vote. Option one, we can decide to find a nice spot in the woods. Build up a camp and try and see if we survive or we could take our chances and drive up to Fort A.P Hill. While I don't know if the base is still standing. I figured it's worth a try."

"And if the base is gone?" Sabrina asked.

Zack shrugged. "We fall back to option one. Find a place to hunker down. However I would say that far north would bring us closer to the Washington DC area. That's a high population area which means more zombies."

"Perfect." Sophia mumbled.

"Are those our only options?" Sheri asked.

"Yes, unless someone else has another."

"I'm assuming we're not going to take 95 to Fort Hill?" Malcolm asked.

"Hell, no." Zack chuckled. "We're taking the long way around. We'll head west first then go north through the mountains then head east. The further west we go, the less zombies we should run into as the population is less in western Virginia. I have our routes all marked up on the map."

"What's your vote?" Emily asked Zack.

"I vote option two. I think we should head to Fort Hill. We need to get as far as we can away from the Sons of Satan. We're still in Hampton Roads area and hopefully their twisted minds are only in this area. Nowhere else."

"I agree, with you Zack." Emily replied.

"Where Emily goes I go." Victor replied. "It's a yes for me."

"I'm a no." Sophia added. "I've been to more *safe places* than I care to count. Each one turns out the same. I'm tired of getting comfortable in one place and it getting destroyed. I rather stick with y'all in the woods."

Sheri looked at Keshia and the child nodded at her mother. Sheri smiled back at the group and replied, "it's a yes, for Keshia and me."

"Anne?" Zack asked.

"Yes, I agree. Let's go to the base."

Zack looked towards Sabrina. "No, I'm with Sophia. Fort Hill is a long way to travel. Anything could happen between here and there. It's safer if we find a spot here."

"Well, the vote is 5-2." Zack replied tallying up through counts. "Malcolm and Kelsey, any objections?"

Malcolm and Kelsey both shook their heads.

"I'm with you till the end brother."

"I love you, baby. I trust your decision." Kelsey added.

Zack took a deep breath and then looked everyone in the eye. "Then get some rest everyone. We leave at first light."

TWENTY-SEVEN

The group had been traveling for three days. Through their journey they've encountered several zombies and had to fight and run from them. Through it all the small band of people grew closer to each other as the hardships they encountered tested them in more ways than one. The two-vehicle convoy had the machine gun Humvee in front while the truck Humvee drove in the back. In the front car, Sabrina drove, while Sophia sat in the front seat. Anne and Malcolm were in the back seat. Malcolm manned the turret and Anne kept watch however her eyes were constantly drifting over towards Malcolm.

Since their talk in the woods about their relationship status, he'd barely talked to her. While Anne wanted to go back to being friends, she always didn't want to lose out on the deep conversations that Malcolm and her had. Even though they had a fake relationship, she enjoyed his company. She enjoyed his jokes and his laughter. At night when they set up camp, she expected for him to lay be her side and cuddle like they'd done countless times, instead he always either took watch or slept separately from her.

Granted this is how they were before the fall, they were more acquaintances having to deal with each other whenever Kelsey and Zack had them in the same space, but it felt weird now after experiencing so much with him. Anne felt like she was going crazy as a part of her wished to take back what she told him about just being friends. She missed what they had before.

Anne sighed and shook her head. She turned her attention from Malcolm back onto the road.

She frowned knowing whatever she did have with Malcolm was gone. She'd burnt that bridge and there was no coming back from that.

The lead Humvee bounced on the uneven two-lane road. The mountainous terrain was a different sight compared to the coastal plain of Virginia Beach. The group just finished their path up north and was now heading down hill east.

As they went around the bend, Anne moved with the vehicle as Sabrina went around the bend. As the road dropped down to the valley, they came upon a bridge and Sabrina cursed as she slammed on the brakes. Anne's eyes opened wide from the sudden movement.

"Why did we stop?" Anne asked.

"The bridge. It's out." Sabrina pointed to the far section and Anne had squint to see the missing section. Anne was impressed that Sabrina could even see it.

"Wow, good call." Anne replied.

A few seconds later, Zack walked by Sabrina's window.

"Why did you stop?"

"The bridge. It looks to be out."

Zack turned and stared at the bridge before cursing. "Shit, you're right. Stay here. I'm going to check it out."

"Be careful!" Sabrina warned as she watched Zack venture out.

"Zack wait! I'll come with you!" Malcolm replied as he followed Zack onto the bridge over the river. The two slowly crept over the concrete bridge testing its dexterity. As they did, they neared the problem. A semi-truck has driven off the side of the bridge and broke the containment wall, causing the bridge to crack and fall apart.

Malcolm bit his lip and then looked at Zack. "What are you thinking?"

"There's no way we could drive the Humvees over this bridge. I can feel the thing shaking with just our weight. We're going to have to double back to the interstate and drive it east until we can get back on the highway."

"The interstate is a bad idea. It would be too populated."

"If you have any other better ideas let me know. There's not a lot of roads out here in the country. If we go further north we get closer to the Washington DC population, which I don't want to do and if we deter any more I'm afraid that we'd run out of supplies before we get there. Taking the interstate is the only way."

Malcolm shook his head as he knew that Zack was right. "Fuck. I guess we're taking the interstate."

Zack nodded and the duo walked back to the Humvees.

"The bridge is unsafe to cross so we are taking the interstate east." Zack declared.

"Are you sure that's safe?" Sophia asked.

"It's our only option," Malcolm replied. "It's only for a few miles until we run into the highway again. Once that happens we be off the interstate. I trust Zack's judgement."

"I do too. I trust Malcolm and Zack." Anne added.

Malcolm stared at Anne and gave her a small smile before looking at the rest of the group.

"Any objections?" Zack asked.

The group was silent and Zack nodded his head. "The machine gun truck goes first, and then the utility truck will follow. Let's move out." Zack commanded.

Everyone got into their respected Humvees and Sabrina turned the truck around to head down the road towards the interstate. Zack followed behind her as they took the on ramp to get on the four-lane highway. The group drove down the mountain side and Anne recognized that the road was a lot easier to pass than the rough country two-lane road. They were moving at a fast pace, besides the fact that they had to zig zag and weave through several broken-down cars.

As Sabrina cleared a bend, she came down the valley to see a large group of zombies blocking the road. There were thousands of them, all blocking the highway.

"Shit!" She slammed in the brakes, getting the zombies' attention in front of her.

Moaning, they began making their way towards the front Humvee, and Sabrina cursed again as she put the truck in reverse and fished tailed it the other way. Zack attempted to do the same, but the Humvee stalled out.

"No, no, no!" Zack yelled. "Don't do this to me. Come on. Start! Start! Start!" Zack panicked as he attempted to restart the Humvee, but it was no use as white smoke erupted from the hood.

"Fuck. Everyone out! Get to the treeline!" Zack yelled. "Only take essentials with you. We're going to have to run on foot through the woods!" The group of Sheri, Keshia, Kelsey, Emily and Victor all hopped out of the car.

Zack assisted Victor as he hobbled across the highway, while everyone else scrambled towards the trees firing their rifles blindly to keep the zombies at bay. Their attempts weren't enough as they drew closer to them.

"Fuck, we're not going to make it." Zack growled as he dragged Victor beside him.

His prayers were answered when he heard machine gun fire and saw that Sabrina returned.

Sabrina hopped out of the truck and fired her rifle from her door.

"Keep going! We will cover you!" She yelled.

Zack nodded and looked at the rest of the group. "Keep moving. Don't stop!" He yelled.

Malcolm roared as he held down the trigger on the 50 cal. He mowed down the endless horde trying to cover his friends as he made their escape. Sophia and Anne both fought bravely as well as they joined Sabrina providing covering fire.

When the bullets for the 50 cal was spent, Malcolm checked on where the group was and saw that they made it to the tree-line.

"Hey! They made it. Let's go!"

"We're leaving the truck?" Anne asked.

"Yeah, no point. There's too many of them and I don't want to get separated. Come on. Let's move!" Malcolm yelled as he fired a few shots at nearby zombies. Sabrina did the same as she made her way to the tree-line. Sophia, Malcolm and Anne were far behind as they ran. Each of them firing from their hip as they tried to make it towards the trees. As they ran, Malcolm heard Sophia trip and turned around to help her, but he was too late as a zombie was already on top of her. Sophia screamed as the zombies chewed on her flesh.

"Sophia!" Anne cried as she attempted to rescue her.

"It's too late for her." Malcolm growled as he held back Anne.

"We have to help her. She's my friend!"

"She was my friend too, but it's too late. They have her." Malcolm replied.

In the background they could hear Sophia's muffled screams. Her voice became gargled with blood.

"Help me! I don't want to die. I don't want to die. Ahhh! I don't want to die alone. Help me Richard!" She begged.

Malcolm looked at Sophia and frowned. He knew she was gone and aimed at her head.

"I'm sorry Sophia." He took a headshot and ended her pain.

Anne stared at Malcolm and he looked back at her.

"It was the only thing left to do. I didn't want her to suffer."

"It's okay."

Malcolm nodded and grabbed Anne's hand. "Come on. Let's rejoin the group."

Anne nodded and ran next to Malcolm. As she ran, she couldn't stop thinking about how Sophia died. Her wails still echoed in her ears. Watching Sophia die awakened a feeling in her heart that she thought wasn't there. Anne gazed at Malcolm and thought how Sophia begged for Richard to save her. It saddened Anne as she replayed the sounds of Sophia's pleas for the man she knew was long gone. Even though she knew Richard was dead she still wanted him there in her final moments.

Anne wondered what their final moments would be like and who would she call out for. She looked at Malcolm again and pondered if he would be the man she'd call upon.

Sophia's death stung but the feeling of her being alone hurt too. While she knew that she didn't want to love someone again, she also didn't want to be alone either. Perhaps she could find a way to have both. Looking at Malcolm, she considered if he could provide her that comfort.

Eventually, Anne refocused and assisted Malcolm and Sabrina with killing any zombies that got in their path.

They rejoined with Zack and his group as they ran up hill. Zack looked at Malcolm with a wide-eyed stare.

"Where's Sophia?"

Malcolm shook his head.

"Fuck." Zack growled. Zack narrowed his brow and looked at everyone still running up the hill. "Keep moving! We need to put as much distance between us and the herd. Victor, I'm picking you up."

"No, let me run by myself. I don't want to slow you down."

"You're not fast enough to keep up. You're still healing. I will not lose another person today. Come on!" Zack growled as he placed Victor in a fireman's carry over his back.

The group ran and fired randomly behind their backs as the zombies kept coming after them. It felt like an endless wave that continued to attack them.

The group continued to run uphill until the tree-line broke and they arrived at a grassy opening. Emily stopped at the end of the hill. She gasped as the ground ended with a cliff leading into a deep gorge.

"Stop! Everyone stop, there's a cliff here!" Emily warned.

"Fuck me. What are we going to do?" Kelsey asked as she looked down the cliff.

"We could climb down?" Anne suggested.

Zack shook his head. "It's too steep. We don't have the proper equipment. We make our stand here. We've managed to get away from the main horde. If we kill the stragglers after us, we can regroup."

Everyone nodded in agreement.

"Okay, circle up. Victor and Keshia, get behind us. Victor, you're Keshia's last line of defense. Don't let anyone near her."

"I won't." Victor replied as he held his hand out to her. "She will be safe with me," Victor affirmed looking at Sheri.

Sheri nodded and kissed her daughter's head. "You'll be safe over there, baby."

Keshia looked at her mom with tears in her eyes. "I'm scared mommy."

"I know you are, but it's okay. We are going to be okay."

Keshia nodded and joined Victor, who held his pistol in his hands ready for any zombie that broke through the line.

"Okay, y'all this is our final stand." Zack yelled. "It's us or them. Don't let them break our line. Got it?"

Everyone nodded, and when the first zombie appeared from the treeline, Zack yelled, "fire!"

From there, countless zombies poured from the trees. Each one looked menacing and straight from hell. Some were missing limbs others had their bodies mangled. All of them were moaning and snarling as they approached the survivors.

Bullets rained down on the incoming foes. As the bullets met their targets, they were stopped dead in their tracks but the mob of zombies kept coming at the survivors.

"I'm running out of ammo!" Kelsey yelled.

"Here, last mag." Zack tossed a magazine towards Kelsey. "Make them count." Zack growled as he kept firing.

Kelsey reloaded and continued to fire. Anne kept firing until both her pistol and rifle were depleted. As a zombie approached her, she let out a mighty war cry and unsheathed her katana to slice the zombie in half. She quickly moved to stab another. Like her, the rest of their group had limited ammo as they switched from their guns to their blades.

Each one of them hacked and slashed as the endless stream of zombies continued to charge at them.

"Don't let up!" Zack roared as he stabbed another zombie with his knife.

"Tossing a grenade!" Malcolm growled, pulling the pin and tossing it into the center mass. The frag did little damage as zombies kept coming towards them.

"Tossing another!"

"Malcolm, save them!" Zack commanded. "Unless we can get into the middle of all of them, those grenades aren't doing shit."

Malcolm nodded and placed the explosive back on his belt loop.

Zack refocused, taking out zombies as they neared him. As he fought, Zack heard a painful scream nearby and his heart fell when he saw where it came from.

There was a zombie biting Sheri's arm as she tried to get him off her.

Malcolm quickly assisted Sheri and stabbed the zombie in the head, and pulled it off her. Quickly Kelsey and Anne guarded the space as Malcolm and Sheri fell back to the center of the circle.

Zack retreated back as well. His heart slump as he looked at the zombie bite mark.

"Sheri...." Zack began to say looking at the death stamp on her arm. He knew what he saw meant that she was lost. He felt sick to his stomach as his promise to keep Sheri and Keshia safe was a failure. His promise to Charles wasn't met. He failed him. Sheri was going to die.

"It's okay..." she cried, as tears rolled down her cheeks.

"How long do you think I have?"

"Seconds." Malcolm replied, shaking his head.

"Then let me make them count. You still have grenades on you?" Sheri asked Malcolm.

Malcolm looked at Zack and Zack confirmed. "Give them to her."

Malcolm pulled out two grenades and then pulled the pins, holding down the clip. "Just release the clip."

Sheri nodded as she held the explosives in her hands. She stared into Zack's blue eyes, "protect my daughter with your life."

The stare reminded Zack of the way Charles looked at him before he died.

"I will." He growled. It was hard to look at her. His eyes stung from the sadness taking over him.

Sheri nodded and looked at her daughter. "Mommy loves you!" Giving her a loving smile, Sheri took one last look at her daughter, attempting to save an image of her before she met her demise.

"Don't go!" Keshia cried, trying to run to her mom, but Victor held her back.

Sheri blew her daughter a kiss before fearlessly charging towards the horde. As she ran she could feel the zombies biting her flesh, but she didn't stop. She kept running. She wasn't sure if it was God's will or just adrenaline, but she kept moving until she was in the center of the horde.

With a smile on her face she flicked the clip on the grenade and looked up to the sky. "See you soon Charles..."

The explosion rocked everyone backwards and they covered their faces from the falling debris.

By the time the dust settled, there was a large crater where Sheri died. Dozens of zombies laid stretched out, either dead or severed enough where they could barely move. Zack looked at the carnage and shook his head.

"Dammit." He growled. He clenched his fist as he felt of failure of losing another person.

Zack's eyes opened wide as the mangled bodies of blasted zombies rose again. Some were missing arms. Others were missing legs. Their decaying skin barely hung on their bones. It was the hunger that drove them as they crawled towards the survivors.

"They're still coming!" Kelsey yelled.

"Fuck..." Zack growled as he took his knife and drove it into another zombie's skull.

TWENTY-EIGHT

Sweat and blood covered Anne's face as she kept hacking and slashing with her katana. She wasn't sure how long she was out there fighting, but her arms grew tired from swinging the blade over and over again. Her hands hurt from the constant shock of her sword cutting through brittle bone. Her energy was wearing thin. She breathed deeply as she pushed herself like she never did before. She didn't know where her body was getting the energy from, but she did know she didn't want to die, so she kept pushing herself.

Anne was scared. She'd never been more scared than that moment right there. Before there was always a glimmer of hope that she'd survive, but at that moment there was no hope. There was no chance of survival. In the last hour she watched her two friends die. Death no longer seemed like something she could escape. For her it felt inevitable.

She looked at Malcolm who was glaring as he stabbed every zombie that neared. Like her, he was in fight or flight mode. She'd never seen him so worried. Blood and sweat rolled off his cheeks as he roared mindlessly shoving his knife into anything that neared.

She prayed that he'd live through this horrible chapter in their lives. She'd already lost two people today and didn't want to lose any more. She missed being at the base wrapped in Malcolm's arms. That is where

287

she felt safe. She missed sleeping in his arms and listening to him laugh and smile. Those moments shared in their tent seemed like distant memories.

She felt greedy but she wanted more of those moments. She didn't want to be alone. She didn't want to sleep alone one night and die alone the next day. If she was going to go out she'd prefer it to be in someone's arms. Someone like Malcolm.

The more she thought about Malcolm the more she wished that she did more with him. She wished that they did more than kiss. While she didn't know where their relationship would go, she did want to explore it. Life was precious and she realized that she shouldn't waste it worrying about the future pain. Instead she wanted to focus on the now. As she fought, she made herself a promise to pursue a relationship with Malcolm. No matter how she felt about it, she had to know where that road would bring her.

Anne didn't know how much longer she could last. She prayed for a miracle as it looked like there was no end in sight. After slaying another zombie, Anne took several deep breaths before raising her sword once more, but to her surprise she heard several gunshots. To her amazement zombies began to fall as bullets mowed the crowd down.

"Everyone down!" Zack warned, as they all crouched from the raining bullets.

Malcolm placed his arms over Anne protecting her.

When the shooting stopped, Malcolm moved off of Anne and held her cheek. "Are you okay?"

Anne nodded. "I am..." she replied.

Malcolm helped her up and Anne looked at the war zone in front of her as hundreds of zombies in front of them were all slain. Figures emerged from the tree-line with their rifles on their shoulders.

As Anne squinted to get a better look at their saviors, they heard a man yell, "are y'all folks a'ight?"

Malcolm stared wide eyed at the stranger who saved him. He was with a party of mixed individuals including, men, women and different races. They had standard issue military gear, but were wearing civilians clothes.

The stranger who spoke first was a white man, about six foot and two hundred pounds. He had an athletic build and brunette hair peeked out of his backwards baseball cap. Underneath his tactical vest, he wore a black punisher T-shirt and a pair of rip jeans and tan combat boots. He placed the barrel of the rifle in his right hand, while his left finger hovered near the trigger as he approached.

"Hi, I'm Liam. What unit are y'all with?" He asked, observing, the Navy SEALs military fatigues. Liam's voice was deep with a bit of southern twang in it. His brown eyes studied each member of the group trying to get a feel of them.

"Captain Zack Morris. Navy SEALs. Team 2." Zack replied.

"Navy SEALs? What brings you out here?"

"We were heading to Fort A.P Hill. We were trying to avoid the interstate, but the bridge on the road was blocked, making us detour on the interstate. Our Humvee broke down when we found that large horde on the interstate."

"Damn and y'all been fighting since then?"

"Yes, we lost two people."

"I'm sorry to hear that. It's terrible about Little Creek Navy Base too. We had hope that base would still be standing."

"We?"

"Yes, sorry, it's been a while. Staff Sergeant Liam Steele," Liam gave a crisp salute and Zack returned the gesture.

"Where were you stationed?"

Liam frowned. "Fort A.P Hill. The base was overrun a few weeks ago. I'm sorry, if you head there now all you'd find are bodies and zombies."

Liam frowned as he watched everyone lower their heads.

"I'm sorry again. I wish there was a way to communicate that beforehand. Perhaps then you would have never lost your people."

"So where did you come from?" Sabrina asked.

"We're a scouting party, from a community not too far from here. We were heading back to it when we heard the gunfire and then the large explosion. When we got here, we saw y'all struggling with the zombies and decided to lend a hand."

"How far is your community?" Zack asked.

"About a few miles from here. It's called New Haven. I know, it's a corny name. I didn't come up with, but it's a great community. It's safe and has running water and electricity. They are working on even getting a farm started on the outskirts of the fence."

Zack looked at everyone and he could tell that several were warming up to the idea. "Does your establishment have rules or laws?"

"Not many, but we regulate under the be treated how you want to be treated rules. We don't tolerate rape or murder, and any of our laws that do get broken will equal banishment."

"Fair enough."

Liam nodded. "It truly is a safe space, but I won't force anyone to join. You are free to go your separate ways, but I'm not going to lie, y'all look like you need a hot shower and some chow."

"Could you give us a minute to discuss?" Zack asked.

"Take all the time you need." Liam replied, walking back to his group.

Zack turned and looked at Malcolm. "What are you thinking? Sounds legit. I saw the way he was handling that rifle. He's military."

"Yeah, I saw that too. I like the fact that they seem down to earth. I trust them too. Any other objections?"

Everyone shook their head.

"But if we don't like their community..." Kelsey began to say.

"Then we leave..." Zack answered. "... but I don't know where we are going to go. Fort A.P hill is gone. We're obviously going to have a tough time on the road. It's the best option right now. They have walls, running water and electricity. We need those things."

Everyone agreed.

Zack took a deep breath and nodded. "Hey, Liam. We've come to a decision. We want to join your community."

"Excellent. We better get a move on if we want to make it by sundown. Come on." Liam led the group away from the cliff and headed back into the woods.

The group followed the New Haven community members through the woods and Liam walked in the middle of them as he continued to study each person following him.

"It appears that I haven't been properly introduced to all of you." Liam smirked. He looked towards Kelsey, "and you are?"

"I'm Kelsey, I'm Zack's wife." Kelsey replied.

"Nice to meet you, Kelsey."

"Lieutenant Malcolm White, but I guess that ranks don't really matter anymore."

Liam laughed. "True. I would guess by now our entire government has been destroyed."

"You're not wrong," Zack added. "Before we left, we got confirmation that the government is gone. We were self-governing ourselves before our base fell."

"How did it fall? We got overrun at Fort Hill before word was spread."

"We did too, in a way, but there were also some religious zealots who called themselves the Sons of Satan who attacked us as well. They believed that it was their job to make hell on earth in preparation for the Devil's return. They use zombies as their soldiers and attacked our gates."

"Damn. We've never heard of those people, but we've had our share of crazies."

"Yeah, the world went to shit the moment zombies started walking around. I'm glad that the Sons of Satan's reach doesn't go this far. They are a nasty group of men."

"Sounds like it."

Liam looked at Keshia and waved, "Hi, my name is Liam. What's yours?"

Keshia didn't say anything as she hugged tightly to Sabrina's leg.

Liam gave her a small smile and then looked at Sabrina. "What's your kid's name?"

"Oh, she's not my daughter."

"Oh my...I'm sorry. I just assumed..."

"It's cool. We're both black. I understand. Her name is Keshia. My name is Sabrina."

"Nice to meet you. Her mother wasn't one of the people you lost, was it?"

Sabrina nodded.

Liam frowned and looked Keshia in the eyes. "I'm sorry to hear about your mother. I'm sure she was a brave woman."

"Thank you," Keshia wept as she wiped her tears away.

Liam gave her a small smile and then looked at Anne.

"And you are?" He asked.

"My name is Anne Yamaguchi." She replied. Anne felt weird not saying White-Yamaguchi. It was the first time she didn't use Malcolm's last name. A part of her missed using the surname.

"Nice to meet you, Anne. Before we assisted you, I saw you and Kelsey with your swords. You two move with such grace."

"Thank you. Kelsey and I have been studying kendo for years."

"Aww well, that explains it," Liam smirked.

He studied Emily and then asked, "Ma'am, judging by the bloodied lab coat, are you a doctor?" We could sure use one in the community."

"I am, Dr. Emily López."

"Nice to meet you Dr. López. What did you study?"

"I'm a Virologist."

"What's that?" Liam asked as he climbed up a steep hill.

Emily took a deep breath as she too hiked up the hill. Liam helped her up, and Emily smiled at him. "Thank you, Liam. To answer your question, I study viruses. I was actually studying the zombie virus before the base fell. Luckily I kept my research safe." She patted her bag around her shoulder.

"You're trying to make a cure? That's amazing. Our resident doctor in our community is trying to do the same thing. Perhaps you two can put your heads together. Two heads are better than one, right?"

"That's actually a great idea. I can't wait to meet them."

Liam gave her a small smile and then turned his attention to Victor who was following Emily closely.

"I'm sorry about your injury."

"It's okay. I just wish that I could help more. Name's Victor."

"Nice to meet you, Victor. It's okay. I'm just glad we have four Navy SEALSs joining our community." Liam replied, noting Victor's bloodied military outfit. "We don't have many soldiers. Most of the members of our community are just families looking for a place to be safe. The more veteran fighters we have the better off we are when the zombies come-a-knocking."

"I understand. I'll be in fighting shape in the next couple of days."

"Don't push yourself. Take some rest. In fact, all of you take some rest when we get to New Haven. When we get to the community, take a day or two. Y'all have been through hell. Now come along, we're almost there." Liam replied as he rejoined the lead upfront.

After a three-hour hike, the large group came to a clearing in a valley that was surrounded by mountains. In front of them was a village of several homes and townhomes. Each home and townhouse had this mountain cabin aesthetic, with wooden walls, green roofs, and large bay doors. On top of each house were large solar panels collecting the sun's rays. Surrounding the neighborhood was a metal fence but nearby was a concrete barrier that was being made as men and women poured concrete in wall molds. Along the fence lines were several watch towers with armed guards posted at each one keeping watch. In the outskirts of the small community there were several plots of land with various fruits and vegetables being farmed by the citizens. People picked the food placing it in containers that were pulled by horses. A guard kept watch as people harvested the food.

"Welcome to New Haven." Liam gestured with an open palm.

"Wow, this place is amazing," Malcolm commented, looking around. "What was it before the fall?"

"It was supposed to be a modern zero carbon ski resort. They built the infrastructure to be green including the electrical system. Fresh water comes from the stream nearby."

"Impressive." Malcolm replied, looking at the area.

"Was this a safe zone at one point?" Zack asked.

"Yes, they opened their gates as soon as the government asked gates communities to register. Since that time, people have stumbled across the place and have joined the community."

"That concrete barrier they're building..." Zack asked.

"That was the leadership's idea. After the fall of Fort Hill they realized that a simple metal fence wasn't going to hold. So we've been taking the containment sound walls from a nearby highway expansion site and using the materials there to build a wall. In the next few months the wall should be completed and it should be strong enough to hold back any horde that comes through here."

"Who are the leadership?" Zack questioned.

"It's four individuals including myself. Each represents a leader from the groups of the warriors, farmers, builders and general population. Each group votes for a leader to voice their concerns. The leadership also votes on laws or rules and punishments."

"You guys have like a small democracy here. I like it." Kelsey admitted.

"Yes, we try to keep a little bit of America here. Despite how much the world is fucked up out there."

Liam led them inside the gates and Malcolm could feel every eye on him and his group as they walked down the road.

"Is everyone usually this curious?" Malcolm asked Liam.

"Yeah, don't mind them. We don't get many new visitors. They are all good people. Trust me." Liam replied. "So we tried to make it as normal as possible. Over there we have the community center." Liam pointed to a large building in the center of the village. "It used to be the ski lodge but we converted it into a supplies area and food distribution center. Anything we scavenge or grow could be found in there."

Keshia heard kids screaming and searched for the origin to see multiple kids running on a playground.

Liam smiled, watching Keshia's eyes light up. "It looks like someone found the playground."

Keshia grinned back at Liam.

"Beside it is the school too."

"I don't want to go to school." Keshia pouted.

Liam chuckled. "It's not the school you're used to. There we teach kids scavenging and survival techniques. There's some reading and math but not as much as you expect. You'll like it trust me."

Keshia grinned once more before turning back to watch the kids.

Malcolm thought it was good to see her smile considering that she'd lost her mother only a few hours ago. Keshia had a strong heart and that was needed to survive this plague.

"Next to the school is the infirmary. Dr. López, that is where you will find our medical team. Feel free to do your research there."

"Thank you," Emily replied.

Liam nodded and continued to lead the group down the road. They ended their journey in front of a large house.

"Well, this is y'all. I'm sorry, space is limited so I hope you don't mind sharing a house. I figured y'all won't be considering you guys were out in the world surviving together."

"No, it's okay. We are welcomed by your hospitality." Zack replied.

Liam nodded. "Each room is furnished, but there's only five rooms available, so some of you might have to bunk together. I know Kelsey and Zack are married, so y'all could stay together, and I'll let you all choose the other pairings. There's fresh linen in the house already. I will have someone drop off some food for you later. In the meantime, get some rest tonight and we will meet tomorrow to discuss duties around the community, okay?"

Everyone nodded.

"Have a good night y'all. If you need anything I'm only a few streets down. House 588. Goodnight." Liam waved goodbye and left the group of seven together.

"I guess, we should go inside and explore our new home," Malcolm suggested.

"Sounds good to me. I can't wait to see the inside." Sabrina grinned. "The outside is already impressive. I love the wooden log and stone brick exterior."

"I agree it's very rustic. However, I'm more interested in the beds. I'm exhausted." Emily commented.

Everyone laughed and agreed. The group walked inside the large mansion and was impressed with what they saw. The large mountain home had a large fireplace in the living room. In the living room, there were several brown leather couches spread around a flat screen tv. Next to the living room was an open concept kitchen with beautiful sand-stone countertops.

"Wow this place is amazing. It's a lot better than the tents at Little Creek." Anne replied.

Everyone laughed, but soon their laugh turned into tired smiles as they looked at each other. Each one of them were dirty and exhausted.

"Well, I don't know about you but I'm tired," Kelsey replied. "I'm going to take a hot shower and go to bed."

"Me too," Emily replied stretching out.

"Wait, we still need to decide who will bunk with who." Zack stated. "Like Liam said, Kelsey and I can get one room, who wants the others?"

"I'll take it." Anne replied. "Malcolm, you can bunk with me."

Malcolm's jaw dropped as he looked at Anne. "Are you sure?"

"Yeah, I mean we bunked back at Little Creek you don't have a problem with that, do you?"

"No, if that's what you want, then I'm okay with that."

Zack looked in between the two and then shrugged. "If that's settled, let's call it a night. Good night everyone. Get some good rest tonight as tomorrow I have a feeling we will be put to work. This ride ain't free."

Everyone nodded and said their individual goodbyes before retiring to their bedrooms. Malcolm followed Anne to their room and shut the door behind him.

"Anne, I'm confused. I thought..."

Before Malcolm could get his words out, Anne kissed Malcolm. He breathed deeply as he stared at her.

"Anne?"

"I've come close to the brush of death today and during that time realized that I didn't want to die alone. I was wrong to push you away. While I don't know how I truly feel about us, what I do know is that I want to be with you. I choose to be with you. Do you choose me?"

A smile spread on Malcolm's face as he charged back into Anne's lips and kissed her passionately again.

As his lips left hers, Anne gasped and looked into Malcolm's eyes.

"Does that answer your question?" He smirked.

Anne smiled, "come here," she pulled him close and kissed him sensually again.

TWENTY-NINE

"Shower?" Malcolm asked in between kisses.

"Yes, please." She moaned.

Malcolm picked up Anne and carried her towards the shower in the bedroom. Anne's legs crossed around Malcolm's back, her hands held his chin, and her tongue was buried deep inside his mouth massaging his own. Malcolm groaned from the erotic movement and clutched Anne tighter.

They reached the bathroom, and Malcolm placed Anne back down to turn on the shower. When he turned back around, Anne was standing naked in front of him.

"Goddamn." Malcolm muttered looking at her beautiful figure in front of him. He breathed deeply and felt his cock grow as he ogled her curves.

Malcolm hastily moved his clothes, and when he ripped off his underwear, Anne's eyes fluttered, looking at his erected manhood.

"Fuck Malcolm..." Anne trembled, imagining what he would feel like inside her.

Malcolm gave Anne a coy grin and then dragged her to his lips once more. The two kissed as they hopped into the shower together. As the water cascaded around them, they cleaned off all of the dirt and dried blood they collected through their travels, but after cleaning each other, their lips were on each other once more.

Malcolm pulled away from kissing Anne and stared into her eyes. He laughed and Anne furrowed her brow.

"What's so funny?"

"I honestly never thought this day would come. Now that it's here, I don't know how to react."

"I feel the same way." Anne smirked.

Malcolm leaned forward to kiss Anne once more. His lips then left her mouth and traveled south towards her neck. He sucked on her skin and Anne tilted her head back moaning from the arousal creeping up her spine. Malcolm's fingers had a mind of their own as they explored every inch of her. She felt his hands squeeze and slap her ass, she then felt his fingers massage and knead her breasts.

Her toes curled as she exhaled deeply. She closed her eyes as her need for him grew. She couldn't deny the feelings anymore. There was a burning desire in her core, and only Malcolm could extinguish it. Second by second her need grew. It was an inescapable hunger to have him. As he nibbled on her skin, rubbed her breast with his palm, and prodded her lower lips, she grew eager for that first time she could feel his cock inside her.

"Oh Malcolm..." she uttered.

Malcolm's mouth traveled even further south towards her nipple. He held her tit in his hand and circled his tongue around her nipple making it hard. With his teeth, he lightly sucked it causing Anne's body to lurch forward.

She held him tightly as her pleasure grew once more. Her breathing quickened and her heartbeat tripled. Something about the way Malcolm touched her made her go wild. His touch was like no other. It felt like pure electricity. There was no denying that there was a spark.

Her hand lowered down to his crotch and grabbed his stiffness. She softly stroked him causing Malcolm to groan. He lifted his head up and nestled it in the nook of her neck as she pleasured him.

"Oh Anne..." Malcolm whispered as Anne's hand jerked him.

Malcolm removed his head from her neck and looked into her eyes. He kissed her softly, and in a low growl, he said, "I must have you."

The look in Malcolm's eyes felt different. Gone was the friend that she once knew. Instead, there was almost a primal look in his eyes as he shut off the water in the shower. From the look alone Anne knew there were no more games, no more ruses, no more lying about who likes who. From Malcolm's deep stare, she knew that she was his.

They shut off the water, and Malcolm lifted Anne up by her sides. Anne wrapped her arms around Malcolm's broad shoulders and her legs twisted around his muscular ass. Malcolm groaned as his lips slid over Anne's. He loved the way she tasted and the feeling of her body sliding across his. He craved every inch of her. Like a barbarian, he carried Anne out of the bathroom and into the bedroom.

At the bed, he laid her on her back, and leaned backwards to bask in her beauty. Words couldn't describe her exquisite features. He couldn't decide which of her he liked more. Each part of her was ravishing. In the end, he didn't care to decide. He knew that she was all fucking his, and he didn't plan on ever letting her go. Not once, and let God have mercy on that motherfucker's soul if they were dumb enough to part him from her.

His cock trembled as if it was begging to be buried into her folds. Reaching forward, he touched her breasts, and then his hands, slid down her smooth beige skin, towards her wet opening. Anne shivered from his touch as he sunk lower. As soon as his fingers touched her wetness, she was captured. Her back arched as a soft moan filtered out of her clenched teeth. Slowly, his fingers slipped in her wet canal, and massaged her flesh. She ground her body on his fingers, as he stretched her opening.

She closed her eyes, groaning as her hands combed through her wet hair. Seconds later she felt his tongue inside her. With every lick, her breathing increased. The feeling of him inside her, felt like no other. She loved every second of it and couldn't wait for more.

"What are you waiting for?" Anne asked with bated breath. " Fuck me..."

Malcolm grinned at Anne, before stroking his dick. He centered himself before entering her. Anne gasped the moment she felt his thickness. She held his back tightly as Malcolm pumped in and out of her.

Her legs arched towards the ceiling, allowing Malcolm to deeper penetrate.

Laying there, Anne felt her world turn upside down. On her back, she witnessed the man that she had denied feelings for give her the greatest pleasure in the world. Every grunt, every gasp, every moan turned her on. Her hands twitched as her fingertips slid down his dark skin. She noted every curve and ridge. His skin was rigid, and she could smell the fresh soap he used. Her hand rose to the nape of his neck. She held him tight as waves of pleasure crashed into her.

Opening her eyes, their eyes connected. Not a word was shared as the two emotionally bonded. No words needed to be spoken to prove how they felt about each other. The proof was there. By the way Malcolm kissed her. By the way he worshiped her. By the way he groaned fucking her hard. Every single detail of proof was shown.

He had claimed her. She was his. He was hers. Nothing could deny those facts.

She held on to him tightly and her toes curled. Anne moaned as she tasted him once more. That feeling of his tongue touching hers was exhilarating, heart pounding, and out of this world. Every inch of her was on fire as his masculine musk hypnotized her. Her fingers pulsed as they slid down his smooth dark skin, and her eyes couldn't bear to look away from the God like shape of Malcolm's sculpted core. Every sense she had seemed to be on fire. She was almost there.

Malcolm grinned, listening to Anne's moans. Her sounds of pleasure were music to his ears as he continued to rapidly fuck her. Anne felt amazing. That feeling of having her in his arms and being inside her was beyond anything he expected.

Leaning back, he held her hips and gazed at her beauty. He loved the shape of her hips and the curve of her breasts. He loved that with every thrust into her, her tits would bounce and she would shriek, creating an erotic image that stirred his heart's desire. Everything about her turned him on. From the scent of her hair, the sounds of her moans, the feeling of her wetness wrapped around his cock, the look of her loving eyes, all the way to the way her mouth tasted when he kissed her. She satisfied each one of his senses and then some.

He was almost there.

The couple rolled in bed and Anne gained the dominant position. Malcolm laid on his back, holding Anne's hips, his grin grew watching her reach her climax. Listening to her moan, Malcolm couldn't stop smiling. He knew he brought her to completion.

There was something about watching her come that made him happy. It could have been the glow that she had, or the way her skin glistened in the limited light of the bedroom. Or it could have simply been the fact that as she came his name was on her lips.

Needless to say, watching her enjoy her pleasure was enough for Malcolm to experience his own. Grunting, he came inside Anne, moving his hips at a feverish pace until he was spent. When he was done, Anne rolled off him. Her smile barely fit on her face as she held his face cheek.

"That was amazing."

"And then some." Malcolm smiled.

"I'm not going to lie, I'm a bit disappointed that we didn't do this sooner."

"I'm not. I'm just happy that we go to this point. For you, it was well worth the wait."

"Oh, Malcolm." Anne grinned as she kissed him. "Well, I guess your wait is over. Did you want to do it again?"

"I never thought you'd ask." Malcolm grinned as he kissed her once more.

He got on top of her, and the couple made love once more.

THIRTY

Anne woke up with Malcolm's arm casually draped across her breasts. She palmed her head, smiling as she remembered their incredible sexual night. Getting up, she slipped her underwear on and then looked back at Malcolm who was still sleeping softly. His bare black ass was protruding from the sheets.

She grinned looking at his muscular figure and her body trembled as she relived the feeling of his cock in between her legs once more. She took a deep breath trying to compose herself.

After months of flirting and staring they finally got to express their feelings for each other, and Anne was delighted at the outcome.

Anne walked towards her bag and took out a clean pair of yoga pants and placed on a cami top. She crept towards the door, trying to be quiet to not wake up Malcolm and snuck out the room. Walking out into the hall, Anne could smell coffee and she followed the scent to the kitchen where she found Kelsey sipping the contents from the mug.

"My God, I can't tell you how much I missed coffee. Where did you get it from?" Anne asked, grabbing a mug that was nearby, and pouring herself some.

"It was part of our welcome package that the community got us."

Kelsey pointed to a large basket of food, including several canned perseveres, fruits, bakery items and jerky."

"Oh, when did this get here?"

Kelsey laughed, about an hour after we retired to our rooms. We ate a lot of it. Sorry."

"Why didn't anyone tell us it arrived?"

"We tried," Kelsey smirked. "Until we got to y'alls room and heard you two moaning like a banshees."

"Oh my..." Anne's cheeks became flushed as she combed her fingers through her hair.

"Yep. We all know. Spill it." She grinned.

Anne smiled and closed her eyes. "Malcolm and I hooked up last night."

Kelsey squealed. "I knew it! How was it?"

Anne gave her friend a guilty smile as she pushed back a strand of her hair. "It was good. Really good..." Anne's thoughts once more drifted to the night, imagining how Malcolm held her as he buried himself inside her. Anne looked at her friend and took another sip of her coffee.

"So what does that mean between you? Are you guys together?"

"For the most part, yes. I mean we still haven't clarified what stage our relationship is in, but for the most part, we are a couple."

"I'll take it! Ugh that sexual tension between you two was too much for all of us."

Anne laughed and shook her head. "Sorry about that." Anne looked around the kitchen and then back at Kelsey, "where's everyone else at?"

"They're getting ready. They should all be down here in the next couple of minutes."

Anne nodded and poked through the basket to find a peach. She bit into it and moaned from the sweet flavor.

"Damn, this tastes good."

"Yeah, I guess all of this food is from here. Which is good, this is what we were trying to work to at Little Creek, but I'm glad that they were able to get their system down."

"Yeah. What do you think about this place?"

"Honestly, it's a little too good to be true."

"That's what I'm thinking too. It's almost like we died and gone to heaven."

"Exactly." Kelsey smirked.

"How does Zack feel about this place?"

"He's skeptical, but he likes it."

"Malcolm feels the same way," Anne admitted.

They heard footsteps and Zack approached the coffee pot that was behind Anne.

"Good morning," he smirked, grabbing a cup. "Did y'all have a good night?"

"Go ahead. Lay it on me. I know everyone knows about me and Malcolm."

Zack laughed and shook his head. "I'm just glad that y'all finally hooked up. I swear the would-they-won't-they trope was getting old."

Anne punched Zack and he laughed placing his hands up. "Hey now!"

Sabrina, Victor, Emily, and Keshia all walked downstairs.

Victor had a goofy grin on his face as he winked at Anne.

"Oh God. How many people know?" Anne placed her hands on her face as her cheeks turned red once more.

"We all know." Victor smirked.

"Know what?" Keshia asked. Everyone laughed at her innocence and Sabrina shook her head placing her hand on Keshia's back.

"It's nothing, sweetie." Sabrina gave the group a dirty look before looking back at Keshia. "How about we eat some breakfast in the living room and see if that tv has cartoons?"

"Okay," Keshia grinned.

Sabrina grabbed a couple items from the welcome basket and then pointed at the group, "y'all are a bad influence on her."

Everyone laughed again and Sabrina looked at Anne and winked at her. "I'm glad y'all finally hooked up."

"Ugh, now I'm starting to regret living in this house with y'all crazy people."

Malcolm walked downstairs and entered the kitchen. Once Victor saw him, he started clapping and Zack chimed in as well.

Kelsey held her head, and Anne once more felt embarrassed as she looked away.

"Let's give it up for the hero!" Victor joked.

"What?"

"We all know." Victor smirked.

"Know what?" Malcolm looked at Anne and she made a sexual gesture.

"Oh, no, we didn't do that..."

"I swear, if you say we're just friends..." Zack shook his head.

Malcolm grinned and looked at his friends. "How did y'all know?"

"Trust me we all heard." Kelsey grinned.

"Oh, wow...I'm so embarrassed."

"Now you know how I feel," Anne added. "At least you're here with me in the trenches."

"I don't know. I'm about to put up the white flag and retreat if this is how y'all are going to be."

"Hey!" Anne smacked Malcolm's arm. "How dare you leave me to the wolves."

"It's either you or me."

Anne laughed shaking her head. "You're such an asshole."

"I know." Malcolm grinned as he dragged her close and kissed her.

The group cheered and clapped. Anne pulled away from Malcolm smiling from the group's outburst.

"Alright, Alright, calm down." Anne waved her arms attempting to settle down Kelsey, Zack and Victor who seemed even more excited after their kiss.

"What's there to calm down about? You just gave everyone a private show." Victor teased.

"You know..." before Anne could finish her sentence, there was a knock at the door. Anne looked at everyone before looking towards the front door.

"I wonder who that could be?" she asked.

"I got it." Malcolm walked towards the door and opened it to discover Liam standing in the doorway.

"Morning. From the sound of it, everyone is awake and is in good spirits."

"Yeah, something like that come on in."

"Thank you," Liam grinned as he entered the home. "This won't take long, I know you all are still healing from your travels. If everyone could meet in the living room?"

Sabrina muted the tv and the rest of the group all walked into the living room. Everyone sat on the couch looking at Liam who stood in the center.

"So I talked to leadership, and they are delighted to have you here." Liam looked towards Keshia and smiled. "Whenever you're ready Keshia, we told the school that you'd be attending. We have several kids your age so you'd fit right in."

"Will I be learning how to farm? I always wanted to learn." Keshia asked.

Liam nodded, "Yes, that and much more." He turned his attention to Emily.

"Dr. López, Dr. Blake would be expecting you at the infirmary. He can't wait to see your developments on a cure. He has already had a couple attempts, but he believes that with your help, they can make some decent progress."

"That's excellent. I'm going to get my research and head over there now."

"You don't want to rest?"

Emily shook her head. "The longer we take to find a cure the more innocent people die. I want to find a cure as quickly as possible."

"I understand. You remember how to get to the infirmary?"

"Yes, I will find my way. Thank you." Emily left the living room to grab her research in her room.

"So what about the rest of us?" Sabrina asked.

"Well, given the fact that four of you are SEALs, and Kelsey and Anne are amazing with their swords, the leadership believes your best fit would be as soldiers and scavengers. You will be serving under me, going on missions to find additional supplies, and if needed defend this place if any hordes show up."

"Sounds good to me." Zack replied.

"Yes, we are all eager to do our part." Malcolm added.

Liam nodded. "I figured." Liam stood up and smiled. "Enjoy the day guys."

"Wait, where are you going now?" Sabrina asked.

"A few guys and me are going to scout a Walmart a few clicks out. See what we could find."

"Do you need back up?" Sabrina asked.

"We can handle it, just take the day and relax."

"No, I want to earn my keep." Sabrina told Liam. "Trust me, soldier, I don't like relaxing too much. Let me get back in the fight."

"I'm with Sabrina." Zack replied. "Us SEALs don't really do breaks."

Malcolm nodded in agreement.

"Okay, we leave in thirty minutes. Get your gear and meet us at the armory."

"Yes, sir. See you then." Zack replied.

Liam nodded and then left the house.

"You guys go ahead. I'll stay here with Keshia. I don't want to be a hindrance." Victor replied.

Zack nodded and then looked at Kelsey and Anne. "Are you guys coming or staying?"

"Well, come. Like you said. We have to earn our keep." Anne replied.

Kelsey nodded in agreement.

"Then it's settled. Like Liam said, get your stuff. We meet downstairs in five minutes."

Everyone nodded and dispersed to their rooms. Malcolm and Anne walked back to their room and placed on their tactical vests, gathering their weapons.

"It's crazy that we're going back out here." Anne replied.

"Are you sure you want to come? You don't have to put yourself in danger anymore."

"Malcolm..." Anne placed her hands on his cheeks and looked into his eyes. "I have skills that not many people have. While I know it's dangerous, I want to be with you. I know you will protect me, just like I will protect you. Right?"

"Right." Malcolm grinned.

Anne smiled back at him and kissed him. "Come on, let's meet everyone downstairs."

THIRTY-ONE

"It's good to see y'all." Liam grinned. Behind him were four other soldiers. Each wore similar outfit to Liam of jeans, shirt and tactical vest. They held their rifles in their hands as they looked at the group of Sabrina, Anne, Kelsey, Zack and Malcolm.

"Thanks for inviting us." Zack replied. "This is your opt, so we're just following your commands."

"Sounds good to me. I knew it was a good idea to include SEALs on my team. We went ahead and got some additional ammo for your rifles and pistols. Go ahead and get stocked up and then we could head out."

One of the soldiers held a crate filled of ammo clips and placed it in front of the group.

"Oh, it's like Christmas again. Damn have I missed having ammo." Sabrina grinned as she placed several clips in her vest and replaced one in her rifle.

"Where did you get all of this?" Malcolm asked, reloading his gun.

"Most ammo is from Fort Hill. The other comes from various stores and homes we've raided. You got to say one thing about Americans is they love their guns, so we haven't had trouble finding it when we're out. Everyone set?"

They all nodded and Liam smiled. "Good, let's go."

The group split up in two teams, taking two electric trucks. Zack drove one truck while Liam was the lead driver. They drove twenty miles from New Haven to the abandoned shopping center. When they arrived, there were dozens of zombies stretched out in front.

Liam stopped the truck and got out. Zack did the same and everyone huddled around Liam.

"This is the plan. We form a line and take out the zombies in the parking lot. Once they're gone, we go to blades only in the store. I would imagine that place is still crawling with zombies, but we want to conserve as much ammo as we can. Understood?"

Everyone nodded.

"Good. Make those headshots count."

Everyone spread out in a line in front of the trucks and Liam held up his hand counting down from three. At one, he whistled getting the zombies' attention and by the time they turned their heads, multiple shots rang out as the group of ten killed every zombie in their path with accurate precision.

When the last zombie in the parking lot fell, Liam raised his hand. "Cease fire! That's the last of them."

The firing stopped and Liam observed the carnage left from their destruction. With a grin, he laughed, "damn, I knew I had a good feeling about y'all. Whew, all of you are top shots."

"Thanks," Sabrina grinned.

Liam winked at her and then looked at Zack. "I'm glad y'all decided to tag along. Sure makes clearing out hordes like these easier."

"I'm just glad we're no longer on the road. Are we looking for anything in particular in the store?"

"No, like I said, food and supplies. Anything that you think would be useful. We don't have to get all of it today. We'll come back here in spurts, collecting various items we think are necessary for the community. We'll split in groups of two."

Anne was about to ask Malcolm before Kelsey grabbed Anne's hand.

"Hey, did you mind tagging along with me?"

Anne rose her brow and replied, "yeah that's cool. Malcolm, I'm going with Kelsey."

"That's fine. Zack and I will just goof off together. Y'all be safe."

"Yell if you need us," Zack added.

"We will. I love you." Kelsey replied. Zack grinned and held the small of Kelsey's back giving her a passionate kiss.

Malcolm held Anne's hand, and stared into her eyes. "We never really talked about how to do a proper goodbye. Should I kiss you or..."

"If you don't kiss me now..." Anne smirked.

Malcolm laughed. "Yes, ma'am." Malcolm leaned forward and placed his lips on Anne's. Once more he was brought to a happy place he didn't want to leave. The kiss heartwarming and lingering, making him want more of her.

Anne felt the same way as she held Malcolm's chin. When he broke away she took a deep breath, shivering as she stared into his eyes.

"Come back to me." She uttered.

"I don't plan on going anywhere." Malcolm replied as he removed his knife from its sheath and placed his flashlight in the other hand. "See you soon."

"Yep, see you soon," Anne replied, watching Malcolm disappear into the store with Zack.

Anne removed her katana, like Kelsey did and held her flashlight on her opposite hand. "You ready?"

"Yeah, let's go."

The duo walked into the store and Kelsey pointed her flashlight at the opposite direction that everyone was walking.

"Hey, Anne, come with me towards the pharmacy section."

"Okay," Anne replied. They both walked in silence shining their lights down the aisle making sure there wasn't any hidden zombies in the store.

"Hey, is there a reason why you asked me to come with you?" Anne asked.

"Yeah, there is. This morning I was sick. At first I thought it was something I ate, but I started adding up the days and I realized that I'm late."

"You serious? Do you think you're pregnant?"

"I'm not sure, but the signs are pointing to it. I wanted to take a pregnancy test here. You know, just to be sure."

"I got you. Have you told Zack yet?"

"No, I wanted to wait until I got the results. No need to raise the red flag if there isn't one to be raised, you know?"

"Yeah, I get you."

Kelsey and Anne walked down the family planning section and Kelsey reviewed the different tests.

"Do you know which one is best?" Kelsey asked.

"Honestly, I have no idea."

"Ugh...I guess I'll just take this one." She grabbed a pink box and pointed to the restroom that was nearby. "Let's go in there."

"Okay." Anne replied.

The two walked into the women's bathroom and Kelsey placed her flashlight on the counter to provide more light in the darkened room.

"So how do you think Zack is going to react?" Anne asked, exploring her surroundings.

"I'm not sure. I mean we always wanted kids, but since the zombie apocalypse, I think having a kid would be impossible. The constant danger, limited doctors and medications. It doesn't bode well for new mothers."

"True, but we are no different from our ancestors. I mean they had to live under all of those conditions and threats and they still managed to have us."

Kelsey laughed opening up the nearest bathroom stall. "I'm pretty sure that..." before she could get her next words out a zombie poured out of the bathroom. Kelsey screamed but quickly dodged its lunge at her. Its arm was missing as it attempted to grab her. For a second, fear gripped her chest as she evaded its grasp. The creature growled, overextended itself to yank Kelsey's blonde hair towards its opened mouth. With a scream, Kelsey yanked her head back, side stepped, and then brought down her sword on the zombie's head.

"Whoa, I guess Liam was right about this place still having the creepy crawlers lurking around. That bitch took some of my hair..." Kelsey claimed looking at the zombie still clutching her blonde locks in its fingers.

"Yeah, it was close. Hurry up and take your test. I'll guard you."

"Okay thanks." Kelsey closed the stall doors and peed on a stick. Once she was done, she walked out and placed it on the counter.

"How long do we wait?" Kelsey asked.

"The package said five minutes."

Anne nodded and looked out in the distance for a minute or two. She turned back to Kelsey and asked, "Is there a gender you prefer to have?"

"Zack and I have discussed a girl, but honestly as long as it's a healthy baby, I don't care."

"Speaking of kids, I feel bad about Keshia. She lost her mother, Sheri last night. How do you think she's taking it?"

"She's buried her emotions. I tried getting her to talk about it today, but it's clear she's dealing with her trauma her own way."

Anne shook her head. "That's sad. She's seen so much death already that she's probably numb to it."

"You're right, it is terrible. Her entire childhood was robbed by these fuckers."

"Perhaps we can make it better. I mean all of us in the house care for Keshia. Perhaps we can do something for her to show her how much we care."

"Yeah, I would like that."

Anne nodded, "do you think it's been five minutes yet?"

"Yeah, I think it has."

Kelsey looked at the test and then back at the box. "What does the double lines mean again?"

Anne reviewed it and grinned, "it means you're pregnant."

"What! Are you serious?" Kelsey shrieked.

Anne nodded.

"Ahh!" Kelsey screamed again as she hugged Anne. "I'm having a baby!"

"Yes, you are! How did you want to tell Zack?"

"Oh I have a fun idea..." Kelsey grinned.

After leaving the bathroom they collected various items from the pharmacy section including prenatal vitamins and put it all inside a crate. When they walked out of the store they found Zack with Malcolm putting away several crates in the truck.

"There you are. We were getting worried when we split up. Where were you two?" Zack asked.

"Oh, we were just getting some items. Including this..." Kelsey flashed him the test and Zack's eyes went big as he stared at her.

"Oh my God. Does that mean..." he pointed to his chest and Kelsey laughed and nodded her head.

"I'm going to be a father! Oh baby! This is the happiest day of my life. I can't wait to take this next step with you."

"Me either."

Zack dragged Kelsey close and kissed her. He then picked her up and spun her around causing her to laugh uncontrollably.

THIRTY-TWO

Kelsey and Zack held hands as they sat in the laboratory. Zack's leg was bouncing endlessly until Kelsey placed her hand on his thigh.

"Hey, are you okay?"

"Yes, just nervous."

Kelsey laughed. "Captain Zack Morris is nervous? Now I really know it's the end of the world."

"Hey..."

"It's funny. You have to laugh a little bit."

Zack chuckled and then looked at Kelsey's blue eyes. He rubbed her cheek and kissed her. "You're right. It was funny."

"What are you nervous about?"

"Being a dad. I mean if you really are pregnant. What type of father would I be? You know me and my old man never got along. What if I'm like him?"

"You're nothing like your father. You're a good man. You're going to make an excellent father."

Zack grinned and kissed Kelsey again. "Thanks babe."

The two stared at each other until Emily walked in.

"Hey, I got your blood work."

"And?"

Emily nodded. "You are pregnant. Congrats."

"Babe!" Kelsey shrieked.

"I know!" Zack grinned as he hugged her.

"I'm happy for the both of you. Kelsey, in the next coming days, you and I will work out the details in your pregnancy. You're still in your first trimester, so you can do a lot of things you were doing before, but I wouldn't push myself. When we get towards the second and third trimester, I don't think you should leave the compound. Just to be safe."

"I agree," Zack admitted. "Honestly, I don't think you should leave New Heaven at all now."

"Seriously, Zack? You can't bench me. You heard Emily, I should be fine the first couple of months."

"True, but outside these walls it's dangerous."

"I know but we just got here. We are still trying to prove that we belong. Let me help. What would I be if I just sat around playing house. You know me. That's not me. Please. All I ask for is two months. Two months of putting in the work to prove to these people that I'm no slob. After that, I'll stick around the house."

Zack crossed his arms and stared at his wife. He didn't like the idea of her risking her life outside the walls however she did have a point. They were new to the community and the last thing they needed was trouble and people whispering that they weren't pulling their weight.

"Fine. Two months, no more. Also if you're going out, Sabrina, Malcolm , Victor or me need to be with you at all times. It's not that I don't trust Liam and his people, I just know we'd look after you."

"Understood."

"And if Emily tells us you need to stop, then you stop. Got it?"

"Got it."

"Good," Zack grinned. "Thanks Emily. See you at dinner?"

"Yes, I'm going to hang back and work with Dr. Bruce a bit more. We are really making headway understanding this zombie virus."

Zack nodded, waved goodbye and then held Kelsey's hand as they left the infirmary.

The couple walked through the community of New Haven waving at the people walking around. Everyone seemed friendly to their new arrivals. To Zack it felt weird to wear just jeans and a shirt, as the last couple of months he was always wearing his military fatigues.

"What do you think of New Haven?" Kelsey asked.

"It's nice. Honestly it's better than what I thought it would be. It's a good community that we could raise a family in. I just wished Sheri was here to see it. She always talked about a place like this."

"I agree." Kelsey said.

"How do you feel about losing her?"

"I still feel like shit. Skipper told me to watch out for her, and I failed that. She died on my watch. I failed the mission. I never fail."

"Oh, Zack. You haven't failed yet. There's still Keshia. She's without parents."

"Yeah, I know. It's terrible."

Kelsey nodded and placed her head on his shoulder. "Zack, I was thinking. Keshia doesn't have anyone here. Did you want to adopt her?"

"Adopt?"

"Yes, she doesn't have any parents and you and I can take care of her. Watch out for her and help raise her. I figure it would be good practice for us because we got another one in the oven."

Zack grinned. "Yeah, I like that. Do you think she would want us as parents?"

"Of course! She's in love with you."

Zack chuckled. "True. I guess we should tell her the good news."

"Yeah, she'd like that. She's been up in her room since we got here."

Zack nodded and the couple continued to walk to home. When they got in they went upstairs to Keshia's room and knocked on the door.

"Yes?" She asked.

"May we come in?"

"Yes," Keshia replied.

Zack and Kelsey walked in and Keshia was in bed watching tv.

"Hey, how are you feeling?" Zack asked, sitting on the bed.

"Okay, I still miss my mommy."

"I know you do. We do too. We were actually talking about that... with your mom gone we wanted to know how you would feel if we watched over you?" Zack asked.

Keshia's brow moved. "What do you mean?"

"Well, sweetie..." Kelsey paused and sat beside her. "While we know we can never replace your mom or dad, we wanted to adopt you as our own. You know just to watch out for you. Would you like that?"

Keshia smiled and nodded. "Yes, I would." She replied. She hugged Kelsey.

"Ahh," Kelsey exclaimed, looking at Zack smiling. Zack returned the gesture before leaning forward and hugging Keshia too.

"I know it's been rough the last couple of days, so if you need anything. Let us know."

"Well, there is one thing..."

"What's that?"

"I want to pay respects to my mommy. I want to do one last final goodbye."

Kelsey and Zack looked at each other and nodded. Kelsey held Keshia tighter and replied, "I think that's a great idea, sweetie."

THIRTY-THREE

"Here's to Sheri, Sophia, and Richard. They gave their lives so that we could have ours." Zack replied, raising his glass up.

"To Sheri, Sophia, and Richard." Everyone replied.

Everyone took a sip of their beverages. Most of the beverages were alcohol accept for Kelsey's and Keshia.

The group of survivors stood in their house, in a celebration of life ceremony for the lives that were lost on their journey to New Haven. They quietly all took a sip and then smiled at each other.

"Keshia, how are you feeling?" Zack asked.

"I miss her, but I know I'm loved here."

"Oh, you are!" Kelsey replied, hugging Keshia.

"It's different without her. She would have liked it here."

"This was what she was fighting for." Zack admitted. "I promise we won't let her death be wasted."

"Thank you."

Zack gave her a small smile and then looked towards Liam who was also in the room, " Liam, thank you for being here. You didn't have to."

"I wanted to be here. I feel bad that we didn't arrive sooner to assist you all."

"You came at the right time. If you didn't come we would've all been dead. Thank you," Zack replied.

"Keshia, are you ready to light this lantern for your mother?"

"I am."

The group walked into the backyard of the house where three paper lanterns were lying on the ground. Zack held the lantern that Keshia decorated for her mother, and Kelsey helped Keshia to light it before sending it up in the sky. Malcolm and Anne lit the lantern for Sophia, while Emily and Victor lit the light for Richard. Once all three lanterns were lit, they launched them into the sky, and watched the bright lights rise lighting up the darkness.

"Let these lights carry their souls to heaven..." Zack replied, watching the lanterns rise higher and higher with the wind. "...allowing their souls to finally find peace. Amen."

Keshia wiped her tears away and clung to Kelsey's leg.

Kelsey rubbed her back as she cried as well. The group stood silently watching the lights rise in the sky until they were too far to see any more. Afterwards they all walked in from the sobering moment.

"I needed that," Anne added, wiping her tears away.

"Yeah, me too. I felt like that was a good way to respect the dead." Emily added.

"There are other ways that we can remember them. Drinking. Who wants a shot?" Victor asked.

Everyone rose their hands except Keshia and Kelsey. Kelsey placed her hand on Keshia's shoulder and smiled, "I think that's our cue to head to bed. How about we lay in the room and watch some cartoons until we pass out?"

"That sounds amazing." Keshia grinned.

"Come on." Kelsey led Keshia away from the group and stopped near her husband. "Have fun. I'll see you upstairs. I love you."

"I love you too," Zack replied, kissing her.

Kelsey and Keshia left as Victor finished pouring shots for Malcolm, Anne, Sabrina, Liam, Emily and Zack. He poured himself some vodka and then place the bottle in the center of the table that they stood around.

"To the fallen."

"To the fallen..." everyone repeated and then everyone took a long swig.

"Oh, that's good. When did you find that, Liam?" Malcolm asked, looking at the shot glass.

"A week ago. You know one good thing about the zombie apocalypse is all the top shelf stuff is extremely cheap these days."

"You mean the five-finger discount?" Sabrina joked.

"Yeah, something like that," Liam winked. "Who wants another round?"

Almost everyone rose their hands as Liam went around the table pouring out drinks. Two shots led to three to four to five, as the group began to feel the effects of the alcohol.

Liam burped. "Any one down for another?"

Sabrina and Zack rose their hands as Liam walked over to them and poured the shots.

"One for you, beautiful," he smirked at Sabrina.

"Oh, now I know you're really drunk if you're hitting on me?"

"Why do I have to be drunk to know when I see a beautiful woman in front of me?"

"Yeah, he's drunk..." Zack replied, taking his additional shot. "I'd be careful. Those looks could kill."

"It's okay. I'm nowhere near water. You Navy SEALs have no effect on me."

"Is that a challenge?" Sabrina grinned with her eyebrow arched.

"Maybe. Maybe not. I would hate to kick your ass in front of your squad."

"I eat Army rangers for breakfast."

"How about a quick sparing match outside. See who walks away?"

"You're on."

"Oh! You're going to need a referee!" Zack yelled as he followed the two outside. The rest of the group laughed and Anne shook her head.

"That is not going to end well."

"I agree. I bet my rations that Sabrina would kick his ass." Emily replied.

"Pssh, Sabrina is all hot air. I beat her when we spare. She's not that great." Victor replied.

"You're saying that because she's a woman?" Emily questioned.

"No, I'm saying that because she has a tell. You could see it a mile away. You know what. I'll take that action. Make it two rations though. I'm a hungry boy."

"You're on!" Emily grinned shaking his hand.

"So, Emily it's been a while since we caught up. It seems like you're buried in the lab all day. How is that?" Anne asked.

"It's good. Dr. Bruce's research rivals my own. He has this mega brain. It's almost superhuman. I think with the two of us we can crack it. I mean we were already coming up with solutions to our problems that we both had."

"That's good," Anne replied.

The sounds of shouts from Zack could be heard as Victor stood up and looked out the window.

"It looks like they stared and Liam has the upper hand."

"What!" Emily yelled getting up. She stared at the window and shook her head. "That's because she has no one in her corner." Emily walked outside and yelled, "Come on, Sabrina! Kick that man's ass!"

Victor followed Emily and laughed. "Come on, Liam. I really don't want to miss out on two meals."

Anne laughed and placed her head in Malcolm's shoulder.

"That Victor..." Malcolm smirked. "Did you want to head out there and watch?"

"We could...you know...we could retire early?" Anne grabbed the nape of Malcolm's neck and leaned forward giving him a sensual kiss. Malcolm didn't have to read her mind to know what she wanted.

"Yeah, let's call it a night," he grinned.

Before the door was even closed to their bedroom, Malcolm and Anne were on top of each other. Kissing, they fell into the bed and hastily removed their clothes. Malcolm kissed Anne and then worked his way down to her neck, sucking her skin. Anne closed her eyes and moaned as her hand drifted lower to Malcolm's crotch.

She softly jerked off Malcolm and he groaned, closing his eyes.

"How does that feel?"

"Amazing."

"Yeah..." Anne lowered herself to his cock and sucked on its tip.

After a few seconds she gasped, and jerked him off. "What about now?" She seductive grinned.

"Even better..." Malcolm breathed as his body tingled.

Anne smirked and then lowered herself to his dick once more sucking him off. Malcolm groaned and softly massaged Anne's body as he enjoyed her oral. His fingers crept to her wet center and then entered her. Anne moaned as she felt his fingers touch her. She loved the way they slid in and out of her.

Malcolm grabbed her hips and lifted her towards his mouth. While Anne sat on his face, Malcolm leaned forward and he ate her out. He groaned tasting her juices. Anne's body shuddered and she closed her eyes as her body quivered from the pleasure collapsing into her.

"Oh, Malcolm..." she muttered. Her hand kept softly stroking him as her pleasure grew. Every so often she would place him in her mouth but by the second it was becoming harder and harder too. She was on a pleasure cruise and she didn't plan on getting off.

Ecstasy poured across her, and there was no escape. Her legs buckled, her breathing became shallow, and her heartbeat tripled. Her world was spinning and she couldn't stop it. Her small beige fingers clenched his bulky dark thighs. They pressed hard into his skin, leaving an deep imprint, but he didn't stop his relentless assault. He didn't let the pain detour him from his goal. He wanted her. He wanted to listen to her moan. He wanted to feel her squirm. He wanted to taste her come.

Laying there, Anne was smitten and paralyzed by her own pleasure. She closed her eyes feeling the rush that stared in her toes going through her spine and hitting every nerve she had in her body.

Minutes later in their shared oral experience, Anne came. Her body trembled from her passionate orgasm that rocked her to her core. She rolled off Malcolm's body and planted a deep kiss on his lips before sliding onto his dick.

Riding him, the two shared a close embrace. The passion and love the two shared was shown from the way they kissed and held each other. Emotions were shared as Anne rolled her hips up and down. She placed her hand on his buff chest and her mouth was agape as the pleasure coursed through her veins. He took her breath away as a silent celebration left her lips.

Malcolm squeezed and held her ass, as he laid there gazing upon her beauty. He gasped and bit his lips as waves of pleasure swelled in his body. He was adrift in an ocean of warm feelings he didn't want to leave.

She opened her hips wide and rhythmically swayed. Lying there, Malcolm couldn't do anything but smile. Anne was like a priceless work of art. She was exotic, stunning and awe-inspiring. Malcolm didn't even know what to do with his hands as she watched her work. The woman knew how to shake it. The way her curves shook were hypnotic. Like an addict all he wanted was more.

Slowly his hands crawled up her shapely thighs, they rolled across her beige hips, to her plump ass. He gently slapped her cheeks and Anne squealed from the playful tap.

She leaned forward and whispered into her ear, "You like that?"

"Yeah, baby..." Malcolm muttered from the sensation.

"How does it feel?" She asked, slowly jerking his cock in a circle with her hips.

"Amazing. You are..." Malcolm pushed back Anne's black hair, behind her ear and stared into her brown eyes. "...Fucking Amazing."

"Then prove it to me. Fuck me."

Malcolm grinned and held her hips and powered into her. Anne moaned and closed her eyes from the aggressive strikes that Malcolm gave. The bed creaked and rocked from his quick bursts. With his eyes narrowed, Malcolm looked like a madman. His mind was blank. He didn't think of anything but her. She was his woman and he planned on satisfying her to her fullest.

Malcolm wrapped his arms around her back and tossed her in the bed, to be on top. He held her leg up to his shoulder and pumped into her at a rapid pace. Reaching up, Malcolm grabbed her breast and squeezed it.

"Yes, that's it, baby. Fucking take me..." Anne encouraged as their sex became more physical.

Malcolm grinned as his hand drifted lower to her exposed clit. His thumb pressed her delicate bud and Anne's back arch as a new round of pleasure entered her system. Her eyes rolled in the back of the head as her body involuntary flailed.

"Oh, Malcolm." Anne wheezed. Her eyes were closed and her breath was ragged. Her mind was scattered as she laid there taking Malcolm's thickness. She wondered why it took her so long to be with him. She felt like a fool to be missing out on this performance. Malcolm was like no other and she loved that. For the second time that night she came.

Looking down, Malcolm thought he was with an Angel. Something about the glow that Anne gave send him to a place he never thought was possible. With her, Malcolm thought heaven was on earth. There's nothing like watching her skin glisten with sweat from their passionate session or the way she moaned his name. Each one of them, drove Malcolm to completion.

He held her tightly as his body spasmed. With a groan he released inside Anne. When he was spent he pulled out of her and held her face cheek. He kissed her and looked into her eyes.

"I'm so happy that you're in my life."

"So am I." Anne grinned.

Malcolm smiled back at her and gave her another final kiss before laying in his side of the bed and falling asleep.

———

THE NEXT MORNING, Anne woke up with a naked Malcolm draped over here. This was the second time she woke up like this and she didn't want it any other way. Anne kissed Malcolm's cheek and headed downstairs for a cup of coffee.

Anne found Kelsey reading a book while Keshia was watching tv in the living room. Anne grabbed a cup and poured its contents in a mug.

"How did you sleep last night."

"Okay, but pregnancy ain't no joke. I threw up again last night."

"I'm sorry."

"It's cool. Part of the game I guess. Did you know what happened last night? Zack came in late last night."

"Not really. Malcolm and I went to bed early last night."

"Bullshit."

"You really can't just let me have the lie?"

"Nope. Not when your fucking one of my friends."

Anne laughed and shook her head. Before she could say something else, they heard footsteps and saw Sabrina and Liam. Both had black eyes as they smiled and looked each other in the eyes.

"I guess I'll see you at the start of our watch?" Sabrina grinned.

A guilty smile spread on Sabrina's face as she rubbed the back of her head. "Yeah. Last night was fun. We should do that again some time."

"Yeah we should," Sabrina smirked. Just looking at the two, Anne knew something else went on other than a boxing match.

"See you soon?"

"Yeah sure." Liam replied before kissing Sabrina's cheek. The two held a lingering stare before Liam left the house with a toothy grin on his face.

Sabrina walked to the coffee pot and poured herself a cup.

"Good morning, ladies."

"Good morning indeed." Kelsey smirked. "Oh, I can't take the suspense. Did y'all fuck?"

Sabrina nodded taking a sip of her coffee. "He was good. Really good."

"So, wait how did this happen?" Anne asked.

"We'll, after y'all went to *bed*,"

"Hey, we really did go to sleep." Anne interjected.

"*Sure*. Anyways. When y'all left. We play fought and I won. So naturally were both licking our wounds. He's shirtless. I'm shirtless next thing we know we're doings the horizontal cha-cha."

They all laughed and as they did, Emily and Victor walked down the steps.

"Be sure to visit me in my lab, okay?"

"Yeah, I'll be there today. It was fun last night."

"It sure was." Emily kissed Victor and left. The threesome watching it all had their jaws drop.

"What! When did this happen?" Kelsey asked Victor who was getting himself a cup of coffee as well.

"Last night. After I lost my bet we changed the terms to sex and let's just say that Emily and I are together now."

"Yep, now I know this world went to hell if Emily hooked up with you." Sabrina joshed.

"Hey now, I'm not that bad."

"Ehh…" Sabrina shrugged and everyone laughed.

"Hey, now I least I got some last night. I like Emily, I want to see where this goes."

"Hey, No need for bragging. I got some too." Sabrina added.

Victor laughed, "With Liam?"

Sabrina nodded.

"Oh, you sly dog. Anne did you get some?"

"A lady never kissed and tells."

"Yeah, Malcolm and her hooked up again."

"I can't confirm or deny."

"Hey, that's usually my line." Sabrina mocked.

The group laughed again before Kelsey shouted, "Wait. Oh my God, I can't be the only one who didn't have sex last night. What is the world coming to?" Kelsey asked.

The foursome all looked at each other and shared a big laugh.

THIRTY-FOUR

K
eshia sat in the swing by herself watching the other kids play.
They were playing warriors versus zombies. One side would
growl and act like zombies while the other side would fight
them off. Keshia observed them with intensity as memories of her own
fight against zombies replayed in her mind. Unlike the children in the
gated community, they never had to be out in the world like she had to.
They never had to actually fight to stay alive. They never had to lose a
loved one.

They were all naïve.

Since joining the school, she excelled in learning the surviving tips.
Keshia even proved to know a thing or two that the teachers didn't even
know about. What she lacked was the social interaction. Before the fall,
she was always a social butterfly, but after losing her mother and father,
she became a shell of her former self.

Sitting there alone, she frowned. She missed the way the world was.
She missed playing soccer in her backyard with her parents, and going
out to the movies with them. She even missed the times they disciplined
her, because even then they were still present in her life. She missed her
parents' love. It wasn't that Zack and Kelsey did a bad job, it was just the
smaller touches she missed. Like the kisses on the head from her dad, or

the warm hugs she got at night from her mom. The little things were what she missed most about her parents.

Keshia didn't notice her teacher, Mrs. Lewis, sit next to her. She was an older black woman, with grey hair and a round face. She gripped the swing chains and gave Keshia a small smile.

"Is everything okay, Keshia?"

"Yeah, I'm just watching everyone play zombies versus warriors."

"Did you want to join? I'm sure they would let you play."

"No, thank you. Why play the game when I lived it."

Mrs. Lewis paused and nodded. "That's a good point. Did you want me to swing with you?"

Keshia shrugged. "If you want."

Mrs. Lewis nodded and slowly pumped her legs back and forth.

"I've enjoyed having you in my class this week. I know it's been hard on you with all of these changes, but you've taken them well."

"Thank you."

Mrs. Lewis nodded. "How's home life? I know Zack and Kelsey Morris have been your guardians."

"It's good. I've known Zack all of my life. He and my father were good friends in the Navy. It's different now because he's watching over me."

"Yeah, it's tough being without your birth parents. I would know. Did I ever tell you that I was adopted?"

Keshia's brown eyes opened wide as she stared at her teacher.

Mrs. Lewis chuckled. "Yes, I didn't know my birth parents, but I was adopted when I was a baby. Like you my parents were both white. Growing up, it was tough because I always got stared at. My parents got the worst of it because they were raising a black baby in a time where different races stayed apart from each other. As a kid, I knew they weren't my parents, and I even thought about running away a couple of times."

"Did you?"

"No, I learned eventually that no matter what people say, those were my parents and they loved me no matter what."

"How long did it take you to feel that way?"

"Years, but trust me it will eventually come. From what I've seen, Zack and Kelsey are good people. Just give it some time, okay?"

Keshia nodded.

"Is there anything else I can do to make you feel more welcomed?"

Keshia thought about telling her that today was her 8th birthday, but decided against it. She shook her head.

"No, I'm fine."

Mrs. Lewis nodded, and stopped swinging. "I'll be in the classroom if you need anything else. School is about to be over and Zack or Kelsey should be picking you up soon. Remember, if you ever want to talk, I'm here."

Mrs. Lewis waved goodbye before leaving Keshia.

Keshia studied her teacher as she walked up to a group of boys and talked to them about something.

Sighing, Keshia resumed swinging until she heard Zack's Texas twang.

"Keshia!"

"Zack!" Keshia grinned, hopping off the swings. She gave him a big hug along with Kelsey who was also standing there.

"Are you ready to go?"

"Yep! Bye Mrs. Lewis!" Keshia waved.

Mrs. Lewis looked up and waved goodbye watching Zack, Kelsey and Keshia walk away. Leaving the school house the threesome walked on the sidewalk of the community towards their shared home.

"How was school?" Zack asked. Standing beside him was Kelsey who had an equally expressive grin.

"It was good." Keshia gave a half smile. "We learned how to create fires, but I already knew how to do that. I ended up having to teach the entire class how to do it."

Zack chuckled. "Sounds like Skipper taught you well."

"He did." Keshia gave a small smile as once more she was reminded of what she'd lost.

"Did you play with the other kids?" Kelsey questioned.

"Yeah, I did." Keshia lied.

Kelsey and Zack looked at each other. They didn't have to say a word to know that she was lying.

"Did anyone say happy birthday?" Kelsey inquired.

"No, I didn't tell anyone that it was my birthday."

"Why not?"

"There's no point. I don't want to get close to anyone, because what happens if this place falls like Little Creek did. What happens if we get attacked again. There's no point."

Zack narrowed his eyes and stopped walking. He kneeled in front of Keshia, and held her hands.

"Keshia, no. Don't you go down that road. Don't think like that. Sure, we got dealt a crap hand, but there's still life in our lungs. Your parents wouldn't want you to stop living life. Yeah, there's no guarantees about this place, but as long as we're together, we're home."

"Zack is right." Kelsey grinned. "We're family. No matter what happens. We love you."

Zack nodded and unexpectedly hugged Keshia. She was surprised at first by the gesture but it quickly felt familiar to her as she hugged Zack back. Kelsey joined in the duo's hug wrapping her arms around Keshia.

"We love you, Keshia. Don't forget that." Kelsey whispered.

Keshia closed her eyes and felt the warmth of Kelsey and Zack. Their hug, although foreign, was a gentle reminder of what she lost. Her mind then thought of her mom and dad, and the thing that Mrs. Lewis said about loving her adoptive parents. Right there, she realized that she was glad that Zack and Kelsey were in her life.

After their lingering hug, Zack and Kelsey both smiled and held Keshia's hands.

"How about we head back to the house. We have something we want to show you."

"Okay." Keshia grinned.

The threesome walked another block before heading towards their home. Opening the door, Keshia was surprised as the lights of the house turned on and everyone shouted, "surprise!"

Keshia giggled with glee as Malcolm, Anne, Sabrina, Victor, Emily and Liam were all in the room with large smiles on their faces. Behind them was a large banner that said Happy Birthday, a cake and multiple presents.

Keshia's jaw dropped as she looked back at Zack and Kelsey. "A birthday party?"

"How could we not throw one?" Kelsey smiled. "We knew you had a tough couple of months, so we wanted to give you something positive."

"Wow! Look of all this stuff, and cake too! How did you manage to bake a cake?"

Liam chuckled. "That's my present to you, Kelsey. I managed to find some cake mix on our last scavenger hunt. After bartering for some eggs and milk from our local farmers, I was able to bake it."

Sabrina elbowed Liam hard and he gave her a small smile. "Correction, Sabrina and me both baked it."

Sabrina winked at Keshia and then grabbed a small box on the table. "This one is from me."

Keshia smile triple as she stared at the box. "Oh, can I open presents first?"

Kelsey chuckled. "Of course you can, sweetie. It's your party. You can do what you want."

Sabrina rose her eyebrows and smirked. "Go ahead."

Keshia squealed and quickly wrapped the box, throwing wrapping paper everywhere. Unboxing the item, she gave Sabrina a questionable stare, holding up the empty gun holster.

"What is it?"

"It's a side arm gun hostler. I had to make some adjustments so that it could fit your leg, but it should fit."

"So I can start shooting? No one in my class is doing this!" Keshia beamed.

"Yes, I will teach you, assuming it's okay with Kelsey and Zack."

Kelsey nodded while Zack chuckled, "Of course. I was shooting squirrel in my backyard when I was her age."

"Really going all in on that Texas stereotype, bruh..." Malcolm quipped.

Zack stuck out his tongue towards Malcolm and everyone laughed.

"Can I wear it now?" Keshia asked.

"Sure, I'll help you put it on." Sabrina grabbed the hostler and tied it against her leg.

"There you go, you're a regular cowgirl." Sabrina commented.

Keshia laughed with joy as she inspected the new item on her hip.

"Speaking of which, I know something that is going to look great on your belt. Open this one next." Malcolm added, handing Keshia a long-shaped item wrapped in cloth and tied with a string bow. Keshia untied the knot and opened the gift. Inside was a small knife sheathed in leather pouch.

"Wow! My own knife!"

"Yep, it's a great utility knife, plus it's good for protection. Remember that's not a toy. It's sharp."

"I know." Keshia replied, adding the knife to her belt loop.

Malcolm nodded.

"Here, open mine," Victor replied.

The package was small, and took little time to unwrap. Keshia smiled, inspecting the small red metal compass in her hand.

"Do you like it?" Victor asked her.

"I love it."

"It's so that you'd always find your way home."

"Thank you so much." Keshia clipped the compass to her belt and saw Emily approach her with a microscope with a green bow attached to it.

"Sorry, I didn't have time to wrap this."

"While I didn't get you a gun or knife, I did get you something cool. It's a microscope, it's a tool I use to view something up close. I can see tiny microorganisms that are naked to the eye. When I was your age I got one of these and I've been hooked to science ever since."

"Wow..." Keshia looked into the viewing tube and then smiled back at Emily.

"I love it."

"Great. When you have time I can bring in some samples in and we can check out some cool creepy crawlers."

"I'd love that!" She shrieked.

Emily gave Keshia a small smile before retreating back to Victor. She placed her arms around him and held him tightly watching the young girl play with the knobs on the device.

"Here you go, Keshia. This is from me." Anne replied, handing her a gift bag.

Keshia peeked her head inside and squealed. "Clothes!"

"Yes, I had to guess your sizes based on what you have. If nothing fits we can always exchange them. I'll just get more. We got shopping for days now." Everyone laughed including Keshia who was placing a pair of jeans up on her body.

"No, I love them. This is so cool!"

"If you think that is cool, check this out," Kelsey replied, handing her a training sword.

"What is it?"

"It's a shinai or a kendo training sword. It's made of bamboo."

"Wow..." Keshia replied, looking at the object. Her eyes then grew wide as she looked back at Kelsey. "Wait, does that mean I'm going to learn kendo?"

"Yep, daily lessons will start soon. Are you ready?"

"Yes! Oh, I can't wait to be a warrior like you and Anne."

Anne and Kelsey shared a look before smiling back at Keshia.

"I'm happy to train you." Kelsey replied.

"There's one last gift." Zack added. "This is from me, Charles and Sheri."

Keshia gave a strange look to Zack before unwrapping the gift. As soon as she saw it she shrieked.

"A karaoke machine!"

"Yep! This is the one you wanted, right?"

"Yes! How did you know?"

"Charles and I had a lot of conversations about you Keshia. I know that it's tough with Kelsey and me, but know that we're going to be there for you."

"Thank you! I love it." Keshia smiled giving Zack a big hug.

Zack chuckled and rubbed Keshia's back. "You're welcome."

The rest of the night was filled with singing and dancing as everyone had a turn with the karaoke machine. As Keshia sang her favorite Taylor Swift song, she grinned at her Zack and Kelsey. While she knew that they could never replace her mom and dad, she knew that she was lucky to have them in her life.

THIRTY-FIVE

Malcolm smiled as he watched Anne sleeping. For the last three weeks, Anne and him had been sleeping together. Every night was the same. They would go to bed. He would kiss her. She would kiss him. Next thing he knew they were both naked, making love. He loved having sex with her. There was something about being with Anne that made his stomach turn. She knew how to touch him and how to kiss him. Every inch of her drove him insane and like a love crazed man he had to have her.

Every night that they laid together was special with him. Laying in bed. He remembered the last night that they shared. Something about the curve of her ass, as he took her from behind made his blood rush. The memory alone was making him hard again.

Caught up in his sexual fantasies, there was a knock at the door, and Malcolm heard Victor's voice.

"Hey Malcolm, are you up?"

"Yeah...what's going on?"

"Emily needs another live test subject for her research. I need your help to catch them."

"Yeah sure, let me get dressed. Meet you downstairs in five?"

"Yeah, sounds good."

Malcolm could hear Victor leave the door. He turned to Anne who woke up.

"Be safe out there." Anne mumbled.

"Always am. I'll see you later today?"

Anne nodded and then kissed him. Malcolm smiled and rubbed her cheek before leaving the bed. Walking around the room, he grabbed his underwear, jeans, shirt and placed his tactical vest over his shirt.

"I'll see you soon. Bye," Malcolm waved.

"Yep, see you."

Malcolm smiled at Anne once more before leaving the room. As he walked downstairs, Malcolm felt weird saying goodbye to Anne like that. While he's not sure he loved her, he did have feelings for her, and the way they said goodbye felt like they were still friends, but they were more than that. They were together. Shouldn't they have a more romantic goodbye, he wondered.

Victor was waiting for Malcolm downstairs and grinned when he spotted him.

"You ready?"

"Yeah, let's go."

The two left the house with their rifles in tow and headed to the nearest gate. Malcolm followed Victor and they hiked through the woods looking for a zombie.

"How's you and Anne doing?" Victor asked, pushing bush out of his path.

"We're good. Every night I fall asleep with a smile on my face and every morning I wake up with one. Anne she's one of a kind. I've never been with a woman like her. It's a shame that it took a zombie apocalypse for us to get together. I often wonder what if we found each other before the fall. What would our relationship be before."

"I often think the same thing with Emily. I mean on paper we don't mix. A smart scientist like her and a military grunt like me. The odds of us being together are low, but yet here we are. I have a strong relationship with her now. I fucking love that woman."

"Really? Things are that good?"

"Yeah they are. Emily she's like no other woman I've ever met."

"This is saying something considering how much you got around before all of this."

"Hey now..."

"I'm just saying. You've grown. A one-woman man? That's impressive."

"Thanks, it's just that Emily gets me. She makes me smile. Makes me want to be around her. Makes me want to run through a fucking brick wall for her. She does all those things. It's hard to explain..."

"No, I get you. Anne makes me feel the same way. Ha, who would've thought we'd have two special women in our lives?"

"Not me. Now that I have her though, I can't see myself any other way."

"Me either, Bruh."

The two soldiers came up to a clearing and saw three zombies roaming.

Zack tapped Victor's shoulder and gave him a silent command. Victor understood and replied with his own. The two Navy SEALs tracked the zombies' path and then advanced ahead of them. Crouching down they aimed at the crowd coming toward them.

"You want left or right?" Victor whispered.

"You go left. I got right. On three..."

The two soldiers didn't need to count down out loud. They've done this countless of times against foes. At three seconds both fired and killed their respective zombies leaving one left alive.

"You got him?" Malcolm asked.

"Yeah, you go." Victor replied.

Malcolm nodded and backtracked away from the path that the zombie was heading. Victor did the opposite as he walked casually towards it.

"Umm excuse me, you wouldn't happen to know where the nearest McDonald's is? I would kill for a Big Mac?"

The zombie growled and charged at Victor. However, Victor stood relaxed as it got closer. Before it could lay a finger on Victor, Malcolm roped the zombie like a cowboy as he strung up the zombie. He pulled the zombie down to his back and then hog tied its arms and legs with the rope. He then removed a large black body bag from his backpack and pushed the zombie inside.

"Easy as pie." Malcolm breathed.

"Easy for you to say, you're not the one being live bait."

"But you can't swing the rope like I can." Malcolm winked.

"Says the guy who isn't from Texas. Don't get cocky. The only reason why Zack isn't here is because he prefers missions with Liam and Sabrina."

"Oh, now you're just breaking this Cowboy's heart. You're telling me I'm second string?"

"More like third. I think Kelsey can rope too, but Zack thinks this is too dangerous for her. Thus I'm stuck with your ass."

"Ouch. Words hurt you know."

The two looked at each other and laughed, before Malcolm began to drag the body bag.

"Ugh, this is the worst part."

"Tell me about it. Come on, they're waiting for us."

The two dragged the zombie a mile back to the infirmary compound. As they did, they got strange looks from the citizens as they saw the large black bag kicking and moving.

"Don't mind us. Just another delivery to the doctors." Victor waved. Most people turned their heads and others looked disgusted at their actions.

"Well, we're certainly not the most popular people." Malcolm commented, judging everyone's stares.

"No, we are not." Victor chuckled. "It's fine, they won't be judging us once we come up with a cure. Then we'd be considered heroes."

"Oh, I like the sound of that. Heroes get laid, right?"

"All the time."

The two men chuckled and entered the infirmary. They took the zombie to the lab where Dr. López and Dr. Bruce were discussing something with great excitement. Like Dr. López, Dr. Bruce was wearing a white lab coat over a pair of jeans and a shirt. The doctor was in his sixties and had a white hair ponytail that reached his back shoulders.

When Emily saw Victor she squealed and leaped into his arms to kiss him.

"Whoa, now if delivering you fresh zombies turns you on, I will start doing that every day."

Emily laughed and then kissed him once more. "It's not the zombie that I'm excited about. It's the cure. Dr. Bruce and I think we finally managed to make a headway."

Victor's eyes opened wide as he looked at Dr. Bruce. "Wait, are you serious?"

Dr. Bruce chuckled. "Yes, so far the simulations are showing positive reactions. Of course, this is just a computer simulation. We won't know how the cure reacts to tainted blood until we test it against our new guest."

"Did you want us to put this guy in his restraints?"

"Yes, please. Dr. López, while they do that, let's prepare a sample for a trial run."

"Yes, of course." The two doctors walked towards the computer and began typing. Seconds later, a machine beside it began humming as it began to synthesize the chemicals together.

"A'ight, just like before." Malcolm muttered as he unzipped the black bag.

"Easy for you to say, you're not the one who has to push the fucker onto the bed."

"We can easily switch. You want to be the one to hold it down while it tries biting you?"

"Point taken."

"Okay, we do this in three. I hold it down while you strap it down."

"Yep, I got it."

He counted down to three and then opened the bag. The zombie kicked and groaned attempting to grab Malcolm, but he was quicker, as he picked up the specimen and shoved it on a gurney.

"Strap him down! Strap him down!" Malcolm yelled.

The zombie came close to biting Malcolm several times as he narrowly avoided the deadly bites each time. Victor placed the leather straps around the zombie's arms, chest and legs pinning it to the bed.

"Okay I'm done."

"Whew, that was close."

Victor nodded and then turned towards Emily.

"The zombie is ready."

"Good. So are we." Emily replied, walking with a needle. She drew some blood from the zombie and looked at its contents. Inside the vial was its black opaque blood. She brought it towards Dr.Bruce who was studying the cure through a microscope.

"I have the cure, Doctor."

"Perfect. If this works, then we could save humankind. Instead of me watching this, how about we put this on the big screen so that we can all watch."

Dr. Bruce tapped a few buttons on the microscope and on a tv beside him, a projection of what he saw was on the screen.

"So Malcolm and Victor. This is the cure. In its pure form, it's blue. It's full of antibodies that were designed to kill the virus, stopping the effects of a zombie bite."

"So this won't cure the current zombies?" Malcolm asked.

"No, those who turn can't be saved. They have too many underlying injuries to survive the turn back to human. This cure will only be for those who have survived so far."

Malcolm frowned but Dr. Bruce smiled at his reaction.

"It's a sad truth but it's worth it. Think of how it would turn the tide of this war against the zombies. If we are no longer turning due to bites, we can finally get a chance to be on offense instead of defense. We can take back this country."

"Good point. So what are we expecting to see?"

"The antibodies should destroy the virus upon contact. Once I add this blood to the cure, you'll see the effects on the screen. Dr. López, if you would?" Dr. Bruce asked.

Emily took a deep breath and did a silent prayer hoping that this would work. She squirted the contents into the cure and everyone watched with bated breath as the antibodies fought against the cells in the zombie's blood. At first the blue and black blood was indistinguishable, but minutes later the entire sample turned red.

"It looks like blood now. Did the antibodies work?" Victor asked.

Dr. Bruce studied the blood sample and muttered to himself as he focused the microscope on the cells in the blood.

"I'll be..." he whispered. "Dr. López, could you check this sample? Please say what I'm thinking. Did we do it?"

Emily's eyes opened wide as she studied the cell structure. "Oh, my God. We did it."

"Did what?" Victor asked.

"We found a cure."

"Oh babe! What are we waiting for. Shoot me up with that stuff."

"Victor, it doesn't work like that. We still have to do additional tests and..."

"Wait! Look..." Dr. Bruce pointed at the screen where the red blood began turning black again. "Fuck. Dammit," he cursed as he reviewed the cells once more. He looked at Dr. López and shook his head. "They reverted."

"Wait, I thought the cure worked."

"It did work, but it only delayed the turn. The cure didn't stop it. This isn't the right formula." Dr. Bruce concluded.

"But we're on the right track. I mean, this is better than nothing. Not to mention, the delay. That's a good thing. Before a bite the person would have less than a minute. This cure can extend that time. Perhaps to a three or five minutes. That's a lot more time to say goodbye to your loved ones or allow people to get away from you before you turn."

"Good point. We'll do more tests, but I can't see why we can't talk to the leadership to see if they would allow us to administer it to anyone who would want it." Emily added.

"Good point. Let's improve what we have but in the meantime let's give some time to our loved ones. I like it. Let's go to the leadership now to discuss."

THIRTY-SIX

The vote to administer the cure to the population in New Haven was unanimous and was open to anyone who wanted to take it. Malcolm didn't hesitate to sign up as did Anne. Kelsey didn't want to because of the baby and Zack still wasn't sure yet. Even though Malcolm took the cure it still didn't make him feel confident.

Even now as he's shooting dozens of zombies, he still wonders if the cure works. He questioned that if he got bit would he have time to tell Anne how he felt.

Thinking of Anne, Malcolm looked to his left to check on her. As usual she looked fierce. She was firing her pistol with one hand while slicing zombies with her katana with the other. She was a killing machine, ripping through the zombies like they were paper.

Malcolm grinned thinking that this woman was his. Words couldn't describe how much he cared for Anne. Not to mention, watching her be a total badass took his breath away and made him hornier than a rabbit during mating season. He wanted her like the air he breathed.

A zombie grew close to him and Malcolm's shoulder checked it to the ground before firing a shot to its skull. He then aimed his gun at two incoming foes, taking them both out with precision. He looked toward his left and saw that Anne was about to be flanked by two zombies and he quickly rushed to her aid.

"Anne, watch your six!" He growled, removing his knife. Quickly Malcolm stabbed one in the head and spun around to kill the other. By the time Anne turned, two dead zombies laid at Malcolm's feet.

"Thanks for covering my ass."

"I'm always covering your ass. With an ass like that, it deserves to be covered."

"My hero. Perhaps a hero deserves a hero's thank you."

"What do you have in mind?"

Anne shrugged and then kissed him. Her hand grazed his cock and she whispered in his ear, "anytime anywhere baby." She winked at him before joining the others to clear the store.

Malcolm had a goofy grin on his face as he attempted to regain his composure. With a deep breath he grabbed his rifle and rejoined the fray.

When the last zombies were dead in the department store, Liam yelled, "cease fire. You know the drill break up in twos, search for anything thing useful. I'm not sure what we would find here, as this place already looks picked clean but you never know."

Anne was about to leave with Kelsey before Malcolm took her hand.

"Hi, what do you say if we search together this place?"

"Yeah, sure. Kelsey, you're cool with that?"

"Yeah, I will go with Zack. Come on baby." Kelsey took Zack's hand and walked away to search the baby section in the store.

"It's cute that they are going to look for baby supplies. Every day I'm always amazed that Kelsey is pregnant."

"Me too. They are going to be good parents. You've seen them with Keshia."

"True. So why did you want to team up with me?" Anne asked.

"Well, I recall something about anytime, anywhere. Watching you back there killing zombies and looking like a total badass got me hot and bothered. What do you say we find a place to put these flames out?"

Anne smirked and wrapped her arms around Malcolm. "I wouldn't mind that. I actually have a spot in mind. Follow me..." she grinned, holding his hand.

Anne led him to a tent in the outdoor section and unzipped it. "Care for a quickie?"

"Fuck, yes." Malcolm crawled inside, followed by Anne. Malcolm zipped up the tent and then turned to find that Anne had already removed her tactical vest and sword. She was working on her pants, while Malcolm did the same. Once his pants were off, he grabbed her chin and dragged her close.

Anne moaned as their tongues met with a fiery passion. Her fingers trembled as the excitement of what to come was too much to bare. Malcolm pulled away from her lips and nuzzled his head into the nook of her neck. Anne tilted her head back and gasped, feeling Malcolm lightly nibble on her skin. The suction from his mouth was erotic and pulse pounding. Her whole body trembled as she was peppered with kisses.

"Damn, do I love doing this with you." Malcolm's husky voice was heavy with need as he gripped her tightly. His hold on her was over-bearing as if he knew if he let her go he'd never get a chance to hold her again. It was primal, and Anne loved it. She played along, allowing him to take over. She batted her eyes at him, stroked his hard cock, egging him on. "So do I, baby..."

"Yeah?" Malcolm breathed as he took in every inch of her delicate features.

"Fuck yes. Are we going to keep talking or are we going to get it in?"

A sly grin spread on Malcolm's face as he looked at the woman he cared most for, "Yes, ma'am. Turn around."

Anne smugly got on all fours with her ass in the air.

"Goddamn..." Malcolm muttered. His hand slid down her backside, and he could feel her body twitch from the anticipation. The urge to bury himself in her slick heat pounded him. He was hungry with desire and his mouth salivated at the feast of flesh yet to come. When his hand neared her rear, he slapped her butt, admiring the way her cheeks jiggled. He licked his lips like a wolf preparing to devour a meal, grabbed his cock, and slowly entered her. As he slid in, he groaned at her wet tight-ness, and gripped her ass. Closing his eyes, he attempted to keep his composure as the velvet pleasure he felt was like no other. Slowly, he rocked his hips back and forth, allowing her to get used to his size. As he moved, Anne's moans grew in volume.

Malcolm loved looking at Anne's backside. Her curves were perfect and the feeling of her felt amazing. She was one of a kind. He loved the way she would call out his name, begging him to go faster. He grinned watching her hands squeeze the tents material as her body quaked from his blows. From the way her insides trembled, he knew that she was almost there.

There was something basic that he loved about Anne. She didn't need to do much to turn him on. Just a smile here, or a touch there made him a pawn to her will. Her sweet scent drove his lust, and the shape of her eyes made him a slave to her will. The little things that were often overlooked were kryptonite for him.

Right there, he realized what he had with Anne was special and nothing could replace it. That feeling. That connection. That bond. He was on a level with her that he never thought possible.

He wanted her in the morning, afternoon and evening. She was that good. There was something about the way she backed it up on him, the way she uttered his name with bated breath, and the way she twerked her ass. All of which, teased him to go faster and harder. She was the total package and he was glad that she was in his life.

Anne exhaled deeply as she buried her head between her arms. The entire tent seemed to spin as she felt the most incredible pleasure imaginable. Every strike, every move, every inch was felt. She was his as he bent her to his will. He was aggressive, demanding, sexy. He was hers taking what he wanted as he pummeled inside her. He rocked her world and then some. Burying his cock from tip to hilt.

She didn't know if there was an explanation for her feelings, but she couldn't escape it. At first she thought she was going mad. She thought there was no way she could feel those feelings. Those feelings that she thought were a figment of her imagination were becoming more real by the second. Lying there, emotions swelled within her making the sex more passionate. She couldn't contain herself even if she tried. Her shrieks shook the tent's walls as she wailed from the powerful emotions that swept her. Her body convulsed as the aftershocks of her pleasure spread.

Malcolm closed his eyes as her wetness engulfed him. It choked him, making his own pleasure unbearable. His fingers clenched her body and his cock twitched. He groaned, as his body produced his own orgasm. He pulled out of her exhausted, breathing heavily as if he just ran a marathon. Anne turned around to kiss Malcolm. He grinned and held the back of her head deepening their kiss. He pulled away from her lips, and pushed away her wet matted hair behind her ear.

Anne smirked and touched his sweaty bare chest. She could feel his heart beat against his rib cage. She looked into his eyes and they shared a loving gaze, breathing as one as they both came down from their highs.

"Once more you didn't disappoint. That was amazing." Anne beamed.

"It was also stupid. I could hear Anne two aisles over, God knows who else heard." Zack growled outside the tent.

"Zack?" Malcolm questioned.

"Don't worry, your secret is safe with me. Just get dressed. I need to show you something."

"Yeah, sure..." Malcolm's voice trailed as he looked back at Anne. She snorted, causing him to erupt with laughter. The couple quickly got dressed and then exited the tent.

"Did y'all really thing that fucking in a tent in a zombie infested shopping center was wise?"

Anne and Malcolm shared a look before cracking up again.

"Honestly, when you put it that way it sounds like we're idiots, but when the both of you are feeling each other, there's no better time than the present." Malcolm quipped.

"Oh, how the tables have turned." Kelsey joked. She placed her hands on her hips and shook her head. "One minute you're yelling at me about just being friends, now you two are humping like rabbits."

"Yeah, sorry about that." Anne replied.

"It's okay, but remember we are counting on you two. I don't mind some fooling around but if it becomes a habit I'm benching you. You put others in danger when y'all are distracted." Zack scolded.

Malcolm looked down ashamed and nodded his head. "You're right. It won't happen again. Sorry, Zack."

"It's fine, Malcolm. Come over here. I want to show y'all something," he replied as he led them to the group that was surrounding a figure. When Malcolm joined, he saw what they were looking at. The body was disfigured, but it did have a distinguishable scar on its head. The letters of SS were carved in its skull. There was no denying that was the mark of the Sons of Satan. Malcolm's heart started beating twice its pace as he looked at Zack.

"Do you think they're scouting this area? I thought they were only exclusive to Hampton Roads."

"So did I, however, if I'm learning one thing about these motherfuckers then it's always expect the unexpected with them. This guy looks fresh. There's no way he traveled with a horde from where we were at. Those fuckers are somewhere near here."

"Are the Sons of Satan what overran Little Creek?" Liam asked.

"Yes, they are bad news. Regardless of how this fucker got here we need to be ready for an attack."

"I understand. I will call an emergency leadership meeting when we get back to New Haven. I will have you explain the situation to the leadership."

Zack nodded. "Let's head back. We need every second to plan for them."

Liam agreed and the group left the shopping center. Each survivor was serious as their horrible memories of their time at Little Creek replayed in their heads. When they arrived back at New Haven, they followed Liam as he collected the members of the Leadership, including the farmer's leader Maria Garcia, builder leader Tyrese Johnson and the general population leader Dr. Tanner Bruce. Once all of the members were gathered in Liam's living room. They all looked at each other and then back at Liam.

"Why the emergency?" Dr. Bruce asked. He straightened his white lab coat, adjusting himself in the chair.

"I called this meeting to discuss a new threat that we found while we were out. The group that forced Zack and his people from Little Creek has been found."

"Who are they?" Tyrese asked. Tyrese was a large black man, with a goatee. He wore a pair of brown steel toe boots, dirty khaki pants and a red shirt.

"Sons of Satan," Zack replied. "They are a group of dangerous individuals obsessed with the devil. They believe that they are heralds of Satan, here to make hell on earth. They believe that the zombies are their soldiers and are brutal to all living humans. They kill without remorse and rape women for sport. It's a bad group of people."

"Wow..." Maria closed her eyes and shook her head. Maria had brown hair and was wearing a pair of jean overalls over a pink shirt. "Do you know if they followed you?"

"No, I don't think so. We didn't have anyone following us when we left. Not to mention we've been here close to a month. My experience with the Sons is they don't wait too long before attacking a community. If they were following us, they would've made themselves known. I think that was a scout. They haven't found us yet, but this doesn't mean we shouldn't take precautions."

"What did you have in mind?" Liam asked.

"We need to get that wall up as quickly as possible. We need to double the amount of watch along the wall, and send out scouts to find any other movements from the Sons. All citizens that are of fighting age need to be ready at anytime for an attack. And if they do attack, we do not underestimate them. That was the downfall of Little Creek. The moment they show up on our doorstep we fire. No questions asked. These people are sick and use zombies as their own personal army."

"Dear God..." Dr. Bruce muttered.

Liam looked at Tyrese. "How much longer do you need for the concrete barrier?"

"Two months, I can get more done with more people though, but you can't rush concrete drying."

"You'll have your men. I'll give you some of my people to help."

"Same here." Maria added. "There's no point of harvesting if there is no one to have food for. Take some of my people too to speed up the project."

Tyrese nodded. "That should help."

"In the meantime, Dr. López and I will continue our work on a cure. Now that we delayed the effects of a bite that should give us some time if they do decide to use zombies. Someone who's bit could keep fighting longer before they turn. However, if we can perfect the formula, it wouldn't matter that they have an army of undead. We can protect ourselves and wipe them out."

Liam nodded. "Good. It sounds like we have our jobs. Most importantly, we shouldn't let panic settle in the community. It's a new threat, but we know what to expect with them. We will be ready for them when the time comes. Let's go to work."

THIRTY-SEVEN

"Let's try sample number 615." Dr. Bruce suggested.

"Okay, testing it now," Dr. López replied as she added the blue liquid to the black blood of a fresh zombie. They watched on the projector as the usual scene played out. The serum turned the black blood back to red, but like the rest of all of their samples, minutes later the blood turned black once more.

Emily slammed her hand in the counter and cursed in Spanish. "Why aren't the antibodies holding?" She muttered.

"I'm not sure, but don't get frustrated. We will figure it out."

"Yes, but time is not on our side. We know the Sons of Satan are out there and I've seen how they use zombies as their army. If they come here and we don't have a cure, they could wipe us out. We need to figure this out now."

"Dr. López, you and I both know it doesn't work like that. Science isn't something that can be microwaved. It needs to be respected. We need to take our time to figure it out. We are close. We are at this virus' doorstep and it's fighting with all of its worth to keep us from killing it. We are there. The light bulb wasn't invented in a day and neither would this cure be. I have faith in you."

"Faith can only take you so far..." Emily muttered as she reviewed the biological structure of sample 616.

"True, but I don't think God intended us to submit to this virus the rest of our lives."

"I didn't know you were religious."

"I was one of those Only Easter-Christmas people."

"Ah, that explains it." Emily joked.

Dr. Bruce winked at her and explained, "before you came I prayed for a solution to my problem with this cure and then you arrived the next day and within weeks we made more headway than I ever made before. I'd like to think that's God's Will."

"Eh, that's debatable. It's more like two heads are better than one."

"I take it you're not religious?"

"I was at one point, mi abuela took me every Sunday until she died when I was ten." Emily paused and stared out in the distance.

"What happened then?"

"I stopped going. I questioned if there even was an all powerful God, why does he let bad stuff happen? I don't buy it."

"God works in mysterious ways. His wrath and his mercy could often be misunderstood. He has a reason for everything."

"I just don't understand. He's taken a lot of people I care about. How could you still stand by him when he's done such terrible things?"

"The same way that you believe that we can find a cure. Faith."

Dr. Bruce smiled at Emily before the computer beeped letting the doctors know that formula 616 was ready to test.

"Well, that's our time for today's religious lesson."

"Oh, I can't wait for the talk tomorrow."

"Oh, you'll like tomorrow. We'll do communion. I have a great vintage I could bring to the lab."

"Now you're speaking my language." She winked.

Dr. Bruce chuckled softly as he resumed reviewing the results.

"I'm going to grab the blood from our patient." Emily called out, stepping away.

"Yeah, sure, I'll get the sample ready. Be careful getting the blood. Victor stepped out for a bit, you don't want that zombie rocking those restraints. Do you need help?" He asked.

"No, I got it. He's pretty secure."

Dr. Bruce nodded and resumed working. Emily walked into the containment cell and crept closer to the zombie. His face was disfigured and his black eyes were cold and soulless. His teeth chomped at Emily as she inched near him. Its strained body kicked and rocked inside the gurney attempting to get near her.

"Easy, Mister. You can't be trying to bite me on the first date. I got a boyfriend." She quipped. Biting her lower lip, whispered, "Now hold still...I just gotta get some blood from you." Emily grabbed a capsule, and stuck inside the IV connected to its arm. The zombie continued to wiggle, until it snapped its bonds. With its free hand, it tried to grab Emily.

She screamed, backing away, but she was too slow as it grabbed her hair, dragging her closer to its mouth. She tried to break free but the zombie's grasp on her hair was tight.

"No, no, no!" She yelled as she attempted to break free. She struggled, but was losing the fight. Closer and closer she got to the zombie's mouth until she felt a hand shove her. She fell onto the floor hard and heard someone yelp in pain. Looking up, she saw Dr. Bruce's arm inside the zombie's mouth. He punched the zombie hard in the face and backed away, holding his arm as he bled.

"Dr. Bruce!" Emily cried as she ran towards him. She held his hand as she looked at his arm. Her heart raced seeing the bloody death mark of a bite.

"Damn..." Dr. Bruce growled, looking at his arm. "Well, it's been over a few seconds. At least we know that the first shot we gave to people works."

"True. Seconds are now minutes, but you'll still turn..."

"Don't think like that. Let's test 616 on me."

"We don't know if 616 will work."

"We don't, but it's worth a try. I have faith."

Emily hesitated and then shook her head. "We don't know what would happen. There's a thousand things that could go wrong."

"And all of that stuff wouldn't matter if 616 works. Take the chance. Don't let me turn without trying it. It's my dying wish. Please."

Emily nodded and grabbed a needle to extract the serum. She injected Dr. Bruce and he growled as she pushed the plunger down.

"Are you okay?"

"Yeah, I'll be fine." He grunted. "Here, take this." He handed her a gun and she stared at it.

"What's this for?"

"Don't be coy with me. We know that it's a possibility that I turn. If I do, I want you to put me down immediately. Don't hesitate."

"Dr. Bruce..."

"Please. Just promise me."

Dr. López sighed and nodded. "I'll do it."

"Thank you."

Emily watched Dr. Bruce for a few minutes before asking, "how do you feel?"

"Good actually. I'm afraid to say that this is working."

"Me too."

"Do you remember your first virus that you cured?"

"Yeah, it was the XR-18. Nasty cold if you caught it."

"Ah, I remember XR-18. I didn't realize it was you who cured that one."

"Yeah, I was fresh out of med school. It wasn't all me though. I had a team. Much like this..."

"No, it was all your genius. Those doctors were just riding your coat-tails just like I did. You're brilliant, and you're going to heal the world."

"Thank you, Dr. Bruce."

Dr. Bruce smiled back at her before coughing. He looked down at his hand and it was black liquid. His smile disappeared as he looked at Emily.

"Remember. Not a moment after..."

"Wait, it could work..."

"Don't be naïve, Dr. López. I'm at the end of the road. It's been an honor, working with you. Remember this is God's Will. Everything that is happening has a purpose."

Dr. Bruce gave her one last smile before he coughed and gasped for air. He dropped to the ground in pain, clutching his heart. Emily cried as she aimed the gun at his head. She felt sick to her stomach to have to put down her colleague. He'd done so much for her since she arrived at New Haven. Tears rolled down her cheeks as she watched the change.

A low growl emitted from Dr. Bruce's throat and his eyes opened not blue and bright, but black and soulless. He stood and began to move towards Emily.

"I'm sorry," she wept before pulling the trigger.

The undead Dr. Bruce dropped to the ground as did Emily as she fell to her knees crying. Emily looked up and her fists were clinched looking at Dr. Bruce's dead body.

Her eyes narrowed as she growled, "Your death won't be in vain."

She stood up and walked towards the computer to start working on sample 617. Her eyes burned as she worked tirelessly she didn't give up. She couldn't.

"Emily?" Victor asked walking in. He saw the dead body of Dr. Bruce and his heart raced. "Emily!" He yelled, searching for her until he found her at the computer.

"Jesus, Emily are you okay?"

"I'm fine..." she growled as her tears pooled on the computer table.

"No, you're not. Dr. Bruce is dead and you're upset. What happened?"

"Dr. Bruce got bit and the cure didn't work. I'm working to find the next one because I don't want to lose another person that I love."

"I love you too, but you can't just throw yourself into work like this."

"Victor, please, just go. I'm better off working on my own."

"No, I'm not going anywhere."

"Please just go. I know what you and I have is just physical to you..."

"It's not just physical." Victor grabbed Emily's arm and turned her to face him. "I fucking love you. There's nothing else. There's no other feelings but that. When you're in pain, I'm in pain. I'm here for you. I'm not going anywhere."

Emily wrapped her arms around Victor and kissed him. She looked into his eyes and grinned, "I know you do. That's why I must try. I must try for us."

"Okay, baby. I know. I know." He held her tightly and they swayed together embracing each other. Softly, Victor chuckled. "Who would have thought that we'd be together?"

"Not me."

"Me either, but we're here now."

"So what now?"

"You have work to do. The woman I love is going to solve this. First we should pay our respects to Dr. Bruce and give him a proper burial. After that, we come back in the lab and we work our asses off to solve this. Anything you want you got it. I don't know much, but I'll be your lab assistant. Fetching you food or anything in between."

"Thank you, Victor. Thank you for being there."

"I will always be there for you." He grinned, kissing her.

THIRTY-EIGHT

"It's crazy about Emily and Victor." Anne commented as she stood watch. With Sabrina and Kelsey. All three women were patrolling the area watching out for any stray zombies while the builders worked on the wall. The ten foot two feet thick concrete wall had multiple people around it, as they extended it around the compound. They had people flatting the earth for the molds, settling up the molds, pouring concrete, and testing the walls' dexterity. It was almost an assembly line as the workers moved at a frantic pace to prepare for the possible attack. The work speed seemed to double with the additional workers to assist.

"Yeah, who would've thought it?" Sabrina remarked as her eyes didn't leave the treeline ahead of her.

"I did." Kelsey said smugly, holding her rifle close to her chest.

"No, you didn't." Anne huffed. "Like the both of us, you knew that Victor was always a multiple women man, but now he's settling down with Emily. It's crazy."

"I agree with Anne. I've known Victor since I joined SEAL Team 2. He's always been a playboy."

"Well, times have changed. Last I checked , it was the zombie apocalypse. Perhaps he realized it was time to settle down, with a wonderful woman. It's true love. What you two don't believe in true love?"

Anne and Sabrina looked at each other and laughed.

"The only thing I believe is the US Constitution and my rifle." Sabrina added.

"Oh, God, can you sound any more like an army grunt?" Kelsey snorted, rolling her eyes.

"Hey now...don't diss the service."

"I would never..." Kelsey smirked. "What about you, Anne? Do you believe in true love?"

Anne hesitated and looked at Malcolm. He was shirtless, helping to pour concrete into a mold. Her insides quivered looking at his glistening dark skin. She had to stop herself several times as she kept herself from gawking at him. This by far was the sexiest look that she saw on Malcolm. His jeans were low enough to show off the sculpted deep V on his rippled core. Along with his brawny chest and broad shoulders he was a sight to see.

As she ogled him working, she wondered if she was in love with him. While she cared for him deeply, she never thought of it as love. Perhaps it was more lust driving their relationship at this time, but it wasn't love. Love wasn't for them. Or was it?

Anne sighed frustrated at the fact that she couldn't describe her relationship.

"Anne?"

"What?" She breathed as if she was awakened from a dream.

"Are you okay? You seem distracted."

"Yeah, I'm fine."

"Bullshit. She was just checking out her man meat." Sabrina grinned.

"What?" Anne breathed.

"It's fine, girl. I've been checking out my own man meat too. Damn that Liam...watching him work is doing something to me too." Sabrina commented.

"Oh, yeah I was thinking of Malcolm." Anne lied as she withheld the real reason she was pondering about him. The question of love still lingered in her brain as she wondered if Malcolm shared the same sentiment as her. Anne was in her own thoughts until she heard Kelsey ask Sabrina , "Speaking of relationships, are we seeing one grow between you and Liam?"

"Oh, Liam and I are just fucking. A means to make this zombie apocalypse fun."

"Yeah, that's what Malcolm and I are doing."

Sabrina and Kelsey looked at each other and laughed. "Yeah, that's not what you'll are doing. He's in love with you. If he hasn't said yet, he will."

"What? Malcolm? He's not in love with me. We're just doing the friends with benefits thing."

"Seriously? You are both so far from the friends with benefits angle. You are in serious relationship territory. Trust me." Sabrina added.

"I agree, with Sabrina. You guys have chemistry. A real relationship. If he hasn't admitted it now, he will."

Anne sighed and looked back at Malcolm. He caught her eye and waved before turning back to work again. Watching him work, Anne wondered if the girls were right about Malcolm. Perhaps they were right, they were past the whole friends with benefits stage, she thought. However, she didn't want to be labeled as boyfriend and girlfriend. That is when it becomes real. That is when their relationship became something more and that fact scared Anne. She was scared because she already lost something she cared about and she didn't want to lose him. She couldn't bear the thought of losing Malcolm.

The building crew worked on the wall until sunset. When the day was through everyone went back to their homes tired and exhausted. After dinner with the house, Malcolm and Anne retired to their rooms cuddling in the bed staring at the ceiling. Their hands were intertwined as they quietly laid in bed holding each other.

Malcolm cleared his throat and grinned, "I saw you checking me out today. You looked good today too."

Anne laughed, "Malcolm, I was wearing my normal jeans, shirt and tactical vest. You've seen me in that outfit all the time."

"True, but every time I looked you took my breath away. Words can't express how beautiful you are. You make me so happy to be with you."

"Oh, Malcolm that's sweet..." Anne replied.

Malcolm grabbed Anne's chin and brought her mouth close to his laying a passionate kiss on her lips. He held her close as his tongue entered her mouth and massaged her own.

When he looked at her, Anne smiled as cupped his chin. She breathed deeply and placed her head on his chest. Malcolm held her tightly and rubbed her arm.

"Anne, something about you makes me feel like I can take on an entire horde. You empower me. Since we've been together I feel like a different person. Everyday I'm with you is a gift. I still think of that first night we kissed. I didn't know it at that time but, that was the first moment I realized that you were the girl for me."

"Ahh Malcolm..." Anne looked up and kissed him once more. Malcolm held her close as he grounded his body on top of hers. He rested his head on hers breathing deeply, inhaling her heavenly scent.

"Anne?" He whispered.

"Yes?"

"Can I make love to you?"

The way he said *love* made Anne's stomach flutter. His voice was husky and filled with need as his brown eyes pierced her soul. She didn't question his words as she lived in the moment.

"Yes, baby." She replied, kissing him. They rolled in bed and Anne got on top. She smiled at Malcolm as she ripped off her shirt and tore away her sports bra. The moment she revealed her breasts, Malcolm growled like an animal and sat up to suck her tit. Anne leaned her head back and moaned, felling Malcolm's tongue on her skin. He sucked on her nipple making it harder than stone. With every second, Anne's breathing became more ragged. She ground her pelvis on top of him, begging for him to unleash his beast from his cage.

Blood rushed to his cock, and he stiffened. The two tossed in bed, and Malcolm got on top of her. With haste, Malcolm unzipped his jeans and removed them, and watched as Anne did the same. Once she was naked, Malcolm reached down and touched her wetness. From the feeling he knew she was ready for him. Slowly his finger slid in and out of her sex. Anne arched her back from the sensation that spread through her body. She closed her eyes, gasping as the arousing feeling took her.

As he touched her, Malcolm leaned forward and peppered kisses around her neck. Each time he touched her Anne felt a spark and her body lurched forward.

He settled his body over hers and parted her legs with his own as he settled between her. With one hand, he guided his cock inside her, and groaned as he slid in. Anne gasped as his thickness stretched her out. As they had sex something felt different. This wasn't a normal hook up. Malcolm's intentions were different. He didn't rush, he took his time. It was like he was savoring every bit of her. They didn't do multiple positions , nor they didn't stop kissing each other. They stayed together in each other's arms. Holding each other, experiencing something greater than they ever felt before. His movements were sensual and passionate as he thrusted deep and slow.

Anne closed her eyes as her emotions took a toll on her. Malcolm was different in bed. His focus was just for pleasure, and she could feel his feelings with every thrust.

Just the way he held her turned her on. The feeling of his lips grazing hers. Hearing his soft grunts as he pumped in and out of her. Listening to him mutter her name over and over to her made her mind spin. Anne tilted her head back and his hands slid down his backside to his ass. Her nails clawed into the taut muscles encasing his shoulder blades, and she held on tightly feeling him buck back and forth.

"Malcolm..." Anne moaned. "Oh...Malcolm...just like that baby. Just like that... almost there..."

Malcolm buried his head in the nook of her neck and increased his speed. Anne's toes curled as she felt the warm of his breath on her ear. Her fingers tingled, and her heartbeat drummed on her rib cage as her pleasure increased. The slight deviation from the previous slower speed was like a fuse for Anne. Seconds later she exploded as her orgasm took hold.

"Ohhh!" Her mouth opened as waves of pleasure went through her.

Malcolm leaned back and lifted her legs to his shoulders, getting deeper penetration. He flicked his hips as his pace quickened. He groaned, feeling his orgasm approaching.

Looking down he gazed at her beauty. She was a sight to behold. He loved the way she stared deeply into his eyes. Her look told him that she was his. He loved the way feeling of her smooth curves on his fingertips. Every inch of her was desirable. Every inch of her was pure. Every inch of her was perfect, in every aspect of the word.

At first he was uncertain about his feelings, but now he knew. He knew that she was his and he never planned on letting her go. He knew his feelings were true. They weren't false. They weren't fiction. They were facts. It was a fact that he cared for her. It was a fact that he would die for her. It was a fact that he loved her.

That statement alone supercharged his body to a level he never felt. Pleasure raced through his veins and gripped him. He gasped as it took hold of him, and held her tightly as he came. His body shuddered as it felt like he unleashed everything he had into her.

Anne clutched the sheets tightly and came with him. It was the second time of the night. Her back to back orgasms were unexpected, but welcomed. She moaned as her world spun. This man inside her knew every little detail to set her off and just when she thought he knew it all, he found a way to surprise her. Together they embraced their equally appealing moments and when they were through, they held each other, both trembling from the prior excitement.

Malcolm shifted his weight to look at Anne. He noted the small dimples on her cheeks and her way her button nose curves. Slowly he pushed a strand of her hair back. He couldn't help but smile at the woman in his arms.

"Malcolm, that was amazing..."

"...I love you." He finally admitted.

Anne's eyes opened wide at his expression.

"Malcolm...I..."

"You don't have to say it back. I understand if you don't feel the same way. I just wanted to let you know how I feel."

Anne hesitated. She wondered if she should say it too. However, she knew that would be a lie. She liked him, but she wasn't sure if it was love or just strong feelings.

"I'm sorry Malcolm..."

"It's okay. As long as you're mine. That's all I care about."

Anne smiled and kissed Malcolm. "I really like you though. What we have, is nice."

"It is, isn't it? It's okay you didn't say it back. Seriously I'm okay with it." Malcolm kissed Anne and held her cheek. "Goodnight, Anne."

"Night."

Malcolm kissed her cheek and turned to fall asleep. As he slept, Anne laid in bed awake wondering if she made the right decision not to tell him how she truly felt.

THIRTY-NINE

"You see! I called it!" Sabrina grinned.

"Yeah, you did. I saw it too. In the winkle of his eye. I always knew he loved you. Did you tell him you loved him back?" Kelsey asked Anne.

Anne sighed and looked ahead in the woods that they were patrolling. They were a distance away from the wall as the girls wanted to stretch their legs so they came up with the excuse to search the area. It was early morning as the dew was rolled off the leaves on the fall day. Honestly, Anne just wanted to get away from Malcolm. Every time she looked at him she was reminded of their sensual night the other night. However, her plan was turning sour as all Kelsey and Sabrina wanted to talk about was Malcolm's big confession and her lack of confession.

"No, I didn't tell him." Anne admitted.

"Why not?"

"Because I don't feel the same way."

"Bullshit," both women replied at the same time.

"Anne, Sabrina and I both know that's a lie. Tell us the truth. Since you've been with Malcolm, admit that you haven't felt this way about anyone else and that everyday you wake up with a smile on your face. You know that Malcolm is the reason why. Malcolm is your everything.

The fact that you stand here and deny that fact means that you are lying to yourself. You deserve to be happy."

Anne paused and wanted to explain her piece before the group of women heard a tree branch snap.

"Zombie?" Anne asked.

"I'm not sure.." Sabrina began to say before they heard a chuckle.

"Oh, I'm not a zombie. Just a ghost..." From behind a tree, Sawyer appeared. He was wearing a leather jacket and jeans. In his hands was a rifle and on his side was a pistol. His most distinguishable feature was the scarred SS on his forehead.

When Anne saw it she immediately knew it was trouble. She looked back at Sabrina and Kelsey who had similar worried expressions.

"Sawyer? You're alive?" Kelsey asked. "I thought Zack killed you."

"I thought he did too. There I was bleeding out like a pig, zombies surrounding me, trying to take a bite out of me. I didn't stop fighting though. Not once. Eventually I got free of the horde that Zack set upon me, but I ran into the leader of the SS. He wanted to kill me, I had other plans. The fucker went down like a pussy. So there I was, expecting the rest of the Sons to attack me, but it turns out, they are so devoted to faith that they believed in a Alpha. After killing that fucker, I was the new alpha, I was their new leader. When I first got the job, I didn't want it. I thought these people were freaks..."

"They are freaks..." Sabrina growled.

"No, they just see the world clearer. Whatever they want they take it. Women, guns, food. The world is ours. Now that I see, I am happy to lead them. However, there was one thing always bothering me. Zack and Malcolm. With Malcolm's lies, he got to have the one thing I wanted to have on the base..." Sawyer growled as he stared at Anne.

"While you and him got to play house, my real girlfriend died out there. So I tried to move on. That's when I found Sophia."

"Sophia wasn't yours." Kelsey yelled.

"She wasn't yours either!" He snapped. Sawyer's eyes grew wide as he glared at Kelsey. "Where is Sophia now? I've been watching you. She's not in that community. She died, didn't she?"

Kelsey hesitated and then nodded. "She did. On the road."

"Ha! You see! I told you. She wasn't safe. If she would have stayed with me, she would have been alive."

"You would have taken advantage of her, you sick freak." Anne growled.

"So? It's just sex. She may have not liked it at first, but over time she would have accepted it. I've broken in many women. It always starts the same and ends the same. She would have broken too. They always break..." Sawyer grinned as he ogled Kelsey and Anne.

"For months, I've been planning this, my revenge against the men who took everything from me. Malcolm took my girlfriend, so I should take his. Zack left me for dead. He took away my respect and Sophia, so in turn I should take his wife."

"Over my dead body..." Sabrina growled. "You should count your odds, Sawyer. We outnumber you."

"Do you?"

Sawyer whistled and seconds later a shot rang out. Sabrina hunched over, grabbing her stomach. She looked at her hands and saw blood.

"Sniper? I always knew you were chicken. What ever happened to a good ole fight to the death?"

"Oh, you're right. Where are my manners. Let's make this interesting. If I win, you can leave with Kelsey and Anne, but if I win, they come with me."

"Fuck you." Sabrina growled.

"Is that yes or no?" Sawyer smirked.

"Sabrina..." Kelsey began to walk forward but there was another shot at Kelsey's feet.

"Did you forget that I have a sniper? If I were you I would stay put. He was a marine so his aim is pretty good." Sawyer winked. He turned his attention to Sabrina and grinned, "so what would it be? Do you want to be a hero?"

"Fuck you. Give me a knife then. You are obviously too chicken shit for it to be a fair fight."

"It will be a fair fight. I promise." Sawyer chuckled tossing a blade at Sabrina's feet. He took out another knife behind his back and then signaled Sabrina to attack. Sabrina screamed as she charged at Sawyer, slashing her blade wildly. Sawyer dodged most of the attacks and then punched her bullet wound. Sabrina cried in pain as she took a few steps back.

"You see this is why the SEALs shouldn't have let a woman join the ranks. You are weak. You are pathetic. I know hundreds of men who deserved to be in your spot, but instead the Navy advanced you. Another PC thing shoved down our throats by those fucking left wing pussies. Thank god America fell. This country was going to hell anyways."

Sabrina glared at Sawyer and spat blood. She gripped the blade tightly and got into a stance.

"America may have had its problems, but it's going to come back. I believe it will. Assholes like you will always lose."

"Such brave words from a woman about to die."

"Wrong. I'm a Navy SEAL. Ah!" Sabrina charged fearlessly towards Sawyer and attempting to stab him. Sawyer deflected Sabrina's knife, but Sabrina was quicker than Sawyer anticipated as she switched the blade from one hand to the other dropping down to his unprotected stomach. She took one swipe and landed a cut across his chest. Sawyer opened his eyes surprised at the move, but before he could register it, Sabrina was moving quick tossing the blade in the air before catching it and scratching Sawyer's face.

"Ahh!" He growled as he held his cheek. "You bitch!" Sawyer attempted to attack Sabrina but she was too quick for him. However, the more she moved the more she bled out. Sabrina attempted to counter, but she felt too weak. She tired pushing through the pain but it was too much. She attempted to attack, but Sawyer was too strong for her as he blocked it and stuck her with her own blade. He gutted her, making sure the knife hit her vital organs.

Sabrina choked on her blood before staring at Sawyer. "Fuck you. Assholes like you will always lose."

"Says the dying bitch." Sawyer pushed her down in the ground and smiled as Sabrina took her last breath. He looked up at Anne and Kelsey and smiled.

"Ladies, if you would please accompany me to our temporary housing."

"We're not going anywhere with you. You're going to have to shoot us like Sabrina."

Sawyer smacked his mouth, "Oh, I don't need to shoot you. I just need to out man you." Sawyer clapped his hands and a dozen men all ran toward them. Anne quickly drew her rifle and tried to shoot them, but she couldn't kill all of them before they collapsed on top of her and Kelsey. Kelsey and Anne kicked and screamed as they were handcuffed and bond by their feet.

"Where to, sir?" One of the Sons asked.

Sawyer drew his blade, and began to carve SS on Sabrina's forehead. "Back to our base, to start phase two of our plan." He ordered as he butchered her.

"What of the other women? Should we cover our tracks."

"No, we are going to leave her right here..." Sawyer paused and stood up admiring his mutilation of her body. A wicked grin spread across his face as he looked back at his soldier. "I want to put the fear of God into them. Besides they need to know it was us who took Anne and Kelsey."

"Yes, sir," the Son assisted the others bringing Kelsey and Anne with them, leaving Sawyer alone. He laughed hysterically looking at Sabrina before pulling out a flare gun on his gun belt. He fired the flare and grinned watching the red light fall back down to Earth.

"Your move Zack and Malcolm. Come out. Come out, wherever you are."

FORTY

"So, did she say it back?" Zack asked, wiping the sweat off his brow.

"No, she didn't, but I'm okay with that." Malcolm replied, feeling the sun radiating on his skin. The building crew had taken their midday break and was either eating lunch or resting. Malcolm, Zack, and Liam all sat in the circle. They had finished their lunch of jerky, dried fruit and nuts and were enjoying the last few minutes they had before rejoining the crew.

"Seriously? You're okay?"

"Yeah, as long as I'm with her, I know things will work out. She may not say it now, but perhaps in the future she will." Malcolm responded.

"That's a lot of faith in someone," Liam added.

Malcolm shrugged. "I'm telling y'all, she's the one. I ain't never felt this way about a woman. With Anne she makes me feel things I never felt before. Not only is she sexy, but intelligent and funny. I mean who wouldn't want to spend the rest of their lives with her?"

"Wait, rest of their lives? Are you thinking of proposing?" Zack asked.

Malcolm grinned and reached into his jeans pocket. "I've been having this thought about Anne for some time now. So the last time we were out salvaging, I took a stroll in the jewelry section and found this engagement ring. Malcolm brought out the ring and showed it off. Both guys whistled at the expensive diamond ring.

"Surely you didn't pay for that. That sucker looks like it cost twice of what uncle Sam's paid us." Liam remarked.

Malcolm laughed. "Benefits of the zombie apocalypse. Free jewelry."

"Speaking of that, I think it may be time for Kelsey to get a ring upgrade. Which place did you swipe that?" Zack asked.

Before Malcolm could answer there was a shot that rang out and Zack, Malcolm and Liam all looked at each other concerned.

"Where did the girls say they were patrolling?" Zack asked.

"In that general area." Liam replied, standing up.

"You think it was them?" Malcolm questioned.

"A single shot like that? No, if they were under attack it would've been multiple shots. That sound was like a...sniper." Zack gasped and looked at the other men. Before they even had time to question anything else they were already grabbing their guns and gear nearby and heading into the forest. The three men ran with haste. Their hearts were beating rapidly as they didn't know what to expect and the lack of additional gunfire concerned them.

When they arrived at a clearing they found Sabrina lying on the ground.

"Fuck! Sabrina!" Liam yelled as he rushed to her side.

Zack and Malcolm frantically searched for Anne and Kelsey, shouting their names hoping that one of them would appear.

"Goddamnit, she's dead!" Liam gasped, checking her pulse. Liam punched the ground enraged. His body shook with fury as he screamed. His eyes narrowed as he clutched Sabrina's body close to him.

Malcolm walked back and placed his hand on Liam's shoulder as he mourned. Zack followed and studied his dead comrade. He felt remorse. He still saw Sabrina as his little sister. They were the only SEAL team who welcomed her into the unit with open arms. Because she was a female, she was often shunned, but not SEAL Team Two, they were always there for her. She was one of the bravest sailors he knew. His fist clenched staring at her before his eyes noticed the bloody SS on her forehead.

"Those fuckers..." he breathed as he inspected her forehead. "Malcolm look..." Zack pointed to her symbol.

"Sons of Satan..." Malcolm breathed.

Zack nodded.

"Do you think they took the girls?"

"I'm willing to bet that was the shot that we heard. I know Kelsey and Anne wouldn't give up without a fight." Zack commented as he searched the ground for clues.

"It appears that Sabrina didn't either. Look, she has a gun wound and several cuts on her body. She fought until she couldn't anymore. A warrior's death." Liam added.

"I expected nothing less from Sabrina. She was the toughest among us. She went through twice as much shit we had to during hell week to become a SEAL." Malcolm replied.

"I promise you, Sabrina, we are going to make those fuckers pay. We are going to make them wish they stayed in whatever fucking hole they crawled out of. By the time I'm through, there will be nothing left of the fucking Sons of Satan. Just saying their fucking name will be a warning to anyone who decides to fuck with us." Zack growled.

"You thinking what I'm thinking?" Malcolm asked.

"If you thinking about killing every single one of those sons of bitches then yeah, that's what I'm thinking."

"Good, I'm itching for a fight. Plus those fuckers made it personal taking Anne. If they touch a hair on her, they better wish to whomever they fucking worship for mercy because I know I won't show any."

Zack nodded and looked down at Liam who was still tending to Sabrina. "Take her body back and bring enforcements. We will make the trail with an X on trees."

"Fuck that. I'm not leaving just so you can kill all of those bastards. I want blood. I know what Sabrina and I had was new, but her death still hurts. I really liked her and I saw a future with her. No, I will not leave. I'll come back to bury her body later. Right now, all I want is payback. All I see is red and all I want is blood."

Zack grinned, "I wouldn't have said it better myself. I guess there's only one thing left to do. Boys, let's go hunting."

FORTY-ONE

Anne and Kelsey kicked and attempted to break free the entire way to the Sons of Satan's stronghold. The building was an old two-story warehouse with broken windows and a rust fence around the building. Anne could hear the moans and growls of the zombie army that patrolled around the perimeter outside.

Kelsey was shoved hard into a room with a bed, along with Anne. In the room was a four-post bed, along with a desk and chair. Litter across the room was clothes and beer bottles. With their hands still bound, they were tied up at opposite ends of the bed posts and then the men with Sawyer left the room leaving Sawyer with Kelsey and Anne alone.

"You like what I did with the place?" Sawyer asked. "Most of the sons sleep on the floor, but I prefer the little comforts in life."

"Fuck you." Anne growled.

"No, I'll be fucking you, but I like the spirit. I prefer the women to fight back."

Kelsey spat at Sawyer's face and he wiped the spit away from his face. "Aww, yeah, I'm going to have a real nice time with you." He slapped Kelsey back and she yelped in pain.

"Fuck you Sawyer! Untie me and let's see who can really fight." Anne growled.

"Oh, Anne...I can see why Malcolm likes you. Filled with such grit and care for others. You're very similar to him, you know? I'm going to enjoy breaking you in."

"Good luck with that..." Kelsey smirked. "By the time you manage to pull your pants down, my husband will be kicking down that door and killing you."

"Oh, I'm expecting that. Knowing Malcolm and Zack, they are rushing head on into my little trap. You saw those zombies out front. I have a massive horde out there surrounding the compound. I know that they are going to attempt to distract them like they did last time, but that's not going to work. I have my sentries around to attack them as soon as they near. They aren't even going to make it to the front doorstop."

"You shouldn't underestimate them." Kelsey replied.

"Oh, I don't. That's why I'm leaving fifty men here too. To guard my prized possessions."

"Wait, you're not going to be here? Where are you going?"

"Oh that's right you don't know part two of my plan. When I said that I'm going to take everything from them, I mean that. The rest of the Sons and I are going to pay New Haven a little visit. Thousands of zombies will descend upon that community, and wipe it from the face of the earth."

"Sawyer, you can't be serious. There are women and children there. Are you that far gone?" Kelsey asked.

Sawyer smirked, "why do you think we're going? You have to feed the monster, Kelsey. These men have urges just like you and I. They want to eat. They want to kill. They want to fuck..." Sawyer leaned forward and forced his tongue in Kelsey's mouth.

Kelsey closed her eyes and tried to break away from Sawyer's kiss, but he held her down as he took advantage of her. Kelsey bit Sawyer's lip and he roared taking a step back.

He licked the blood off his lip and moaned, "Mmm, tastes like cherry."

"Yeah? Come over here and kiss me again and I'll rip those fucking lips off you."

"Oh, I like it rough, baby." Sawyer barked and winked at her. "Save that energy for tonight during our threesome. Bye Bye, ladies."

"Fuck you, Sawyer." Anne spat.

Sawyer laughed and waved Kelsey and Anne goodbye. At the doorway he spoke to his guard.

"No one is allowed in here. Anyone who tries to open that door, kill them on the spot."

"Yes, Alpha."

"Those women aren't to be touched. Understood."

"Yes, Alpha."

"Good." Sawyer left the room and the door shut behind him.

Once the door was closed, Anne looked at Kelsey.

"Are you okay?"

"Yeah, I'm peachy. Wish I had some mouthwash though. That was disgusting."

"I'm sorry, but I'm not planning on sticking around to find out what else Sawyer has in store for us."

"Yeah, me either. Let's get out of here."

"Any ideas?" Anne asked, attempting to break the rope bindings around her wrists.

Kelsey looked around to see a beer bottle near her foot.

"I could smash the beer bottle and use the glass to snap the rope."

"Okay, but be careful."

"I will." Kelsey removed her boots from her feet going barefoot. She stuck out her foot and grabbed the bottle with her toes. Lifting the bottle up, she smashed it to the ground and it broke into pieces. Using her feet, she attempted to grab a large chunk of glass. As she did, she cut herself and growled through her gritted teeth.

"Are you okay?"

"I'll live." Kelsey replied. It took her a couple of minutes to finally grab the glass shard she wanted. By the end, her feet were cut up and bloodied. Holding onto the glass with both feet, Kelsey flipped her legs up to her hands and transferred the glass from her feet to her hands.

"Damn, girl. You're flexible."

"You see, cheerleading paid off in high school."

"You had to ruin the moment, Miss Braggerton."

Kelsey winked at Anne as she used the glass shard to cut the bindings. As she did ,the women heard voices outside causing Kelsey to stop.

"Who's in there, Derrick?" A voice asked.

"Sawyer has two women in there that I'm guarding. Wants to make sure no one touches them."

"Oh, and if I told you I wanted to go in there and get my fill, you would say?"

"Let me have the Asian, and I'll let you in."

The man laughed, "you see I always knew you were a smart man, Derrick. We can find two grunts and kill them. We'll lie and say it was them."

"Perfect plan, Ryan. Shall we?"

Derrick laughed as the door opened and Kelsey hid the glass in her hands.

"Mmm what do we have here? Two sexy women tied up for us. It's like they're gift wrapped."

"You touch me, you die..." Anne growled as Derrick approached her. He snickered as his finger trailed down her cheek.

"I'd like to see you do that..." he teased.

Ryan got closer to Kelsey and held her tight. "You know I always had a thing for blondes."

"Why is that?" Kelsey asked.

"Because..."

Before he could get the words out, Kelsey snapped her bindings and shoved the glass piece into the man's throat. He gurgled blood as he fell back to the ground. Derrick turned in shock and removed his knife in his hands.

"You bitch!"

"Come on motherfucker!" Kelsey growled. Derrick charged at Kelsey with the blade and Kelsey dodged it. She placed him in a tight arm bar and kicked the blade away. Derrick broke free of her grasp and scrambled for the knife on the floor. Kelsey did the same as they fought throwing punches trying to get the dominant position. Derrick was one hundred pounds heavier than Kelsey and was easily able to manpower her. He grabbed the blade and sat on top of Kelsey trying to press the blade into her chest.

"You'll pay for killing Ryan, bitch."

Kelsey screamed as she felt the blade enter her stomach. Panicking, she reached out and dug her nails into Derrick's eyes. He screamed in pain as blood leaked from his face. Using the open opportunity, Kelsey removed the blade from her stomach and then stabbed Derrick with it several times. When she was through, her face was covered in blood and guts from her brutal killing of Derrick.

Kelsey held the knife in one hand and stood up to cut Anne free.

"Kelsey!" Anne cried.

"I'm fine." Kelsey coughed, holding her stomach.

"No, you're not. You're bleeding. We need to take you to the doctor. At New Haven they could patch you up and..."

"Anne, I'm not going to make it. There's no way you're making it through all those guards. I don't want to slow you down. Leave me here."

"I will not abandon you."

"Go! Save yourself." Kelsey replied.

Anne held Kelsey close wondering what she should do until she heard a large boom followed by gunfire. Looking out the windows Anne saw a figure. Her smile soon grew larger as she realized that there was an answer to her prayers.

"Kelsey! It looks like Zack and Malcolm are here to save us!"

"That's good. I can't wait to see my husband again." Kelsey held her stomach and slumped down.

"Kelsey, stay with me. We're almost out of the woods."

Kelsey grinned, but soon her eyes got heavy and she drifted away. Noticing this, Anne wrapped her in her arms, and held her tight.

"Hang in there. You got this Kelsey. Fight. Don't you dare leave me. Come on Kelsey! Don't die on me!"

FORTY-TWO
THIRTY MINUTES EARLIER

"So how'd you want to do this?" Malcolm asked. "Did you want us to make a distraction to lead the zombies away?"

"No, there still could be Sons that remember how we breached their stronghold last time. They may have countermeasures. We need to do something unexpected."

Malcolm reviewed the warehouse searching for something that could make a difference. He expanded his search outside the perimeter of the warehouse and spotted a rig truck.

"Hey Zack, do you see that rig truck at our seven o'clock?" Malcolm asked.

"Yeah, what are you thinking?"

"If we get a head of steam with it, we could drive through the zombies and into the fence. Granted when we get through, not only will he have to fight the zombies that leaked through the broken fence and the guards in the warehouse, but we will have the element of surprise, plus zombies don't discriminate. A human is a human. They will attack anyone who's close."

"That's madness..." Liam replied.

"True, but we are running out of time. God knows what Sawyer is doing to Anne and Kelsey." Malcolm added.

"No, Malcolm is right. This is a solid play. Let's go fuck them up."

The threesome sunk down from the hill that they were perched on and crept to the rig truck. Malcolm got into the driver's seat and Zack and Liam crammed themselves on the passenger's side. Malcolm hot wired the truck and it roared to life, making all the zombies turn to their direction.

"Well, if we wanted to get their attention, we got it." Malcolm joked as he placed the truck in first gear and pressed down on the accelerator. The truck gained speed and as they neared the crowd of zombies in front of them, Malcolm yelled, "prepare for impact!"

Seconds later, the truck slammed into the ocean of undead. Bodies flew as the truck sliced through the horde. Blood spattered everywhere from the carnage, as pools of human parts were created from the impact. Malcolm screamed as he pressed down on the accelerator. He couldn't see a damn thing with all the blood on the windows, but he didn't care about that. He only cared about getting to Anne, and not a damn thing was going to stop him.

The truck slammed into the fence, there was a loud bang as the metal splintered making a hole for them.

"Knock, Knock, Motherfucker!" Malcolm growled, as gunfire began to hit the truck.

"Let's join the party. Come on, follow me. Let's find Kelsey and Anne and get the hell out of here." Zack commanded.

Malcolm and Liam nodded, and Zack and Malcolm opened the truck doors. They laid down cover fire as they advanced forward.

"Keep pushing! Don't give them an inch!" Zack roared.

Liam pressed ahead firing as they took cover behind anything that could protect their bodies like metal drums and tires. Behind Malcolm, he could hear the low growl of zombies as they filtered through the broken fence.

"Watch your six! Zombies are through the fence too!" Malcolm reminded, firing at two zombies that drew near.

"Save your ammo, Malcolm. Only attack the biters if they get closer. Use them like the Sons do. Keep pushing." Zack yelled.

Malcolm nodded and continued to press with Liam and Zack. Bullets zipped past him as the group jumped from cover to cover. It seemed like there was an endless train of Sons of Satan as their enemy kept charging at them. To make matters worse, Malcolm, Liam and Zack had to deal with close encounters with zombies.

Malcolm had his own close call while he was focused on firing at the Sons and didn't notice when a zombie came near. It growled low, and then touched his shoulder. In shock, Malcolm turned around, and slapped the zombie with his rifle before finishing it off with a bullet to the head.

"Fuck me," Malcolm muttered as he refocused on a group of Sons shooting from the nest near the door.

"We need to get that nest out of the way, if we are ever going to get inside." Zack yelled.

"I got it!" Liam replied. He took a deep breath and then exited his cover. As he ran to the next cover, he fired from his hip, hitting one of the men in the nest. He did the same thing again as he got closer to the nest. With only twenty feet in front of him, he looked at Zack and yelled, "cover me!"

Zack and Malcolm nodded and proceeded to unload their clips distracting the rest of the men in the nest. This gave Liam enough time to leave his cover and sprint to the nest. He leaped over the sandbags, kicking one man. He killed all three men posted there in a blink of an eye.

"Clear!" He yelled.

"Good job Liam. Let's head inside." Zack replied.

Liam nodded and headed towards the front door. Malcolm and Zack regrouped with him and Zack looked at both of them. "We breach in three." He commanded.

"One, two, three! Go! Go! Go!" They opened the door and were immediately greeted to gunfire. Malcolm closed the door behind him, leaving the roaming zombies outside. The three men got into cover again firing at the remaining Sons.

Liam poked his head out and fired a couple of rounds before taking cover. He missed his mark and cursed under his breath before biting his lip. He took a deep breath and left his cover again, but was met with gunfire. He got hit in the shoulder and growled, "motherfucker!"

"Liam!" Malcolm yelled.

"I'm fine. Keep going."

Malcolm nodded and kept pressing.

Liam gritted his teeth and left cover again yelling a war-cry as he fired his gun.

Malcolm looked back to check on Liam, and his heart dropped as he watched Liam get tore up by bullets.

"Fuck. We lost Liam!"

"Fuckers...they will pay! They will all fucking pay! Argh!" Zack roared taking out two Sons of Satan with accurate shots.

"Do you see Anne or Kelsey?" Malcolm questioned.

"No, I don't. They're here. Trust me. I have a feeling. We just have to keep moving."

"Easier said than done, Bruh. It's just to two of us. We lost Liam. We need back up. There's a lot more of them than us."

"I know, but we have to keep pushing. We have to reach Kelsey and Anne."

Malcolm nodded as he reloaded. He turned from his cover and roared firing multiple shots.

Malcolm had been in his share of uneven battles, but this one he felt like was the worst of them. With ten to one odds, it wasn't in their favor, but Malcolm kept pushing. He kept fighting. He knew that Anne needed him. He loved her and through that love it gave him the strength to keep fighting. That love was like an adrenaline shot for Malcolm, super charging him into a super soldier that was able to perform incredible feats.

Malcolm didn't know how, but the battle was turning in their favor. Twenty Sons of Sam turned into ten, then five, then two, then one. When the last Son fell, Malcolm checked his cover and looked back at Zack.

"You good?"

"Yeah, I'm whole. What about you?"

"Yeah, I'm good. Let's go find our ladies, and get the fuck out of here."

Zack nodded and shifted from his cover. Malcolm followed Zack as they ran through the maze of the warehouse. It took twice as long to get through it as they had to check each and every corner.

As they got deeper into the warehouse, Malcolm heard a noise and held up his fist to stop. He pointed towards the noise and Zack confirmed it.

Malcolm took a deep breath and turned the corner expecting to find more soldiers instead he found Anne holding bloody Kelsey. Anne had tears falling from her face as she cradled her best friend in the hallway.

His first thought was thank god Anne's alive but as he reviewed Kelsey's wound his heart slumped. She was fatally stabbed. Anne's hands were covered in blood as she attempted to stop the bleeding.

"Kelsey!" Zack shouted as he slid to his knees. He cradled her head as he looked down at her.

"It's about time you showed up. You stop for doughnuts?" Kelsey joked. She coughed and blood rolled out of her mouth.

"You know me. I couldn't pick a flavor," he smiled gingerly.

Zack knew what the wound meant. He didn't want to though. He wanted to have hope that she'd pull through, but in his years in service he's seen this stomach wound several times. They were too far away to move her to get to the doctor. She only had a few more minutes before she bled out.

Anne stood up and cried on Malcolm's shoulder. "I'm so happy you guys are here. We didn't think we'd make it out." Anne sobbed.

"What happened?" Malcolm asked.

"It was horrible. Sawyer's back."

Zack looked up and glared at Anne. "That's impossible. I killed him."

Anne shook her head. "No, he survived and he's out for revenge. Kidnapping us was only the start of it. He wanted to draw you guys out here. He's attacking New Haven right now with an army of undead."

Malcolm's eyes opened wide, "All those innocent people. Just for revenge? What the hell happened to Sawyer?"

Anne shook her head. "He's a madman. Truly gone. He killed Sabrina."

Zack growled and clutched Kelsey tighter. "Did he do this to Kelsey?"

Anne shook her head. "No, Kelsey and I were trying to escape, but the guards watching us interrupted us. They tried to rape me and her, but Kelsey broke free. She killed one man, and fought the other. I would've helped...I'm so sorry Zack. I was tied up. I tried breaking loose..."

"It's okay Anne."

Anne sniffed and wiped her tears away. "They fought and Kelsey got stabbed. She ended up killing the man though. She saved my life."

Kelsey chuckled, "that's what heroes do."

"Shh, don't speak." Zack shushed, pushing her blonde hair behind her ear. "Save your energy. We're going to get you to the infirmary." He kissed her forehead and Kelsey weakly held his cheek.

"You and I both know I won't make it. It's okay. At least I got to see you again. I love you."

Zack sobbed loudly and he couldn't find his words as he got choked up. "I...I...I love you too," he whimpered.

"Promise me, you'd keep living life. Raise our daughter, Keshia, up to be a strong woman. I want her to have my katana so she could defend herself in this world, Anne would you teach her?"

Anne nodded. "Every day. Just like we were taught."

"Thank you, Anne..." Kelsey croaked. She was on death's door as she coughed up blood. She looked back at Zack and held his cheek. "I'm the luckiest woman in the world to be married to you. I love you Zack Morris. I love..." before she could get the final word out, Kelsey took her last breath. Her eyes remained open as she stared at her husband.

Zack's body shook as he was filled with emotions. He held her tightly sobbing like a madman.

"No, no, no, no, no..." he repeated rocking her limp body back and forth. "Come back to me. Come back. Don't leave me. Don't leave me. Please baby. Don't go. Baby please..." Zack cried.

Malcolm held Anne as he watched his best friend break down. He had never seen Zack in this crazed state before. Zack was always confident. He seemed invincible, this was the first time he'd seen him unhinged.

"Zack... I'm sorry." Malcolm whispered.

Zack didn't say anything as he kept rocking back and forth with Kelsey's corpse.

Malcolm reached out to touch his friend but he pulled away. "Just leave me be." He growled.

"Zack? Let me help you."

"Don't fucking touch me!" He snapped.

"Zack..."

"She's gone. She's fucking gone. She was my everything and now she's gone. I can't live without her. I can't." He shook his head.

"She wanted you to live on though. You promised her." Malcolm reminded Zack.

Zack shook his head. "I thought I could, but I can't. Life without her is a life I don't want to live." Zack reached for his side arm and pulled it out.

Malcolm's eyes opened wide as he connected the dots on what Zack wanted to do.

"Zack whatever you're thinking, don't do it. We need you."

"I can't live without her brother. I can't."

"Don't do it. You still have a mission to fill. Remember your promise to Charles, Sheri, and Kelsey. You gave them your word that you'd watch Keshia. That is *your* mission. You end it here, you will *fail that mission*. The Zack Morris I know does not fail missions. How would you explain yourself if you see them in the afterlife? How could you explain that you abandoned Keshia in her hour of need. Right now, Sawyer is attacking New Haven. *Keshia* is in New Haven. They need our help. They need *you*. Please, don't do this. Don't kill yourself."

Zack looked at Kelsey's body and back at Malcolm. He shook his head. "I can't do it. Sorry."

"Zack, No!" Malcolm took a step closer to him in an attempt to get the gun away from him, but Zack turned it towards him.

"Don't come any closer. Just leave me be."

"Zack..."

"I said go! Go save New Haven. Just leave me alone." Zack sobbed.

Anne and Malcolm shared a look. Anne shook her head and pulled his hand back. Malcolm knew that she was telling him that Zack was too far gone. He saw it too. His friend was a former shell of himself.

"I love you, bruh. In this life or the next. Come on Anne. Let's get out of here."

Anne nodded and looked at Zack. "We're heading back to New Heaven. We will watch out for Keshia until we see you again. We love you."

Zack didn't reply as he continued to stare at Kelsey's corpse.

Malcolm took one last look at his friend and then turned his back. There was nothing left to say. The decision to live was his.

"Come on Anne, let's go."

Anne nodded and looked at her friends one last time. She didn't like leaving Zack in this state, but she knew there were bigger things happening than just them.

"Okay." She replied.

The two jogged away and as they turned the corner they heard a single gunshot. Anne and Malcolm looked at each other and they assumed the worse. They didn't turn back. They wanted to, but they knew that there were people in New Haven counting on them and their lives meant a lot more.

FORTY-THREE

Malcolm and Anne ran through the forest as fast as their legs could carry them. As they got closer to New Haven the sounds of gunfire could be heard.

Malcolm looked back at Anne and frowned. "It sounds like they already started fighting."

"Are we too late?" Anne asked.

"No, I don't think we are. The gunfire is a positive sound. Means we're still in it."

Anne nodded as they approached the hill overlooking the town. The duo stopped and took a breath as they looked down at the compound below. Hundreds of zombies had made their way into the community as they watched groups of survivors fighting off the horde. Malcolm could make out who were the citizens of New Haven and the Sons of Satan. Compared to the people from New Haven they outnumbered the Sons attacking them, but the Sons had the advantage of the zombies attacking the citizens as well.

"There are so many zombies. What do we do?" Anne asked.

"We focus on the Sons. We know their MO. They will use the zombies as their cover and shoot people who are trying to defend themselves."

"Okay. Who do we go after first?"

Malcolm looked at the valley searching for an answer until he spotted Sawyer yelling at multiple Sons members to attack different targets.

"We go after Sawyer..." Malcolm pointed at him. "Take the head off the snake. We make him pay. We make him pay for Sabrina, Kelsey, Liam and..." Malcolm paused as he got choked up. "We'll make him pay for Zack. He took so much from us and he will not take anything else from us. Are you ready?"

Anne double checked her ammo in her rifle and nodded. "Let's get that motherfucker."

Malcolm grinned and kissed Anne. Her eyes opened wide from the expression but she didn't fight it. When they finally broke, Anne shivered, taking a deep breath. That kiss was different. It was everlasting, emotional, and passionate. It left her speechless as she stared at him.

"I love you." Malcolm told her, rubbing her cheek.

Anne hesitated. She didn't know what to say. Her heart and mind were saying two things as her lips felt glued together.

"I know. It's okay. You don't have to say it back. Just having you in my life is enough." Malcolm kissed Anne once more and a smirk grew on his face. "To paraphrase a friend, let's go hunting."

Anne nodded and followed Malcolm down the hill and the closer they got to Sawyer the more resistance they got from the zombies. They hacked, slashed, and shot their way through the massive crowd of zombies. They didn't stop pushing their way through until they were close enough to yell his name.

"SAWYER!" Malcolm growled with fury. The rage in his voice shook the ground he stood on.

Sawyer turned around and grinned. "Malcolm! Anne! What a surprise! However, I don't see Zack or Kelsey. It looks like my plan to kill you had some results. Well, how did you want to die? By bullets or knife?"

"You don't deserve bullets. Your death will be slow and agonizing. You will suffer for every life you have taken!" Malcolm growled.

"Ha! I'd like to see you try!" Sawyer aimed his rifle at Malcolm, but before he could fire, Malcolm pushed a zombie into him. Sawyer's bullets ripped into the corpse in front of him and before he could adjust, Malcolm was on top of him.

His blade was out as he quickly gutted Sawyer.

"You motherfucker!" Sawyer growled as he clutched his stomach. He aimed his gun at Malcolm, but he was quicker disarming him, kicking the rifle away.

Sawyer attempted to remove his pistol, but Malcolm pushed the gun up in the air. Holding his arm up, Malcolm punched Sawyer's wound several times. Sawyer cried out in pain, and growled as he used his strength to pull the gun back down. Malcolm struggled against Sawyer's brute strength as the pistol moved towards his face. With his opposite hand, Sawyer punched Malcolm multiple times. Each punch felt like a freight train hitting Malcolm. Each punch drew blood as Malcolm's face became bloodied and bruised.

Inch by inch, the gun moved towards Malcolm's face. Malcolm's eyes grew wide staring down the barrel. He tried to push the weapon away but Sawyer was too strong. Malcolm was losing the fight. With all his might he tried fighting back, but Sawyer was too strong. A strong head butt from Sawyer made Malcolm see stars. His eyes open wide as Sawyer took aim with his pistol. Right there, Malcolm knew this possibly could be the end.

Before Sawyer could pull the trigger, Malcolm heard a mighty war cry. Before he could react, Anne stabbed Sawyer in the back.

Sawyer screamed as Anne's blade went through his body. Anne yanked her blade out and lifted it high to sever Sawyer's head. However, Sawyer was quicker as he growled, and aimed his gun at her.

"No!" Malcolm yelled, tackling Sawyer.

Malcolm got on top of Sawyer and pummeled him with multiple strikes. Rage flowed through him, and he roared with every punch.

In between strikes, Malcolm heard the familiar sound of a zombie nearing, and he waited for it to get closer. At the last second, he stood off of Sawyer and dragged the zombie on top of Sawyer.

Sawyer screamed as the zombie ripped into his flesh.

Another zombie came, and Malcolm pushed it into Sawyer again.

Malcolm watched with satisfaction as the zombies tore into the person he hated.

Sawyer's screams became gargled by his own blood as he painfully died from being eaten alive. Malcolm wiped his face off, from his own blood and spat. He picked up his rifle from the ground, and picked off the zombies that were feasting on Sawyer's flesh like crows. A satisfied grin spread on Malcolm's face as he stood over Sawyer's corpse, watching as he turned.

As soon as his eyes turned black, Malcolm shot him, firing multiple shots into his skull.

Standing above him, Malcolm growled, "That's for Zack, Liam, Kelsey and Sabrina. Walk away from that, motherfucker." Malcolm fired an additional shot into Sawyer's skull and wasn't paying attention when another zombie came roaring next to him.

"Malcolm, watch out!" Anne cried as she defended him. She unsheathed her katana and cut the zombie's head clean off.

"Thanks..." Malcolm breathed.

Anne nodded and then turned their attention to another nearby Son. He wasn't paying attention until Malcolm shot him in the back. He turned around briefly to see Malcolm and Anne charging towards him, before slumping over dead.

One by one, Malcolm and Anne focused their attacks on the Sons that were scattered across New Haven. They showed no mercy to the extremists, killing each one in their path. Malcolm wanted to wipe them off the face of the earth. So did Anne. With malice in their eyes, and charged by grief, they left none alive.

"Argh!" Anne yelled as she stabbed the last Sons of Satan in the chest. He coughed up blood before falling to his knees and dying. "That's for Kelsey..." Anne growled.

Malcolm placed his hand on Anne's shoulder and breathed. "I think we got them all."

"Yeah, but look, they already did enough damage. There's zombies everywhere."

"We can take them if we do it together."

Anne nodded and turned to face the rest of the horde. "Looks like we're going to be here for a while."

"I like our odds though. Come on."

Anne smirked back at Malcolm and followed him into the crowd of zombies. She couldn't count how many she killed. They kept coming at them. They were endless. Nonstop. They didn't get tired. They didn't quit.

They fought their way through the crowd into New Haven.

"Malcolm! Anne! You're alive!" Victor shouted as he fought off two zombies.

"Yeah..." Malcolm gave Victor a half smile before shooting another zombie nearby.

"Where's everyone else?"

Malcolm shook his head. "They didn't make it. The Sons killed them all."

"Motherfuckers."

"Yeah, I know, but we blindsided them. We made them pay for every person they took from us. They're all gone. It's just us and the zombies now."

"Good, let's get rid of this nightmare."

Malcolm nodded and rejoined Anne as she sliced through another zombie. Malcolm fired a couple more shots before his gun clicked and was out of ammo.

"Shit, I'm out. Do you have any more ammo?" Malcolm asked Anne.

"Yeah, last clip. Make it count." Anne replied, tossing him a mag from her tactical vest. Malcolm reloaded and continued to fire at the endless stream of zombies.

"They keep coming!" Anne yelled.

"I know don't give up!" Malcolm replied. "We are almost through this!" Malcolm turned to check on Anne and saw a zombie approach her from behind. "Anne! Behind you!" He yelled, but Anne didn't notice as she continued to fight the zombie in front of her. Without hesitating, Malcolm charged into the zombie knocking it onto the ground. He removed his knife and stabbed it in its head. Before he had a chance to regroup, two more zombies were on top of him. He stabbed the first but wasn't quick enough for the second as its teeth sunk into his arm.

Malcolm growled as she shoved the zombie away and stabbed it with his knife.

"Malcolm!" Anne yelled as she looked at his injury.

"I'm okay," he winced as he continued to fight the zombies that charged at him.

"No, you are not!" Anne cried, as she killed another one in front of her.

"I'm fine. I took the serum. I have a few extra minutes. Let me keep fighting."

"No, I can't let you."

"Anne...please."

"Malcolm, no! I can't lose you. Not you." She sobbed.

"It's okay Anne..."

"It's not okay!" Anne snapped. She stopped fighting and looked back at Malcolm, she stared into his eyes and held him. She didn't care about the zombies. She didn't care about dying. All she cared about was him.

"I don't want to lose you. You are too important in my life."

"Anne, it's okay. Just let me go." Malcolm told her.

Anne shook her head. "I can't let you go. I was afraid to say this before, but now I know. I know that *I love you*. I can't lose you."

"I love you too, Anne. I'm with you *till the end*." Malcolm gazed into Anne's deep brown eyes and as he did , seconds turned into milliseconds, and milliseconds turned into nanoseconds as time froze for him. Staring at the woman he loved, he didn't want his last moments to be fighting. He didn't want his last memory to be of blood and violence , he wanted it to be of love and passion. He wanted to feel her warm body on his. That is what he wanted to take away from this world.

Without thinking, he grabbed Anne and dragged her close. Mayhem was going all around him, but he ignored it. He didn't hear the growls or the screams. Upon looking at her beauty, all he heard was silence.

A smile curved across his lips as he held Anne tightly. His heart was beating out of his chest, not because of the action around him, not because he was becoming infected by the zombie virus, it was Anne that made his heart jump. It was her that made him feel unnatural. She was his everything, and by her saying that she loved him, only proved that fact. He brushed her raven hair behind her ear, leaned forward and gave her a passionate kiss.

As Anne felt Malcolm, her entire body went numb. Feeling his kiss took her breath away as she stood there stunned at his emotionally charged kiss. It was amazing that she could feel so much from something so simple. Right there, in that millisecond, she felt everything they've been through. She felt his passion, she felt his respect, she felt his love. She didn't know the future, but she knew that she was his. Right now, she was his, and that was all that mattered.

As the zombies inched towards them they didn't fight them. Instead, they accepted the love that they shared. Malcolm held Anne's cheeks and he knew that if this was his last moments on Earth, this is how he would want it to go down. Didn't want it any other way.

As they made out, they heard the snarls from the creatures of hell. They could feel their heated breaths on the back of their necks, and could smell their rotten flesh as they neared. They were on death's doorstep, but they didn't break apart. They embraced their deaths, because they knew if this was how it was going to end, they wanted to go out on their terms.

They waited for their end, but it never came. Instead, shots rang out and several zombies that were near them all dropped to the ground. The rapid firing continued as Anne and Malcolm looked at each other puzzled before looking for the origins of the shots. They were surprised to see Zack firing a fifty-caliber gun from a Humvee. The shots cleared the remaining zombies, allowing the citizens to gain the upper hand in the battle.

When the last zombie fell, Zack hopped out of the truck and ran towards Malcolm and Anne.

"Zack? You're alive?"

"Yeah, after what you told me about being a father, it rang with me. I realized that you were right. I was giving up. I fired that shot to the ceiling and said my final goodbyes to Kelsey before finding that Humvee. Looks like I came in at the right time."

"You sure did, thanks, bruh." Malcolm grinned giving Zack a big hug.

After hugging him, Zack stared into Malcolm's eyes. "Is Sawyer dead?"

"I put him in the ground myself. He's not getting back up. I made sure of it."

"Good." Zack's eyes looked at Malcolm's wound and he frowned. "Apparently I wasn't quick enough. You got bit."

"It's okay. You're alive. That's what counts."

"There has to be something that we can do." Zack wondered.

"Perhaps we can see Emily?" Victor suggested. "While she hasn't found a cure yet, she can try her latest sample on you. Something is better than nothing, right?"

Malcolm nodded. "It's worth a shot."

The group walked towards the infirmary where they found Emily defending herself behind a barricade. Beside her was Keshia. Upon seeing Zack, Keshia squealed and hugged him.

"Zack! You're okay!"

"Yeah, I am Keshia. Kelsey is...it's just us now, but I promise, we're going to get through this together."

"Okay..."

"Malcolm, what's wrong?" Emily noticed his wound and frowned. "Did you get bit?"

"I did. Thankfully the serum is holding back the effects. However, I'm feeling weak though."

"Here sit down..." Emily helped Malcolm sit down.

"Victor told me that you had another sample to test out?"

"I do, but last time I did this it didn't work out."

"Emily please." Anne begged. "We just need a chance."

Emily nodded and walked into her lab. She came out with a needle with the blue formula inside.

"Are you sure you want to do this?" She asked.

Malcolm nodded. "I would rather go out with a fighting chance."

"Okay, here goes nothing." She stuck the needle in his arm and emptied its contents into his arm.

Malcolm winced as the formula entered his blood stream.

"Now what?" He asked.

"We wait..." Emily breathed.

The group stood quietly around Malcolm. Seconds turned into minutes and minutes turned into hours.

"How do you know if this is working?" Malcolm finally asked.

Emily shrugged. "Honestly, this is the longest I've seen the cure work on a bite. I don't want to jinx it, but I need to run more tests."

"Sure, run all the tests you need."

Emily nodded. "First I need to get a sample of your blood."

"Okay."

"If you guys want to leave you can. This will take a while."

"I'm not going anywhere." Anne replied. "I'm staying."

"Thank you Anne." Malcolm grinned. "I love you."

"I love you too," Anne replied. She leaned forward and kissed Malcolm.

Zack rubbed Malcolm's shoulder and smiled, "you got this brother."

"Thanks, bruh. I'll see you soon."

"You better." Zack grinned, before walking away with Keshia.

"Malcolm, it's going to be okay. You're in the best hands." Victor grinned. "Emily, do you need anything?"

"No, baby. I'll be here in the lab checking these results. I just can't believe this. Malcolm's results are...unbelievable..."

Victor nodded and kissed Emily goodbye before leaving the lab. Emily stayed at the microscope reviewing her findings while Malcolm and Anne remained in the chair together.

"Did you think it worked?" Anne asked.

"I'm not sure, but what I am sure is that you love me."

"Yes, I know I picked the worst time to admit it, but I couldn't live with myself without you knowing my true feelings."

"It doesn't matter when you say it, just matters that you did."

Anne smiled at Malcolm and kissed him. She placed her head in his shoulder and cuddled close to him. They stayed like that for a few minutes before Malcolm whispered, "Anne?"

"Yeah?"

"Marry me?"

"Are you serious?"

"Yes, I don't know if I have an hour on this earth or fifty years, but what I do know is I want to spend every second I have with you in my life. I know this proposal is out of the blue, but for the last months we've been together, I have never met someone like you. I don't want to waste time anymore. I see what I want and what I want is you."

Anne smiled and nodded. "Yes, I would love to marry you." She leaned forward and kissed Malcolm.

"I love you, Anne. I will love you until my last breath."

"Malcolm...you've been this strength that I haven't realized that was in my life the entire time. When I needed you, you were there. From the start of this zombie apocalypse you protected me. From there, you truly showed me how much you loved me. I was blind then, but now I see how much you love me. I love you too. From now until the end. I can't wait to marry you."

Malcolm grinned and held her cheek before leaning forward and kissing Anne again.

Emily walked back in smiling at the couple. "Malcolm, I have some good news. Now, I don't want to say that you're out of the woods yet. I'm going to keep you here for another twenty-four hours to see if the results are conclusive, but for all intents and purposes, I want to say you've been cured of the zombie virus."

"Really? Did it really work?" Anne asked.

Emily nodded. "Sample #999. Go figure, right?" She laughed. "Your blood doesn't have any trace of the virus. Almost like it wasn't even there. When I compared it to the samples that I had, sample #999 attacked the cells of the zombie virus and destroyed them. Every sample I looked at there was no trace of the virus and like you it hadn't returned. I know it's early to say, but I think we did it. I think we cured the zombie virus."

Anne laughed along with Malcolm as they hugged Emily.

"Thank you so much for saving Malcolm."

"You're welcome, guys. Malcolm, get some rest. The next twenty-four hours are critical."

Malcolm nodded and watched Emily leave the lab to go study more of sample #999.

"You know you don't have to stay here with me. It's uncomfortable in this room." Malcolm told Anne.

Anne shook her head and held Malcolm's hand. "I'm not going anywhere. I love you, Malcolm."

"I love you too, Anne."

Anne leaned forward and kissed her future husband. As they shared a passionate kiss she knew that as long as they were together they could accomplish anything.

EPILOGUE

"Okay, Keshia, let's see it again." Anne said, holding her katana on her hands.

Keshia nodded and practiced her forms as she hacked and slashed with Kelsey's katana.

"Good. Remember to keep your blade up high."

Keshia nodded and continued to hack and slash invisible targets.

"Nice. That's it. Perfect form." Anne complimented.

Malcolm and Zack stood on the sidelines smiling at Keshia and Kelsey. Zack was drinking coffee as the sun was rising up behind him. In Malcolm's hand was a young baby boy. The mocha skinned baby was sleeping in Malcolm's arm as he smuggled close to his father.

"How's little Liam?" Zack asked, taking a sip of his coffee.

"He's good. It's been months, but I still can't believe Anne and me are parents. You guys are doing great. Coming from a single dad I can tell that Liam loves you."

"You can tell that?" Malcolm asked.

"Yes, Liam shares the same look that Keshia shares with me. The way they smile is the tell."

"Really? I think you're just bullshitting me."

417

Zack laughed. "No, it's true." Zack's eyes turned to Keshia as she bowed with Anne.

"It's nice to see Keshia practicing with Kelsey's sword."

"She's gotten better at it."

"Yes, she practices with it every day just like Kelsey. I would sit outside and watch her. She reminds me so much of Kelsey..." Zack's voice trailed as he closed his eyes and took a deep breath. "She would've liked to see what New Haven became. This community has grown so much."

"It has. Between the wall and the cure, it truly has become a safe haven for any survivors out there. Did you hear what the leadership was considering?"

"Yeah, to expand the living quarters. They wanted to build more homes with an additional wall around them. It's crazy to see the community grow so big."

"People heard of the cure, and they come here to live a life away from the zombies and the crazies out there."

"Do you think we'd ever get back to the way it was before?" Zack asked.

"I'm not sure, but what I am sure about is that as long as we're together we can do anything." Malcolm grinned, looking back at his wife. Anne looked at Malcolm and grinned. She sheathed her katana and joined Malcolm and Zack.

"Zack, Keshia has gotten so much better. It's amazing how much she's picking up." Anne complimented as she watched Keshia practicing.

"Yes, I was telling Malcolm that. Soon it would be Liam's turn to learn kendo."

Anne laughed. "First, he's going to have to learn to walk."

Everyone laughed and Anne walked up to Malcolm to grab Liam. "Oh, come here baby. Mama wants you." Anne picked up Liam and held him in her hands. She leaned forward and kissed him. "I love you, Malcolm."

"I love you too," Malcolm grinned.

The two stared at each other until they heard Victor shouting towards them.

"Zack and Malcolm! You need to see this!" He yelled.

"Is it a zombie horde?" Zack asked.

"No, it's the US army."

Zack shook his head, "the army is gone."

"That's what I thought, but it's legit. They've heard about the cure and wanted to see it for themselves."

"Really?" Zack looked at Malcolm and he shrugged.

"Perhaps they're right." Malcolm replied.

"We can't take the chance though. Anne, do you mine watching Keshia?"

"Yes, I'll take her and Liam back to the house. You two be safe."

Malcolm nodded and kissed Anne. They shared a loving embrace before she took Liam away with Keshia. Zack and Malcolm grabbed their guns nearby and joined Victor at the gate.

As they approached they saw the crowd gathering at the front gate. They made their way to the front and saw the military in front of them. Malcolm was surprised to see the formed military as he believed that there wasn't any form of government left. Dr. López was there as well as she talked to the commander with a four stars on his shoulders.

Victor waved at the commander and pointed at Malcolm. "This is Lieutenant Malcolm White. He was bit and took the cure twenty-four months ago, and he hasn't shown any signs of turning yet."

"Impressive." The commander replied, looking at Malcolm. "How do you feel?" The commander asked.

"I feel the same. The cure works. I'm not the only one who has taken it. All the others have shown the same results."

"Yes, I'm currently working on creating a formula to prevent the virus in total, but right now the cure must be taken at the time someone gets bit. Once they take it, it will kill any traces of the virus in the system." Emily added.

The general nodded. "I'm sold on it. Dr. López, you may have just turned the tide of this zombie apocalypse. With your cure, we can take America back. We can cure the world."

"Thank you sir," Emily grinned.

The general looked back at Zack, Malcolm, and Victor, "we are going to take this country back. I'm going to need warriors. Along my way here I've been putting a band of soldiers back together. I'm going to need more with experience. Would you like to join up?"

Zack looked back at Malcolm and Victor and they both nodded back at him. Zack grinned and looked back at the general. "Sir, it would be our pleasure. Let's take this country back. Boys, let's go hunting."

ABOUT THE AUTHOR

Remy Marie is an interracial romance author who loves to write about charming heroes and brave heroines. While writing never came naturally for Remy, he continued to strengthen his craft, by constantly reading and writing. If he is not writing or reading, he is usually watching TV with his supportive wife, loving his toddler, aggressively cheering for his college and professional sports teams, playing video games, or crunching numbers at his daytime job. If want to learn more, please go to the social media sites below.

https://twitter.com/remymarieauthor
https://instagram.com/remymarieauthor
https://remymarieromance.blogspot.com/
https://www.goodreads.com/user/show/72321338-remy-marie

WORKS BY REMY MARIE

Short Stories
Saved by Him
A Christmas Dinner
Undercover Lovers
What is Love?
Second Chance
A Study Date
Second Rate

Eastcliff Romance University Series
Short Story #1: Never Have I Ever
Short Story #2: Duet
Short Story #3: Rivals
Short Story #4: An Unexpected Surprise
Short Story #5: A Tale of Two Jackie's

Novellas
Blurred Lines: Hill Springs Warriors MC
A Debt Owed
It's Just Business
The US Marshal's Bride

Novels
I'll Be There

I'll Be There

Jasmine Phillips has always had her sights set high, and it seems like she has everything figured out. She has the grades, the looks, the money—and let's not forget her perfect boyfriend. To anyone on the outside looking in, she has the perfect life. Little do they know, it's not what it seems. Despite her stellar grades and top percentile MCAT score, her parents still aren't happy. Jasmine's surgeon parents want her to follow in their footsteps while she wants to pursue a career in pediatrics. However, this turns out to be the least of her worries. Her perfect, med student boyfriend is determined to ruin her future along with his own. When he lays his hands on her for the first time, Jasmine's life is thrown into turmoil and Brock Givens seems to be the only one able to keep her life from spinning out of control.

Brock Givens might seem like an average dumb jock at a glance but to people who know him, he's much more that. While a football star, he's also smarter than most give him credit for and has a passion for more than just football, but that doesn't mean he's without issues of his own. Brock's troubled past and childhood trauma are impacting his football career and threatening his future. Jasmine tries to be there for Brock as a friend but they seem to be getting closer and closer each day while denying there is anything more than friendship until their mutual need for comfort and support brings them closer than they anticipate.

Content Warning, contains scenes of domestic abuse, sexual assault, and racism.

Available Now on Amazon!

Pretty Young Thing

Love can cross any distance. Including a football field.

Tiana Brown is a model student. Meticulous, driven, and hardworking, the last thing she expects when she arrives at the VBU campus for her freshman year, is to be schooled in love.

Sure, she doesn't have a lot of experience in the field, but that's what college is for, right?

She'll meet new people, go to a party or two, and spend the rest of her time focused on her studies.

That's where she's wrong.

When Tiana meets Quay Thompson, local college football star and heartthrob extraordinaire, any plans she had before fly out the window.

Quay is charming, chivalrous, hot as hell, and completely captivated by her.

He's also a notorious womanizer.

As Tiana struggles to accept his past and let the two of them have a future, Quay resolves to prove himself to her and fight for their relationship.

All he knows is that this is a match he can't afford to lose...

Available Now on Amazon!

I Wanna Rock With You

Sammy Deans is obsessed with VBU football. She has been the biggest fan of the Pirates for years, and when the opportunity came to hook up with a player on the team, she didn't hesitate to jump his bones.

Jamaal Johnson has always wanted to be in an interracial relationship, but has always avoided them, due to pressure from his parents. However, after meeting Sammy, he was smitten by her southern charm and her plus sized curves.

There were instant sparks between the two, but after one night of unprotected sex, the new couple's relationship is challenged. Between parents, marriage, and finances, their love is put to the test. Is their love strong enough for the trials ahead or will they split due to the outside forces?

I Wanna Rock With You is an interracial, accidental pregnancy, Insta love, curvy girl, college football sports romance. It is book three of the VBU Pirate series. This is a stand alone title of the series and could be read alone or with the other books in the series. This book contains multiple spicy scenes and is for mature readers only.

Available Now on Amazon!

The Alpha Nanny

She needs money. He masks his pain. Life gives them a second chance, but reality may tear them apart.

Deena Zheng is in over her head. With her father's mounting medical bills, a townhome in disrepair, and more stress than one person should bear, she does all that she can do to stay afloat. Out of options and desperate to pull her family out of the red, she must get out of her comfort zone and accept a nanny position with her firm's notoriously impossible client or risk her family's livelihood.

Jesse Grant struggles to get past his grief after losing the love of his life. Ever since her death, the billionaire hedge fund manager has used alcohol to mask his pain and, in the process, lost a part of himself. With a young son to raise and a business to run, he must pull himself together before he jeopardizes everything he's worked so hard to build.

When they meet, the physical attraction is undeniable, but their personal demons and new professional relationship will make any hopes of pursuing a relationship too complicated for either to handle. Will they ignore their growing feelings for each other and keep their relationship strictly professional or will outside forces force them to reveal the truth?

Find out in this steamy second chance interracial AWBM contemporary romance!

Available Now on Amazon!

The Date Lottery

Victoria Evergreen has nothing going for her: she's a mere store clerk, reeling from the after-effects of a terrible breakup, and the only saving grace in her life is her best friend, Sherri. But when Tori chances upon a $10,000 lottery ticket to an invite-only date contest, her life takes an unexpected turn. Enter Dhruv Patel, Olympic skier, international lawyer, dream hunk. The two chance upon a beautiful, electrifying romance, but little does Dhruv know that Tori stole the lottery ticket. And little does Tori know... Dhruv holds secrets of his own. Will their respective secrets cost the couple their newfound love, or will they move past them and emerge stronger? Find out in this sizzling bwam romance.

Available Now on Amazon!

**Do you want to have updates on all things Remy Marie?
Subscribe to my monthly newsletter!**

http://eepurl.com/c6fynz

Made in the USA
Middletown, DE
03 March 2023

26091567R00257